THE QUESTING HEART

GEORGE SAND, the nineteenth-century female French novelist, had a series of famous lovers: Alfred de Musset, the romantic poet; Prosper Mérimee, the novelist and short story writer, and finally Chopin, the immortal composer and pianist. Born Aurore Dupin, the daughter of a Napoleon lieutenant and a beautiful actress, she was raised on a provincial estate and schooled in a Paris convent. Married unhappily at eighteen, she started writing at first for her own amusement and later left home for Paris' Left Bank with a young playwright. There she took the pen name of George Sand and established herself first as a journalist and later as a romantic novelist. George Sand was known and respected by all the intellectuals of her time. She herself was an enigma: both a devoted mother and a daring Bohemian.

In THE QUESTING HEART F. W. Kenyon once again demonstrates his unique ability to see inside the heart of a great woman.

THE

QUESTING

HEART

A Romantic Novel about George Sand

By F. W. KENYON

DODD, MEAD & COMPANY, *New York*

Printed in the United States of America
by Vail-Ballou Press, Inc., Binghamton, N. Y.

*Dedicated with gratitude
to William Poole*

1265976

I

AND SOON, the child thought, as she bobbed up and down on the hard seat of the jolting carriage, she would see Papa again. The thought was so exciting she could scarcely bear it, yet all she remembered of her father, who came home on leave only rarely, was his splendid uniform. Closing her eyes, she indulged in a favorite daydream. Papa, far more important, far more real than any fairy prince, strode before her flourishing his mighty sword. Papa, the commander of all the armies of the world! She sighed tragically. If only she were a boy and could grow up to wear a uniform like Papa's!

The carriage, a *calèche,* belonged to Madame Fontanier who was going to Madrid to join her husband, a purveyor of some consequence to the French army. Out of the kindness of her heart but with certain misgivings, Madame Fontanier had made room in the *calèche* for Madame Dupin and her young daughter Aurore. Privately she considered the child, who was not yet four, too young to travel, and she feared that Madame Dupin, now heavily pregnant, might suffer a miscarriage at any moment. She grasped at her smelling salts and inhaled shudderingly.

"Ever since we crossed the Spanish border," she gasped, "I

have realized the folly of my own decision to journey to Madrid. For all we know, my husband may be dead, slaughtered by the Spanish. Take, for example, the dreadful news we learned at Vitoria!"

"Madame, I beg of you!" Sophie Dupin exclaimed, glancing anxiously at her daughter.

"A rising in Madrid itself!" Madame Fontanier ran on unheedingly. "Blood flowing in the streets—French blood! Two whole battalions wiped out! Have you no fears, Madame, for the fate of your own poor husband?"

Again Sophie glanced anxiously at the little Aurore, but to her relief she saw that the child was smiling dreamily. Was it possible that to her daughter this story of bloodshed meant nothing? Children, to whom reality was often a mere game, were apt to be like that, and in any case it was always difficult to know what Aurore, so advanced for her age, was thinking.

"Chérie . . ." Sophie ventured.

Still daydreaming, Aurore said brightly: "Is Papa the Emperor?"

Sophie smiled indulgently. "Ah, an important question, that."

"He is, Mother, I know he is!"

"Very well, then, your father is the Emperor." And Sophie added softly, "My Emperor and yours."

"The Emperor Napoleon, Mother!"

"As you wish, Aurore."

Madame Fontanier shot Sophie Dupin an indignant look. What a way to bring up a child! Fairy stories. Fantasy, sheer fantasy! Yet she knew Sophie to be a good mother in many other respects, a pleasingly stern disciplinarian, even if inclined at times to unreasonable fits of temper. Controlling her indignation, she studied her traveling companion critically. Sophie Dupin was fashionably dressed and wore her clothes as regally as if she were the Empress Josephine. Careful questioning and a rapid calculation of dates and events had revealed her to be thirty-five, which was perhaps a little late in life for more child-bearing. Even so, despite her pregnant condition, she was pretty, possibly beautiful when her face was in repose. The dark, glossy hair and the pale, almost transparent skin made an entrancing combination. There were scandalous stories about her past life before she married Maurice Dupin. It was said that she had been a camp follower, that she possessed an illegitimate child, but one must be charitable in the absence of known facts, especially when one considered the importance of her husband's birth and his position in the army.

"Child," Madame Fontanier said, addressing Aurore mildly, "your father is a colonel. He is also aide-de-camp to Marshal Murat who has been sent by the Emperor to conquer Spain."

"The Emperor is my father," Aurore pointed out with childish insistence.

"There!" Madame Fontanier expostulated. "Hopeless!"

Sophie's burst of gay laughter was cut suddenly short as the carriage lurched and came to a shattering halt. Aurore was thrown forward into Madame Fontanier's lap. Sophie herself retained her seat and smiled mischievously when Madame Fontanier asked if all was well. Both women alighted cautiously. The horses were pawing the ground and the coachman was wringing his hands in despair. The low wheels of the *calèche* were firmly embedded in the deeply rutted road.

"Trapped!" Madame Fontanier wailed. "The Spanish will descend upon us with murder in their hearts!"

"The Emperor my father will save us," Aurore announced confidently. She had jumped down from the carriage and was gazing about her expectantly. "But look," she cried. "Look!"

Their savior was neither the Emperor Napoleon nor Colonel Dupin but a French cavalry officer who, bowing gallantly, introduced himself as Captain Perrault. He bowed even more gallantly on learning the ladies' names. Only three days ago he had had speech with their husbands who, far from having been killed in battle, were in the best of health and spirits.

"But—but the rising in Madrid?" Madame Fontanier quavered.

It transpired that the rising had been put down. True, there had been much loss of life, but when the ladies entered Madrid, they would find that order had been completely restored. They had nothing whatever to fear. Captain Perrault took Aurore into his arms; the little one would have the great joy of living in a palace. Aurore was fascinated. The Captain's uniform was not as grand as Papa's, but she kissed him on the cheek and remained in his arms while his men released the carriage.

As they rattled on to the next posting station, Sophie was in the gayest of moods. She sang a nursery song softly and later told Aurore the true story of Captain Perrault's sudden and providential appearance. He had been sent by the Emperor who, with the god-like foreknowledge of all emperors, had known just what was going to happen to the *calèche.*

"Such nonsense," Madame Fontanier muttered.

"A palace in Madrid—that is true, too?" Aurore demanded.

Sophie smiled challengingly at Madame Fontanier. "Certainly, *chérie."*

And sure enough, a palace it was, the palace of the former prime minister of Spain, but now, with the prime minister in exile like King Ferdinand himself, the headquarters of Marshal Joachim Murat. Colonel Maurice Dupin came out to greet the travelers, and, after embracing his wife, he swept Aurore up into his arms. His uniform, or so it seemed to the child, was smothered in more gold lace than ever. Still carrying her, he led the way into the palace and up the wide marble stairway to his apartments with their damask hangings and gilt furniture. There he set her down in one of the great bedrooms and, with the air of a conjurer, he placed a white rabbit in her arms.

4

"Yours, my pet. Be gentle with him."

"Papa, I'm hungry," Aurore said flatly.

"Soon we shall have an enormous meal, a veritable banquet," her father assured her and turned with a wry smile to his wife. "It was scarcely wise of you to travel so far, Sophie, with your time so close."

"I felt it my duty to be at your side," Sophie said demurely, then her eyes flashed angrily. "The Spanish women are very beautiful and you were always susceptible, Maurice."

"Ah, the motive was jealousy—not duty," Maurice teased.

Aurore, stroking the white rabbit absently, was thinking how different this new home was from the attic apartment in the Rue de la Grange-Batelière in Paris. Although Aurore gazed at the rabbit's twitching ears, she saw only the attic. There she was, sitting in the middle of the floor, penned in by a number of chairs. The chairs were really stout stone walls which formed Aurore's own ancestral castle. Because of that, escape was never contemplated. Besides, the foot warmer was comforting and the endless supply of picture books exciting. There was Caroline to play with, too, when Caroline wasn't feeling too grown-up for childish things. Aurore conjured up a picture of Caroline's pretty face—Caroline who was her elder sister but not, for some reason or other, Papa's daughter.

Sometimes Aunt Lucie spent the day with them. Aunt Lucie lived at Chaillot. There were donkeys at Chaillot. That was certainly a vivid memory. Aurore remembered Caroline telling her that she had been sent to Chaillot to be weaned, whatever that meant, while her parents were in Italy. It had been such fun riding from Chaillot to Paris on the back of a donkey. Aunt Lucie was rather bossy. Aurore could remember her quarreling often with her mother, but always about a person referred to as "that old woman," "that unspeakable ogre" and "that unbending aristocrat." The ogre-aristocrat, according to Caroline, was Papa's mother. She lived in a great house at Nohant. Aurore had no memory of having seen her, but her presence was always felt, a very cruel presence. "She keeps you on the edge of poverty," Aunt Lucie said once. Poverty—the word meant little to Aurore. She was happy, she adored her mother and she had all the clothes she needed. The dress she was wearing now was beautiful, an exact copy of her mother's. She had never been hungry, except, of course, on occasions such as this, after a long, long journey.

"Papa," she said again, "I'm hungry!"

II

Marshal Murat stepped lightly onto the balcony and smiled fondly as his eyes fell on the little Aurore. He had grown to love her during the month that had passed since her mother had brought her to Madrid and he knew that she, in her own childish way, had grown to love him. His bull-like roar, which made senior officers as well as humble soldiers tremble in their shoes, had not the slightest effect on her. She would fold her arms, straighten her back, and imitate his voice in the deepest tone she could produce.

"Who is your playmate today?" he asked.

"François," said Aurore, pointing a finger at the youthful figure only she could see.

Murat bowed gravely and the invisible François, Aurore assured him, bowed, too. A strange child, he thought, self-sufficient rather than self-possessed. Most other children would be lost without the companionship of playmates their own age, but Aurore, alone so often, seemed never to be lonely.

"François is really my groom," Aurore confided. "We are going riding. The horses are down there near the fountain."

Murat gazed at the sparkling, dancing waters of the fountain in the center of the square. There were, of course, no horses visible. The whole square, in fact, was completely deserted.

6

Much troubled, he knew that all the other squares and streets of Madrid, apart from the presence of French soldiers, would be deserted, too. Ever since the rising, the Spanish people had remained in hiding during the hours of daylight, hating the French more than fearing them and without doubt plotting another rising. To the south, the east, and the west, the position was growing desperately serious. In not a single town or village dare a French soldier venture forth alone. The Spanish, once considered a conquered nation, were gathering together their ragged forces. How long, Murat asked himself, could he hold Madrid? How long, for that matter, could he hold the thin French line northward to the Pyrenees? He knew, and his master, the Emperor, knew that unless a miracle happened withdrawal would soon be inevitable.

"The white horse, the one with the beautiful tail, is mine," Aurore announced.

Murat, his bulky figure towering over her, took her hand in his. "Before you go riding, you must come with me to your mother's room. She has a surprise for you. You now possess a baby brother."

Aurore, her mind still occupied with the white horse, nodded casually. During the night Papa had entered her own special bedroom, muttering about the agony he was suffering. He wore a nightgown and carried a flickering candle in one hand. Papa in a nightgown was a very different person from Papa in uniform. She had been convinced then that he was not the Emperor after all. He had darted out again, still muttering about his agony and adding, as he closed the door, that the prolonged labor meant only one thing—a boy this time. She trotted along at Murat's side, skipping now and again to keep up with his long, steady pace.

Sophie for once showed only a faint interest in her daughter when Murat led the child into the room. She lay in her bed, exhausted and resentful. The confinement had been long and difficult and the Spanish doctor, the only doctor available, had been cruel and unfeeling. Never in her life had she suffered such torment. Caroline had come into the world so easily and Aurore more easily still. Outcast that Sophie was—at all events as far as the old woman of Nohant was concerned—there had even been gaiety at Aurore's birth. Maurice had brought some officer friends to the apartment. A little thrill of pleasure pulsed through Sophie's breast as she recalled it all. Laughter, wine, some crude but amusing army jokes, then Maurice scraping away at the violin he played so sweetly.

Murat was bending over the cot near Sophie's bed now. "A pretty child," he said, "and none the worse, by the look of him, for his own ordeal."

"We shall call him Louis," Maurice decided.

Aurore, standing on tiptoe, gazed momentarily at the baby. He had quite a lot of dark hair and pale blue eyes. A boy—a baby brother. Envy brought a flush to her tense little face. When he grew up he would wear a uniform. She withdrew quickly to the window and stared hotly at the horses she could still see by dint of very hard concentration in the square below. François, however, had quite disappeared.

"Maman must be informed," she heard her father say. "I shall write to her at once, tell her we now have a strapping son."

Maman? But of course! The mysterious ogre-aristocrat who lived at Nohant. That was in France, somewhere in the country. Would there be donkeys in the stables?

Maurice was bending over his wife. "You agree that Maman must be informed?"

"Whatever you wish."

He caressed Sophie's hands. "She may forgive us, now that we have a son."

Sophie snorted derisively. "She has a heart of stone, that old woman."

Maurice sighed lingeringly. "She would have forgiven us if Aurore had been a boy. I know she would."

Aurore could bear no more. She stole softly from the room. That was all they could think of—a boy.

III

It was Aurore's birthday. She stood before the long mirror in her bedroom at the palace. Was she looking at herself or at her mother? Her dress, a special birthday present, was a copy of her mother's new Spanish gown. The black silk was lovely to touch as the palms of her hands slid over it, but the Marshal had given her a present much more to her liking, a lovely little fawn whose mother had died and gone to heaven. It lay beneath the window now, gazing at her with big, solemn eyes. Staff officers had given her presents, too, dolls and picture books and little Spanish statuettes. But Papa, so forgetful these days, had quite ignored her birthday.

The door was flung open suddenly. Aurore swung round. Papa! Smiling mysteriously, he held behind his back a large bundle which jangled a little as he moved.

"Papa, you remembered!"

His mysterious smile deepened. "A very special present, my pet."

"Let me see! Let me see!"

Aurore darted behind him, but he turned quickly. She tried again and again. It became a frantic game, but always the present, whatever it was, eluded her grasping hands.

"Close your eyes," Maurice commanded.

Aurore closed her eyes.

"Promise to keep them closed until I say 'Open them.' "

Aurore promised.

To her amazement she felt her father removing her mantilla, then her new dress, her petticoat and, finally, her pointed,

9

high-heeled shoes.

"Papa . . ."

"Remember your promise!"

Fighting to control her curiosity, Aurore kept her eyes tightly closed. Papa, lifting her up and down, was dressing her in something that felt desperately exciting. Trousers! There was no doubt about it. Trousers! She held up her arms when commanded and lifted one foot after the other. At last she felt herself being pushed gently across the room.

"Open your eyes, *mon colonel!*"

There, facing her in the mirror, stood Colonel Amandine Aurore Lucile Dupin. The tiny uniform was an exact copy of Papa's—the plumed hat, the cape, the tunic, the trousers, the glossy red-leather boots with their clanking spurs.

"Oh, Papa!"

She was about to fling herself into his arms when she remembered that she was now a man and a soldier.

"One other thing," Maurice said and attached a small saber to her waist.

A bull-like roar made her spin round and face the door. Murat—and laughing at her, actually laughing? She stared at him haughtily until, satisfied, she recognized respect and admiration in his eyes.

"So!" Murat said solemnly. "I now have a new aide-de-camp." He clapped Maurice on the shoulders. "You must look to your laurels, Colonel."

Aurore began to strut about the room, dragging the rattling saber behind her. She reached the window and standing there saw that her regiment was drawn up in the square below, awaiting her command.

Murat took Maurice by the arm. "Leave her to enjoy herself," he whispered. "I have grave news for you. Your wife is distracted, well-nigh inconsolable."

They found Sophie pacing up and down one of the reception

rooms with the baby, now two weeks old, in her arms. Standing nearby was a French army surgeon.

"Blind," Sophie said, in a low, tense voice. "Not born blind, mark you! The Spanish doctor placed a curse on him."

A distraught Maurice took the baby from her and gazed fearfully into his unblinking, pale blue eyes. A whispered consultation with the surgeon confirmed that Sophie had spoken the truth. Blind!

"I demand the arrest of the Spanish doctor!" Sophie shrieked.

Murat made a rumbling, sympathetic noise. Could one arrest the man because of an imagined curse? Even if one could, even if one wanted to make yet another example of yet another Spaniard, the situation in Madrid was far too dangerous. He knew, with an acute bitterness, that within a matter of days his position would be untenable.

With scant success, Maurice tried to comfort his wife, while the surgeon, speaking of the many clever doctors in France, assured her that the case was anything but hopeless. Finally he led her away, insisting that she should rest and forcing her to take a sedative.

Murat turned to Maurice. "I have other grave news."

Maurice, still holding the baby in his arms, nodded briefly. "Withdrawal."

"Withdrawal!" Murat agreed bitterly.

"We shall return," Maurice said automatically.

Murat shrugged. "We shall return." Taking a glittering diamond ring from his finger, he moved it slowly before the baby's eyes. They remained blank and unseeing. "Your personal trouble," he went on, "is all that matters now to you and your wife. You have indefinite leave of absence. Waste no time in returning to France."

Maurice thanked him dully. There had been no time yet to receive a reply from his mother. Would she want to see her grandson? Would she be touched by the child's blindness, or bitterly resentful? He remembered his old tutor, François Deschartres who still lived at Nohant. Deschartres was a man of much medical knowledge. His advice would be invaluable.

"Come what may," he said, speaking hopefully to himself, "I shall take my family to Nohant."

2

SOPHIE DUPIN was horribly seasick. Her clothes were filthy, her hair matted, and her spirits at their lowest ebb. She lay all but helpless on the small, uncomfortable bed in the cramped cabin of the French sloop, the baby whimpering in her arms. Aurore lay on a rough army blanket in a corner of the cabin, listless and uncomplaining.

"Chérie . . ." Sophie whispered weakly.

There was no response. Fever, not seasickness, was Aurore's trouble. She had grown thin and weak and, unable to walk, had been carried aboard by Maurice who was still healthy despite all the privations they had suffered since leaving Madrid. Vaguely Sophie wondered if the living nightmare of that dreadful journey had affected her child. Perhaps Aurore, living in her own imaginary world, had realized nothing of the horror of the dead and the dying by the roadside, the thirst and the hunger, the vermin in the beds at the Spanish inns, the lice in one's hair. The parching summer heat, Sophie thought, was worse than the cold of the coldest winter. Maurice had tried to make light of it, apparently caring little whether they slept in a bed or an army wagon. Stirring herself, Sophie felt a stab of reproach. Maurice had risked his life again and again while fighting rearguard actions. But for him and the men he commanded, they might never have reached the coast and the safety of this sloop which was carrying them to Gironde. Safety! The sloop was plunging and rocking so violently in the storm she expected it to founder at any moment.

Through the tearing, screeching of the wind and the pounding of the sea, Sophie heard the high neighing of a horse. Aurore twisted on her blanket and sat up.

"My white horse! You brought him with us!"

"No," Sophie said sourly, in no mood to indulge in makebelieve. "That is Leopardo."

Leopardo was Maurice's charger, a present from King Ferdinand before His Majesty, hopefully toadying to the French invaders, had been forced to abdicate. Sophie was frightened of Leopardo, a high-spirited, fiery beast from Andalusia. She hated all things Spanish—except, of course, the Spanish dresses. If she survived this voyage, she would cause a sensation in Paris by wearing the latest gown of Spanish design. She fell into a fretful doze from which she woke to find Maurice standing over her.

"He's quieter now. I managed to soothe him."

"Quieter? Who?"

"Leopardo. I know how to control him."

Sophie sat up. "I hate him as much as I hate that Spanish doctor. King Ferdinand placed a curse on you when he gave you Leopardo just as the doctor placed a curse on Louis."

Maurice laughed lightly. "You'll feel better when we land on French soil."

"*If* we land, Maurice."

Maurice bent and kissed her on the brow. "Take heart, Sophie. Gironde within the hour."

"And then?"

"I shall hire a carriage and take you straight to Nohant."

"In the certainty, no doubt, of a warm reception!"

Maurice laughed confidently. "Maman will have heard the news from Spain. She'll think us dead, slaughtered. The sight of us will overwhelm her."

"With regret," Sophie said acidly.

"Chérie . . ."

Sophie made a pitiful noise. "Maurice, I'm going to be sick again."

At that moment, the sloop shuddered violently, then remained surprisingly still while the waves pounded over her bows. Maurice rushed out to the deck, knowing without being told that the sloop had struck a reef. He clung to the rail and waited, uttering a silent prayer. The sea was a terrifying sight, but presently the rising landswell released the vessel. It seemed of immense importance to Maurice that, as he had predicted, they landed in safety at Gironde within the hour.

II

The carriage, a barouche which Maurice had hired, drew up at the inn, the Tête Noire, at La Châtre. There he installed his wife and sickly children and rode off, hopefully if not merrily, to see his mother at nearby Nohant. Sophie herself was in better shape, but the children, especially Aurore, were in a pitiful condition. The poor child swallowed a little broth, then vomited painfully.

Sophie hated the Tête Noire. This was not the first time that Maurice had lodged her here. Her cheeks flushed with anger as she recalled that other woeful occasion. Having wanted to marry her against his mother's wishes, he had brought her to La Châtre and then had gone off to plead with the old lady, only to return after days of arguing with the not-unexpected news that Sophie would not be received at Nohant. Would it be the same this time?

Sophie ordered a meal, fed the baby whose sickly appearance

was beginning to alarm her, and smeared more sulphur ointment on the angry red spots that had appeared on Aurore's face and neck. Maurice came back an hour later, excited but plainly nervous.

"Well?" Sophie asked him stonily.

"It was an emotional meeting. We fell into each other's arms and wept."

"How touching."

"Maman will at least receive you. I convinced her that the children are in urgent need of medical attention."

"From Deschartres?"

"Who else?"

Sophie laughed unbelievingly. Maurice's former tutor was old Madame Dupin's closest friend. He had lived with her at Nohant ever since she had bought the manor and settled there to enjoy the fortune which she had somehow succeeded in preserving during the Revolution. Deschartres! The name would always echo with an ugly sound in Sophie's ears. Oh, such a virtuous gentleman! A loose woman, a prostitute, a camp follower—that was what he had called Sophie when trying to rouse the villagers against her while Maurice was arguing and pleading with his mother at Nohant. A band of them had come to the Tête Noire, solemnly and righteously intent on escorting her from the neighborhood. Well, there was some satisfaction in remembering how she had got the better of them and through pitiful tears and a ladylike demeanor had shamed them into retreat.

"We are much in Monsieur Deschartres' debt," Maurice said propitiatingly.

"We?"

"My mother and I and, through us, you and the children."

"What are you driving at, Maurice?"

Quietly, he began to speak of an event which had occurred during the Reign of Terror. "When Maman bought Nohant but before she had time to take possession of it, she was arrested and dragged before the Revolutionary Committee. We were living at that time in Paris. The house was in the Rue de Bondy. Up until then the Terrorists had left us in peace. Maman felt reasonably safe but thought it wise to hide her jewelry and other possessions behind a panel in her boudoir. An ill-tempered servant, whom she had treated with the utmost generosity, betrayed her. The house was searched and the valuables discovered. We feared, Deschartres and I, that poor Maman would go to the guillotine, not on account of the hidden jewelry, but because there were some incriminating papers in a secret drawer in her escritoire. They revealed her connection and business dealings with proscribed aristocrats. As an admirer of Voltaire and Rousseau, she had welcomed the Revolution; but when the extremists seized power, she began to hate it and helped with money certain exiled princes. The authorities had placed seals on all the visible drawers and would, we knew, make another search. Deschartres eluded the guard that had been placed on the house and succeeded in entering in the middle of the night. He removed one of the seals, found the papers, and destroyed them. But for that, Maman would have gone to the guillotine and all her property would have been confiscated."

"A courageous and faithful friend," Sophie admitted.

"He risked his own life, Sophie."

"I admit it." She laughed lightly. "We now have a new fairy story for Aurore."

"Come!" Maurice urged, encouraged by his wife's near-return to good humor. "Every moment is precious where the children's health is concerned."

Sophie carried the baby out to the barouche. Maurice followed with Aurore limp in his arms. She clutched a doll in one hand, a parting gift from Marshal Murat. The countryside made little impression upon her as the barouche rolled on towards Nohant. Her head felt strangely light, as if it didn't belong to her at all, and the drumming sound in her ears became confused with the steady clip-clop of hoofs. Presently the clip-clop took on a metallic ring, then stopped. They had entered the courtyard of the manor. She felt herself floating. Was she dead now, like the little fawn's mother? She opened her eyes and stared up at a calm, pale-cheeked face. It was lined and wrinkled, and above the forehead was a straw-colored wig. An elderly angel perhaps? This really was Heaven? The face, it seemed, possessed a voice.

"I, child, am your grandmother."

Aurore struggled to sit up. The haziness and the drumming sound cleared for a moment.

"My grandmother?" she asked uncertainly. "The old lady of Nohant?"

"That if you wish, Aurore."

"The ogre-aristocrat?"

"That most certainly," said Madame Dupin, chuckling softly.

Aurore began to feel drawn to her. Such a tiny lady but straight of back, like a soldier. And how quaint she looked in her dark purple dress. Aurore had seen such a dress in a picture book. There were countless folds and the waist was so long it seemed to reach down to the knees. Her mother had laughed over the picture. Could one ever imagine anything so old-fashioned? She herself would never be seen dead in such a relic of the past.

"You have the honor of lying in my own bed," Madame Dupin remarked.

Aurore glanced about her. The bed was bigger than the barouche and much more comfortable. Four large posts towered above her and faded from sight, but the black plumes remained, waving as if in a breeze. Beyond the plumes, flowers danced on the walls. The furniture, a dazzling sight, was edged with gilt.

"The bed is honored to have me," she said with a horrible

18

precocity.

The straw-colored wig bobbed perilously. "In your unspeakable condition? Lice in your hair, horrible spots all over you and—heaven save us—scabies?"

"I'm not old enough to have babies. Mother said so."

"She should know," Madame Dupin said dryly.

Aurore suffered a moment of apprehension. "Where is my mother?"

"Resting with the baby. Both are perfectly safe. Good care shall be taken of them and of you, also. There is no cause for you to feel afraid of anything."

The drumming noise was in Aurore's ears again and behind it the precise rap-rap of heels on the polished parquet floor.

"Leave her to me, Madame," said a new and deeper voice. "She needs a thorough cleansing. The sulphur ointment will drive the fever in, not bring it out."

Aurore saw the white stockings first, then the breeches drawn tightly over scrawny knees. Her eyes traveled upwards and came to rest on the face. She repressed a screech of terror. Surely she was in Hell now—not Heaven. The nose seemed to grow larger and larger, but presently as it fell back into its true perspective, she took heart and smiled timidly. The voice had sounded harsh but the eyes held a kindly expression.

"This is Monsieur Deschartres," Madame Dupin announced. "He will make you well again."

Monsieur Deschartres removed Aurore's filthy clothes and flung them to the floor. He carried her to a steaming tub in an outer room and bathed her painstakingly. There was something vaguely soothing in the touch of his gently probing fingers. She was unable to open her eyes because of the stinging of the soapsuds but she knew that somebody was combing her matted hair.

"Who is cracking nuts?" she asked, listening to a new sound.

"Lice were never nuts," Madame Dupin chuckled. "Monsieur

Deschartres is disposing of them."

She dried the child herself, wrapped her in a warm towel, and carried her back to the bed. Deschartres administered a sour-tasting physic. Aurore coughed and spluttered but finally swallowed it. Then she lay back, light-headed still but almost comfortable. The flowers on the wall-hangings were dancing solemnly. A number of them came together in a large bunch and landed softly on her chest.

"Hippolyte," she heard her grandmother say. "A sweet boy to greet you with flowers."

So, they were real flowers and the boy who had presented them looked almost real, too. He was jumping up and down at the bedside, grinning and giggling insanely.

"Hippolyte is nine years old," Madame Dupin said. "When you are able to go out and play, he will let you ride on his donkey."

Donkeys at Nohant after all! Aurore sighed contentedly and fell into a light, untroubled doze.

"What of the baby?" Madame Dupin asked Deschartres. "Can anything be done about his blindness?"

Deschartres pursed his lips. "We must first cure the fever. His condition is far worse than the girl's."

Maurice tiptoed into the room. He thought it a promising sign that so much care should have been taken of the children already. His eyes grew misty at the sight of his mother bending over the sleeping Aurore.

"What do you think of her, Maman?" he asked tentatively.

"She has the look of a true Königsmark."

The pride in her voice was more promising still. She worshiped the Königsmarks who appeared so prominently in the family tree. They were of German and Swedish extraction, aristocratic rogues, cultured gentlemen, lovely ladies of high degree, legitimate and illegitimate alike. Not that illegitimacy mattered, Maurice reflected. A Königsmark was a law unto himself, or—more often than not—a law unto *herself*.

Emboldened, he said, "And what do you think of Sophie now that you have met her?"

Madame Dupin's eyes flashed. "She has the airs and graces of a lady. She is pretty and no doubt vivacious when in good health. But a man, my poor Maurice, is a fool to marry his mistress."

"I fear I disappointed you sadly," Maurice said contritely.

"You would scarcely have done worse if you had married Hippolyte's mother."

The boy Hippolyte was Maurice's natural son by a village girl. Madame Dupin had sent the girl away but had taken the baby into her own keeping, having first made certain in her own mind that there was no doubt about its paternity. She had been motivated, not by *noblesse oblige*, but by family tradition and responsibility. The Königsmarks, Frederick Augustus and even Louis XV, had always been careful to provide for their natural children. Nevertheless, Madame Dupin had refrained from acknowledging him as her grandson. As far as the boy knew, she was merely his guardian.

"How long do you propose to stay at Nohant?" Madame Dupin pressed her apparently unresponsive son.

Maurice squared his shoulders. "Only as long as my wife and children are welcome."

"Have I not made them welcome already?" Madame Dupin demanded brusquely.

3

AURORE WAS PLAYING in the garden with Hippolyte. His full name, she had discovered, was Hippolyte Châtiron. It seemed that he possessed neither a father nor a mother. Aurore thought it sad that he had no memory of his parents, but the boy himself was quite unconcerned. Madame Dupin was kind to him, and so was Monsieur Deschartres who gave him lessons every day. Aurore was looking forward to having lessons, too. It annoyed her intensely that Hippolyte could read the words in the picture books while she could only understand the pictures.

It was a month now since she had been brought to Nohant. The manor house and the farm had quickly become her world. The house with its tall windows was very nearly a modern structure, or so Papa had said when telling her that it had been built during the reign of the late King whose head had been chopped off by the guillotine. Aurore regretted the disappearance of the old castle which this modern house had replaced. It would have been much more exciting living in a castle.

Hippolyte was crawling across the front garden on his hands and knees. Aurore followed him half-heartedly. She was growing tired of his pretending to be a dog. Soon she would insist on a new game, perhaps a well-planned battle, for she was

22

wearing her uniform. But for the uniform, she would have forgotten Murat and those joyous days in Madrid.

"Hippolyte!" she commanded.

He crawled on unheedingly and disappeared through a gate in the garden wall. When Aurore caught up with him, he was squatting before a small house which was partly hidden by elm trees.

"Colonel Châtiron!" she commanded.

Hippolyte sprang to attention. "Sir?"

Aurore led him back to the garden, picked up a rag doll she had left on the grass, tore it apart and flung it down.

"That's a corpse, a dead Spanish soldier."

Hippolyte took up another doll. Its long dress was of thin scarlet silk. He tore the dress asunder and scattered the pieces on the grass.

"Blood," he explained and rocked with laughter.

Both he and Aurore turned and looked up at the windows of the manor, their attention held by a shrill, piercing scream. Another Spanish soldier killed by her men, Aurore thought, and trotted to the house to investigate. Madame Dupin intercepted her in the hall and, bending, took her in a fierce embrace.

"Go back and play with Hippolyte," she said after a moment.

Aurore obeyed, but she thought it strange that her grandmother should be weeping over the death of a Spanish soldier.

In her bedroom upstairs Sophie was crouching over Louis' cot. Maurice was facing her, tears streaming from his eyes. Deschartres stood withdrawn at the window. Sophie, after her first demented outburst, had grown suddenly calm. But it was, Maurice thought, a dangerous, frightening calmness.

"I cannot believe that Louis is dead," she whispered. "To me he appears to be sleeping more serenely than ever before."

They buried the baby the next morning in the small village

23

cemetery beyond one of the garden walls. Aurore stood with her parents, her grandmother, and Hippolyte at the graveside. She thought it a very small coffin for a Spanish soldier; but when she remarked on this, Madame Dupin told her that the soldier was really her baby brother who had gone to Heaven. Aurore accepted this simple statement of fact philosophically. Heaven must be a very large place since people were always going there. It was a pity she wouldn't see little Louis again until she went to Heaven herself, but she would try hard to remember him, however long she had to wait.

During the night she was awakened by the sound of violent weeping. Rubbing her eyes, she tiptoed to her mother's room. The door was ajar. Papa was pacing up and down, his long shadow bobbing on the wall in the candlelight. She heard her mother blow her nose and clear her throat.

"Would you leave me to do it myself, Maurice?"

"Sophie, I beg of you!"

"Louis is only sleeping. You buried him alive. Would you have him die of suffocation?"

Aurore drew back as her father came out of the room, dragging on his civilian trousers. She followed him cautiously downstairs to the hall. There he lit a lantern and went out to the gardener's toolshed. A new sort of game was being invented, Aurore decided, as she hurried after the flickering light of the lantern. Papa carried a spade and was soon digging in the cemetery. He worked hard and furiously, muttering to himself from time to time that there was only one way to save poor Sophie from insanity. The gray light of dawn was spreading over the cemetery. Fearful of being discovered, Aurore hid behind a bush and only just in time, for her mother had come out to watch and instruct. It was then that something most peculiar happened. Papa stepped back and uttered a cry of alarm as a great coffin reared up behind him. He cried out again and fell into the hole he had dug.

"The wrong grave!" Sophie shrieked.

"No, the two are close together," Maurice said, scrambling out of the hole.

He lifted out the small coffin and replaced the large one.

"Hurry!" Sophie urged.

Maurice began to shovel back the earth, saying that the village people were superstitious, that the graves must be left to look as if they had not been disturbed. Aurore was shivering with cold. It was a warm enough summer morning but her feet were wet with dew. She hurried back to the house unseen and was soon asleep again in her warm bed. When she woke up, the sun was streaming through the window. She remembered the adventure in the cemetery and wondered if she had dreamed it, but when she went to her mother's room, there was Louis lying in his cot, covered in flowers. Madame Dupin, who was present and looking most severe, took Aurore by the hand and led her away.

"Do people ever come back from Heaven?" Aurore asked.

"No," said Madame Dupin, "and I doubt if they would want to."

A day later, Louis was buried again, not in the cemetery but beneath a pear tree in the orchard. The villagers must never know, Aurore heard her father say, his voice sounding like the sighing of the wind. It was all very secret and exciting. Aurore enjoyed it enormously, but her enjoyment was tinged with envy. Would she ever be as fortunate as her baby brother and go to Heaven twice?

II

Stormy weather had brought an early autumn to Nohant, with brown-green leaves falling in cascades from the trees. Aurore and Hippolyte helped to sweep them up while Madame Dupin watched from her chair at one of the windows. Only rarely did she walk in the garden. It wasn't that she was too old or crippled, Aurore discovered, merely that she wore shoes so small and tight that walking was agony. It had something to do with pride or so Papa said.

Aurore had seen little of her mother since the baby's second burial, for Sophie remained in her room, either weeping or lying as if in a stupor. Hippolyte was almost always on hand to play with Aurore in the garden or the nearby farm.

Occasionally Maurice played with the two children in the garden, but mostly, when not sitting with Sophie, he was riding furiously about the countryside on Leopardo. Soon there was heavy rain and the children were kept indoors, Hippolyte studying with Monsieur Deschartres, Aurore playing with her dolls but fretting at being confined to a room. She loved the smell of the grass and the earth and all the rich smells which came from the farm.

One night, eleven days after the baby's death, Maurice failed to return to Nohant before darkness fell. Sophie, who had left her room for the first time that day, grew anxious and her anxiety was conveyed instantly to Aurore. Had Papa gone back to Spain? Madame Dupin said there was nothing to worry about. More than likely the torrential rain had delayed him. But Aurore sensed that she, too, was anxious, for she turned quite pale when Monsieur Deschartres observed that Leopardo was a difficult beast in wet weather.

"Hold your tongue!" Madame Dupin told him sharply.

Aurore went to bed, said her prayers obediently, and, at her mother's command, added a special one for her father. Hours later—maybe years, or so it seemed—she sat up in bed and wondered what had disturbed her. The rain beating against the window? No, not that, but a great commotion downstairs. Jumping out of bed, she went to investigate. Her mother was sitting on the edge of a chair, a dazed expression on her face, while her grandmother, wearing comfortable slippers, was wrapping a heavy winter dressing gown round her still slim body.

"Take the child back to bed," she instructed Sophie.

It was daylight when Aurore saw Madame Dupin again. The old lady was bending over the bed. Her dressing gown was wringing wet and her straw-colored wig was in a sorry state. A queer, choking noise was coming from her throat, but at last she managed to speak intelligibly.

"Be brave, child. Papa has gone to Heaven."

"With Leopardo, Grandmama?"

"Leopardo is still tied to a tree by the roadside."

"Poor Leopardo."

Aurore glanced at the window. The rain had stopped. The sun was shining. Fairies were dancing in the slanting, watery rays that reached down from the window to the foot of her bed. So Papa, more impatient than she, had gone to Heaven to join dear little Louis.

"Be brave," Madame Dupin repeated. "Promise, child."

"I promise," Aurore said dutifully.

She began to cry. But whether she was crying for poor Leopardo who hated to be tied up, or for Papa whom she wouldn't see again until she went to Heaven herself, she found it hard to decide.

III

"We cannot wear mourning forever," Madame Dupin said. "Nor can we grieve forever. Life, whether we like it or not, goes on relentlessly, demandingly."

Facing her at the other side of the leaping flames of the log fire, Sophie looked at her stonily. Willfully she refused to believe the truth, that the harshness of her mother-in-law's words was a deliberate attempt to hide the sadness of her heart. A month had passed since Maurice, thrown by Leopardo, had

27

suffered a broken neck. Sophie had wept and raged. She was indeed still capable of both, but her grief was fading and there was, strive as she did to repress it, a rising tide of the old ebullience, the old optimism, even the old gaiety.

"We must think of Aurore," Madame Dupin went on. "She is our only concern now."

Our only concern, Sophie thought. Aurore was the link that held them together now: Madame Dupin, the unbending aristocrat; she herself, the undoubted daughter of the people. If one felt inclined to laugh, one's sides would ache intolerably.

Sophie glanced across the room at her young daughter. The child was playing beneath the window, arranging in opposing ranks the two armies that would soon engage in violent battle. How fortunate that, to the very young, death had no real meaning. Aurore had asked what it meant to be dead and had been told, as usual, that it meant that one went to Heaven.

"The child is my responsibility more than yours," Madame Dupin said challengingly.

"So you want to take her from me!"

"Quietly!" Madame Dupin urged, glancing at Aurore. "I see no reason why you should not stay at Nohant also."

"A compromise," Sophie said dryly. "If I leave, obviously Aurore will leave with me." She thought of her other daughter who, for the time being, was living with her sister Lucie. "I want my two children with me—Caroline as well as Aurore."

"Do you hope to bring her *here?*"

Sophie shrugged. "Hippolyte is here."

"That is another matter."

Sophie thoroughly understood. Hippolyte, though illegitimate and unacknowledged, was Maurice's son, the old lady's own flesh and blood; whereas Caroline, the child of an unknown father, was beyond the pale of respectability, Madame Dupin's own particular brand of respectability. Sophie came close to remarking on this acidly, but she glanced again at Aurore and with difficulty held her tongue.

"Let us suppose that you withdraw from Nohant and set up house in Paris with Aurore and Caroline. What then?" Madame Dupin asked, supremely sure of herself. "You will have only a small military pension. Do you want Aurore to become a neglected urchin in some miserable Paris slum?"

"Would you willingly see her go in need?"

"No, Sophie. Would you?"

"I would contrive by some means to keep her from starving. I would see to it that she never went about in rags."

"Yourself also?" Madame Dupin eyed her daughter-in-law grimly. "You are fond of fashionable clothes. I have often wondered how you could afford to dress so well."

Indeed she must have, Sophie thought. Had not the old ogre deliberately kept Maurice short of money during the last four years? It was an absolute miracle that they had been able to scrape along on his army pay.

"I have large debts, Madame," Sophie said airily, then laughed at a sudden though inadequate comparison. "Like the Empress Josephine," she added.

An unexpected smile crossed Madame Dupin's face. "But not, I pray, so mountainous!"

"Mine are a molehill compared with hers."

Aurore looked up from her game. Her mother and her grandmother had been quarreling but now they were laughing together. Whatever the joke was, she had missed it. Not that it mattered; she had more important things on hand.

"Which is it to be," Madame Dupin asked lightly, "Paris and poverty? Or Nohant and every comfort a respectable woman could want?"

"A respectable woman!" Sophie laughed again.

"Try to be serious," Madame Dupin said severely. "Remain at Nohant and your debts shall be paid. In addition, you shall receive a personal allowance sufficient for the care of your other daughter. Come, Sophie, the choice is yours."

"No, Madame, yours," Sophie said, accepting unwillingly.

When Aurore looked up again there was only her grandmother in the room. She was sitting bolt upright in her chair by the fire and apparently talking to herself. "Maurice," she kept saying, "Maurice . . ."

Aurore rearranged the front ranks of her opposing armies. The French were going to triumph over the Spanish. That was a foregone conclusion, but she thought she would like the Spanish to think for a while that they were going to win.

"Maurice!" Madame Dupin said, so loudly and commandingly that Aurore jumped to her feet. "Come here, child. I want to talk to you."

"Yes, Grandmama." Aurore went obediently to Madame Dupin's side.

"You must call me Maman," Madame Dupin said insistently. "You, child, are my son now. There is no one else left. You, Maurice, are the young master of the house. Is that clearly understood?"

"Oh yes, Maman!"

Aurore placed her head in the old lady's lap. The mock-battle was forgotten. She, Maurice, the master of the house! What could be more exciting, more important than that?

IV

"Maurice sees far too much of the village children," Madame Dupin remarked coldly.

"Why must you continually call her Maurice? Her name is Aurore." Sophie's voice rose angrily. "The man of the house! The man indeed!"

Aurore, free of lessons for the day, was lying on the grass beneath the open window. So her mother and her grandmother were quarreling again. Either they quarreled or they laughed

30

together. There was no middle course, no real peace, and never had been during the last four years. Aurore felt sorry for both of them but wanted, now as always, to take her mother's part rather than her grandmother's. Poor, pretty Mother! It was almost as if she were a special doll grown into one's mother, a doll that breathed and talked and often seemed so helpless.

"Time and again I send the village children away," Madame Dupin went on querulously, "but the moment my back is turned you bring them here again."

"Aurore is my child—not yours."

Aurore tried to concentrate on the book she was reading. These ever-recurring quarrels were the only thing that marred the happiness of her life at Nohant. Unlike Hippolyte, she found much pleasure in the lessons given to both of them by Monsieur Deschartres.

First taught the alphabet by her mother, she had quickly learned to read and write and of late had begun to invent little stories which she jotted down in her notebook. Monsieur Deschartres, dry old stick that he was, admitted that she was developing a fine imagination, but all imagination, he said, must be curbed and controlled. Aurore had yet to make up her mind whether she liked or hated the old man. Certainly she hated him whenever he made her swallow a vile emetic. He asserted constantly that the color of her skin indicated some alarming liver complaint, but her mother said that was nonsense: Aurore had simply inherited her own olive complexion.

There were times, too, when she hated Maman. Those tedious lessons in deportment, for instance! What a bore it was walking carefully and unnaturally about the room with a book balanced precariously on one's head. Worse than that, one was obliged to stoop, still straight of back, to pick up a glove; bending, so much easier, was entirely prohibited. Lessons in deportment were even continued at mealtimes, for one was instructed relentlessly in the precise manner of holding a knife and fork.

Her mother laughed and sneered about it all but admitted when challenged by Maman that good manners would no doubt help to turn the child into a lady. Aurore's hatred of Maman, however, disappeared magically when the old lady sat at the harpsichord and to her own accompaniment sang a Mozart aria in a still quite beautiful voice. Madame Dupin had already given Aurore a few music lessons and had promised to give her many more. To be able to play the harpsichord properly, Aurore thought, would give her almost as much pleasure as writing fairy stories.

She looked up at the window and sighed deeply. The quarrel was still in progress. Sophie accused Madame Dupin of not believing in God. Madame Dupin retorted that, as a deist, she most certainly did believe in God. Her quarrel was with revealed religion in which she did not believe. As for Jesus Christ, she held Him in high esteem.

"Heretic!" Sophie shrieked.

There was a long and dreadful silence. Madame Dupin broke it finally, her voice carefully controlled.

"It has occurred to me, Sophie, that you are bored with life at Nohant."

"How could it be otherwise, longing as I do for Paris? The country stifles me."

"It has occurred to me also that you disapprove of the training that Maurice is receiving here."

"Yes, I most certainly do!"

"Yet you want her to be a lady?"

"Of course," Sophie admitted sulkily.

"All you disapprove of, then, is the religious training?"

"Rather the lack of it."

"You are confusing religion with morality. Maurice has a thorough understanding of the Ten Commandments. She is being taught the difference between right and wrong."

"No—between you and me," Sophie said wildly. "You being

right, I being wrong."

"You call me a heretic. I call you a hypocrite. Things have come to such a pass that we cannot continue to live beneath the same roof if Maurice is to remain unaffected by our differences of opinion. This, then, is my suggestion. Maurice must become mine legally. If you will sign the necessary papers, I, for my part, will grant you an allowance more than sufficient for your needs."

There was another long and dreadful silence. Aurore's eyes filled with tears. Maman was offering to buy her from her mother. She sprang to her feet, ran indoors and flung herself into her mother's arms.

"Mother, you can't, you can't!"

"Can't—what, Maurice?" Madame Dupin asked softly.

"Sell me!"

"She has already agreed to do so."

Sophie stroked Aurore's hair. Paris, she was thinking, Paris! Caroline would be with her again. And the freedom, oh, the freedom!

"Chérie," she said persuasively, "it is better for you to remain at Nohant. Here you will grow up to be a lady and here, in time, you will inherit your grandmother's fortune. Meanwhile you may visit me in Paris. There is no objection to that. Believe me, I am doing the right thing."

Aurore looked into Sophie's tear-stained face. Then an appalling thought struck her.

"Mother, you will have no one to protect you in Paris; no man to look after you!"

A quick look passed between Sophie and her mother-in-law.

"Well now," Madame Dupin said thoughtfully, "well now . . ."

Aurore saw her mother toss her head defiantly and wondered why, of a sudden, she should be blushing so deeply.

4

So ENGROSSED WAS Aurore in her secret task that she failed, for the moment, to notice the presence of her grandmother's maid who stood silent and watchful at the half-open bedroom door. Carefully she counted again the money she had hoarded in the trinket box and fingered the little pieces of cheap jewelry. How much could she obtain for the bracelet, the brooch, the imitation diamond necklet? Was it possible that she now had enough money for her purpose?

Aurore was nearly fourteen. But how the years were dragging! Maman, in failing health these days, said they were flying by all too rapidly, but Aurore knew differently. Deschartres laughed dryly and told her not to worry. The time would come when she would long to put the clock back, not forward. He was pleased with her and occasionally, if somewhat grudgingly, admitted it. She was proficient at history, geography, mathematics, and drawing, had gained a thorough grasp of Latin and a useful smattering of what he called the natural sciences. True, she had not yet learned the value and importance of Reason, but that would come in time. Reason meant the unquestioning acceptance of a creator who was all-powerful but coldly aloof, not of God who, according to her mother, loved

34

the human beings He had created. Reason, yes, but did Reason explain the purpose of life? Yet oddly enough, Aurore had been confirmed at her grandmother's insistence. Thereafter, God the Father, God the Son, and God the Holy Ghost had never been mentioned. It was all very puzzling and at times disturbing. Hippolyte, who was now in the army, had thought Aurore's probing questions silly. Life was sufficient in itself. Life was meant to be enjoyed, not questioned.

Aurore gathered her little treasures together now and replaced them in the trinket box. It was then that Julie, the maid, swooped down on her and seized the brooch.

"This is mine, you wretched, thieving child!"

Aurore faced her squarely. She had never liked Julie, and Julie, always resentful, had never liked her either. She was a middle-aged woman with stringy, faded hair and a sallow complexion. Her narrow eyes—so Hippolyte said—were those of a sour and disappointed virgin.

"The necklet belongs to Madame Dupin," Julie added with a snarl.

"And the money," Aurore said defiantly, "to Monsieur Deschartres. It fell from his pocket and he didn't miss it."

"You have everything you need," Julie pointed out. "Why must you steal?"

"Because I want to run away." Aurore was close to tears. "Because I want to be with my mother."

"You see her every winter. What more do you want?"

Aurore remained sullenly silent. The maid snatched up the trinket box. "Thieves have never been known at Nohant. I have no recourse but to report your sinful behavior to Madame Dupin."

"Do so! Do so!"

"God will punish you!"

"The God of Reason? Never!"

Leaving Julie with a silly expression on her face, Aurore

rushed out to the garden, cast a quick glance over her shoulder to make sure she was not being followed, and stealthily entered a little glade surrounded and hidden by trees. This was her own private, secret retreat. Here she had built an altar of smooth stones, and here she worshiped and communed with the god of her own creation. She had seen him first in a waking dream at dawn one calm and glorious summer morning. His name was Corambé. In her mind she saw him mostly in the form of a man, handsome, benevolent, all-powerful and all-loving. But occasionally, when she thought of her mother, Corambé became a beautiful woman. Yet, despite his knowledge which transcended the knowledge of all men, he always remained enigmatically silent when she sought from him the meaning of life and the reason for her being on this earth.

Aurore glanced over her shoulder again. She decided that she had merely heard the wind in the trees, not the snapping of a twig on the ground, and she set about gathering a handful of wild flowers. These she laid on the fern-covered altar. The next step in the ritual concerned the birdcage which hung from a branch. In it, twirping and jumping, was the sparrow she had caught a week ago and had come daily to feed. She placed the cage on the altar, opened it and allowed the bird to flutter away to freedom. Freedom! If only she could give freedom to all the creatures of the earth as well as to herself!

Another twig snapped. She sprang up. "Monsieur Deschartres!"

"So this is where you hide yourself," he said gently, as he glanced at the altar.

"You followed me!" Aurore accused. "Now everything is spoiled. I'll never come here again!"

The maid Julie appeared behind Deschartres. She was panting, gasping for breath. There was an unholy, triumphant gleam in her eyes.

"Wicked child!" she rasped.

"You told Maman? Well, what of it?"

"I told her and the poor old lady has suffered a stroke."

"Because of me?" Aurore gasped. "Oh no, no!"

Deschartres gave Julie a little push. "Go back to the house, woman," he said angrily.

Aurore was growing frantic. "The fault was mine, Monsieur, mine?"

"No," he said. "Madame Dupin suffered the stroke early this morning. That was why she remained in her room. It was only a slight seizure. She was still able to speak. Julie told her about your extraordinary conduct, yes, but strangely enough that seemed to hasten her recovery. Come, we will go to her." He sighed as if in regret. "There is much, I fear, that she wants to tell you."

When Aurore entered her grandmother's room, the scented atmosphere was stifling. She had no memory of ever having seen the windows of Maman's room open. Now, as always, they were heavily shrouded with curtains. She approached the bed fearfully, the same bed in which she had been placed when she had first arrived from Spain. Maman looked like a corpse, except that her eyes were alight, darting and full of intelligence.

"Maurice . . ." Madame Dupin said, her voice surprisingly strong. Then she turned her head on the pillow and studied the girl in a long and contemplative silence.

Maurice, she thought, was a little short for her years, thin and much too pale. There was an intense and no doubt rebellious expression in her dark eyes. Adolescence was a difficult period for any girl, but there was more to it than that. She was moody, alone far oftener than was good for her, and had lost her appetite. Madame Dupin heaved a deep sigh. Neither she nor Deschartres, separately or together, were capable any longer of controlling her.

Aurore fell to her knees. "Forgive me, Maman."

Madame Dupin seemed not to hear. "So you stole in order to

37

go to your mother, your worthless mother."

"Maman!" Aurore's voice rose in agony.

"I have loved only one man," Madame Dupin went on. "My first marriage was arranged for me. My second was, of my own choosing, another marriage of convenience."

"There was a lover?" Aurore asked hesitantly.

Anger flashed in Madame Dupin's eyes. "I speak of your father. I loved him and worshiped him. I gave him my whole life. Judge, then, my suffering when your mother took him from me. He was mine, entirely mine, and she took him from me. Am I to permit her to take you now—you, my other son?"

"Maman, you don't understand!" Aurore said desperately.

"I understand only too well."

"But for Mother you wouldn't have me now," Aurore tried to argue. "Would you rather Papa had never married?"

"I wanted a good match for him. I wanted him to marry a lady, but he married a trollop."

Aurore sprang to her feet. "That is a hateful thing to say!"

"Remain on your knees," Madame Dupin commanded. "I shall tell you the full story."

Unwillingly, Aurore fell to her knees again.

"Your mother's father was a common person," the old lady went on, her voice harsh and contemptuous. "For a time he ran a billiard saloon. Later he sold canaries, hawking them on the quays in Paris."

"But my mother—my mother!"

"She was a wild and uncontrollable child. Stubborn, willful. Gay? Well, no one can doubt that. She possessed a wanton gaiety which susceptible men found irresistible. While she was still young, she became a dancer and performed in a low-class, disreputable Paris theatre. She was much sought after by the type of men who frequent such places, never accompanied by their wives. She had a baby, your half-sister Caroline. Nobody, not even your mother, knows who the father was. She became a camp follower, leaving Caroline with your aunt or with friends. A camp follower, you understand, is a loose woman, a prostitute. Later she took Caroline with her when she went to offer her special services to the army of Italy. She became a general's mistress. She had a preference, you see, for officers. She met your father in Milan and found him more to her liking than the general who was an old man. Her aim was to marry him, but it was four years before she became pregnant and thus found herself in a position to force marriage upon him. He was weak, of course. He need not have married her. I told him only a fool married his mistress. He refused to listen to me. You were born a month after the secret marriage I was helpless to prevent."

"You wanted me to be born illegitimate!" Aurore exclaimed, horrified by the harshness of her grandmother's voice as much as by the story itself.

"Then I did, but not now. In any case, I would have taken care of you. I know my duty." Madame Dupin turned away her head and stared at one of the curtained windows. "Need I tell you more? Your mother was—and still is—a lost woman. Do you want to become one, too?"

"No! Never!" Aurore gasped, the tears streaming down her cheeks.

"Very well. Be sensible in future. 'Forgive me,' you said? There is nothing now to forgive."

Deschartres, his heart aching intolerably, touched Aurore lightly on the shoulder. "Come, Madame Dupin must rest. You have both passed through a dreadful ordeal."

Aurore ran blindly from the room. Her mind was in tumult. Life, which seemed now to have a horrible meaning, was closing in on her, suffocating her. Reaching the altar again, she knelt before it imploringly. The reason for her being on this earth had been revealed with disillusioning clarity. But what of the purpose for which she had been born? It seemed to her, as she knelt there hoping to hear Corambé's reassuring voice, that her mother was in need of greater protection than ever. If only there had been gentleness in Maman's voice, she would have been shaken by anger and indignation, not this gnawing desire to fly at once to her mother.

During the rest of the day, the blackest of Aurore's life, she refused to eat. The next day she refused to study and tore up an unfinished sketch of her grandmother that she had begun earlier. And so it went on, day after day, this rebellion against the law and order of Nohant, and with it, through many a sleepless night, the creeping, ever-increasing feeling of frustration. Life had become a cage from which there was no escape.

Madame Dupin sent for her at last. She sat in a chair in her stuffy, airless bedroom, her face more wrinkled than ever but her voice strongly commanding.

"You seek the meaning of life, Maurice. You yearn for religious comfort. Well, I have no quarrel with that. You are also, though you do not seek it, in need of discipline and the education which neither I nor Monsieur Deschartres can give you. Very well. I shall place you for a time in a convent."

II

The Dupin family carriage, an ancient berlin that had been in Madame Dupin's possession for many years, was rolling through the streets of Paris en route to the convent. It was an enormous vehicle, more like a small, compact room than anything else, and well stocked with food, pillows, blankets, and foot warmers. Madame Dupin, well enough now to make the long journey to Paris, sat in grim silence in her corner seat. Facing her in the opposite corner, Aurore gazed moodily out of the window, hating the thought of the convent but hating even more the purple serge dress her grandmother had forced her to wear. She felt that she had already lost her identity, for Deschartres had told her that all the girls at the convent would be similarly garbed.

"Maman," she said suddenly, "I want to see my mother before I go to the convent."

Madame Dupin seemed not to have heard. The carriage rolled on. Aurore gazed out of the window again. Her heartbeats quickened painfully. Any moment now they would pass the Rue Duphot where her mother lived in a small apartment with Caroline.

"Maman, stop the carriage!" Aurore seized the door handle. "Stop it or I shall throw myself out!"

Madame Dupin smiled brightly. "They have a well-equipped infirmary at the convent."

"What use would that be if I broke my neck?"

"None whatever, I do agree."

Aurore flung open the door.

"Maurice!" Madame Dupin shrieked.

Her cry, alarming the coachman, brought the carriage to a halt. Aurore leaped out, found herself facing the Rue Duphot and raced down it. A fiacre stood at the door of the house where her mother lived. Aurore scarcely glanced at it until a voice called her. There, sitting in the fiacre with an army officer, was her mother.

"Mother, I want to talk to you!"

Sophie laughed gaily. "How funny you look in that horrible dress, chérie."

"Mother, please!"

"Such frantic insistence," Sophie teased and turned to the officer. "Wait for me, Jules. I won't be long."

She stepped down from the fiacre, fashionably dressed and still quite young in appearance. Aurore, after a quick, unhappy glance at the officer, followed Sophie up the narrow stairs and into the apartment.

"Mother, who is Jules?"

"A friend."

"Are you going to marry him?"

"He has a wife already."

Aurore felt a choking lump in her throat. "So it's true what Maman said!"

"And what, precisely, did the old ogre say?" Sophie asked impatiently.

Aurore repeated everything that her grandmother had told her. She spoke haltingly, her voice scarcely above a whisper. Her face was scarlet; there were tears in her eyes. Sophie embraced her briefly but without warmth, or so it seemed to the girl.

"She told you the truth, but not the whole truth," Sophie said at last. "Ah well, the past is the past. Who cares about it now?"

"I do, Mother, I do!"

Sophie went to the window, drew aside the curtain and waved. Then she turned, still with a charming little smile on her lips.

"Jules is growing impatient."

"Mother!"

Sophie shrugged. "As you wish, child. Did your grandmother tell you, for instance, that I was left alone and destitute when I was fourteen, the same age that you are now?" Her voice, Aurore thought, was coolly detached. "Clearly she did not. I was hungry so often I almost grew used to it. On one occasion an unexpected good meal made me sick. Even when I started dancing at the theatre, I earned scarcely enough to keep body and soul together. There were many temptations. All those rich men flattering me, offering me presents. I fell, of course I did! But believe me, Aurore, I didn't know at the time just what that particular sort of temptation meant. When I found out, it was too late. I grew used to the life. There were times when I even enjoyed it."

Sophie's voice was still coolly detached and she kept glancing at the window as if anxious to be finished and rush down to Jules, but Aurore's heart went out to her. Poor Mother, trapped in the cage of poverty, only to escape and find herself in another cage with no hope of gaining her liberty. At least, not until . . .

"Mother, it was different when you met Papa?"

Sophie's face softened. "Yes, it was different. I loved him. How could it have been otherwise when I lived with him, looking at no other man, for four years before he married me?" Her eyes narrowed. "Did your grandmother tell you that I was proud of marrying an aristocrat? She accused me of that often enough. Oh, I was proud of being married, but not of the aristocratic connection. Far from it, Aurore. The lasting pride of my life is that I'm a daughter of the people. Do you blame me for that?"

"No, Mother. How could I? Let me stay with you. I want to be one of the people myself."

"And I want you to be a lady," Sophie said sharply. "Why did I leave you at Nohant and let you remain there?"

Aurore laughed shakily. "I think you're contradicting yourself, Mother."

"Nonsense, child! Are you not an aristocrat by birth? Nothing can change that whatever I am."

Aurore felt lost and desolate. Was her mother despising her because of her birth?

"Only half of me is an aristocrat," she burst out. "I want to forget it. Please don't let me be sent to the convent."

Sophie was at the window again. She turned presently, her smile as charming as before.

"Your grandmother is a cunning woman," she said, quite without rancor. "She has offered me a larger allowance providing I convince you that the convent is essential to your training as a lady."

"That's bribery, Mother!"

"One can always do with a little extra money."

Aurore turned away. So it was true, the conviction that had been growing on her relentlessly: her mother, whom she loved so dearly, no longer loved her. Or was it that the poor lost woman was making yet another sacrifice?

"I am thinking only of you," Sophie said, "you, the heiress of Nohant. Take heart, chérie. Your grandmother is in failing health. Can she live forever? No doubt she intends to, but not even she can get the better of God's will. We'll be together again, perhaps sooner than either of us thinks. Go to the convent. Pray, if you like, for the old ogre's death."

Aurore was shocked. "I love Maman less than I did, but I could never pray for her death."

"And what about me?"

"I love you more than ever before. I—I know you are only pretending. I know there are tears in your heart."

Sophie was at the mirror, readjusting the set of her fashionable hat. "Dear Aurore," she said lightly, "there were tears in my heart when Louis died, again when your father died, but never since, I assure you. Why should my heart weep when you are alive and have such a splendid future before you?" She turned from the mirror with a little dancing step. "But enough! Can I keep the amusing Jules waiting forever?"

Aurore followed her from the apartment and down the stairs. Sophie waved gaily and jumped into the fiacre. Behind it stood the ancient berlin. Aurore got into it slowly, her chin high, her dark eyes glistening with tears.

"Well?" Madame Dupin demanded.

"I am ready to go to the convent," Aurore said tonelessly. "My mother will be happy to receive an increased allowance."

Madame Dupin was well content. "I never doubted it."

The coachman whipped up the horses and soon Aurore and her grandmother were being ushered into Mother Superior's parlor at the convent. Madame Dupin had already given her granddaughter a vivid description of the place. It had been used as a prison during the Reign of Terror, a prison in which she herself had been incarcerated. Now it was a convent again, and the nuns, as the name implied, were English, the *Dames Augustines Anglaises*. The first nuns of that order had come to Paris over a hundred and fifty years ago when driven from their own country by the Lord Protector, Oliver Cromwell.

"You will find happiness here," Madame Dupin insisted, as she and Aurore sat waiting for the Mother Superior.

Aurore doubted it. Deprived of happiness with her mother, deprived of happiness even at faraway Nohant, how could she hope to find it anywhere? Yet strangely, the quietness of the room and the withdrawn atmosphere were having a soothing effect on her already.

"This is Madame Canning," Madame Dupin whispered.

The Mother Superior had entered so softly that Aurore had failed to notice her.

"Do you speak English, M'm'selle?" Madame Canning asked.

"No, Madame."

"French is spoken, naturally, but there are certain hours of the day when only English is permitted. We have between ninety and a hundred students. Thirty, including yourself, are French girls. The others come from England, Scotland, and Ireland. I am told you are a clever child. I trust you will learn English quickly."

Aurore was studying the nun's face. Her eyes were blue, her cheeks rosy, and her expression calm. Her voice was calm, also, compellingly calm, and it carried a ring of absolute authority. Her habit, like Aurore's dress, was of purple serge.

Madame Dupin cleared her throat. "My granddaughter, Madame, has never taken kindly to deportment. She is something of a lout—at times no better than an uncouth boy. She is in need of discipline. I want her to become poised and elegant."

Aurore was greatly taken aback. Her grandmother, addressing her always as Maurice, had brought her up as if she were a boy. Maman was as illogical as Mother who was proud to be "of the people" but wanted her daughter to be a "lady."

Madame Canning's eyes twinkled momentarily. She inclined her head and addressed herself solely to Aurore.

"You will receive full discipline here, more of it than you will at first appreciate. If you are good, you will be praised justly but not immoderately. If you are very good, you will be permitted, as a special privilege, to take English afternoon tea with the good sisters, possibly with me also. It is a strange ritual to the French, this tea-drinking of ours, but I think you will grow to enjoy it. As for deportment, dancing plays a large part in that since most of the students will eventually take their places in society. Our dancing master is Monsieur Abraham, a gentleman once employed to teach your late queen deportment. He is old but skillful still and not unamusing."

Aurore came close to laughing. The Mother Superior, though a nun, was human, after all.

"In addition to Monsieur Abraham, two other men are permitted entry here—our chaplains, the Abbé de Villèle and the Abbé de Prèmord. They will take full care of your spiritual welfare."

"Splendid," Madame Dupin said, a shade too heartily.

Madame Canning touched Aurore lightly on the shoulder. "You may not be happy here, you may often be in rebellion. But in time, I pray you will find peace, and peace is greater than mere transitory happiness."

The words brought a thrill of response to Aurore's breast. Peace! She could almost believe it here in this quiet room. She was rebellious still, that she knew without question, but she was eager, also, to throw herself violently into the new experience of life within Les Anglaises, as the convent was generally known.

"Come," Madame Canning said, "Mother Alicia is waiting to show you to your dormitory."

Aurore bade her grandmother a formal farewell.

"I beg you not to forget Nohant," Madame Dupin said in quick anxiety.

Aurore tried to laugh as gaily as her mother. "I think I have forgotten it already."

5

MADAME DUPIN SAT at her desk in her airless boudoir. She was weary and her head ached throbbingly, but she was determined, even if it meant sitting here all afternoon, to gain a clear account of her granddaughter's conduct during the three years that Aurore had been at Les Anglaises. Reports from Madame Canning and the girl's letters lay before her, and with them were the notes she had made after seeing Aurore on the winter visiting days. She read them all again.

Clearly rebelliousness had marked Aurore's first year at the convent. The nuns, despairing for her, yet loving her, called her Madcap and sometimes teasingly gave the English rendering of her name, addressing her as "Miss Some Bread." She joined a group of girls who took delight in naming their little society "The Devils." Aurore became the chief "Devil," the ringleader when any mischief was afoot—such as scrambling over the convent roofs, meeting in cellars for secret feasts, and composing "confessions" which none of them had any thought of making to either of the chaplains.

Yet she studied diligently, if somewhat sullenly. She could now speak English with scarcely any accent; she had learned to play the harp as well as the harpsichord; and the little old dancing master regarded her as his most promising pupil. Obviously the religious discipline irked her but she submitted to it meekly while at the same time refusing to take Communion. She kept a notebook in which she jotted down a day-by-day account of convent life, blank verse, and stories about imaginary subjects. She also kept a sketching pad close at hand and was reported to have some little talent in that direction.

At the beginning of her second year she entered the ranks of the senior students and was given the privacy of a cell of her own. Madame Dupin chuckled to herself as she read Aurore's clever description of it:

> It is not quite square, not quite round, and measures no more than six paces in either direction. There are no curtains on my hard bed, but I am not complaining even though I bump my head against the beams of the sloping roof whenever I sit up suddenly. Almost every night I have music, for the cats who prowl on the roof above engage in a concert which would have made Mozart shudder. Former occupants have scribbled all manner of names and dates and poems on the faded yellow wallpaper. I shall do the same myself, but in cipher, so that whoever follows me shall spend many puzzling and no doubt fruitless hours hoping, perhaps, to discover some amazing naughtiness.

Having become a senior, Aurore decided that she could no longer remain a "Devil," but thought it unlikely that she would ever find herself a member of that other society, "The Sensibles." They, she wrote, were far too meek and complaisantly holy. Nevertheless, or so Madame Dupin concluded, her granddaughter was herself showing a leaning towards holiness. She was reading "with bated breath" the lives of the saints and was becoming aware, if only vaguely, of something greater and more profound than anything Monsieur Deschartres had taught

49

her. This in part alarmed Madame Dupin for the cult of Reason was departing and that of Mysticism was taking its place. Even more alarming was Aurore's reference to one of the nuns, Mother Alicia, whose eyes were "mirrors of purity" and who had agreed, at Aurore's request, to "adopt" her.

Madame Dupin came upon the girl's last letter which had reached Nohant that very morning. She had set it aside, trying to forget it, but now, reading it again, she faced the problem squarely. It was an emotional letter. When gazing up at the stars one night Aurore had decided that one star, isolated from the rest and brighter, was watching and guiding her. A great faintness had overcome her. In a single blinding flash of revelation, all obstacles had been removed. Now she loved God as truly as did Mother Alicia. She had discovered a vocation. She would never return to the world. She was preparing herself for a general confession, even though she had never yet confessed or taken Communion. Her burning desire, the only desire of her life, was to join the Order.

A problem, Madame Dupin thought, but how serious a problem? Many girls who, while being educated in a convent, fancied they had a vocation; then, outgrowing it after a period of sublime ecstasy, they came back to the world and married. Would the same thing happen to Aurore? Knowing the girl, understanding the intensity of her nature, Madame Dupin felt certain doubts. Seizing the little bell on her desk, she rang it wildly.

"Madame?"

"We are going to Paris, Julie. Make the preparations at once."

"It is a long and arduous journey for one as frail as Madame," the maid argued.

"Do as I tell you, woman. For all we know, this may be a matter of life and death, a living death."

During the journey to Paris Julie complained that Madame

Dupin had already consigned them to precisely that, a living death. Normally the berlin was driven in a leisurely manner, but on this occasion Madame Dupin ordered the coachman to spare neither himself nor the horses and to give no thought to her own discomfort. They reached the capital in the late evening. She was so exhausted she had to be carried from the berlin, but she rose early the next morning, declared herself to be in perfect health and wasted no time in going to Les Anglaises. Madame Canning protested that it was not a regular visiting day; Madame Dupin brushed this aside with an imperious gesture.

"Tell me, Reverend Mother, is my granddaughter in your opinion fitted to become a nun?"

Madame Canning smiled faintly. "In my opinion, no."

"Nevertheless, it is imperative that I see her."

Madame Canning, placing her parlor at Madame Dupin's disposal, withdrew discreetly when Aurore appeared. Momentarily pleased, Madame Dupin saw that the girl walked with the utmost grace. At least that much had been achieved! She could picture her granddaughter in a fashionable *salon* wearing a gown of the latest design.

"Do you want to go about in purple serge for the rest of your life?" she asked angrily.

"But why not, Maman?" There was a dreamy expression in Aurore's eyes.

"You hated it once."

"I love it now," Aurore sighed.

Many questions were forming in Madame Dupin's mind. She seized on one of them and gave expression to it harshly.

"Why did you seek to be adopted by Mother Alicia?"

"It is the practice here," Aurore replied calmly. "All the girls are adopted from time to time by various nuns."

"Have you found in Mother Alicia all that is lacking in your real mother?"

"Mother Alicia and my real mother hold the same religious views."

Madame Dupin's old eyes flashed wickedly. "They give expression to them in a widely different manner."

"God will forgive my poor, misguided mother."

"The truth of the matter is obvious. You felt that your mother had deserted you."

"Yes," Aurore admitted, her calmness unshakable.

"And that, of course, is why you were so unruly during your first year."

"Perhaps, Maman."

"And so you sought solace from Mother Alicia."

"Whether or not I sought it, I found it—and the peace which Madame Canning spoke of the first day." A tinge of red colored Aurore's cheeks, but the dreamy look was still in her eyes. "Your God of Reason! I could never believe in him. If only you could see religion as I see it, Maman, you would be a happier woman."

"So! You seek to convert me!"

"Yes, Maman."

"An insulting attitude, but Deschartres will be most amused."

Aurore looked at her grandmother sadly. "This is no laughing matter."

"By heaven, it isn't!"

"Dear Maman, try to understand what my conversion means. No longer do I need to torture myself with unanswerable questions about the meaning of life. If only you knew the great joy of just believing in God."

"Believe in God if you must, but belief alone will never give you a vocation."

"It has already done so."

"You—a cloistered nun? Ludicrous! I forbid it!"

Aurore was completely calm again. "That is your present

52

privilege, Maman, but when I come of age I shall be free to please myself."

Defeated, Madame Dupin rose to go. "You have been at Les Anglaises too long. It is my duty to take you back to Nohant."

"That will only strengthen my resolve."

"Aurore, be sensible," Madame Dupin begged plaintively.

Aurore walked to the door and turned. "Thank you for not calling me Maurice."

"In other words, for not thinking of you as a boy?"

"Well, yes."

"As a nun you would be neither a boy nor a girl," Madame Dupin said triumphantly.

"Good-by, Maman," Aurore murmured and opened the door.

"Did you enjoy the dancing lessons?" Madame Dupin shot after her.

"Very much, but I have put all worldly desires from my mind."

Madame Canning returned to the parlor while Madame Dupin was trying desperately to control herself.

"You failed, Madame?"

"Yes, I failed."

Madame Canning smiled serenely. "She has no real vocation. Soon she will make her general confession. Let us be patient and leave her to the good offices of the Abbé de Prèmord."

Somewhat reassured, Madame Dupin returned to Nohant and there, a week later, she received a stricken letter from her granddaughter. She had made her general confession, but the Abbé de Prèmord, who at first had seemed so kind and understanding, had laughed softly and imposed a monstrous penance. She, Aurore Dupin, seventeen years of age and fully capable of recognizing the most urgent need of her heart, was to become a child again. In short, she was commanded to resume her earlier interest in the innocent pastimes of youth. Intolerable! Yet what could she do but obey, or at all events make a show of obeying?

Madame Dupin waited patiently and presently learned that Aurore, after weeks of brooding, had organized the production of Molière's *Le Malade Imaginaire*. This was followed by a week of fasting, after which another production, *Le Bourgeois Gentilhomme*. And so it went, a frantic leaping from one extreme to the other. The nuns could do nothing with her, Madame Canning wrote, and many of the girls were alarmed by her wild conduct. Alarmed herself, Madame Dupin decided to withdraw her granddaughter from Les Anglaises. Once again she journeyed to Paris and was joined at the Dupin apartment by a sad-eyed, listless Aurore. Madame Dupin greeted her with forced gaiety.

"First of all, we must get you out of that purple serge. We shall spend a week in Paris. I scarcely have the strength for shopping expeditions but I insist on the purchase of a fashionable wardrobe."

"If you wish, Maman."

"Then home to Nohant. There are several interesting and eligible young men in the district now."

"Young men?" Aurore was appalled.

"I have only a short time to live. It is my duty to find you a husband before I die."

"A husband! I shall never marry! Never!"

"Nonsense."

"I shall run away."

Madame Dupin was gasping for breath. "Run away? To your mother perhaps?"

Aurore grasped at this. "Yes, Maman. I am more capable now of looking after her."

"Have you no pity for me, old and tired as I am and close to death?"

Aurore softened instantly. Her behavior, though reasonable in her own eyes, was clearly a sore trial to her grandmother. There was wickedness in it, too. Loving God as she did, she must force herself to love all God's creatures. But Nohant and marriage!

"What are those marks on your neck?" Madame Dupin demanded. "They look like scars."

"They are indeed," Aurore said proudly. "All last week I wore a tight filigree necklet. I broke the filigree, leaving sharp edges, and tightened the necklet a little more each day."

"In heaven's name, why?"

"The mortification of the flesh."

"Did you also wear a hairshirt?"

Aurore sighed dramatically. "Alas, I was unable to obtain one."

Madame Dupin took full note of the girl's sense of drama. A promising sign, perhaps, but the battle was not yet won.

"Will you come willingly to Nohant," she wheedled, "if I allow your mother to accompany us?"

Aurore looked at her grandmother uncertainly. "Is this a trick, Maman?"

"No, child. I give you my solemn word. You may go to your mother at once."

"Alone, Maman?"

"Certainly not. The streets of Paris are unsafe for a young lady alone. Julie shall accompany you. Instruct her to hire a fiacre. Julie, naturally, will remain in the fiacre while you talk with your mother."

II

Much to Aurore's relief, her mother was at home when she reached the apartment in the Rue Duphot. She had seen very little of her during the last three years. Sophie had visited the convent occasionally, but each visit had been shorter than the last and her conversation had been concerned chiefly with references to new friends and the gay life she was leading. Always, Aurore had been left with the dismaying impression that her mother visited her out of a sense of duty and was anxious to rush away again.

"So they still have you encased in that ghastly purple serge," Sophie remarked after embracing her daughter.

"Maman is going to buy me some fashionable dresses," Aurore said with a broken sigh.

"She can well afford it. Does this mean you are leaving Les Anglaises?"

"Yes, Mother."

"Splendid! You have been out of the world too long."

Aurore was shocked at her mother's appearance. It was midday but she had not yet dressed. Her pink peignoir was badly crumpled, her hair untidy, while her face, devoid of cosmetics, revealed many lines and wrinkles that Aurore had failed to notice before. She was over fifty now but she looked much older.

"Maman has invited you to come with us to Nohant," Aurore announced excitedly.

"Nohant? I loathe the place more than ever. My life is here in Paris. And a very happy life it is, I assure you."

"Mother, for my sake," Aurore pleaded.

"Oh, I'll visit you at Nohant one of these days, but not until the old ogre is dead and buried."

"I want to look after you, Mother. Come, please come."

"I'm perfectly capable of looking after myself."

"Has Maman offered you a larger allowance to stay away from Nohant?" Aurore asked fearfully.

Sophie hesitated. Should she tell the truth? Would she gain anything by lying?

56

"No," she admitted. "But perhaps if I were to threaten a visit . . . ?"

"Mother!"

Sophie shrugged. "Talk to me while I dress if you must. But be brief. I have an appointment."

Aurore stifled a sob. "You don't care what happens to me."

"Of course I do, you silly girl."

"I won't go to Nohant unless you come with me."

Sophie's voice rose impatiently. "Nohant is your home, your inheritance. Be sensible, Aurore."

"Maman is going to find me a husband," Aurore blurted out.

"What's so terrible about that?"

"I have a vocation. I want to join the Order."

"You must be out of your mind!"

"Mother, let me stay with you."

Sophie laughed shrewdly. "Stay with me and I shall find you a husband."

Defeated, fighting back her tears, Aurore went down to the fiacre. Julie shot her a sharp glance but remained silent during the drive back to the Dupin apartment.

"Well?" Madame Dupin asked, more gently than might have been expected.

Aurore sought vainly for an answer, not to her grandmother's question, but to the seething thoughts in her mind. She could run away, yes, but what would happen to her if she did? The same thing that had happened to her mother? The convent was closed to her. Only Nohant remained open, Nohant and marriage. But worst of all, her mother had rejected her. The gaiety of life in Paris was more important. Unsuccessfully she tried to tell herself that her mother was merely putting a brave face on a situation which neither of them could master. Suddenly she felt alone in the world, alone and bereft of human kindness. It seemed to her that even God had turned away from her. Or was He simply testing her? She clung

57

frantically to this thought. Whom the Lord loveth He chasteneth.

"Well?" Madame Dupin repeated.

Aurore heaved a melancholy sigh. "I think I have grown up very suddenly, Maman."

6

MONSIEUR DESCHARTRES CAST a quizzical glance on Aurore as they rode abreast toward the village. Her big dark eyes were solemn. She appeared to be staring into space. He suspected that she was striving to resist the magic of the countryside that had always entranced her. "Give her time," he had told Madame Dupin earlier that morning. "This is only her second day at Nohant." He smiled uneasily and averted his eyes. Aurore's rich black hair was tied back with a pink ribbon. She wore a pink gingham dress which, since she rode her mare Colette astride, was rucked up to her shapely thighs.

"It is most unseemly," he protested, his eyes still averted, "to ride astride in a dress."

"You suggest trousers, Monsieur?"

Deschartres laughed uncertainly. "I should feel more at ease in your company if you wore trousers while riding."

"Does the sight of a girl's legs disturb you, Monsieur?" she asked flatly.

"Not in the way you mean, but it would surely disturb the young men of the village."

Aurore's eyes flashed angrily. "That is the last thing I want to happen."

She remembered her tiny uniform of years ago. She had not worn trousers since though she had often wanted to do so. It would be exciting and convenient to wear them again. Better still, if she adopted a mannish attitude, the young men whom she was sure her grandmother was organizing to woo her would be deterred in their efforts.

"Henceforth I shall wear trousers," she announced, "not only when riding, but on every other possible occasion."

"That will make me even more at ease in your company," Deschartres admitted.

"You mean you will care for me more if I look like a young man?"

Deschartres laughed shyly. "Well, yes, now that you are grown up."

"Do women frighten you?"

He nodded. "With the sole exception of your grandmother."

"Were you never in love, Monsieur?"

"Never!" he said vehemently.

Aurore thought of all that her grandmother had told her about the old man. As a youth he had studied for the church, had even styled himself the Abbé Deschartres, but he had never been ordained. During the Revolution he had abandoned his studies and overnight had become plain Citizen Deschartres. Thereafter, his religion, if religion it could be called, had been the same as Madame Dupin's, deism. He had also studied medicine but had never become a qualified doctor. Nevertheless he practiced medicine of a sort and went on his rounds in the village, tending the sick, setting broken bones, bandaging cuts and abrasions, and sometimes performing minor operations. Aurore, for want of something better to do, was accompanying him now on such a mission.

Their first call was at the Josse cottage. Ursule Josse was one of Aurore's old village friends. Her mother was suffering from a touch of the colic. Deschartres prescribed a vile-tasting remedy. Aurore greeted Ursule with enthusiasm, but the girl seemed shy and tongue-tied. She addressed Aurore punctiliously as "Mademoiselle." They went on to the house of another old friend. The girl's brother, one of the Nohant farm laborers, had a broken arm. Deschartres, while setting it, commanded Aurore to assist him. Once again an old friend spoke to her as "Mademoiselle." Aurore protested, but the girl merely lowered her eyes. At the third call, Deschartres lanced a boil and set Aurore the task of staunching the flow of blood. The sight of the blood sickened her, but she felt pleased in the end that she had not actually fainted. It was necessary, Deschartres said, that she should become hardened to suffering if she was to continue to assist him.

Riding back through the village, Aurore stopped from time to time to greet other old friends. Without exception they all addressed her as "Mademoiselle." They were shy and humble and made her feel like a stranger.

"What have I done to these people I love so dearly?" she asked Deschartres.

"It is one thing for an aristocrat to play as a child with village children, but when the aristocrat grows up . . ."

"But to isolate me like this! It's so unkind."

"That is the way of the world."

"The social barrier is their creation, not mine," Aurore cried hotly.

"That, I assure you, is not unusual."

Aurore fumed and fretted until they reached Nohant. The manor house looked so tranquil in the midday sun that her heart stirred painfully. Did she really hate the place? Of course she didn't! All she hated was what it had come to represent —her grandmother's marriage plans. She took a deep breath of the clean spring air and gloried in the sight of the trees that were bursting into leaf. She had heard the nightingales last night and thrilled now at the thought of them. During the early evening she had walked through the farm and had tried not to enjoy the old familiar farmyard smells and the sight of the lumbering carts. What a fool she was! Did it matter if the villagers, her grandmother's tenants, were setting her apart? Oh, it was hurtful but she was strong enough, she prayed, to stand alone.

The withered old Julie met them at the door.

"A visitor has called, M'm'selle Aurore," she said. "Madame Dupin is asking for you."

Aurore looked at her haughtily. "It is sufficient that you should address me as Mademoiselle."

The maid scowled but looked just a little afraid. "Very well, Mademoiselle."

"She still hates me," Aurore remarked as she and Deschartres went indoors.

Deschartres laughed perkily. "What is the difference between an old maid and a ripe orange? You may squeeze a ripe orange with appetizing results, but an old maid never."

Aurore laughed spontaneously. That was amusing coming from a man who had always been frightened of women. It came upon her suddenly that she had almost forgotten how to laugh. She gave Deschartres an affectionate smile. He knew all about that. He was a wily old devil really.

The visitor was Comte René de Villeneuve, the grandson of Madame Dupin's second husband and therefore Aurore's cousin. He had been a general in the days of Napoleon's empire and still carried himself with a soldierly air. He was fifty-four, handsome, gray-haired, and immensely rich. He had once visited the convent with Madame Dupin. Aurore liked him and thought him very amusing. He bowed before her and kissed her hand as if she were a very great lady indeed.

"Can you use a pistol?" he asked, somewhat startlingly.

"No, René, I can't."

"Then I shall teach you. Naturally you must know how to

protect yourself."

Madame Dupin explained that the count had come to Nohant on family business. She was putting her affairs in order and had made a new will. Comte René de Villeneuve was to be Aurore's guardian if the old lady died before the girl came of age.

"You would in that case live with me at the Château de Chenonceau," he said, "and my wife, a born matchmaker, would present a whole regiment of eligible young men."

"That is a subject I prefer not to discuss," Aurore told him stonily.

The count spent several days at Nohant. He taught Aurore to fire a pistol with reasonable accuracy and went with her on many a wild ride through the nearby countryside. She had started wearing male attire, an old suit of Hippolyte's that a complaining Julie had been forced to cut down to the right size. Unlike Deschartres, René disapproved of trousers.

"They destroy your not inconsiderable femininity, Aurore."

"That is my aim, René."

"Ah, but whatever you wear, can you destroy it within yourself?"

"I shall try my best."

"You actually want to destroy it?"

"No," Aurore admitted. "I am not dissatisfied with being a woman."

"Praise heaven for that!"

When the count had departed, Madame Dupin told her granddaughter that he had married a widow with one daughter but had earlier sought the hand of a much younger woman, indeed a mere girl.

"In short, it was you he wanted to marry. He made up his mind after seeing you at the convent. You were fifteen and to my way of thinking a little too young. Nevertheless, now that you are of a marriageable age, a man like René would be most suitable."

Aurore was appalled. "A man as old as he?"

"To you, of course, he is very old, but not to himself. Believe me, Aurore, old men make the best husbands. They are kind and understanding and, as a general rule, experienced. Your grandfather was sixty when I married him but I had no regrets."

"How old were you?"

"Thirty."

"But I am only seventeen!" Aurore's heart was beating wildly. "Have you an old man in mind for me, Maman?"

"Indeed I have. He is just as handsome as René, considerably more cultured and even richer."

Aurore burst into tears, quite appealing tears, Madame Dupin thought. Some men would find her entrancing when she wept. The old woman studied her tremblingly. Dressed now in male attire, Aurore had become Maurice again. Not that the trousers and the coat gave her the appearance of a youth. Far from it! They served only to emphasize the fact that she was a girl who had achieved the maturity of womanhood. Her breasts were small but not too small. Her neck was slender while her hands and feet were finely formed. Her hair, dark and glossy, was very nearly pure black. The eyes beneath the wide brow were a brilliant black, poignantly beautiful now with the tears pouring from them. Her nose, which Madame Dupin thought her best feature, had a truly aristocratic curve. The girl's only fault, if it really mattered, was her shortness of stature. She measured only five feet and seemed to have ceased growing.

"I shall shoot myself!" Aurore cried.

"Get me your pistol at once," Madame Dupin commanded.

Aurore got it, pointed the barrel at her right temple and fingered the trigger, but then surrendered the weapon with a deep sigh to her grandmother.

"Lock it away, Maman, but there are other means. I—I shall drown myself."

"I have heard it said that drowning is a very pleasant death."

"Splendid!"

Madame Dupin burst unexpectedly into tears. "You are making life very difficult for me."

Aurore turned and ran from the room. She had never felt more rebellious in her life, yet at the same time she experienced a twinge of guilt. She had upset poor Maman, had possibly brought her to the point of another stroke. Would God, who was still testing her, ever forgive her if it happened?

That night, after refusing to eat, she sat in melancholy silence at the window of her room. It was a calm, cloudless night, with the setting sun casting a fiery red haze across the western horizon. The angry beauty of it hurt her intolerably and, trying to ease the agony of her soul, she created clouds above the sun and reduced the fading light to a paleness more in accordance with her somber thoughts. She found a pencil on her little writing table and, returning to the window, began to scribble in English. Never in her life had she felt anything so intensely nor known the need so urgently to record her thoughts in writing. If she died during the night, here on the window frame would be found a sort of epitaph:

Go, fading sun!
Hide thy pale beams behind the distant trees.
Nightly Vesperus is coming to announce the close of day.
Evening descends to bring melancholy to the landscape.
With thy return, Beautiful Light,
Nature will find again mirth and beauty,
But joy will never comfort my soul.

Aurore awoke the next morning to the angry realization that she had slept soundly and dreamlessly. She remembered Deschartres' story about the orange and the old maid, but sternly forbade herself to laugh. An old man was waiting to snatch her up and make her his wife. She was still determined, by some means or other, to kill herself.

II

Hippolyte Châtiron had arrived at Nohant on a dashing charger. Having heard that Aurore had emerged from the convent, he had obtained a week's leave from his military duties. Aurore had almost forgotten him. He had been sent to a school in Paris before she went to Les Anglaises; then he had embarked on his military career. He was twenty-three now, a Hussar who had not yet gained advancement beyond the rank of sergeant. She recalled him as an ugly, clumsy boy. He was still ugly, still clumsy, but the ugliness was so pronounced that one, possibly out of compassion, felt instant affection for him. He chided her about her trousers. Could any man feel respect for a girl in trousers? He mocked her about her horsemanship—or the lack of it—and gave her riding lessons. He also gave her fencing lessons. They went hunting and shooting together, a completely man-to-man affair, and occasionally they recalled and savored some of their childhood memories.

"That altar of yours, Aurore—are you still a pagan?"

A pagan? What an insulting question! Aurore had already written ecstatic letters to Mother Alicia and the Abbé de Prèmord, telling them of her longing to return to the convent. Why, in God's holy name, must she be consigned to the fate of marrying an old man? Before she quite knew what she was doing, her arms were round Hippolyte's waist and she was looking up at him imploringly.

"Hippolyte, elope with me! Maman is going to marry me to an old graybeard."

Hippolyte tried to release himself and that made her feel vastly affronted.

66

"Are you, like Monsieur Deschartres, afraid of women?"

"On the contrary, I adore them, especially the young and pretty ones."

"But me—you don't like me?"

"I'm very fond of you, Aurore, in a—well—brotherly sort of way."

"Is it my trousers? If you dislike them so much, I'll take them off."

Hippolyte succeeded in releasing himself. "Please, I beg of you! Not now, not here!"

"I meant in the privacy of my room," Aurore said with dignity. "I'll never wear trousers again if that will make me more attractive to you."

There was a desperate look in Hippolyte's eyes. "I would do anything in the world for you, but I could never marry you."

"I would make you a very good wife, Hippolyte."

"Dear Aurore," he said quietly, "so they haven't told you."

"Told me what?"

"My father was your father—Maurice Dupin."

"No!"

"I'm your brother. That is to say—your half-brother. My mother was a village girl. Madame Dupin told me about it before I joined the army."

"Poor Hippolyte! Do you mind very much?"

Hippolyte shrugged easily. "Obviously my father couldn't marry a peasant."

"He married my mother, a daughter of the people."

"He was very deeply in love with her."

"But not with your mother. How unfair, how unjust!"

"Oh, he probably thought he was at the time. I always think I am myself, but that conviction soon passes."

"You have illegitimate children yourself?"

Hippolyte strutted importantly. "Who can say?"

Aurore quickly lost interest. All that mattered was that she could not elope with Hippolyte. Escape from that old man was now impossible. There was only one other alternative.

"I shall kill myself. I mean it this time, Hippolyte. I shall kill myself."

She rushed headlong to the stables, saddled Colette and flung herself on the mare's back. Perhaps if she rode furiously enough, Colette, though a gentle beast, would throw her and break her neck just as Leopardo had thrown her father and broken his neck. It would be a fine thing to die the way he had died. Papa would never have permitted her to marry an old man. She reached the village, fully aware that Hippolyte was following her on his charger. Deschartres was in the main street, talking to the village priest. She waved to them gaily as she flew past and, glancing back a few moments later, saw that Deschartres had joined Hippolyte in the chase.

"Colette, do your duty!" she urged.

She put the mare to hedges, fences, and stone walls. Colette sailed over them without mishap. She faltered, however, when crossing a ford. Aurore fell into the water. The stream was in full flood. Her feet touched the bottom, but the current swept over her and she was soon out of her depth. How fortunate, she thought, that she had never learned to swim! But was death by drowning so pleasant? Her mouth was soon full of icy water. She coughed and spluttered but succeeded only in swallowing more water.

"Aurore!"

It was Hippolyte, standing on the river bank. She grew frantic at the sight of him, for Hippolyte had never learned to swim either!

"Seize Colette's mane!" he shouted.

Colette was alongside her. Aurore seized the mare's mane and clung to it desperately. Presently she found herself close to the bank, her feet on a large, loose stone, her chin barely above the water. The bank was so steep she was quite unable

68

to gain a foothold.

"Hurry, Hippolyte! Do you want me to be swept away again?"

Hippolyte was sliding headfirst down the bank, stretching out his hands toward her. Deschartres, coming up behind him, clung to his legs.

"Hippolyte, hurry!"

"Wait!" Deschartres demanded. He was trembling with fear but determined to teach Aurore a lesson. "You want to kill yourself. Very well then, drown. We will give you a splendid funeral."

"For pity's sake . . ." Aurore gasped.

"There will be no more talk of suicide?"

"None, none!"

"You give me your word?"

"My word, my solemn word!"

"Pull her out, Hippolyte."

Colette had already scrambled out of the water further down the stream. A shivering, dejected Aurore mounted her. She was very ashamed of herself and laughed hysterically when, in the village, Ursule Josse curtsied, took no notice of her sodden condition and addressed her as "Mademoiselle."

She was put to bed and instructed to remain there for three days. Having saved her from herself, Deschartres had no intention of seeing her die of pneumonia. He made her swallow some nauseating medicine and placed a burning mustard plaster on her back. On the third day, Madame Dupin, who had expressed her displeasure by remaining aloof, came to see her.

"Did you think about God when you thought you were drowning?" the old lady asked calmly. "Did you pray?"

"Yes," Aurore lied, appalled by the memory that she had neither thought of God nor prayed. "Did you pray that I wouldn't die of pneumonia?" she countered.

"Indeed I did," Madame Dupin avowed surprisingly, "but

not on my knees."

"You don't believe in God, Maman."

"Rubbish! I most certainly believe in the God of Nature."

"And Christ?" Aurore said, remembering a past declaration. "You hold Him in high esteem?"

"I do. He was a great man, a sincere and inspired teacher. As for the Gospels, they express a philosophy that has never yet been equaled. But dogma! Did dogma come from God? As for religious ceremonial—mummery—sheer mummery! For myself, I prefer grand opera. You will come to it yourself given time."

"Never."

"We shall see."

"That old man of yours—is he also of a rational turn of mind?"

"Would it help if I said he believes as you at present believe?"

"A little," Aurore admitted.

"Not that it matters. I have decided—oh, against my better judgment—that there will be no more talk of marriage until you are eighteen."

"Maman, you don't mean it!"

"I mean it, child."

Aurore sighed happily. She was well content. By the time she was eighteen she would, she felt sure, have converted her grandmother to true religion.

III

It was late autumn and very nearly as cold as winter. Deschartres sat dozing in his chair by the fire. Madame Dupin was already asleep in hers. Aurore, from her position at the card-table, glanced affectionately from one to the other and continued to sketch her grandmother's lined old face. But she kept thinking of the letter she had received from her mother that day. It was a letter of protest, the phrasing both indignant and angry. Gossip had reached Sophie from Nohant. The whole village was shocked by Aurore's behavior. Not that the villagers mattered in the least, but what of the neighboring gentry? There was something unnatural about a girl who dressed always as a man and took a positive delight in pretending to be a doctor. So much for her hopes that her daughter would grow up to be a lady!

Aurore had already been reproved in much the same way by the village priest and as a result no longer went to confession. This did not mean that she was turning against the Church. Far from it. She was as devout a Catholic as ever and was still determined to bring about her grandmother's conversion. In addition, she had written to the Abbé de Prèmord asking his advice and was now waiting impatiently for his reply. One thing troubled her. No longer did she feel—at least, not quite so strongly—that she had a vocation. Was Stéphane, she wondered, responsible for that?

Deschartres was taking a special interest in Stéphane Ajasson de Grandsaigne, the son of an old country friend. Recently Stéphane, a medical student, had spent a few weeks at Nohant. Tall and handsome, he had presented Aurore with a skeleton and had given her lessons in anatomy. Though her heart had remained untouched, she had toyed with the thought of marriage. Deschartres, as wily as ever, had chided her, calling her a contrary young woman. Aurore laughed to herself. No longer compelled to rush into marriage, she was finding the idea not unattractive. After all, as heiress of Nohant it was her duty to think of marrying some day and having children. Not that Stéphane, aristocrat that he was, could be regarded as eligible. He came of an old family but, as Deschartres had pointed out, he was all but penniless.

Aurore rose and threw a log on the dying fire. Deschartres emerged from his doze with a little grunt of alarm.

"Forgive me for disturbing your dreams," she laughed. "It's still quite early. Perhaps Maman would like another game of cards."

She turned to her grandmother. The old lady was no longer asleep. Her eyes were wide open but their expression was blank. Her limbs, always stiff these days, had the look of complete rigidity.

"Maman!"

Deschartres hurried to Madame Dupin's side. Controlling the trembling of his hands and the quaking of his heart, he made a quick examination. There was no need for Aurore to await his diagnosis. Her grandmother had suffered a stroke of extreme severity. She was carried to her bed. There she remained for a week before recovering the power of speech. For the rest, she was seriously paralyzed. Her first words, uttered in the driest of tones, brought the tears to Aurore's eyes.

"Soon, Maurice, you will lose your best friend."

Deeply stricken, Aurore realized the truth of her grandmother's words. Thereafter, through the weeks that followed, she devoted herself entirely to the welfare of the dying woman. Every hour of the day and many hours of the night were spent at the bedside. Deschartres himself was often present. When Madame Dupin slept, he went through the household accounts with Aurore, giving her prudent and precise instructions in the matter of controlling the estate and preparing her skillfully for the position which would soon be hers—that of mistress of Nohant.

Her greatest fear was that her grandmother should die a heathen, yet the Abbé de Prèmord seemed in no way disturbed. To alarm Madame Dupin, he wrote, would only hasten the end. Aurore was to forget the mind and obey the dictates of the heart. The heart, he said, was never wrong if one's aim was pure and holy. Aurore was to speak but gently if her heart commanded it. If she felt in doubt, she was to remain silent and pray for the direct intervention of God. Tentatively she broached the subject by asking her grandmother if she would like the village priest to visit her.

"For what purpose?" Madame Dupin asked slyly. "Is it your wish that Monsieur le Curé should take afternoon tea with us?"

"Knowing him as I do, Maman, he would prefer a glass of wine."

A rasping sound came from the old lady's throat. "And wine would loosen his tongue in prayer for a lost soul. We understand each other perfectly, Maurice."

With that, Aurore prayed as the Abbé de Prèmord had directed her to do, and to her absolute amazement, Madame Dupin summoned the priest to Nohant.

"Will it make my passing easier for you," she asked Aurore, "if in my last days I embrace the faith which means so much to you?"

"What I feel is of no account," Aurore said stoutly. "I am thinking only of you, Maman."

"By which you mean my immortal soul."

It seemed to Aurore that her grandmother was making a mockery of religion, yet she knew, in a blinding flash of revelation, that the brave old lady was the strongest character she had ever met and that she herself had been imbued with much of her strength.

The priest, a simple, kindly old fellow, was ushered into the bedroom by a skeptical Deschartres. Aurore started to withdraw, but Madame Dupin insisted that both the girl and Deschartres remain while she made her confession. She thought it likely that she had not loved God wholeheartedly, but she declared that never in her life had she deliberately hurt anyone. She spoke argumentatively as if challenging the priest to question her statement. Later, all the servants of the Nohant estate, even the farm laborers, were present to witness the administration of the Last Sacrament. Madame Dupin herself brought the solemn ceremony to a close by promising to love Almighty God throughout eternity, providing He brought her together with her son once more. Making a condition, Aurore thought more in admiration than horror—actually trying to bargain with God!

"And so I shall die in peace," the old woman said, her eyes on Aurore.

Did she mean it? Did she feel at peace? Had confession and absolution done that for her? She certainly looked at peace and by no means as close to death as everybody thought.

"I am leaving you free but alone," she added. "Be brave, child, for my sake."

When the end came with the strong-minded old lady dying in her sleep, Aurore was too weary for tears. The days and nights had merged into one long, dull vigil. Automatically she made the arrangements for the funeral while Deschartres superintended the digging of the grave. He was distracted almost to the point of insanity, though Aurore was only vaguely aware of it until one bitterly cold night when he knocked wildly on her door and hurried her out to the cemetery. A lantern was burning by the side of an open, earth-stained coffin. For a moment Aurore thought she was gazing at the skeleton which Stéphane had given her. Then the truth dawned upon her with startling clarity. Deschartres lifted the detached skull and held it reverently.

"Your father's, Aurore. I have loved two people in my life. Your grandmother and your father. Now both are gone, but where, where? Kiss your father's skull, child, kiss it!"

Aurore obeyed as if in a trance. Slowly the tears began to roll down her cheeks and she gave way at last to grief. Free, she thought, but alone, as Maman had said, so very much alone.

7

"I CAN ONLY thank God," Madame Sophie Dupin greeted her daughter, "that you have the decency to wear a suitable mourning dress. I had half-expected to find you in trousers."

Unable to reach Nohant in time for the funeral, Sophie had nonetheless arrived for the reading of the will. She wore mourning herself when she would have preferred a ball gown. What fun it would be to dance on the old ogre's grave! Beneath her veil her face was heavily coated with rouge and lip salve. She might feel her age but she had no intention of looking it. Turning again now to her daughter, she laughed immoderately.

"Is it true, Aurore, that a village girl mistook you one dark night for a handsome young man and attempted to seduce you? Well, well, never mind. But what an intriguing situation! Or was it you who . . ."

"Mother!" Aurore protested hotly.

René de Villeneuve came squarely between mother and daughter, thus saving Aurore from further embarrassment. It was he whose task it was to read the will. He had already greeted Sophie politely while she for her part had merely given him a haughty stare. The atmosphere was charged with hostility; Aurore felt it instantly.

"You may think I have no right to be here," Sophie said jauntily, "but I have every right, Monsieur le Comte."

René de Villeneuve bowed stiffly. His eyes were coldly penetrating and remained so while he read the will. It was, as wills went, a brief enough document. Madame Dupin's death had made Aurore a well-to-do young woman. She was now the owner of the Nohant estate, a number of investments, and the Hôtel de Narbonne in Paris, a large house which, divided into apartments, brought in a substantial income. Full control would be hers when she came of age. Meanwhile, according to the wishes of her late grandmother, he, the Comte de Ville-neuve, was her guardian.

Sophie chuckled. "Madame Dupin was a law unto herself, but did that make her the law of the land? I, Monsieur le Comte, am now my daughter's guardian. Madame Dupin's death has returned her to my care until she comes of age."

"So?" said the count.

"You wish to argue the point?" Sophie was enjoying herself hugely.

"Madame, Aurore would enjoy greater advantages under my care than yours."

"A mother's care is more important, Monsieur."

"You feel better equipped than I to arrange for her a suitable marriage?"

"Monsieur, she has no wish to marry. Therefore it is not my wish to force a husband upon her."

"Nor is it mine, Madame."

"How splendid that we should see eye to eye," Sophie purred.

"A mother's care . . ." René pondered. "You willingly gave Aurore to Madame Dupin—or am I mistaken?"

"To Madame Dupin, but not, in the event of her death, to anybody else. We are concerned solely with the letter of the law, Monsieur."

"Why not let Aurore decide for herself?"

Sophie had no intention of taking such a risk. "She is neither old enough nor sensible enough to decide for herself."

René glanced at Aurore. "Let us compromise, Madame. I suggest that she return to the shelter of Les Anglaises."

"Never!"

Free, Aurore thought. How wrong her grandmother had been! She was neither free nor alone, yet wasn't this what she had always wanted—to be with her mother? Not only to be with her but to look after her. Tears of frustration sprang to her eyes, and she asked herself if she still loved her mother. She shook her head just as if René or Deschartres had asked her that question aloud. Gone was the old romantic, idealistic love. Her mother had killed it now if not at their last meeting. All that remained was the tie of blood and, with it, pity and compassion.

"My mother is concerned solely with the letter of the law," she said quietly. "So am I. She shall stay with me here at Nohant."

"I loathe Nohant as much as ever," Sophie burst out violently. "It holds no happy memories for me. We shall live in Paris."

"As you wish," Aurore sighed. She began to think of herself as Saint Aurore, the Martyr.

Sophie clapped her hands in childlike glee. "A dutiful daughter at last!"

Before departing for Paris with her triumphant mother, Aurore told Deschartres that she was leaving him in complete control of the Nohant estate. The old man stammered that he was unworthy of such a trust, particularly since he had treated her so shamefully.

"Shamefully?" she asked in amazement.

"It was wrong of me to open your father's coffin, to insist on your kissing his skull. I was out of my mind with grief.

77

I beg you to forgive me and I pray with all my heart that I harmed you in no way."

"You helped to bring me up as a boy rather than as a girl," Aurore said quietly. "Your training has given me great strength."

"Yes, but has it hardened you?"

"My mind, perhaps, but not my heart. It has given me the fortitude to endure things which would otherwise be unendurable."

Deschartres took her hands in his. "Come back to Nohant as soon as you can," he said emotionally.

"As soon as I can," Aurore promised.

Madame Dupin had died on Christmas Day. It was late January when Aurore and her mother reached Paris only to find the Dupin apartment at the Hôtel de Narbonne cold and desolate. Sophie issued dictatorial orders for many unnecessary renovations and then carried Aurore off to stay with Aunt Lucie. Aurore's half-sister Caroline, now married, came on a brief visit. She had grown into a stranger and took little interest in Aurore. Even Aunt Lucie, once so kind, was aloof and preoccupied with her own affairs.

Aurore was increasingly miserable and began to feel that there was no friendliness anywhere. Certainly there was no understanding. She had nothing in common with anybody. Her mother, her aunt and her half-sister all jeered at her preoccupation with reading which had become her only means of escape. Finally Sophie took possession of the renovated apartment. There, playing the grand lady, she was affronted when the aristocratic friends of the late Madame Dupin refused to call. Her hatred of the dead woman spilled over in a tirade of abuse.

"Thank God, she was your father's mother, not mine!"

Almost hourly she swung from periods of hysterical gaiety

to periods of deep and sullen brooding. Her scorn for Aurore's intellectual pursuits became an obsession. Books would disappear overnight, and when a case of new ones arrived from Nohant, she sent it, unpacked, to a secondhand dealer.

"Why are you treating me like this?" Aurore asked pitifully.

Sophie laughed airily. "No doubt it is my change of life. It is worse for me than other women since I was always so passionate."

Aurore tried to see her mother as a willful child in need of guidance but unwilling to accept it. Pity and compassion, she thought—what could she achieve by either? Death would be preferable to the fate of spending the next three years with her mother. She refused to eat. Perhaps starvation would bring a sweet release in the end. Yet she wanted to live. Life, the Abbé de Prèmord had said in one of his letters, was her true vocation. She knew that now without question.

Sophie, while denying Aurore all but a small inadequate wardrobe, became preoccupied with clothes herself. New dresses arrived in abundance from the fashionable dressmakers and outrageous hats from the milliners. Many were sent back because they clashed with the changing color of her hair. Its natural shade was still black and glossy, but from time to time she returned from the hairdresser's with yet another change. Her hair was a vivid red one week, a sleek blonde the next, a rich chestnut the next, until through constant bleaching and dyeing it became brittle and stringy.

"You are growing thin," she told Aurore one day. "Your face is pale and pinched. You are little more than skin and bone. Remain like that and I shall never be able to find you a husband."

"You said it was not your wish to force a husband upon me," Aurore reminded her.

Sophie's eyes narrowed. "Surely a husband, any sort of

79

husband, would be acceptable as a means of escape from me."

Aurore shook her head, suspecting a trap in this. "No, Mother."

"Nevertheless, I shall find you one, but not an aristocrat. I've had my fill of aristocrats."

"Are you tired of me?" Aurore asked.

"I am certainly tired of a girl who mopes about the house all day and is interested in nothing but books. How far would I have got in the world if I had become a bookworm at your age?"

"Let me go back to Les Anglaises," Aurore pleaded.

"So that is still in your mind! Very well, you shall go to a convent again, but not the genteel and highly expensive Les Anglaises."

After dark one night, Sophie hired a fiacre and took her daughter through narrow and dingy streets in one of the poor quarters of Paris. The fiacre stopped before a tall, narrow building with a rusting iron gate.

"Ample seclusion here," Sophie said.

The gate swung open. Inside, a silent nun led the way through a small courtyard, up a creaking, uncarpeted stairway and along a series of dark and eerie corridors. The nun opened a door and Sophie thrust her daughter into the cell. A candle burned on a small, bare table. The only other furniture was a narrow bed.

"As you see," Sophie said, "there are none of the luxuries nor the comparative freedom of Les Anglaises in this place. But what of it? All you require is that luxury of the mind, meditation. Well, there is nothing to stop you from meditating and growing holy until you come of age."

"This is a prison," Aurore said dully.

"In a sense, yes. You will receive no visitors. The good sisters are well aware of your willfulness and will remain deaf to your complaints. If your friends wonder what has happened to you, I'll never tell them. If they search for you, they'll never find you. I am your legal guardian. The law cannot touch you."

"Why do you hate me so?" Aurore asked.

"Hate you?" Sophie burst into tears. "I love you dearly. You wanted a convent. I am doing my best to meet your wishes."

Emboldened, Aurore said: "I think the law could touch you."

Sophie looked frightened. She dried her eyes, complaining that tears would ruin the appearance of her carefully painted face. "I am only trying to discipline you, Aurore. It is either this place or a husband."

"Very well, Mother—a husband."

Sophie laughed triumphantly. "How sensible of you! Come, I shall take you home and tomorrow buy you some pretty new clothes."

The next morning Aurore found the door of her room locked. An hour later she heard her mother's voice outside.

"You were lying. You lied to escape the convent. You planned to run away."

"Yes," Aurore admitted truthfully.

"We are both in need of a change of air," Sophie went on. "I shall give you a little treat and take you to Plessis-Picard."

"Where is Plessis-Picard?" Aurore asked suspiciously.

Sophie unlocked the door. "Ah, you think I have another convent in mind!" She was smiling brilliantly. "Plessis-Picard is a country house set in a large park near Melun. Will it delight you to stay in the country again?"

"Oh, yes!"

Sophie's voice grew wheedling. "Truly?"

"Truly, Mother."

"Plessis-Picard is the country residence of Jacques Roettiers du Plessis. I met him the other day by chance at Tortini's. He knew your father well. They served together in many a campaign. He was delighted to see me and invited me to take you to Plessis."

II

Mother and daughter traveled to Plessis in the old Dupin berlin. During the journey Sophie was attentive and loving, a really gay companion. Yet in spite of this welcome attitude, Aurore wondered if she was practicing a new and diabolical cunning. On reaching their destination, Sophie was on her best behavior, a grand lady but one not in the least condescending. Indeed, she was at times demure. Aurore was more puzzled than ever. Monsieur du Plessis greeted Sophie circumspectly and Aurore with genuine warmth.

"Do you remember me, Aurore?"

"No, Monsieur."

"Ah, but I remember you! I visited Nohant after your father's tragic death. I fell in love with you the moment I saw you."

"She was only four," Sophie pointed out.

"It was a fatherly sort of love, Sophie."

Aurore liked him instantly. He was a man of forty-five and had long since retired from the army. Why remain a cavalry officer, he was fond of joking, when fate had given him a rich young wife? Aurore liked Madame du Plessis, too. She was twenty-seven but looked considerably older since her hair, which she vowed she would never dye, was streaked with gray. There were five children, all girls. The eldest was nine, the youngest three. They swarmed about Aurore and dragged her away on a tour of inspection of the park. Within a matter of hours, Aurore felt that she had become an important member of this happy, boisterous family.

The next day there was an informal party. Monsieur and Madame du Plessis entertained in a carefree if lavish manner.

Several of their guests were young army officers, and one of them, whom Sophie greeted familiarly as Raoul, paid special attention to Aurore. The girl liked his handsome, soldierly appearance but was taken aback by his proprietary airs, his insistent possessiveness.

"You actually know him?" she asked Sophie.

"Only casually. We have mutual friends in Paris."

"You knew he would be coming here?"

"What of it?"

"Are you matchmaking, Mother?"

Sophie smiled slyly. "Raoul is the only son of a widower. The dear boy will be immensely rich one of these days. Matchmaking? The choice will be yours if Raoul should think to approach you."

That evening Aurore was amazed to hear her mother remark that she had urgent business in Paris and planned to make an early start for the capital the next morning. Mysterious ways indeed!

"In any case, I have no love of country life," Sophie added, "but if Aurore wishes to remain longer, I have no objection."

Monsieur du Plessis looked puzzled. "Have I not agreed already that she shall stay with us indefinitely?"

"True, I had quite forgotten. Well, Aurore?"

"I'd love to stay, Mother."

"Splendid! I shall come back for you within a week."

Sophie departed gaily the next morning. Raoul, who had stayed the night, helped her into the berlin. She leaned out of the window, kissed him on the cheek and whispered in his ear. Aurore, beyond earshot, saw him smile as if at a very amusing joke.

Turning from the berlin, he took Aurore by the arm, led her through the park and there, in the seclusion of the trees, kissed her roughly on the lips. Aurore drew back, gasping and fighting as he tried to hold her in his arms.

"Ah well," he sighed, "I was warned that you would play the coy young virgin at first."

"Warned? By whom? My mother?"

Raoul shrugged and smiled. "It is my nature to come to the point without preamble. I have a comfortable little apartment in Paris. It lacks at the moment the one thing so necessary to that sort of apartment. How soon can you take possession?"

"As your wife?" Aurore asked, still not fully comprehending.

Raoul roared with laughter. "What an amusing question! As my mistress naturally."

Aurore was appalled. So her mother was cruelly and deliberately bent on humiliating her. She picked up her skirts and ran. Raoul followed with long, easy strides. He caught her as she tripped and with surprising gentleness set her firmly on her feet. He studied her for a moment in contemplative silence.

"I ought to have known it," he said at last. "You have the look of complete innocence."

"My mother suggested otherwise?"

Raoul nodded slowly. "She gave me to understand that you were complaisant and had been since the age of fourteen."

"She was speaking of herself—only of herself!"

"That I can well believe."

"Was it her intention to sell me?"

Raoul shrugged easily. "Such a transaction is not entirely uncommon."

"But my *mother!* I can't believe it of her!"

He stroked Aurore's cheek lightly. "I wish you well, M'm'selle. Make a good marriage some day and be happy." He laughed not unattractively. "Of what use would a virgin be to me? I am not yet old enough to have a driving passion for such rare creatures."

Aurore was miserable for the rest of the day, but soon the all-embracing warmth of Monsieur and Madame du Plessis got the better of her. Here, she thought, was an ideally happy marriage. Would she ever achieve one like it herself?

The week drew to a close. Sophie neither came nor wrote. A month passed, then a second month. But for a smoldering desire for Nohant, Aurore was ready to accept Plessis-Picard as her home. She romped with the children during the day and spent her nights in unrestricted reading. She made little sketches of her new friends and wrote vivid accounts of life as she observed it in the nearby countryside. At all events, Monsieur du Plessis called them vivid and suggested that she should write a book. With the passing of the third month she was addressing him as "Papa Jacques" and his wife as "Mama Angèle." They were delighted and insisted that she, an orphan, must always regard them as her father and mother.

After five months of happy and almost contented life at Plessis-Picard, the family paid a visit to Paris where they had a house they occupied during the winter. Mindful of his duty, Monsieur du Plessis took Aurore to see her mother and begged Sophie to admit that her daughter had benefited in health during her stay in the country.

"Well, she is no longer skin and bone," Sophie said languidly.

"Am I to stay with you again?" Aurore asked fearfully.

"Of course. Am I not your mother? Nevertheless, I am much occupied these days." Sophie tossed her head and laughed. "I have many friends. Life is gay and exciting. I feel younger now than I did at twenty."

Aurore stayed with her but found herself amazingly free to discover Paris with the du Plessis family. The realm of art opened up new, never-to-be-forgotten horizons, while the theatre and the opera made her hold her breath in sheer, undiluted joy. She was taken to the circus, too, Monsieur du Plessis saying that such down-to-earth entertainment was a beneficial antidote to too much serious culture. The children, not yet old enough for "culture," went to the circus as a special treat. After one such outing, Monsieur du Plessis took his brood, as he called them, to Tortini's where he found a vacant table on the terrace and ordered ices.

"But look," Madame du Plessis cried, as they sat there watching the world stroll by, "here comes dear Casimir!"

Aurore, glancing up from the ice she was enjoying as if she were a child herself, saw a slender young man approaching. The children greeted him with cries of delight. He pinched their cheeks and rumpled their hair, kissed Madame du Plessis' hand and bowed to Monsieur du Plessis.

"And whom have we here?" he asked, smiling at Aurore.

Madame du Plessis laughed affectionately. "Our new daughter. Her name is Aurore. Her father, Maurice Dupin, was an old army friend of my husband's."

"I was waiting to marry your oldest daughter," Casimir chuckled. "Now I need wait no longer."

Madame du Plessis called him a delightful rogue and presented him to Aurore. He was a bachelor, the only son of Baron Jean François Dudevant who had received his title from the Emperor Napoleon. After serving in the army for a time, the young man was now studying law though not very seriously. Aurore was surprised to learn that, in spite of his youthful appearance, he was actually thirty. Dudevant wore a neatly tied cravat, a long gray coat with narrow lapels, and impeccable narrow trousers. Nobody could call him handsome. His nose was much too long and his lips a shade too thin. Nevertheless, Aurore was taken with his smile and thought it suggested a man of the utmost kindness. She realized with a little start that, possibly because of his bantering remark, she was considering him in the light of a possible husband. Monsieur du Plessis invited him to join them and ordered another ice.

"When are you going to visit us again at Plessis?" Madame

du Plessis asked.

"Is your new daughter returning with you?"

"Aurore is at present staying with her mother, but I shall endeavor to persuade Madame Dupin to allow her to return with us."

"In that case," Casimir Dudevant promised, "I shall waste no time in visiting you."

8

THE CHILDREN WERE romping in the park with Casimir Dudevant, the acknowledged ringleader in all their games. He
looked and sounded little more than a child himself, Aurore
thought, younger even than she was. Gratifyingly enough,
Sophie, immersed at the moment in thoughts of a colonel
twenty years younger than herself, had made no objection to her
daughter returning to Plessis-Picard. Aurore was unbelievably
happy, but she wondered if it would last. Happiness rarely had
before.

"Now a new game," Casimir shouted above the delighted
squeals and laughter of the children. "Let us play house. I shall
be your father and Aurore, I'm sure, will quite enjoy being
your mother."

Aurore looked at him sharply. Just a game, or another joke
such as the one he had made at Tortini's that day? Nevertheless,
it seemed to her that for one brief moment a serious look
crossed his face. She wondered why she should find herself
trembling. How fond was Casimir growing of her? Up to now,
he had been no more than a gay companion, especially when
romping with her and the children. As for herself, was she
falling in love with him? A little, perhaps, though not in the

manner of a heroine in a highly romantic novel. She knew that she admired and respected him, but—love?

Casimir revealed a surprisingly serious side of his nature when browsing with her through the books in Monsieur du Plessis' library that afternoon. They had been discussing the plays and operas she had seen while in Paris; now it was books. When serious, he seemed even older than his years. Aurore smiled to herself as she remembered her grandmother's words: "Believe me, old men make the best husbands." Actually, to a girl of eighteen, Casimir was old. She also remembered her mother's words: "Surely a husband, any sort of husband, would be acceptable as a means of escape from me."

Escape with the du Plessis family had been possible during the last few months but there was always the fear that her mother would swoop down and snatch her back to that intolerable existence in Paris. Escape, then, through Casimir Dudevant? Still, there was more to it than that, for she was beginning to believe that she could be happy with him. Had he not said that by instinct he was a farmer? A farmer-husband for the mistress of Nohant—what could be better than that?

"So you have a fondness for Chateaubriand," Casimir remarked, taking a leather-bound volume from Aurore.

"Yes, and—no," she said, frowning. "I began reading him in a spirit of defiance. I was sure that all philosophers were powerless to turn me from the Church."

"And now you are not so sure?"

"No, Casimir. Chateaubriand has forced me to ask uneasy questions."

"Uneasy questions?" he asked. "Surely they brought you to the brink of new discoveries, not the abyss of despair which your words seem to suggest."

Aurore felt immensely encouraged. "New discoveries! Yes, I did feel that! One of them was a searching for harmony which is not of this world, for a universal freedom." She remembered the birds she had trapped, then freed, at Nohant. "A—a beatific liberty for all the creatures of this earth."

"What an old head you have on those slim young shoulders." Casimir touched her hands lightly, the first physical contact he had yet attempted. "And then . . . ?"

"I hoped to prove the philosophers wrong," Aurore said shakily, "but I soon came to realize that God is closer to us and more real than he had seemed to be while I was at Les Anglaises. Now the philosophers are making me believe that God exists in all earthly things."

"Or do you mean your own interpretation of the philosophers?"

Aurore laughed. "True or false, I am slowly evolving a philosophy of my own. Earlier I was in a great rush to love God; now I am trying slowly and through reason to love and understand Him."

"And—so?"

"I want to be known as the 'Just Man.' "

" 'Man'? Not 'woman'?"

"The Just Person—if you wish."

"A wise woman is more just than any man," Casimir said, tongue in cheek.

Aurore glowed with pleasure. "Are you trying to flatter all women or just me alone?" she asked with a low, deep chuckle.

"I have yet to discover whether you are wise or foolish."

It seemed to her that he spoke crushingly. She instantly regretted the unintentional coquettishness of her words.

"Tell me more about your private philosophy," Casimir went on, sounding eager now rather than crushing.

Quickly she matched his eagerness, if eagerness it really was, with her own. "I believe in the brotherhood of man. It may be hard to achieve but I am ready to work for it."

"The brotherhood of man, with God playing no part in it?"

"Oh no, not that, Casimir! But it is becoming difficult for me to believe that the Supreme Being, the Creator of all things, is a personal God. When I touch a flower, I touch the Creator. When the wind strikes my face, God touches me, small and insignificant as I am. Please, please, Casimir, do not get the impression that I am vain enough to believe that I am God. A part of me is—yes—and that part will in time return to God."

"Tell me about the Just Man."

"He is proud of his status but by no means vain. He is penniless and binds no other person to him as a slave. Everything he possesses belongs to the whole world. He . . ."

"If he is penniless, how can he possess anything?" Casimir interrupted with a quizzical smile.

"Now you are trying to confuse me! He possesses everything that is not concerned with money. Money in itself is evil."

"Ah yes, money is the root of all evil."

"No, no, Casimir, the 'love of money.' That is the exact quotation."

Casimir seemed to withdraw into an aloof, adult superiority. "Proceed, M'm'selle."

"The Just Man," she ran on, "is, in fact, neither man nor woman. He can, of course, be either, if the Almighty decrees it. He . . ."

"You are trying to tell me that you have a passionate belief in the equality of men and women?"

"Yes, yes! And I shall try to achieve it."

"The man you marry, like all the self-satisfied members of his sex, may have other ideas."

"So you would have me become a meek and subservient wife!"

"I prefer you as you are, Aurore."

"You—you are laughing at me? You think me inexcusably pompous?"

"Pomposity in the young is never inexcusable. I was pompous myself when young, but happily I grew out of it. The saving grace is that one does grow out of it."

"You are still laughing at me, Casimir!"

Casimir bent over her and kissed her lightly on the brow. Was he playing the elder brother or the tolerant father? A little of each, she thought, her heart sinking in tragic disappointment.

"Since God is in all things," he went on slowly and thoughtfully, "in you, in me, in a flower, in the wind, and since you love God as I do, then I am compelled by the dictates of your philosophy to love you, knowing that, in the same sense, you love me."

In the same sense? What, in heaven's name, did that mean? A spiritual love, she could but conclude, a love based on the brotherhood of man and the sexless, unromantic equality of man and woman. Tragic disappointment swamped her again. She felt like bursting into tears of wild frustration and wished with all her heart that she had remained silent.

Casimir left for Paris the next morning, saying that urgent legal matters called him. He, with his provocative questions, had appealed to her mind rather than her heart or so she tried to tell herself, yet her heart ached and she missed him intolerably. Was it possible, she wondered woefully, that the passionate, uncontrolled blood of her mother, that poor lost woman, was coursing in her veins shamelessly demanding expression?

She was delighted but timidly uncertain of herself and him when, less than a week later, Casimir returned to Plessis-Picard.

"The urgent legal matters were not so exacting after all?" she greeted him, and she felt herself blushing.

Casimir looked at her gravely. "In point of fact, they were personal matters. I wanted to be alone. I wanted to think, to argue the pros and cons, to make up my mind."

Aurore blushed more deeply. "And . . . ?"

"I admit that I should ask my father to approach your mother first, but I was never a conventional man. Will you marry me, Aurore?"

She wanted to fling her arms round his neck and hold him close, but she drew back. A proposal but not one word of love? Quickly, as if escaping from a distasteful situation, she fell into her self-imposed role of the Just Man. Something far more valuable than mere romantic love had sprung up between them. Casimir understood her and appreciated her philosophy. What more could she want?

"Well?" he asked softly.

"My mother must be consulted," she said, fearful suddenly of Sophie's attitude.

"That is not answering my question."

Aurore's heart leaped joyfully. "Of course, I'll marry you, Casimir!"

Casimir wrote to his father at once. The baron replied that he was delighted at the thought of his son marrying at last and added that he had wasted no time in writing to Aurore's mother. Casimir himself wrote to Sophie who remained silent for a week, then came storming to Plessis-Picard.

"I'll never give my consent," Sophie said when she and Aurore were alone together. "That long nose of his! You have a rather long nose yourself. Two such noses would breed an absolute monstrosity."

"Really, Mother!" Aurore protested weakly.

"When he grows old and wrinkled, his nose will almost touch his chin. Your children would be positively ugly. People would say to me, 'Are they really your grandchildren?'"

"Happiness is more important than ugliness, Mother."

"Happiness? Casimir Dudevant would make you miserable, treat you abominably. I realized that at first glance. Believe me, I have an instinct in such matters."

"Is that your only objection apart from his long nose?"

Sophie shook her head vigorously. "I have made inquiries about him. He was born out of wedlock. His mother was Augustine Soulés, a lady's maid. Oh, the old baron acknowledged him and gave him his own aristocratic name, but nevertheless . . ."

"My father married beneath him," Aurore was taunted into retorting.

"But I was legitimate."

"Does illegitimacy really matter?"

Sophie considered this. "You have a point there. In some quarters, aristocratic quarters, it is even fashionable. Your grandmother was illegitimate, her father also." Sophie stared at her daughter with wide, challenging eyes. "Are you shocked?"

Aurore had long ago heard the full story from her grandmother and had grown up to accept highborn bastardy as a matter of course.

"No," she said stoutly.

"Then you ought to be!" Sophie shouted.

"Ought I to be shocked, also, that Caroline is illegitimate and that I only just escaped illegitimacy myself?"

"So you would throw that in my face!" Sophie burst into unconvincing tears. "You are cruel and vindictive."

"Mother, I am only trying to be reasonable."

"Reasonable!"

"You have no valid objection to my marrying Casimir."

"Indeed I have! I want a handsome son-in-law. More important still, I want a devoted one. Oh, he was polite to me just now, but I sensed at once that he disliked me. Given the chance, he would treat me with contempt."

Aurore tried to laugh. "He was probably taken aback by the color of your hair." Her mother's hair was now a startling red.

"Other men have admired it," Sophie said and returned to the attack again. "Casimir Dudevant has an evil reputation in Paris. Mistresses by the score."

94

"Are you growing virtuous in your old age?" Aurore asked quietly.

"Old age, by heaven!" Sophie shrieked. "I see you are determined to antagonize me."

"Forgive me," she said quickly, "that was spiteful of me."

"Casimir Dudevant is unsuitable for another reason. He was once a cafe waiter."

Aurore controlled the urge to laugh hysterically. That, from her mother—a child of the slums, a one-time dancer in a disreputable theatre—was comic indeed.

"He told me about it, Mother. He worked in a cafe for a week. He did it for a bet, as the English say."

"Frivolous, you see. Irresponsible!"

"He is good and kind and honest," Aurore said warmly. "I once thought I was strong enough to protect the whole world, but I know now that I need protection myself. Casimir will protect me and love me and cherish me. He will be a wise friend as well as a loving husband."

"Romantic twaddle. All he wants is your money."

"How can you possibly say that? He receives a good allowance from his father, and he will be almost as rich as I am when the baron dies."

Sophie was instantly nonplussed. "Why am I arguing with you?" she asked airily. "If negotiations are to take place, they must take place between the parents, between me and the baron."

Baron Jean François Dudevant, when acquainted with this *impasse*, came at once to Plessis-Picard. It appeared that, apart from being a Baron of the Empire and an ex-colonel, he was also a member of the Legion of Honor. Sophie was much impressed. She found him to be a jolly, if blustering, old fellow even though he was badly crippled with gout. He reminded her of the elderly general whose mistress she had been before becoming Maurice Dupin's, and she roared with laughter at his

95

somewhat stale barrack-room jokes which she had heard during her youthful, camp-following days.

"Now to business," she said, when closeted alone with him in Monsieur du Plessis' study.

The baron looked at her shrewdly. "My son has no need to marry an heiress."

Shrewd herself, Sophie said: "You will provide an adequate marriage settlement, Monsieur le Baron?"

"Assuredly."

"I am not prepared to provide one myself."

"What of it?"

Sophie pressed her advantage immediately. "My daughter's estate is a valuable one. I must insist on it remaining in her own name."

"Agreed."

Sophie laughed gaily. "I can smell fish."

"Fish, Madame?"

"In short, something fishy. Why are you so anxious for your son to marry my daughter?"

"My dear Sophie, you have adorable red hair. Is it natural?"

"As natural as the day I was born."

"And so it will remain until the day you die."

"My dear baron, what an old rogue you are!" Sophie's eyes narrowed. "You have yet to answer my question."

The baron shrugged lightly. "Casimir led a wild youth. There is nothing more distressing in a man who tries, through middle-age and old age, to continue such wildness. I want him, at thirty, to settle down."

"You find my daughter eminently suitable?"

"Eminently."

Sophie pounced at once. "She has the blood of kings in her veins. Naturally you find her eminently suitable."

The baron gave Sophie a sorrowful look. "The blood of kings? Yet she possesses no aristocratic title." He heaved a sigh

and turned away. "My natural son, who is also my acknowledged son, will inherit my title."

"How can that be possible?" Sophie asked suspiciously.

"In this case the title goes with the property."

"So my daughter will be a baroness one day!" Sophie exclaimed.

Old Dudevant looked back at her over his shoulder. "And—
so?"

"Since all my conditions are acceptable to you," Sophie
answered haughtily, "I will give my consent to this marriage."

II

The marriage took place on September 10, 1822, at Plessis-
Picard, with an outrageously attired Madame Sophie Dupin the
most prominent, if startling, person present at the ceremony.
Before Aurore and Casimir left for Nohant where they were
to spend their honeymoon if not the rest of their lives, Sophie
took her daughter aside.

"It has perhaps been remiss of me not to have given you any
explanation of the facts of life. However, better late than never.
Am I embarrassing the new Madame Dudevant?"

"No," Aurore said truthfully.

Sophie looked cross. "Like all young people, you imagine you
know everything."

"We have a farm at Nohant, Mother. I have been well acquainted ever since I can remember with the processes of con-
ception, gestation, and birth."

"Such shocking immodesty!" Sophie exclaimed. "In any case,
you are speaking of animals." She laughed crudely. "Ah well,
your husband is undoubtedly in that respect an animal."

Aurore checked her rising anger. "I assisted Monsieur Deschartres many times in the delivery of village girls."

"You witnessed the result, not the cause. Be that as it may, the facts of life are one thing; experience, especially the first experience, is quite another. Mine was anything but pleasant. Yours, I suspect, could be even more unpleasant. All I ask is that you listen to your poor mother and cope with the situation more skillfully than I was able to do."

"You are embarrassing me now," Aurore cried hotly. "Please say no more."

"Very well," Sophie said huffily. "All I can do is consign a willful and stubborn girl to her fate."

III

En route Aurore and Casimir spent the night at a village inn. They reached the inn after dark, Aurore so tired and sleepy that her husband insisted on her going to bed at once. Shyness overcame her at the thought of undressing in his presence. Casimir smiled as if in complete understanding and withdrew discreetly. She was in bed when he returned, carrying a tray of food and a bottle of wine. It seemed to her as she tried to eat that the food would choke her and the wine, if she attempted to sip it, make her sick. Casimir, smiling understandingly again, stretched lazily when he had finished eating and remarked that he would take a brisk walk in the village.

"Sleep well, little Aurore," he said, kissing her lightly on the cheek. "Our honeymoon begins at Nohant."

Gratitude swamped her. "Dear Casimir, how kind and thoughtful you are!"

When they arrived at Nohant, they found that Deschartres, warned in advance of their impending arrival, had brought together a little party of friends to celebrate the important occasion. A sumptuous wedding feast had been prepared. There was gaiety and music, Aurore playing the harp, Deschartres the harpsichord. Casimir, much to his young wife's surprise, took no real part in the festivities. He remained aloof and withdrawn. What, she wondered, had happened to the boyish enthusiasm that had entranced her so much? She saw a scowl distort his face as he glanced at Deschartres. Was he beginning already to resent the old man's presence and the position of trust he held at Nohant? She put this disquieting thought from her mind and joined Deschartres at the harpsichord.

"What are you playing now, Monsieur? I don't remember having heard it before."

"It's a polonaise. A friend who is traveling in Poland sent it to me. You like it, Aurore?"

"Oh, yes indeed! The originality is shattering."

"You echo my own opinion. The young composer has a brilliant future."

"Young?"

"A mere boy—twelve or thirteen. His name is Frédéric Chopin. A Polish mother, I believe, and a French father."

Aurore turned away, still troubled by Casimir's attitude. "Our honeymoon begins at Nohant," he'd said. Was he moved solely by impatience? The hour was late. One by one, the guests began to take their leave, offering hearty congratulations again.

"And so to bed!" Casimir said briskly the moment the last had gone.

Madame Dupin's old room, with its vast bed, had been prepared for the newly married couple. Casimir slammed the door, undressed rapidly and stood waiting before his wife, a thin, hard smile on his thin lips. He was much more slender than Aurore had first thought him, but his fingers, covered in black hair and splayed out now over his naked, olive-skinned hips, had the look of frightening power.

Aurore averted her eyes. Physical desire in relation to love was as disturbing to her as the confusing difference between the dictates of conscience and the dictates of the heart. But she was Casimir's wife. She had made her vows. The marriage exacted of her a wifely duty. Carefully, almost meticulously, she began to undress. Her slowness infuriated him. He all but danced with rage. Finally he fell upon her and took her with brutal force, then a second time after only a short respite, leaving her to sob in agony and humiliation. So her mother had been right. Casimir Dudevant in that respect was an animal.

Later in the night, with her husband breathing heavily in a deep, exhausted sleep, Aurore slipped from the bed, dragged on a dressing gown and went downstairs to the deserted *salon*. There, scarcely knowing what she was doing, she lit the candles that stood on the harpsichord. The young composer's music was still open on the music rack. She tried to play it but knew at once that she lacked the skill to interpret the most difficult music she had ever encountered. Frustrated, she crashed her hands down on the keys and burst into tears.

"Frédéric Chopin," she sobbed as if crying for the unknown boy as much as for herself.

9

JUSTINA CHOPIN opened the door softly, tiptoed across the room and seated herself in a chair near the window. She smiled fondly. Her cautious entry was quite unnecessary. Not even a thunderbolt could disturb her son Frédéric when he was deeply engrossed in his work. She wondered what he was composing this time. One moment he was trying out a ringing phrase, the next he was scribbling wildly. It sounded like a mazurka. At thirteen, she thought he was working far too hard, but what could she or anybody else do to prevent it? She heard him cough and her heart leaped instantly in alarm. She had been anxious about his health, his most delicate constitution, since the day of his birth.

The boy swung round from the piano, sprang to his feet and darted to the window.

"Mother!" There were tears of frustration in his eyes.

"Does my being here trouble you, Frédéric?"

"No, of course not." He stared somberly out of the window. "If only I could get it right!"

He was a graceful boy if not quite tall enough for his age. His every movement, his mother thought, was like the line of a beautiful poem. He had her own blue eyes and oval chin, and his father's rather curved, aristocratic nose.

"Those little phrases sounded just right to me," Justina commented.

An affectionate smile crossed her son's face. "Your ear for music is not very good, Mother."

Justina could but smile. "So you thought when you were only five years old."

Frédéric looked aghast. "And did I say so?"

"No, you burst into tears."

"What a horrible exhibition I must have made of myself!"

Frédéric returned to the piano, leaving Justina to dwell at length on the past. She was forty-one, the daughter of an impoverished Polish nobleman. Since her marriage to Nicolas Chopin in 1806, she had borne four children—three girls and a boy. Frédéric, her second child, was and always would be her favorite, but neither her husband nor her daughters resented this. Indeed, Nicolas was, if anything, more indulgent than she, while the girls spoiled Frédéric outrageously. To them his well-being was of the utmost importance and even the slightest hint of a cough alarmed them beyond all reason. As far as music was concerned, they considered him a genius, a prodigy.

Music . . . And yet at first Frédéric had seemed to hate it. This was a great blow to Justina and Nicolas. They were very fond of music themselves. Their musical evenings had caused something of a stir in Zelazowa-Wola, the village where Frédéric was born, and were even more appreciated here in Warsaw. Justina sang and played the piano a little; her husband played both the piano and the flute. Her lips broke into a gentle smile as she remembered the horror they had felt when Frédéric, then five years old, had been given a flute, only to break it in an apparent fit of temper. But worse had followed during one of their musical evenings. Justina was singing a Mozart aria to the accompaniment of their friend, Adalbert Zywny, when Frédéric burst into the room. Another tantrum, and with it great sobs racking his chest and tears rolling down his cheeks.

"No, no, Mother! You must stop, you must stop!"

His father tried to be stern. "Frédéric! What is the meaning of this?"

"You should be in bed and asleep," Justina said, trying to be stern, too. She turned to her guests. "I must apologize. Frédéric is a little difficult where music is concerned."

Adalbert Zywny, Justina remembered, had looked at the boy with a peculiar, searching expression in his eyes. Presently he took him on his knee at the piano and, guiding his right forefinger, picked out the air. Frédéric, still in tears, freed himself angrily, but remained on Zywny's knee and ran the fingers of both hands up and down the keys. His tears vanished. He placed his finger in Zywny's hand and the whole air was picked out. Justina began to sing to this accompaniment, but that only caused more trouble. There was another outburst of sobbing, with Frédéric at last running from the room.

"To possess a child who hates music," Nicolas Chopin said sadly, "a sorrow, my friends, a deep sorrow."

Zywny shook his head. "I think you are making a grave mistake, Nicolas."

"Oh, come!" Nicolas protested in laughing disbelief.

"The music causes the tears—that I admit. But they are tears of emotion."

"Emotion!" Nicolas mocked. "You hear that, Justina? Emotion! Ah well, anger is in itself emotion."

"You really mean what you say, Adalbert?" Justina asked quietly.

"With all my heart. I also believe that the seeds of genius exist in your little boy. Smile if you must, but the years will reveal the truth."

Adalbert Zywny, the Czech violinist who had settled in Poland, was right in one respect. An emotional response to music had caused the tears. Certainly there was anger too, Justina reflected wryly. Her ear for music was not as good as she had first thought. The boy, young as he then was, had detected this instantly. He had the ear of a perfectionist even before he could make music for himself.

But genius? Dotingly fond as she was, Justina was unprepared to accept that assertion. Talent, very great talent, yes, and talent was an important social asset. It had opened many doors for Frédéric in the great houses of the Polish aristocrats and would in time open many more. His elder sister Louise had given him his first piano lesson and his father had tried to give him more. Frédéric submitted to this inadequate instruction impatiently and only seemed really happy when attempting to produce the sounds which, he claimed, came out of his head.

Finally Nicolas Chopin, unable at that time to afford the expense of a professional teacher, asked his friend Zywny to give the boy lessons. Zywny agreed gladly but pointed out that, as a violinist, he knew practically nothing about the technique of the piano. Later he proclaimed that perhaps that was just as well, since his ignorance was forcing the boy, whose head was full of music, to discover a technique of his own.

Frédéric made his first public appearance when he was eight. Justina glowed with pleasure at the memory. It was a concert given in the interests of charity. The boy played a concerto—a whole concerto! It was of no consequence that the composer would never amount to much. Frédéric played it. That was all that mattered. There was much applause and one music critic, quite carried away and in tears, proclaimed Frédéric François Chopin a genius. The boy himself was dissatisfied with his performance but not with the special clothes he wore for the occasion.

"People were more interested in my beautiful lace collar than in my playing," he said.

"And you, darling?"

"I was more interested in it myself."

After that came a series of small concerts and numerous invitations to the great houses of Warsaw. The most important invitation came from Prince Casimir Sapieha in whose private orchestra Adalbert Zywny played the violin. Justina very nearly burst with pride. The patronage of a prince!

Nicolas Chopin had prospered a little by the time his son reached the age of twelve. Nicolas had come to Poland when he was sixteen, seeking change and adventure. He was born in France. Rumor in the family had it that he was of aristocratic descent; a Polish forebear of his had gone to France over a hundred years earlier, following a dethroned Polish king, and there had been given a French duchy. As far as Nicolas himself was concerned, the rumor was without foundation. For a time he worked as a cashier in a tobacco factory; then, with his sound knowledge of French and his rapidly acquired knowledge of Polish, he began giving French lessons. One of his pupils was the future Countess Maria Walewska, perhaps the most celebrated of the Emperor Napoleon's mistresses. Later he became a professor of French at the Lyceum in Warsaw. Now he was running a boarding school and still teaching French at the Warsaw School of Artillery and Engineering, where his son, shamelessly privileged and pampered, was one of his own pupils.

But the time had come, Justina thought, to send Frédéric to the Lyceum where his education, apart from music, would not be so shockingly neglected. Tentatively she was waiting for Nicolas to whom she had broached the subject to make up his mind. They could afford it, by a little scraping and pinching, but Nicolas, clearly unwilling to let Frédéric out of his sight, had uttered an uncompromising no. Her lips curved in a little secret smile. When Nicolas said no so ferociously, it generally meant that in time she would get her own way.

"What are you playing now?" she asked her son, startled at

the banging and crashing noise that was making the ornaments rattle on the mantelpiece.

"Leapfrog, Mother."

The door opened. Nicolas Chopin entered the room, his eyes veiled, his footsteps self-consciously firm and deliberate.

"Frédéric," he said in a soft, loving voice which he imagined to be a thunderous roar, "have you eaten that special broth your mother prepared for you?"

Frédéric was still playing leapfrog on the piano. "I think so, Father."

"You think so!" Nicolas turned up his eyes to the ceiling and quivered with rage no more violent than the gentlest summer breeze. "It is still there untouched on the dining-room table."

Frédéric laughed gaily. "How strange that I should still be able to taste it in my mouth."

"That imagination of yours! We must have a serious talk, you and I."

Frédéric continued the mad gallop across the keys. "Whatever you wish, Father."

"Frédéric, we are all very worried about your health."

"I'm not worried about it myself." Frédéric forgot the leapfrog interpretation. "Listen! Father worried about my health!"

The most doleful music imaginable came from the piano. Justina and Nicolas rocked with laughter, but Nicolas soon grew serious again.

"It is all very well to have a great love of music, but to give one's whole life to it, and at your age . . ."

"Music is my whole life, Father."

"Your education in all other matters is being badly neglected."

Frédéric turned with an impish smile. "That, dear Father, is your concern."

Reproached by his son, Nicolas thought, and browbeaten by his wife! All he could do was refuse to listen even to himself.

"You are still a child, yet have you ever lived as a normal child lives? Your young friends are out there now in the square playing hide-and-seek."

Frédéric attacked the piano again. His touch at first was light, then he interspersed a few shrill treble notes.

"I, too, am playing hide-and-seek!"

Nicolas felt himself weakening but sternly bent himself to his task. The boy could speak fluent French, but that was only to be expected when, at home, he had the opportunity to grow up bilingual. There were many other things to be learned if Frédéric was to become an accomplished gentleman as well as an accomplished pianist.

"The time has come to send you to the Lyceum," he said ponderously. "I have already enrolled you."

Frédéric jumped up in alarm. "But, Father, what of music? Why should I care about arithmetic, for instance? I can add up quite well on my fingers. As for history, I know that Louis XV died on the guillotine . . ."

"Louis XVI," his father corrected.

"Does it matter? As for geography, I know that the River Seine flows through London."

Nicolas threw up his arms. "No, through Paris."

"But of course! In one city, the Thames, in the other, the Seine, but—*what about music?*"

Nicolas laughed triumphantly. "Music will not be neglected. I have also enrolled you at the Conservatoire. Professor Elsner will take a special interest in you. He is a composer of no mean worth. He has written operas and symphonies and cantatas and masses by the score."

"What does he know about the piano?"

"Well, now . . ."

"Is he not a violinist like our good Zywny?"

"True," Nicolas admitted.

"Then I can't complain, Father. Instructed by Professor

107

Elsner, I shall continue my studies unhampered." Frédéric ran his fingers lightly and tinklingly over the keys. "Listen! Professor Elsner giving me a lesson in harmony."

Nicolas tried to sound severe. "The professor has agreed to instruct you in both harmony and counterpoint."

"And the violin? Listen! Professor Elsner playing the violin!"

Justina had never heard the piano sound like a violin before, but she felt a need, a strictly motherly need, to speak as severely as her husband.

"Frédéric, you must take that special broth. Your health is more important than anything else in the world. Come! I shall reheat it at once."

IO

Casimir dudevant smiled charmingly. "If the baby is a boy, you shall choose the name yourself; if a girl, the choice shall be mine. Agreed?"

"Agreed, Casimir."

He drew his chair closer to the bed. "What a pretty domestic picture you make sitting up on your pillows doing needlework." He touched Aurore's hand lightly for a moment. "Will you make a good mother? For that matter, will I make a good father?"

"Time alone will tell."

"Are you beginning to love me a little?" Casimir sounded anxious.

"There are times when I love you more than a little."

"Ah! That makes me the happiest man on earth."

Aurore had discovered herself to be pregnant a month after arriving at Nohant. Thereafter, Casimir, the attentive husband, had shown her every kindness—except when making love to her! Now, with her time drawing close and with Deschartres ordering her to bed for a few weeks in order to build up her strength, no further demands were being made on her. It was sheer bliss to sleep alone and dream romantically of the baby now stirring in her womb.

She glanced about the room in delight. What a transformation since her grandmother had occupied it! New light curtains at the windows and more fresh air than Casimir himself relished; it was an extremely cold winter but she had insisted on having at least one window open. Unable to venture out-of-doors, Aurore had brought a little of the country she loved so much right into the room. The black plumes that had adorned the bedposts in her grandmother's day were now replaced with branches from the fir trees. Birds rescued from the snow and ice perched on them, chirping merrily. The linnets, the robins, the chaffinches were all amazingly tame and fluttered down to peck the seed from Aurore's open hand. Casimir ascribed this "eccentric" behavior to his wife's "condition" and merely smiled indulgently.

"I like your half-brother," Casimir remarked. "He and I have become great friends."

Hippolyte was staying at Nohant. Aurore, fully aware of her duty to her father's illegitimate son, had given him an allowance. She had also given her mother an allowance and provided small pensions for a number of old servants, including the hated Julie. Casimir and Hippolyte went hunting together and indulged much too frequently in drinking sprees. With other people, especially Deschartres, Casimir was unfriendly and sullen, revealing a part of his nature carefully hidden from Aurore until their marriage.

"You still have a craving for bonbons?" Casimir asked.

"An almost unbearable craving!" Aurore laughed.

"Very well! I shall order a new supply from Paris."

"You are much too kind."

Casimir jumped up and strode to the window. "Old Deschartres has decided to retire."

Quick tears sprang to Aurore's eyes. "But I don't want him to retire!"

"Be reasonable, Aurore." Casimir's voice was flat, unemotional. "He is no longer capable of running the estate. I've been going into things. The rent roll is in arrears, the farm hardly pays its way, and the whole estate has fallen into a disgraceful condition. A glance at the garden alone is sufficient to reveal that. I cannot bear the sight of so much neglect."

"Have you forced the decision upon him?"

"No. He made up his own mind."

"You quarrel with him often. I've heard you."

"I'm not a patient man when faced with neglect and waste. I'll run the estate more efficiently than Deschartres ever did."

Aurore at once sent for the old man, intent on forcing him to remain at Nohant, but his decision, or so he said, was unshakable. He stood before her smiling vaguely, a dignified figure in his old-fashioned coat and knee breeches.

"The time has come for me to make a life of my own," he said, fingering one of the tarnished gold buttons of his coat.

"At your age, Monsieur?"

"What does age matter? One lives a thousand lives and endures a thousand deaths. Each day, to me, becomes a new life. Let that life be sufficient unto itself."

"But where will you go? What will you do?"

"I shall buy a small house nearby and a few acres of land. What will I do? I am interested in the cultivation of rape which, as you know, is a sort of cabbage. The seeds yield a most valuable and beneficial vegetable oil. My aim is to invent some means of producing a greater yield than has ever yet been thought possible."

His pretended enthusiasm was pitiful, but Aurore took some small consolation from the fact that he would not be leaving the district. Perhaps in time he could be persuaded to return to the manor. She had hoped that he would take care of her baby just as he had taken care of her father and herself. Timidly she put this hope into words. Deschartres shook his head.

"I am too old for that, dear child."

"Tell me the truth. Has my husband forced you to retire?"

Deschartres' eyes grew veiled. "Why blame Monsieur Dudevant because I have come to see the writing on the wall?"

Deschartres' retirement was the beginning of a new era at Nohant. Casimir busied himself from daylight till dark. Nobody could deny that he worked hard. Dead and dying trees were felled; ancient farm animals that had outlived their purpose were destroyed. Thieving servants were tracked down and dismissed without notice. The neglected garden was transformed and showed promise, with the coming of spring, of being the show place of the district. The manor itself blossomed under a new coat of paint. The tenants who had been backward with their rents were brought sharply to order or evicted. There was no doubt that, with Casimir in control, the estate would soon yield a greater profit than ever before. Aurore praised her husband but with a sinking heart. She felt, when emerging from her bed for a tour of inspection, that she had become a stranger in her own home. Nohant, as she remembered it, scarcely existed any longer.

"I have an orderly mind," Casimir said pridefully. "If Deschartres had remained," he added, "I would have got him into a new suit."

That, Aurore thought, would have been the complete end of her world.

A few weeks before her baby was due, Casimir took her to Paris. Sophie had left the apartment at the Hôtel de Narbonne and it had been let at a good rent. Why, then, turn out a valuable tenant? Casimir found a cheap and reasonably comfortable apartment in the Rue Neuve-des-Mathurians and there, the day before her nineteenth birthday, Aurore's baby was born. It was a boy. She called him Maurice after her father. Sophie, whose visits were rare since Casimir's icy politeness repelled her, came to see her grandson.

"Amazing! Positively amazing! He is by no means as ugly as I had expected. Is Casimir really the father?"

"That," said Casimir acidly, "is a remark unworthy even of a woman of your low character."

Aurore hated to see her foolish mother hurt, but she thought that Casimir, thus taunted, had spoken not unreasonably.

Soon after the baby's birth, he took her back to Nohant, warning her that her mother must never visit them there, and there he threw himself with renewed zeal into the running of the estate. Aurore, although dreading their nights together, found a new and blissful happiness in motherhood. She adored little Maurice and was free, during Casimir's daily absences, to read and study. In addition, she filled her notebooks with philosophical ideas, sketches of country life, and comments on political theories.

The months slipped by. Occasionally the neighbors called and occasionally Aurore and Casimir went visiting, but mostly they spent quiet evenings together playing piquet. When Casimir was too tired for that or had drunk too much wine, Aurore read while he dozed and snored in a chair. Once, waking suddenly, he snatched the book from her hands.

"Books!" he sneered. "This pretentious intellectualism of yours!"

Aurore had been shocked to discover that he was no longer interested in her philosophical searchings and probings. Nor was he as interested in music as she had first believed. It seemed to her that he was growing jealous of the things he either could not or would not share with her.

"It's only a light romance," she said apologetically.

"Romance! Small room there is in a married woman's life for romance!" He rose with a muttered apology. "The truth of the matter is, I'm restless. Country life is beginning to bore me."

"It always bores my mother."

"Then she and I have at least one thing in common."

Casimir went off to Paris to confer, he said, with his agent there. Much to her amazement, Aurore missed him sorely, just as she had missed him when he had departed briefly from Plessis-Picard. He wrote loving letters from Paris and she, as if penning a romantic novel, wrote loving letters in reply. On his return, he was surly when alone with her but gay and light-hearted in company. He was being careful in public, she decided, to present a picture of a happy marriage: Casimir Dudevant, the ideal husband and exemplary father!

"We have an invitation to Plessis-Picard," he said one day. "It will be a relief to get away from Nohant again."

The du Plessis family welcomed them warmly. They called Aurore "the little mother" and made a great fuss over the baby. Their hospitality was as unstinting as ever. There were private theatricals, with Aurore producing the plays, musical evenings and gay parties. Once again Aurore found herself surrounded by young army officers. Unable to resist their flattering words and ravishing glances, she indulged in a mild flirtation. Casimir grew sullen even in company, and on one occasion slapped his wife's face. Madame du Plessis was shocked.

"I cannot understand what has come over him," she said.

Later Casimir took Aurore aside. He was still in a rage and reminded her that a wife who committed adultery could be sent to prison.

"Prison?" Aurore was disbelieving.

"That is the law."

"But adultery, Casimir! I was only enjoying myself in the most innocent manner in the world."

"Innocent! You are not Sophie Dupin's daughter for nothing."

Aurore touched her still stinging cheek. "Why did you marry me, Casimir?"

"It was a matter of expediency. My father threatened to disinherit me unless I settled down."

"And this is settling down? I saved you from disinheritance only to become disinherited myself."

Casimir uttered a foul oath. "What do you mean by that?"

"I surrendered my freedom. I became a slave, a chattel."

"No, you became a wife."

"Is there any difference, Casimir?" Aurore touched her cheek again. "I'll never forgive you."

"Where a husband is concerned, it is not a wife's right to accuse or forgive."

Casimir left at once for Nohant, saying that if he remained away much longer, the estate would fall into ruins. No longer able to enjoy the pleasures of Plessis-Picard, Aurore followed him miserably a few weeks later. He greeted her brusquely, making her feel immediately unwelcome. Thereafter he avoided her whenever possible. They occupied separate rooms. Only rarely did he make any physical demands of her. He had, he said, other more satisfying interests in that direction. Aurore began to write a novel, but the plot remained vague in her mind and the telling phrases she sought to set down on paper continually eluded her. It was stupid, she thought, to try and escape unhappiness by writing about it, but with the exception of her love for little Maurice, what else was there to write about?

"We must have a council of war," Casimir said one day. "An intolerable situation has been allowed to drag on far too long."

"A council of war? I am actually to be consulted?"

"Exceedingly weak of me, but yes."

Aurore's heart began to beat with a new wild hope. "Are you suggesting a judicial separation?"

Casimir's thin lips curled. "That would please you immensely, but you are my wife. You belong to me."

"What have we to discuss, then?"

"How we can continue to live together in this insufferable country isolation."

"Are you thinking of Paris?"

"Paris would be delightful, except that we cannot afford to live there. We are not rich enough for a completely civilized social life. However, there is a compromise. We shall rent a house on the outskirts of the city."

"You have made up your mind?"

"Yes."

"What of my own wishes?"

"I have made up your mind for you. That is my privilege."

It was his husbandly privilege also, Aurore reflected, to control her entire estate, even though it had remained in her own name.

During the autumn which followed Aurore's twentieth birthday, they occupied a cottage at Ormesson with tall trees and an English-style garden. Casimir was rarely at home during the day and quite often failed to return from Paris at night. Aurore enjoyed an almost unbroken spell of peace. She worked in the garden with the hired gardener, read to her heart's content, and wrote long letters about her baby to friends and relatives. She entertained her neighbors, dull company as many of them were, and even her mother—when she felt reasonably sure that Casimir would not surprise Sophie at the cottage.

"That monster, Casimir Dudevant, is having a gay time in Paris," Sophie remarked. "I wonder how many servant girls are now with child by him?"

One morning Casimir picked a quarrel with the gardener. It was a senseless quarrel; Casimir had merely tripped over a rake. Aurore sprang to the gardener's defense and the quarrel grew into an even more senseless domestic storm.

"Life is no more pleasant here than at Nohant," Casimir raged. Then, controlling himself, a slow smile crossed his face. "Time and again before you married me you longed to return to Les Anglaises. I see no reason why you should not do so now. It is not unusual for a disgruntled married woman to make a retreat at some convent or other."

Aurore's heart leaped for joy. "But what of Maurice? Are you trying to take him from me?"

"Babies are a mother's concern, not a father's."

"But a baby at Les Anglaises! They wouldn't permit it."

Casimir laughed uproariously. "Maurice is far too young to disturb the fluttering nuns."

He took his wife and child to Paris where he possessed, Aurore discovered, a small bachelor apartment. She herself went at once to Les Anglaises and poured out her heart to Madame Canning who was still the Mother Superior. Madame Canning agreed without preamble that nothing could be more suitable to Aurore's present need than a short retreat. The baby? Well now, that would be an innovation! Mother Alicia was consulted, then the convent's housekeeper, a large and muscular nun who was in many ways a great power at Les Anglaises.

"Our reputation would suffer," the housekeeper said, "if a man were seen entering by the main gate. It would suffer even more if he were to enter by the back gate."

Madame Canning hid a smile. "What of the *tour?*"

The *tour* was a cylinder set in one of the thick walls. Tradespeople placed their goods in it, rang a bell, and a nun, turning the cylinder, received the goods within.

"How large is the man?" the housekeeper asked.

It was discovered that Maurice was not too large. He fitted comfortably into the *tour,* crowed happily when revolved in it and showed every sign of wanting to remain there when Mother Alicia herself dragged him out.

"You must feed your baby in the utmost privacy," Madame Canning warned.

"He's been weaned," Aurore explained.

"Providing food suitable for a baby will not be an easy matter here," the housekeeper barked.

"We shall contrive," Madame Canning said calmly.

Aurore was so happy during the first few days that she forgot to speak of certain religious doubts which had crept into her mind, doubts all the more distressing because of her disillusionment in marriage. When at last she remembered, it was Mother Alicia to whom she opened her mind.

"Rest here and pray," Mother Alicia instructed her softly. "Your mind will grow less troubled then. I know without question that you love God, and God in His infinite wisdom knows it, too."

"If only I could have remained at Les Anglaises," Aurore sighed, but not too deeply.

"Ah yes, that vocation of yours! Remain content with what you are now and what you have."

"With what I have?" Aurore asked in wonder.

"Your child. Devote your life to him and God will reward you."

II

"So my daughter-in-law has come of age at last," Baron Dudevant chuckled. "Now we are all in awe of her."

He and his wife had come to Nohant for the celebrations which were as much an affair of the village as of the manor itself. Aurore found it difficult to believe that she was now twenty-one, that she had been married to Casimir for almost three years, and that Maurice was a growing, healthy child of two years and one day. As for the retreat at Les Anglaises, that seemed like a dream which was a part of somebody else's life.

"I am very nearly in awe of myself," she laughed.

The festivities began at midday when a procession of gaily dressed village girls trooped out to the manor bearing garlands of flowers. They were followed by the local mayor, a pompous fellow who made a pompous speech to which everybody listened with uneasy, straying attention. Later, Aurore distributed gifts among the children, while Casimir, already drunk, regaled the men with wine.

There were fireworks in the village square that night and a dance at which everybody wore masks. Undaunted by Casimir's scowling presence, Aurore danced with gay abandon and presently found herself in the arms of a slim young man. She wondered idly if he was a villager, the son of a local gentleman, or one of the many visitors attracted by the festivities. Presently he said he knew who she was in spite of her mask and wished her a happy birthday. His voice was soft, his accent that of a provincial gentleman. She tried to place it and remembered that a young widow who had been at Les Anglaises during her retreat had spoken with much the same accent.

"Gironde, Monsieur?"

He laughed pleasantly. "How clever of you, Madame."

Casimir lurched between them, muttering that he saw no reason why his wife should dance with every other man but himself, but he was much too drunk to keep his feet and would have fallen but for the press of dancers about them. The baron saved Aurore from further humiliation by persuading his son to go home to bed.

She found him waiting in her room when she returned to the manor. He fell twice this time while trying to get out of his trousers, but he was less brutal this time, sheerly because drink had deprived him in part of control and purpose. Aurore awoke at dawn. Casimir was already up and dressing rapidly.

"I'm going hunting with Hippolyte," he explained.

"It isn't the hunting season."

"Every day in the year is the hunting season for the game we have in mind." He turned at the door. "Strange to wake and find myself in your bed. Did I touch you last night?"

"You don't remember?"

"Oddly enough, I don't. What a waste of energy."

Casimir returned during the early evening. The young man with whom Aurore had danced the night before was with him. She would not have known him without his carnival mask but she instantly recognized his voice.

"Aurélien de Sèze," Casimir said by way of introduction. "He's a lawyer, here on business from Bordeaux. The two of you should have much in common." He slapped de Sèze on the back. "My wife is an intellectual, too."

The visitor dined at Nohant that night. He had a sensitive mouth and, Aurore thought, the soulful eyes of a doe. She discovered that he was twenty-six, highly thought of in legal circles and engaged to be married. She discussed poetry with him and felt a strange thrill of response when he quoted lines with which she was very familiar.

"Next it will be philosophy," Casimir said, smiling as if at a great joke. He rose and stretched. "I'm off to bed. I've had a heavy day. But don't rush away on my account, Aurélien. Do you like music? My wife plays the harp quite sweetly."

The young man rose, too, and bowed. "I fear I must take my leave, Monsieur."

"As you wish, but why not call again tomorrow? Call in the afternoon when I'm busy on the estate. Nothing is more disturbing than the presence of an ignorant oaf when people want to argue about God."

Aurore was much puzzled. Was her husband trying to throw her and this interesting young man together? Aurélien de Sèze did call the following afternoon, but in the company of Deschartres whom he apparently knew quite well. The three of them strolled in the garden. It was a joy to see Deschartres again, a greater joy to exchange views on art and literature with Aurélien de Sèze. She was discovering a mental affinity which she had never thought possible with any man or woman. Aurélien had no physical attraction for her. When she looked at him, she felt no stirring of the blood; but when she listened to him, she heard a vital part of herself speaking back to her. It was love at first sight, she thought tremblingly, but love on the highest of possible spiritual planes. If Casimir was trying in his crude way to tempt her to the other thing he would be sadly mistaken.

Aurélien left Nohant the next day, promising to write to her and send her some books. His departure filled her with a strange longing. She felt as bereft as if the whole of her spiritual being had gone with him. They began an exchange of letters and continued to write when, a month later, Casimir took his wife and child to stay at Guillery, the Dudevant estate in Gascony. It appeared that Aurélien had business in nearby Nérac. When he wrote of this, Casimir was away shooting eagles. Or was he once again hunting the game available to him every day of the year? Aurore cared not at all and took advantage of his absence to drive into Nérac where she dined with Aurélien at a small, secluded hotel. She knew she was behaving unconventionally, but independence, she told herself, was all that mattered. A mention of Aurélien's fiancée brought the conversation round to love and marriage, and Aurore at once took on the airs of a matron of vast knowledge and understanding.

"In how many marriages does love play the part it ought to play?" she asked rhetorically. "Very few, I do assure you, Aurélien. Yet marriage is indissoluble, even if only sacrifice and despair remain."

Aurélien looked at her with an intentness she failed to recognize. "Are you warning me to pause and think well before committing myself to marriage?"

"Yes, Aurélien, I am. I gave insufficient thought to the subject myself. The important question is this: have you as much in common, spiritually, with your fiancée as you have with me?"

Aurélien shook his head slowly. "Once I thought that she meant everything to me spiritually, but not now—not any more." He leaned across the table and kissed Aurore on the cheek. "What a noble relationship it is, yours and mine."

"Noble, indeed!" she exclaimed ecstatically.

"Sacrifice and despair . . ." he murmured, thinking that Aurore was as innocent as if she had never emerged from her convent.

Casimir, restless as ever, now moved his family from Guillery to Cauterets in the Pyrenees. He thought Aurore should take the waters at Cauterets while he went mountain climbing. Aurélien, brought to the spa by some legal business or other, stayed at the same hotel. Casimir greeted him with a sly smile that Aurore noticed and puzzled over. Yet his friendliness was amazing; once again he seemed intent on throwing her and Aurélien together. Privately but not nastily he remarked that if they should move—say, to Madrid—Aurélien would doubtless discover business there, also.

"Did you really have business here in Cauterets?" Aurore asked Aurélien one day when she was taking a country walk with him.

Aurélien laughed apologetically. "To be honest, no." His face grew grave. "As a matter of fact, your husband wrote to me suggesting that I should spend a few days at Cauterets."

"I can't imagine why he should do that. You have nothing in common with him."

"He said he wanted you to enjoy with me the things which he cannot share with you. I thought it most generous of him."

"Most," Aurore said skeptically.

They walked on in silence for several moments. A strained atmosphere not of her own making, certainly not of her own seeking, was springing up between them. Suddenly tongue-tied, Aurore wondered how best to bring the conversation round to the things of the mind. A reference to music, perhaps?

Aurélien had admired her piano playing in the hotel's *salon* the night before. She remembered the polonaise that Deschartres' friend had sent from Poland and wondered what had happened to the young composer.

"Have you ever heard of Frédéric Chopin?"

"No."

"He is a young Polish composer of great promise."

"Indeed?"

"He wrote some exquisite music three years ago when he was only twelve. Strange that the world has not yet heard of him."

"Strange."

Aurore laughed wryly. "What has happened to you, Aurélien? 'No,' you say; 'Indeed?' you say; 'Strange,' you say. Have you suddenly lost the tongue that usually wags so freely?"

Aurélien caught her arm. "You, Aurore Dudevant, have happened to me. I love you with all my heart."

"But I know that, Aurélien. I've known it from the first. I love you in the same way, too."

"The same way?" he asked heavily.

Her eyes shone brilliantly. "Spiritual love is the most ennobling love in the world. We are very fortunate people, you and I, dear Aurélien."

"Fortunate."

"Aurélien . . ."

"Are you satisfied with that alone?"

"Yes. Are you?"

"Yes."

Aurore freed her arm. They turned and walked back toward the hotel in silence. Guilt touched her of a sudden. Aurélien's moroseness was making her feel as if she had actually committed adultery. Was she free to give him her spiritual love? It was—or should be—the greater part of marriage. Her spiritual love belonged to Casimir even though she saw no hope of attaining it with him. She was a married woman. She was bound to Casimir legally and, through her marriage vows, spiritually as well. Duty—how irksome it was, and how exacting, too! She sighed tragically and broke the silence which was becoming unbearable.

"Aurélien, I can no longer give you my spiritual love. Nor can I any longer accept yours."

"As you wish."

Aurore struggled on. "A platonic friendship is beautiful and precious, but does the world—the suspicious, wicked world—believe it possible? It is wrong of me to be alone with you. I see that now."

Aurélien shrugged. "Wrong?"

"Spiritual love, more than anything else, calls for sacrifice and black despair. We are faced, my poor Aurélien, with renunciation."

"Renunciation!" Aurélien turned on his heels. "You may be a saint but I'm not!"

Sorrowfully she watched him stride into the hotel. Saint Aurore but not Saint Aurélien! Much as she wanted to laugh, laughter was impossible. Another sort of despair swamped her as she realized that she was beginning to feel both angry and bored with Aurélien de Sèze. But why, in heaven's name, when their noble platonic friendship had meant and still did mean so much to her? A strange new emotion which she could think of only as restlessness was stirring within her.

Listless and heavy-hearted, she stood brooding in a corner of the terrace that night. She had seen no more of Aurélien. As far as she knew, he had gone home to Bordeaux. She turned at the sound of a light footstep behind her and was taken completely by surprise.

"Aurélien!"

"Renunciation," he said. "Well, I accept it."

Her voice fell miserably. "I'm so glad."

"May I kiss you before I go? Will you accept the chaste kiss of renunciation?"

Aurore stood immobile. Aurélien's lips were hot on her cheek.

"Well, well! A most entrancing sight!"

It was Casimir, "surprising" them with all the triteness of a contrived scene in a play. Still, she was not in Aurélien's arms and all Casimir had seen was Aurélien kissing her on the cheek.

"A brotherly kiss," Aurélien said pompously. "I am leaving for Bordeaux in the morning."

Casimir swayed drunkenly on his feet. "With your business uncompleted? How distressing! Would you like me to place my bedroom at your disposal?"

Aurélien turned and fled, a not very dignified figure.

Casimir roared with laughter. "A frightened little rabbit. Shall I run after him and thrash him? Or would it be better if I thrashed you?"

"It was all perfectly innocent," Aurore said, thinking that if her husband had come upon them a few moments later, innocence would have been anything but evident.

Casimir nodded sagely. "If that is the case, I was much too impatient. I should have waited and watched a little longer."

Was he reading her mind? Aurore wondered.

Casimir then took her roughly by the arm and led her up to her own bedroom. There, to her absolute horror, he burst into tears. She realized that he had been drinking more heavily than usual. Was that the reason for his tears?

"I have sad news," Casimir said at length. "My father died yesterday. Word has just reached me."

Tears sprang to her own eyes. "I'm so sorry, Casimir. I was very fond of the baron."

"The gout got the better of him at last, but I'm not crying about that."

"No?" Aurore said in wonder.

"I lost my temper just now and ruined everything."

"Everything? What do you mean, Casimir?"

He laughed harshly. "You must have wondered why I threw you and Aurélien de Sèze together. Well, I wanted to see how far intellectualism could go in the realm of purity." He sat down and held his head in his hands. "Would purity and innocence emerge triumphant? I doubted it, but now I'll never know."

"You ought to be ashamed of yourself, Casimir!"

"I am, believe me, I am."

Aurore looked at him coldly. "Simply because you are drunk enough to feel sorry for yourself."

Casimir glanced up somberly. "No, Aurore. I shall feel just as ashamed in the morning. And I shall know, too, as I know now, that I have failed myself and you. I have spent too much time drinking, too much time whoring. My physical senses are jaded. Why have I never experienced the spiritual love that means so much to you?"

"Because you never wanted it."

"But I want it now!"

"Tell me that in the morning and I may believe you."

Casimir stayed with her that night and made no physical demands. Perversely, with the memory of Aurélien's hot lips on her cheek troubling her, Aurore felt a deep, unreasoning frustration. Casimir woke at dawn. He kissed her softly and, oh! so chastely, on the lips.

"I'm a reformed man. Tell me what to do to attain spiritual enlightenment."

Aurore could scarcely believe her ears. Had drink deranged his mind? This for the Casimir she had known was out of character. Then she remembered his father's death. That, though he pretended no grief, was having a softening effect on him. She glowed with a missionary zeal. Instantly she was caught up by the idea of her husband finding spiritual love.

What an ideal marriage they would have then!

"Believe me," he said eagerly, "I shall never sneer again at your search for knowledge. Tell me what to read to begin with."

Aurore puzzled over this for a moment. "Pascal. Especially *Les Pensées*."

Casimir kissed her softly again. She clung to him and held him close but, freeing himself, he jumped out of bed.

"Not until I have proved myself worthy in every respect!"

He left that day for Guillery and his father's funeral. And now, Aurore thought, I have two sons instead of one. It was gratifying, since she had never been permitted to protect her mother, to know that she now had Casimir to look after and guide as well as Maurice.

II

Maurice's new nurse, Pepita, entered the *salon* where Aurore was busily writing in her diary. The girl was Spanish, with a slim waist, full swaying hips, and languorous dark eyes. Casimir, writing in praise of her ability, had sent her to Nohant from Guillery. Detained at Guillery for quite some time, he was now in Paris busy with his late father's affairs. Aurore, alone at Nohant, was very much the mistress of the whole estate. The "Queen of Nohant," the servants and the village people called her, and the title had a pleasing ring in her ears. Her rule was an easy, charitable one, for she was very much concerned with the well-being of all her "people."

"What is it, Pepita?" she asked.

"Madame, Monsieur de Grandsaigne has called."

Aurore remembered him instantly. Stéphane de Grandsaigne, the dear Deschartres' one-time protégé. The old man was now living in Paris. No doubt Stéphane, en route to visit relatives in the district, had brought a message from him. She hurried from the *salon* and there stood Stéphane waiting in the hall. He looked very grave. There was a black mourning band round his right sleeve. Aurore felt her heart grow cold.

"Stéphane!"

He led her into the *salon* and closed the door.

"Stéphane, is it—is it Monsieur Deschartres?"

Stéphane took her gently in his arms. "You must be brave, Aurore. He died peacefully in his sleep."

Aurore sobbed in his arms. With Deschartres' death she had lost a man as precious to her as the father she could scarcely remember. Stéphane held her lightly and tried with soft words of sympathy to comfort her. She saw that there were tears in his own eyes.

"Do you remember the skeleton I once gave you?" he asked.

She smiled wanly. "Yes. I still have it."

"It?"

"Does a skeleton have any gender?"

"Such a poor memory you have for anatomy, Aurore."

She drew away from him slowly, reluctant to leave the comfort of his arms. "What a great solace you are to me, Stéphane. You'll stay the night? Oh, but you must! I couldn't bear to be alone. You shall have our old friend's room. It hasn't been used since he left Nohant."

While dining together that evening they talked about themselves. Aurore insisted that nothing of any importance had happened to her except the birth of her son, but what about Stéphane? It transpired that he had abandoned his intention of becoming a practicing doctor and was now on the staff of a Paris museum. Natural history was his main subject. Privately, since he had a thorough understanding of Latin and Greek, he was translating into French the works of the great Roman and Greek writers. He was interested in literature generally and was gradually collecting a personal library. More important than that, his great ambition was to establish a public library for the use of those who could ill afford to buy books.

Aurore was enthralled. This was a Stéphane very much in tune with her own ideas. Timidly she spoke of her own writing efforts which up to now had ended always in frustration, a sort of mental impotence. Stéphane nodded understandingly. It was a feeling with which he was all too familiar, but if one worked hard, if one could forget the world, if one refused to be sorry for oneself while working, the frustration and impotence would be quickly overcome.

"How your words inspire me!" Aurore exclaimed warmly.

Later, Stéphane remarked that he had met Casimir just before leaving Paris. A hint of dryness in his voice made Aurore look at him sharply.

"Was he in good health?"

"Intoxicated with good health, I'd say."

"He was—drunk?"

Stéphane nodded. "Perhaps I should not have mentioned it. Forgive me."

"He promised me he would never drink again!"

"His lady friend was rather tipsy, too."

"So! Another mistress!"

"It is common knowledge in Paris. I thought the gossip would have reached you."

Aurore remembered Casimir's last letter. He was living the life of a monk, he'd written, reading avidly under her direction and, since he planned to enter the business world, studying English, the language of the world's shopkeepers. He regretted that he had been such an idle, shiftless fellow during the years of their marriage, but all that was now changed. Angrily Aurore began to confide in Stéphane, telling him about the supposed reformation. Less angrily she spoke of Aurélien and the spiritual love which alone had not been sufficient for him.

"Am I always to be disappointed?" she asked dramatically, forgetting that it had not been quite enough for her, either.

"Dear Aurore," Stéphane said, "you are far too trusting. Worse! For in your search for spiritual love, you have fallen into the habit of thinking too much."

"I thought I was following my heart—only my heart."

"It is easy to deceive oneself."

At bedtime she went with her guest to the room that had been prepared for him to make sure that Pepita had fully obeyed her orders. A fire glowed in the grate; the sheets had been changed and turned down; flowers had been placed beneath one of her black and white sketches of Deschartres. The sketch and the books the old man had left in the bookcase brought tears to her eyes.

"So many memories," she said brokenly.

Stéphane took her in his arms. He kissed her on the lips, gently at first, then demandingly. Not knowing at first what she was doing, then not caring, she responded wildly.

"Grief intensifies one's feelings," she heard him murmur.

Then he began slowly and gently to undress her. There was an air of reverence about his every movement, but was reverence what she wanted? Without glancing at the bed, he carried her to the thick carpet in front of the fire. It was soft and warm and comforting beneath her. She stretched lazily while Stéphane, kneeling at her side, caressed her breasts and thighs and, bending, kissed the base of her neck.

Presently, without haste, he too undressed. Now he lay down at her side and took her in his arms. She remembered her first night with Casimir. How different this was! Stéphane was holding her lightly, the length of his smooth body scarcely touching hers.

"You are still thinking too much," he chided her. "Standing aside, looking on, appraising, assessing. You are still living through the mind."

"No, no, the heart!"

"That is all very well if you feel through the heart, but you use the heart as a thinking machine."

Aurore turned on her back. Stéphane knew so much about her he might well be her other self. Shadows danced on the ceiling. One looked like her grandmother, another like Deschartres. Why had this not happened before she met Casimir? Why hadn't she married Stéphane? He was too poor to be eligible, she remembered.

"Relax," Stéphane whispered. "Don't think. Feel. Live this endless moment through the senses . . ."

She closed her eyes and stretched up her arms as he slid lightly over her. She felt herself tremble but not with fear or dread. Relax, relax. . . It was becoming easier now as if, sleepless, she had taken a drug which was beginning to have a dreamy effect upon her. How gentle Stéphane was! Powerful beyond belief but gentle. She knew hazily, as all conscious thought disappeared, that she wanted this—not with her mind but with every fiber of her quivering body, and because she wanted it, she was helping the gentleness and contributing to the power. It was her power now as well as his.

Presently Stéphane moved as if to leave her. The thought was unbearable. She held him close for a moment longer, extending the ecstasy. It was like the tide running out, rolling back, then out a little further.

"I never knew it could be like that," she sighed.

Stéphane rose and threw more fuel on the dying fire.

"Stéphane . . ." she begged.

He smiled understandingly, snatched a blanket from the bed and lay down at her side again. During the rest of the night, she was vaguely conscious at times of the fire dying in the grate, then flaming up again. The embers were still red at dawn.

"Stéphane, how often?"

"Now you're beginning to think again."

"I can't live through the senses all the time."

"True," Stéphane laughed. "You're going to use your mind, your writer's mind, until you drop from exhaustion." He laughed again. "Mental exhaustion. I want to see you make a name for yourself."

Aurore giggled. "I ought to be able to write some lovely romances after this." She sat up, tugging the blanket round her, and looked at him gravely. "In spite of marriage and motherhood, this is the first time that I have felt completely a woman. I'm so proud, Stéphane!"

II

Casimir refilled his glass.

"I lost twenty-five thousand francs," he said angrily. "Not a very great sum, you may say, but a fortune to me."

"It is a considerable bite out of my fortune," Aurore said, just as angrily.

Casimir looked sulky and drained his glass at a single gulp. That day he had returned to Nohant from yet another protracted stay in Paris where, falling in with a plausible rogue, drinking champagne with him, and sharing his mistress, he had bought a non-existent merchantman. Aurore felt a little sorry for him. His father's will had disappointed him greatly, for the baron had left his fortune tied up for the use of his wife, rich though she was in her own right, during the rest of her life. He was not even entitled to style himself Baron Dudevant since the title would only really come to him when the property did. Not that Casimir cared very much. It was the money that mattered to him. Hence his frantic desire to do well in the business world, a world which he would never understand. Still this made Casimir more dependent on Aurore financially. She was, in a sense, gaining the upper hand.

"Have you done any more serious reading?" she asked, changing the subject.

Casimir poured more wine into his glass. "The menu at Tortini's is the only serious reading I care about these days."

"To say nothing of the wine list."

"A veritable termagant, this wife of mine. How did I permit

it to happen?"

Aurore, her nerves on edge, was well aware that she was snapping at her husband and also that he, in his drunken state, was cringing a little instead of raging.

"The dressmaking accounts presented by your current mistress—are they serious reading also?"

"By God, they are!" he tittered, then scowled heavily. "What of your own serious reading? Stéphane de Grandsaigne is a comparatively poor man. Are you keeping him in comfort in Paris?"

"Stéphane and I are merely good friends," Aurore said, hating the need to lie.

"Is that so?" Casimir jeered. "It's common gossip in the district that you've been his mistress since you were seventeen."

Aurore tried to keep her voice steady. "I was a virgin when you married me."

"You were?" Casimir shrugged heavily. "I was too drunk to notice."

Aurore jumped up from her chair. Running to the window, she stared out at the long shadows cast across the garden by the setting sun. Stéphane had left for Paris a week ago. She was missing him as intensely as she always did when unavoidable separation came between them. Soon she would flaunt her new independence again by joining her lover in Paris. Thinking of Stéphane she grew calmer.

It was a year or more since Stéphane had come to Nohant with the news of Deschartres' death. Since then she had met him frequently either here in the country or in Paris where together they had often gone to the theatre and concerts and had visited art galleries and museums. She had met many of his scholarly friends and had sat entranced while listening to their long and often heated discussions on art, music, and literature.

That he professed to be an atheist mattered not at all. That was actually a fiery challenge; in time she would convert him to her own beliefs, tenuous and unformed as they were. That he was in poor health, threatened with consumption, filled her with anxiety but aroused as well her maternal instinct. Their only quarrels concerned his refusal to take greater care of himself. She loved him in every possible way as she had told her mother when that unpredictable woman had attacked her, calling her a loose woman and an adulteress.

"It is a love of the heart and mind and spirit, Mother," she had said.

"How delightful! What if you become pregnant? You have a pregnant look already. I swear it!"

Aurore, examining her face carefully in the mirror, had seen no sign of pregnancy. Her figure was still slim, too.

"A married woman is always likely to become pregnant, Mother."

Sophie nodded wisely. "I'm told Casimir no longer sleeps with you. You'd better tempt him into bed a few times, just to be on the safe side."

Conscious now of Casimir's eyes on her, Aurore turned from the window and walked to the new piano that had replaced her grandmother's old harpsichord. Why—she could even play better music, both on the piano and the harp, since her love for Stéphane had engulfed her; and under his tuition and guidance she was writing steadily and satisfactorily, with scarcely any of the old depressing frustration. She wondered what her husband would say if he were to read the ten-page description she had written of him.

Casimir sprang to his feet. "Go back to the window!"

When she stared at him coldly, he dragged her to the window, placed her against it so that her right shoulder touched the glass and stepped back several paces.

"Draw your dress tightly against your body!"

Aurore obeyed without protest. Casimir would have to be

told soon. This was as good a way as any.

"Pregnant, by God!"

"Yes, Casimir. Isn't it time we had another child?"

"We? That creature in your womb isn't mine! Aurélien's, perhaps? Or Stéphane's?"

"You're out of your mind, Casimir." Aurore was not ashamed of having conceived a child by Stéphane. Far from it! She was proud, but she felt a pressing need to protect the name of the unborn child. "You're insulting, too, crazily insulting."

"When do you expect to drop the baby?"

"About the middle of September."

Casimir counted the months on his fingers. "So you conceived last December. Why have you delayed so long in telling me?"

"You are telling me."

"Why? Come, madame, answer me! A guilty conscience undoubtedly."

"We were together in Paris last December."

"We were?"

"We slept in the same bed."

"I don't remember."

"You were too drunk to remember."

He was working himself up into a violent rage. "You and Stéphane de Grandsaigne! That sickening stench of intellectualism! A child of the mind, if you wish. What will you give birth to—a volume of poetry?"

12

IT WAS FRÉDÉRIC CHOPIN's eighteenth birthday. The young man, in the gayest of moods, was enjoying himself immensely. His father and mother, his sisters and all the guests were rocking with laughter at his boyish antics. Count Wodzinski's daughter, the twelve-year-old Maria, was actually rolling on the floor in an agony of mirth.

"Come now," Frédéric asked as he stumped across the floor, his shoulders bent, a heavy frown on his face, "who am I this time?"

"Who but myself!" Professor Elsner chuckled, in no way put out by Frédéric's accurate miming.

Frédéric dashed to the piano; his fingers jumped and pranced over the keys.

"And now?" he demanded.

"Myself again."

"And your mood, sir?"

"Rageful."

"The rage directed at a clumsy pupil?"

"Naturally."

"Now be serious," Frédéric's father interposed. "You must play for us, my boy. You have kept us waiting all evening."

Frédéric seated himself at the piano, composed his features solemnly and began to play a Bach minuet. Now and again he shot a mischievous glance at Professor Elsner. He had played Bach for Elsner on his first day at the Conservatoire, and the good professor, saying that Bach was no favorite of his, had declared that henceforth he would come close to liking Bach as interpreted by Frédéric François Chopin. "Am I the teacher or the pupil?" he had asked.

Justina Chopin watched her son with pride in her heart as he played. The social success that had come to him through his music during the last few years would never cease to amaze and gratify her. His fame had spread far beyond Warsaw. There had been visits to Prague and Berlin, and in each of those cities he had played brilliantly in many a fashionable *salon*. He had met and been flattered by princes and grand dukes and had come to carry himself, when not playing the fool, with an air which was nothing if not princely.

But proud as Justina was of him, she often wondered anxiously if the success, the adulation, and the importance of his position in society were likely to ruin a character which up to now had been becomingly modest. She was anxious, too, about the problem of money. It was necessary that her son should be well and finely clothed for his constant appearances in the great houses of Warsaw. How much longer, she asked herself, could they continue to support him in his role of fashionable amateur pianist? The time had come for Frédéric to choose a profession. She had said as much to her husband that morning. Distasteful as the subject might be to her son, there would have to be a serious family discussion.

Professor Elsner lingered on after the other guests had departed and the girls had gone to bed. Smiling, he reminded Nicolas and Justina Chopin of his prediction of four years ago —that, by the time Frédéric was eighteen, he would be the greatest pianist in Poland.

"I want you to remember certain things," Professor Elsner went on, speaking a trifle pontifically to the boy. "To think of nothing but playing the piano is the wrong approach as far as you are concerned. Playing must be considered solely as a means to a complete understanding of music. Nor must you spend too much time on one method or one point of view. It is not sufficient that a pupil should equal or surpass his master; he must create an individuality of his own. And, lastly, my dear boy, an artist should be subservient at all times to his surroundings and by and through them attain his real self."

"My real self!" Frédéric exclaimed. "I am always seeking it, always!" He flung out his arms dramatically. "But will I ever find it? Tell me that, sir."

"Now we are growing fanciful," Nicolas interrupted. "We must come down to earth." He glanced quickly at his wife for support. "The time has come for a serious talk."

"It has indeed, Frédéric," Justina said gently. "We would like to know, your father and I, what you intend to do with your life."

Frédéric's voice rose in shrill amazement. "What I intend to do with my life?"

Nicolas cleared his throat uneasily. "All your friends have made up their minds and are following some profession or calling. Wilus, for instance, and Jan Matuszynski . . ."

"Father, you amaze me! I thought that you, Mother, that everybody knew what I wanted to do—what I am doing!"

Justina was no less uneasy now than her husband. "Music, yes, but . . ."

"But what, Mother?"

"We know that all your time, all your thoughts are given to music, but will music wholly satisfy you? And if it does, will it provide you with a living?"

"A living!" Frédéric's voice was tragic. "What then must I do? Teach French like Father or music like Professor Elsner?"

"We are not poor," Nicolas said quietly. "But we are not rich, either, and your sisters must be provided for, too."

"You feel then," Professor Elsner interjected quietly, "that music is your life—your entire life?"

"Yes, I do!"

"Does it bring you happiness?" Nicolas asked.

Frédéric indulged in another dramatic gesture. "Happiness is for the peasants. A hard day's work in the fields, a good meal, sound sleep at night . . ." He blushed suddenly. "And the rest!"

Nicolas looked at his wife in embarrassment. He felt a great relief when Professor Elsner rose to go. Taking him by the arm, he accompanied him to the front door, leaving mother and son together.

"There is happiness in marriage, Frédéric," Justina said shyly. "Some of your friends have married already. Others are preparing for marriage. We have often wondered about you. Count Radziwill's daughter, for instance . . ."

"Wanda? I can scarcely remember her."

"We thought you were falling in love."

"A divine creature," Frédéric said airily. "She plays the piano quite prettily. But—love!" He was blushing again. "She contrived again and again to be alone with me. I had to be quite rude to her. What would people have thought if I had permitted a tête-à-tête?"

Justina hid a smile. "What of Alexandrine de Mariollés? It was she, I seem to remember, who sent you a laurel wreath. Weren't you touched by such a lovely gesture?"

"Very much indeed. I thought I had found a true friend until the shameless, languishing glances she cast upon me in public filled me with terror."

Again Justina hid a smile. "Has there been no one, darling?"

A dreamy look crossed Frédéric's face. "There was a girl once

140

at the Conservatoire. I dreamed about her. I longed for her. My spirit soared to unearthly heights. I followed her everywhere. Just to be in a crowded room with her was bliss. She never seemed to notice me and I never had the courage to speak to her."

"My poor boy . . ."

"Oh, it passed, Mother. Why, I can't even remember her name now."

Nicolas came back, his step light and jaunty. There was a broad, hopeful smile on his face.

"We shall scrape the money together somehow," he said gaily.

"For what?" his wife asked.

"Elsner is full of enthusiasm. He is talking now of a concert for Frédéric in Vienna. Just think, Justina, an important concert in that important city! I agree with him that our son's life is dedicated to music. Elsner applauds Frédéric's ambition and so do I."

"Ambition?" Frédéric questioned. "Yes, that is what everybody would call it. But I know it as something else. Something greater than myself." With that he rushed from the room.

II

"So they regard you in Warsaw as a genius," Count Gallenberg said dryly. "Very well then. Play for me!"

Nervous under Gallenberg's piercing eyes, Frédéric seated himself at the piano and began to play one of his own recent compositions, the *Rondo à la Mazur*. He had journeyed to Vienna with three young friends, more in a spirit of adventure than anything else, but with the hope of receiving recognition in the home of such great musicians and composers as Haydn, Mozart, and Beethoven smoldering in his mind. Professor

Elsner, for all his enthusiasm, had not been able to arrange a concert for Frédéric in Vienna after all. Nevertheless he had provided many letters of introduction and, as a result, the young pianist was now playing for Count Gallenberg, the director of the Royal Opera.

"Stop!" Gallenberg commanded suddenly.

Frédéric obeyed and bowed his head in shame. Failure, humiliating failure!

"Am I a very terrifying person?" the count thundered.

"Very," Frédéric admitted faintly.

"That is as it should be. Any pianist who can face me without a qualm can face a thousand audiences. Now begin again. Forget everything but your music."

Encouraged, Frédéric began again, first conjuring up a picture in his mind of Constance Gladkowska, a young singer he had met in Warsaw before leaving for Vienna. How much did she mean to him? Was he falling in love with her? Inspired, he played on.

"Your mind is still on other things," Gallenberg shouted. "Begin once again or take your music and go."

Hurriedly Frédéric forgot Constance Gladkowska and played —or so he believed—as never before. When he had finished, he stole a glance at the count who was pacing the room and snapping his fingers as if in anger.

"Play something else," he said at length.

"Beethoven, sir? Mozart?"

"No, no. Some other composition by this would-be genius, Frédéric Chopin."

Frédéric leafed through his music and then, thoroughly cowed, began to play his variations on the theme of *Là ci darem la mano*. Count Gallenberg was still pacing the room.

"Enough!" he cried at last.

"You are disappointed in me, sir?"

The count shrugged this aside. "Have you met Haslinger?"

"Yes, several times." Haslinger was a music publisher to whom Professor Elsner had already given Frédéric an introduction.

"Is the idiot interested in your work?"

"He has offered to publish these variations, sir."

"Ha! Then if you were to give a concert a reasonably good circulation might follow."

"A concert?" Frédéric asked faintly.

Count Gallenberg looked more fierce than ever. "You are unknown in Vienna. Payment for performing at the Royal Opera House would be out of the question."

"The Royal Opera House!" Frédéric sprang up in vast excitement. "As if payment matters!"

"So! It is arranged. I, Count Gallenberg, will present you before one of the most exacting audiences in the world. Am I out of my mind? The music critics will provide the answer."

III

Justina had stationed herself at the window. She kept twitching aside the curtains and straining her ears. Presently she heard the sound of carriage wheels and turned with a glad cry to the little party of friends she and her husband had gathered together to welcome their son on his return from undreamed-of success in Vienna.

"Here he comes!"

A tired and travel-stained Frédéric, overwhelmed by the welcome he received, submitted patiently to being shaken by the hand, slapped on the back, and kissed again and again on the cheek. Justina stood aside and nodded approvingly. She was quick to see that her son had eyes only for Constance Gladkowska whom she had carefully included among the guests.

"Tell us everything—everything!" Professor Elsner demanded

when Frédéric was seated at the table eating sparingly.

"There isn't very much to tell, Professor."

"Such modesty!" Elsner's eyes swept round the table. "He went, he saw, he conquered!"

"What of the press notices, the critiques?" Nicolas Chopin asked.

Frédéric took some crumpled clippings from his pocket. Professor Elsner jumped up and seized them before Nicolas could take them from his son. He read them avidly, then a second time.

"Listen, listen! 'A master of the first rank.' I am quoting the *Allgemeine musikalische Zeitung.* 'Exquisite delicacy of touch . . . remarkable finger dexterity . . . subtle finish of tonal gradations . . . interpretation of his own compositions bears the stamp of genius!' " Elsner was weeping unashamedly. "I can read no more, my friends."

Frédéric felt the hot blood rise in his cheeks, not because of the applause which rang through the room but because Constance Gladkowska's eyes were fixed on him unfalteringly. There was a secret little smile about her lips—or was he imagining it?

"Frédéric will soon be the most famous pianist in the world," she said and sighed deeply.

The steady gaze of her cornflower blue eyes entranced him. She was almost as tall as he was. Her figure was slim but fully developed. He thought she looked unutterably lovely in her white dress with its touch of lace at the neck. He jumped up impulsively.

"May I take you home, Constance?"

She lowered her eyes demurely. "Thank you, Frédéric."

It was a clear, calm September evening with yellow stars blinking in the sky. Daringly Frédéric took Constance's hand in his as they sat together in the hired carriage. She made no protest. Her fingers were cool and firm.

"I thought only of you while I was in Vienna, Constance. You inspired me. But for you, I would never have impressed those pale and jaded music critics."

"You make me very happy," she said gravely. "I thought of you, too, and—well—I prayed for you."

Frédéric grew dizzy. There was only one person in the world as good as his mother, her name was Constance Gladkowska. Constance! The name itself was all the inspiration he needed.

"Had you noticed the music of the horses' hoofs?" she asked softly. "There's even music in the clatter of the wheels on the cobbles."

For a moment Frédéric found speech impossible. What had Professor Elsner once said? An artist must be subservient at all times to his surroundings and by and through them find his real self. Surroundings! The stars and the music of the horses' hoofs meant nothing to him. But Constance—she meant everything!

"I shall compose some music for you," he said emotionally.

The next morning, very early, he resumed work on a concerto he had already begun in F minor. During the weeks that followed, he wrote and rewrote the slow movements until in his heart he was sure that they gave full expression of his love for Constance. When the concerto was finished, he accepted an invitation to visit her home and there he played it from beginning to end. Her parents, receiving him guardedly, expressed a tight-lipped pleasure in his music. Perplexed by their attitude, he asked himself miserably if they disliked him.

Constance herself was showing a new gaiety now, going about a great deal in society and rehearsing for a leading role in an operatic production. She had many admirers and was seen often in the company of one or other of them. Loving her to distraction one moment, trying desperately to forget her the next, Frédéric's courage deserted him and he was miserably silent.

Meanwhile, just before his twentieth birthday, he performed in his first important public concert in Warsaw, playing an operatic overture composed by Professor Elsner, a number of folk songs, and his own new concerto. Warsaw received him with far less applause than Vienna, but Elsner, saying sagely that a man was rarely a prophet in his own country, encouraged him to give a second concert. Toward the end of the year Frédéric had composed another concerto and this he now played with the orchestra at the Warsaw Theatre. Constance sang an aria at the same concert and together, with the applause ringing in their ears, she and Frédéric bowed before the audience.

"I shall drive you home later," he whispered, trying to sound masterful.

"My father . . ."

"Please, Constance! There's something I want to tell you."

"Very well."

Frédéric seized her hands in his the moment they were in the carriage. He thought she looked lovelier than ever. She wore another white dress with more lace on it and a red rose in her honey-colored hair.

"Surely you know that I love you!" he blurted out.

Constance shrugged. "How could I know? Have you ever told me?"

"I'm telling you now. I—I can't make romantic speeches except in my music. I've told you over and over again that way. Will you marry me, Constance?"

She turned her head away, then looked back at him slowly. "Frédéric . . ."

"Wait!" he begged, his heart sinking. "When I was coming back from Vienna last year, I met a blind beggar on the roadside and gave him some food. He fell into a trancelike condition and told me that my name would become famous throughout the world."

"That's more than likely, Frédéric."

"Yes, but listen! He also told me that I would search and search for happiness but never find it. Fame would be mine but it would bring me no joy. In the end, he said, I would be deserted by everyone. I—I would be sad and bitter and alone."

"What an unpleasant man—to repay you like that for the food you gave him!"

"Are you going to desert me now, Constance?"

She stared at him in silence for a moment. "How much money did Count Gallenberg pay you for that concert in Vienna?"

"None at all."

"How much did Haslinger pay you for the music he published?"

"I can't remember."

"Pocket money perhaps?"

Frédéric laughed wryly. "Pocket money, if you like, but not enough to provide a child with sweets."

"There! You see! A musician, however much fame he achieves, is likely to remain poor all his life."

"Your father said that?"

"What if he did? I know it to be true."

"That is your answer then?"

Constance sighed in faint regret. "I admire you greatly but I've never loved you."

"Oh Constance! Constance!"

The carriage came to a halt. She opened the door. "I am engaged to Joseph Grabowski. My father will make the announcement soon."

"Grabowski! A landowner? a city merchant old enough to be your father but very wealthy. You love him? You actually love him?"

Constance's eyes hardened. "What place does love have in a marriage of convenience? I respect him. That is sufficient."

Frédéric leaped from the carriage. It was raining and bitterly cold, but he scarcely noticed as he tramped the streets struggling with the agony of disillusionment. Was the fault his or Constance's? Love! He would never love again, never! He arrived home in a sodden condition, coughing and sneezing. His mother, crazy with worry, put him to bed and piled blankets over him.

"I'll send for the doctor."

"Can a doctor cure a broken heart?"

Justina stroked his hot brow. "Has Constance been unkind to you?"

"Constance? Do I know anyone by that name?" Frédéric sat up. "Mother, I'm going away. Vienna again, then Paris, then London."

IV

The little village of Wola, Frédéric Chopin's birthplace, was *en fête,* for the young pianist was coming home as the guest of honor for a farewell party before he started off on his travels. Most of Frédéric's friends had already gathered at the inn where the largest room had been reserved for feasting and speechmaking. Professor Zywny was there and Professor Elsner, too, with the choir from the Warsaw Conservatoire.

"Frédéric is late," Zywny said anxiously.

Elsner nodded. "He hates speechmaking."

A few moments later, Frédéric arrived with his parents and sisters. There were only two sisters now, for the youngest had died tragically of consumption. Frédéric had almost died himself after that soaking a month ago. He still looked pale and drawn, but his eyes danced in delight as his friends rushed out of the inn to greet him. He wore a new brown traveling cloak, an immaculate white lace cravat, and highly polished black boots. He bowed and waved and looked, his mother thought, more princely than ever.

"Vienna, Paris, London. Then home to Warsaw!" Professor Zywny cried.

"Of course, Professor." But Frédéric was beginning to feel that once he left his homeland, he would never return.

He was led inside the inn almost as if his enthusiastic friends were carrying him. Endless speeches followed the feasting until Professor Elsner, growing impatient, tapped his baton imperiously and the choir broke into song. Frédéric felt the tears stinging his eyes. Then Jan Matuszynski, one of his closest friends, calling for silence, stepped to Frédéric's side and offered him a small silver urn. He saw at a glance that it was filled with earth.

"The soil of your country, the precious soil of Poland," Jan said, his voice quivering with emotion. "Take it with you. Never forget us. Never forget Poland!"

Frédéric took the urn. He was too overcome himself for speech. Two other old friends, the Wodzinski brothers, stepped forward.

"Come now, why this sudden shyness?" one of them said, turning and looking back.

With that their sister Maria approached and curtsied. She looked, Frédéric thought, like one of the flowers in the bouquet she carried. She was fourteen and already showing signs of mature beauty. He had known her all his life, had romped with her and her brothers, had teased her and pulled her hair. Yet it seemed to him now that he was seeing her for the first time.

"With all our love," Maria whispered gravely as she offered him the bouquet.

Frédéric trembled violently as he took it. He was leaving home, never to return. Why, at such a moment, must he discover that he had fallen in love? He plucked a rose from the bouquet and placed it in Maria's hair.

"I shall never forget you, Maria, never!"

149

13

"I HAVE COME to Nohant to see my daughter," Stéphane de Grandsaigne said challengingly.

Aurore looked at him sharply. "You have a daughter at Nohant? That is a surprise to all of us."

Stéphane's voice rose angrily. "Why must you pretend even when we are alone?"

Aurore turned away from him. "Solange is Casimir's daughter."

"No one believes that—Casimir least of all."

Aurore's second child, a girl, was now almost two years old. Casimir, by no means convinced that she was his, had accepted her without protest if only to save face. He had named her Solange. Thereafter, husband and wife had lived their separate lives even though they often shared the same roof at Nohant. Aurore loved the manor as much as ever, but she was often bored and restless when Casimir was present. They had very little to talk about except domestic matters and the running of the estate. They slept in separate rooms. Casimir never entered Aurore's; she never entered his. Occasionally they spent an evening together, Aurore reading or writing, Casimir falling asleep in his chair before going early to bed—often enough with the nursemaid, Pepita. Aurore was happy with her two children and, taking advantage of her new freedom, she escaped whenever possible to visit friends in the neighborhood. She entertained freely in spite of Casimir's sneers about the "intellectual" conversation of her friends.

"You have a bad cough, Stéphane," she said now, trying to change the subject. "Will you never learn to take care of yourself?"

Stéphane laughed harshly. "No, never, my dear mama."

"Stéphane, I don't want to quarrel with you."

"We do quarrel a lot these days, don't we."

"Almost every time we meet."

"It was religion last time, wasn't it? I'm very comfortable with my atheism. Why waste your breath trying to convert me? Be honest with yourself, Aurore. There is no God, no hereafter. When we die, that will be the end of us."

Aurore refused to argue with him once again.

"Are we falling out of love with each other?" she asked sadly.

Stéphane shrugged elaborately. "Who knows?"

"We are falling out of love," she repeated, as if beseeching him to contradict her.

Stéphane shrugged again. "A little love, a little hate, and then—good-by." He sounded as if he were quoting a favorite line.

"Hate? Oh, no, Stéphane!"

"Life is short, Aurore. Mine will probably be shorter than most. For that reason if no other, I want to see more of Solange. I want the world to know that she is mine. I want above all else to acknowledge her."

"Solange is not your daughter."

"You and your ideas of freedom! How can you believe in them and at the same time play the hypocrite?"

Hypocrite! Aurore tried to be honest with herself. A hypocrite, yes. Yet all she wanted was to protect Solange from the sneers of the world. If only she could tell him that!

He looked at her with his head on one side. "Are you afraid of Casimir taking legal action?"

"He won't do that. He has suffered further business losses. He is more dependent on me now than ever."

"That, of course, is what you like—men dependent on you, the 'Queen of Nohant.' I'm your lover. Please remember that. Not one of your children."

Aurore could bear no more. "You mean you were my lover." Then she flung his own words back at him. " 'A little love, a little hate, and then—good-by.' "

She rushed from the room and out of the house. Reaching the stables, she found herself gasping for breath. She saddled a horse, mounted it, and raced along the road to La Châtre. Self-pity swamped her. She felt so much alone, so isolated from human contact. Stéphane had once said that one must learn to be alone but not lonely. Would she ever master that lesson?

Her horse shied suddenly and very nearly threw her. Looking about for the cause, she caught sight of a body lying beneath the hedge. She dismounted to investigate. Some poor tramp dead of starvation? Only the trousered legs were visible; the rest of the body was at the other side of the hedge. Tentatively she touched the legs with her riding whip. They moved and disappeared. Then, as she watched in amazement, a boyish head and shoulders emerged.

"You gave me such a fright," she said. "I thought you were dead."

"Dead to the world no doubt. I was reading a book. Go away and leave me in peace."

"Tell me your name first."

"Sandeau, Jules Sandeau. And yours?"

"Aurore Dudevant."

"Ah yes, the 'Queen of Nohant.' We have mutual friends, the

Duvernets. I'm staying with them at the château."

The young man leaped to his feet. He was slim and straight and looked like a mere child with his blond hair in disarray.

"Isn't there a family called Sandeau at La Châtre?"

"Yes. My family. My father is the collector of taxes. A poor man, in spite of all the money he takes from others."

"What were you reading?"

"Victor Hugo. He's my special hero."

Aurore was delighted. "I, too, am a liberal when it comes to politics. Jules Sandeau and I must have much in common." She made up her mind instantly. "The Duvernets are coming to dinner at Nohant tomorrow. Will you accompany them?"

Jules laughed. "You make it sound like a command, Madame. What can I do but obey?"

Charles Duvernet and his wife were old friends and neighbors; Charles was Aurore's senior by only a few years. Of late, they had formed an earnest little group of liberals and romantics. Casimir, being a liberal himself, approved of Charles and stayed talkatively awake whenever the Duvernets called. On this particular occasion they arrived later than usual. There was no sign of Jules Sandeau.

Aurore laughed lightly. "Has the little angel disobeyed my royal command?"

It turned out that Sandeau had gone first to La Châtre and would join the company as soon as possible, bringing whatever news he had been able to obtain from the mayor. A revolution was taking place in Paris.

The final fall and exile of the Emperor Napoleon fifteen years ago had been followed by another return to monarchy with first Louis XVIII on the throne, then, in 1824, his brother Charles X whose reign up to now had been a growing reaction against liberalism. Tyranny, Aurore and her friends had cried, sheer tyranny! Now, at last, the people had risen in revolt. What would the result be—a new and greater republic? According to the news which had so far reached Nohant, six hundred barricades had been erected in the streets of faraway Paris, students had placed tricolors on the towers of Notre Dame, while the Tuileries and the Louvre were being stormed, and possibly even the Hôtel de Ville.

"Young Sandeau regrets having left Paris too soon," Charles Duvernet remarked.

Aurore smiled. "Yes, I can imagine him breaking into Notre Dame with a tricolor. Tell me about him, Charles."

She learned then that Jules Sandeau was nineteen. His parents, knowing him to be intelligent and sharp-witted, had denied themselves many a small luxury in order to send him to the Collège de Bourges where he had shown amazing promise. Now he was studying law in Paris and spending only his holidays at La Châtre. He was really a gentle creature, Charles Duvernet claimed. Society meant little to him and he had no interest whatever in such country pastimes as hunting and shooting.

"He is a most voracious reader," Duvernet added, "and is showing some ability—or so I believe—as a writer."

Jules Sandeau arrived at that moment.

"Well?" Aurore demanded.

"The Hôtel de Ville has been taken. There's talk of the King abdicating."

"He'll be no loss to France."

Casimir followed Jules into the room. He was so flushed that Aurore feared he had been drinking more heavily than usual, but apparently he was merely stirred by soldierly thoughts and ambitions.

"I've joined the National Guard," he announced excitedly. "For the time being I'm a lieutenant. I've recruited a hundred men already. Soon I'll have a strong enough force to repel any troops the royalists may send over from Bourges."

Much to Casimir's disappointment, no such emergency arose

in the district. King Charles abdicated and the *bourgeois* party, fully in control of the government, placed Louis-Philippe, Duke of Orleans, on the throne. This was somewhat more acceptable to Aurore and her friends than the dictatorial rule of Charles X, for King Louis-Philippe, an amiable fellow, went about freely in public and insisted on shaking hands with everyone. He seemed likely to become a reasonable, middle-class little monarch. "The Citizen King" was what he called himself proudly.

Meanwhile Jules Sandeau came often to Nohant. The children liked him and romped with him in the garden. Aurore, finding herself growing deeply attached to him, talked to the young man by the hour about music and art, literature and politics. He listened attentively, his eyes shining with admiration. Was he falling in love with her? Aurore thought it possible and did nothing to discourage him. After the disillusionment forced upon her by Stéphane, the love of an innocent boy would be a welcome change. Presently, when she encouraged him to talk freely himself, he did so shyly, even timidly, yet he revealed a knowledge of many subjects that outstripped her own.

"But why? Why?" she asked. "Clearly I have read and studied much more than you have."

Jules replied with the single word, "Paris."

Paris! Filled suddenly with envy, Aurore questioned him sharply about his life there. Her envy increased as she listened to his eager account of *la vie bohème*. What, she asked herself, did Paris mean to her? A convent that might well have been isolated in any other part of the world, a little taste of art and the theatre with the du Plessis family, a further taste with Stéphane. That and no more. Certainly no exciting intellectual gatherings in the cafes on the Left Bank. How much she was missing here at Nohant! One day was much the same as another. Oh, the country would always be her first love, but in it, right now, she was stagnating.

"You must come to Paris and meet my friends," Jules said. "Or do you feel too old and dignified?"

Aurore looked at him obliquely. Was he, at nineteen, regarding her, at twenty-six, as a somewhat staid and passée matron? She laughed with forced gaiety.

"As far as your own special world of Paris is concerned, I am a babe in arms."

Soon she began to regard Jules as a composite of Aurélien and Stéphane. But she now felt very old and very wise. She would play the role of mentor and Jules the role of a most promising protégé. He was delightfully immature in spite of all the learning he had crammed into his curly head; he was even weak where others were concerned. She, so strong herself, would guide him step by step, and he, touchingly grateful, would submit like an obedient child.

Uneasily then she remembered Stéphane's words: "That is what you like—men dependent on you." Well, what of it? It scarcely mattered if a man was dependent on a woman, or a woman on a man. Strength in the one, weakness in the other—that was the ruling factor.

The two had long discussions about their common interest in writing. Aurore showed Jules some of her notebooks and spoke of her ambition, brought to life again by his interest, to become a novelist. He, too, had the same aim in mind. He had written some sketches about the theatre and the actors and actresses of his acquaintance. One sketch, which he showed her diffidently, impressed her deeply.

"You have painted a vivid picture of a young and ambitious actress dedicated to her chosen profession," she commented.

"As dedicated as any nun."

"Why not a novel about an actress and a nun?"

Jules chuckled. "Nuns are complete strangers to me."

"But not to me, my dear boy."

"What better, then, than a collaboration?"

156

Aurore was instantly attracted by the suggestion. Taking Jules impulsively in her arms, she kissed him on the brow.

"There, child! The contract is sealed!"

"Child!" he cried petulantly. "Do I mean no more to you than your son Maurice?"

"You mean a great deal more," she said steadily. "Is Maurice old enough to write a book with me?"

Jules was not to be propitiated. "You treat me as if I were merely your clever elder son. I won't submit, Aurore! I won't!"

With that, he rushed headlong from the room, looking more like a child than ever, a badly thwarted one, she thought.

Much troubled by his attitude, Aurore spent the rest of the day attending to tiresome domestic duties. Solange was feverish. Aurore gave her a dose of medicine prescribed by Deschartres in her own young days and put the child to bed. Maurice, seven now and a manly little chap, had an earache. Aurore applied another of Deschartres' remedies, a heated onion placed on the ear and held tightly by a bandage round the head.

Then, tired and still troubled, she went early to bed after attending once more to the children. Her grandmother's old yellow drawing room on the ground floor had long since been converted into a nursery. She herself, since the breaking of marital relations with Casimir, used a small room nearby. It was both a study and a bedroom and pleasingly isolated from the rest of the house. She slept in a small narrow bed and, in the place of a desk, worked on a panel that came down from the wall on hinges. She often thought of this private, personal room as her "cell." Occasionally, when she left by the window instead of the door, she told herself comically that she was jumping over the convent wall.

She undressed now and slipped naked between the sheets. The long twilight of the summer evening filtered through the window which was wide open with the curtains drawn back. There was insufficient light for reading, but drowsily she decided against lighting the oil lamp that stood on the little table near her bed. Vague ideas for the proposed novel stirred in her mind, and soon, as she hovered on the edge of sleep, two faceless figures, an actress and a nun, floated through that dreamworld of neither sleeping nor waking. A rustling noise disturbed her. She sat up, rubbing her eyes.

"Jules!"

"I tried to be quiet. I didn't want to wake you. At least not just yet."

"How did you get in?"

"Through the window."

Jules' clothes were soon scattered about the floor. His smooth young body looked red in the afterglow of the sun. Naked, he slipped into bed at her side.

"I had to come to you like this tonight, Aurore. You see, I'm leaving for Paris tomorrow."

Struggling with an overwhelming emotion, Aurore held him away from her, but he wriggled like an eel and moved closer.

"The bed is much too narrow," he whispered. "Either take me in your arms or kick me out. Which is it to be?"

Aurore took him in her arms.

"I'm a virgin," he said, his voice quivering but with an edge of wry humor to it.

Aurore kissed him on the mouth. Her hands strayed lightly over his body. The shoulder blades were prominent and the slightly rounded hips more like a woman's than a man's. It was soon over, but she found his clumsy eagerness so touching that the tears streamed down her cheeks. Later, after they had slept a little, Jules took her of his own account, manfully determined to prove himself. And again Aurore wept.

"Did I hurt you?" he asked, sounding both anxious and not ill-pleased with himself.

Aurore ran her fingers through his golden curls. "No, my darling." She laughed lightly. "Would you say that I'm still treating you as if you were merely my clever elder son?"

Jules chuckled. He propped himself up on one elbow, leaned over her and kissed her lingeringly on the cheek. "Do you love me with your heart and your soul as well as your body?"

"Of course, I do!"

His voice rose strongly. "There's only one thing for it. You must join me in Paris."

"How commanding you sound in the dark."

He laughed triumphantly. "I can't see those piercing black eyes of yours. I'm the master in the dark—not the slave. Join me in Paris!"

"What can a poor slave do but obey?"

"Promise!"

Aurore suppressed the joyous laughter that was bubbling up in her.

"I promise," she said in a low, meek voice.

II

Casimir Dudevant, strutting about and shaking his clenched fists, was suddenly asserting himself as the lord and master of Nohant, and more important, as his wife's lord and master.

"So you want to go to Paris! I won't permit it, by God!"

"You made no objection when I used to go there alone," Aurore reminded him. "You seemed glad. It pleased you to be alone here or in Paris when I was at Nohant."

"Things have changed. I see that I must take my family responsibilities seriously. You, my wife, are in need of correction and restraint. Nohant is your home. Remain here."

"We could go to Paris together."

"Ah yes! You expect me to play the complaisant husband!"

Frantic letters had come from Jules Sandeau in Paris, but Aurore had held back until now from taking the definite step of joining him. The children were her main concern. She loved them and hoped that she was a good mother. Though loathe to part with them, she recognized the impossibility of taking them with her. In Paris, she would be Jules Sandeau's mistress, and, scorning dissimulation, she would live with him openly.

"You can't prevent me from going to Paris," she told Casimir angrily.

"You think not?" There was a threatening look in his eyes. "Try me too far, madame, and you will learn a sorry lesson." He smiled cunningly. "Is Stéphane de Grandsaigne the attraction?"

"It's months since I've seen Stéphane . . ."

"Precisely!"

"Be sensible, Casimir. Stéphane and I are no more than friends. We correspond occasionally, but even so the friendship has become an uneasy one."

"Who is it then—that pretty little boy, Jules Sandeau?"

"It's life," Aurore evaded. "I want to live and can only do so fully in Paris."

Casimir laughed. "As you grow older you choose younger and younger lovers. Go too far in that direction and I'll bring you before the magistrates on a charge of seducing infants."

"Casimir," she said quietly, "I'm going to Paris."

He laughed jauntily. "Well, we'll see, madame."

Aurore spent the rest of the afternoon going through the household accounts, a task which for years she had left entirely to Casimir. He was a good manager of the estate, if a poor business man in the world at large. At the bottom of a bulky file, she came upon a sheet of notepaper, folded and sealed. Several words were scrawled beneath the seal: Not to be opened until my death. The handwriting was Casimir's. As far as she was concerned, Casimir was dead; certainly their marriage was. Breaking the seal, she began to read what purported to be a testament directed entirely at her. The vile accusations and the barrack-room language left her shocked and trembling

Casimir cursed her over and over again, yet asserted that he was writing with loving tenderness in the hope of bringing her in the end to salvation. Was he crazy, or merely malicious? A little of each, she thought. Verging on hysteria, she flung the testament at Casimir the moment he returned from the farm.

"So I'm a bad wife!"

"There never was a worse one." He had been drinking as was his habit with the farm laborers.

"This is the end, Casimir. I mean it. I shall leave for Paris the moment I have put my affairs in order. Nevertheless, I am willing to compromise. Appearances shall be kept up if only for the children's sake. I shall in future spend six months out of every year in Paris. The rest of the time I shall reside at Nohant."

"The obedient wife—the loving mother," he tittered.

"The latter but not the former."

Casimir flung himself sulkily into a chair. "The children must remain at Nohant."

Aurore agreed with a pang in her heart. "Maurice is too young to go to boardingschool. I shall engage a tutor for him."

"And Solange?"

"A new nursemaid."

"Pepita is more than adequate."

"I cannot have the child growing up in the belief that your mistress is her mother."

"Stéphane de Grandsaigne's child."

"Must we argue about that again? She was born in wedlock. You have made no move to disown her."

"It so happens that I've grown fond of Solange." Casimir jumped to his feet. "I control the estate and shall continue to do so. The income is good, but the burden of an additional allowance for you in Paris will be heavy."

Aurore began to feel more in control of the situation. He was no longer threatening to prevent her from leaving Nohant.

"Two hundred and fifty francs a month will be sufficient for my needs."

"You'll starve on that."

Aurore smiled confidently. "I shall earn money writing."

"Put me in a book and I'll sue you, by God!"

"Would anyone want to read about a foul-mouthed monster like you?"

"Monster?" Casimir burst into maudlin tears. "I'm the kindest and most considerate of husbands. I could have had you sent to prison years ago for adultery, but out of the kindness of my heart I held my hand."

Disgusted as she was with his weeping, Aurore pressed her advantage. "During my periods at Nohant we shall have a new way of life. I for my part will conceal nothing from you; you for yours will conceal nothing from me."

A little spurt of rage broke through Casimir's tears. "You are thinking of any lover you might take while at Nohant."

"You hate music," she went on hurriedly. "When I play, you either sing coarse songs loudly or rush from the room. In the future you must be as tolerant of my music as I am of your excessive drinking."

Casimir flung himself into the chair again. "If you insist."

"For the sake of the children, there must never be any bickering. If you speak an angry word, I shall reply with a soft one. The past is the past. If we discuss it at all, it must be without bitterness."

"Are you still a Catholic?" Casimir asked suddenly.

"I am, at all events, still a Christian."

"A nice distinction, that! Do you ever go to confession these days? Of course, you don't! I myself, a true son of the Church, confess my sins regularly and enjoy the relief of absolution."

"Until the next time, Casimir."

He flew into another small rage. "Sin in Paris to your heart's content, but absolution will be denied you and your sins will lie heavy on your soul."

"I have never yet sinned in the eyes of God!"

Casimir's mood changed instantly. He staggered to his feet and took her clumsily in his arms.

"What has happened to us, Aurore? Why have we never been able to find true love? God knows, I've tried hard enough."

Aurore released herself. "So have I, Casimir."

"Shall we try again, both of us?"

"Are you willing to?"

He scowled heavily. "No. It would bore me. Go to Paris. I shall be glad to see the last of you."

A month later, with a tutor and a new nursemaid installed, Aurore left Nohant for Paris, believing that the finger of fate was beckoning her. The real life, the full life, she told herself confidently, was just beginning.

III

Jules Sandeau, wrapped in a heavy greatcoat, was jumping up and down excitedly. He had hardly been able to sleep since receiving Aurore's letter, and now at any moment the diligence that was bringing her to Paris would roll into the coachyard here in the Rue Racine. His friend Emile Regnault, who was waiting with him, smiled tolerantly. This country housewife under whose spell the little fellow had fallen must be a paragon beyond compare. The diligence lumbered into the yard; the tired passengers began to alight.

"Here she is!" Jules cried and ran forward eagerly.

Regnault looked puzzled. For a moment he thought that Jules was embracing a rather plump little man; Aurore, as a symbol of her new freedom, was wearing male attire. Casimir had always disapproved of it, so for the sake of peace she had put away her suits and heavy country boots. Now all that belonged to the past.

"How cold it is in Paris!" she said.

"Well, it's the middle of winter, isn't it?"

Jules introduced Emile Regnault. Aurore shook his hand firmly.

"*La vie bohème* awaits you," he said. "Become a vital part of it."

"Oh, but I shall!"

"You look so old-fashioned," Jules laughed. "That suit of yours must have come out of the ark."

Aurore realized then that her suit, which had not been worn for years, was badly outmoded. Well, that would soon be remedied! She would feel quite comfortable, she thought, in a redingote such as Emile Regnault was wearing—warm in it, too, during the winter months, for it reached down to the middle of the calves. A tall gray hat would be excellent as well, would give her the appearance of greater height. Taking the initiative she summoned a fiacre, and in it the two men accompanied her to the apartment in the Rue de Seine that her half-brother Hippolyte had placed temporarily at her disposal. She had two trunks, a large one crammed to bursting point with books and papers, a smaller one containing the few clothes she had brought with her and, inevitably, more books and papers.

Jules made coffee fussily like an old maid; Regnault slipped out for some croissants. Then, although it was after midnight, they talked their heads off. Aurore scarcely noticed the chilly atmosphere of the unheated apartment. She had never been so thrilled and happy in her life. Writing was one topic of conversation, for Jules had already published some articles in *La Revue de Paris* and was thinking of giving up law. Free love was another. Aurore maintained, tritely but earnestly, that love could never be love unless it was free.

The philosophy of Saint-Simon who had died only a few years ago was yet another topic. Saint-Simon, said Jules, had

had and would continue to have long after his death a profound influence on the thought of the century.

Aurore laughed apologetically. "In a small way I myself am a plutocrat. I am, shall we say, the master of Nohant. I do all I can for the people who work on the estate, not one of whom has the ability to run the estate. I'd be wealthy if I kept all the income for myself."

"If you did that, the estate would deteriorate and you would be ruined," Regnault said darkly. "I can see, madame, that you and I are going to have some lively arguments." He rose to go. "How old are you? Come—be brave and honest!"

"Twenty-six."

Regnault bowed gallantly. "In those clothes I would put you at seventeen or eighteen. You have the look of a young student trying out his wings at the Sorbonne."

Jules was looking a trifle sulky. Aurore smiled fondly. How delightful to see him torn, if only mildly, by jealousy.

Regnault turned at the door. "By the way, I've found a snug apartment for you and Jules. It's on the Quai Saint-Michel."

"Which is on the Left Bank?"

"Of course."

"How splendid!" Aurore cried ecstatically.

She and Jules moved into the apartment a week later. The house was on a corner, the apartment itself on the top floor. The rooms with their slanting beams reminded Aurore of her cell at Les Anglaises. There were three of them, each quite small, and a dilapidated balcony. She ran out to the balcony and took a deep breath. Below her she saw the river and the constant movement of life upon it. More entrancing still, she could see, by peering out and down, the river bank with its trees and many bookstalls.

She darted back into the apartment and surveyed herself as best she could in an old cracked mirror. In celebration of the occasion and to emphasize her freedom, she was wearing a newly acquired suit. The redingote, perhaps a little too long, nearly touched her heels. It was gray and had a warmly fitting hood that would keep out the cold winter winds. The tall hat, set at a jaunty angle, quite became her. The trousers, dark gray in color, fitted excellently. She tore off the woolen muffler, a mixture of black and gray, telling herself that she no longer needed it when glowing with an inner warmth. What had her new clothes cost? She could not remember exactly but she knew that this gross extravagance would make serious inroads upon her meager, self-imposed allowance. Well, what of it? Was she not on the point of earning vast sums of money through the use of her inspired pen?

Once they were settled in with a few sticks of furniture about them, she and Jules began most seriously to discuss the proposed novel. They argued a little, even quarreled a little, until a plot was devised, characters created, and pages of notes jotted down. Meanwhile she busied herself rewriting a novel she had brought with her from Nohant. This completed to her satisfaction, armed with a letter of introduction provided by Charles Duvernet, she went to see Henri de Latouche, the publisher.

Latouche glanced at her sourly. "Charles has already written to me, madame. He regards you as a young woman of great talent. Is he a misguided friend or an over-zealous lover?"

"He is merely a friend and not misguided, monsieur."

Aurore tried to speak confidently but she was over-awed by Latouche. Publishers were great men and this one, she told herself, held her future in his hands. He was forty-five, rather stout, and, judging by his clothes, vain and conceited. She studied his face quakingly. He was blind in one eye, an alarmingly disfigured eye, but it was the sneering smile on his lips that really upset her.

"Few people approve of female writers," he remarked.

"In that case, monsieur, I shall use a male pseudonym."

"My interest is in the quality of your writing, madame."

"Very well. I shall read you my novel."

"Not all of it!" Latouche protested as she unrolled the bulky manuscript.

Aurore inclined her head. "A chapter here, a chapter there."

Latouche listened to three chapters with growing impatience. "Charles ought to have known better than to send you to me," he groaned.

Dismayed as Aurore was, she stood her ground. "You see no talent whatever in my writing, monsieur?"

Latouche laughed mockingly. "A hint of journalistic talent perhaps, but no more."

Aurore rolled up the manuscript and rose.

"You have been most kind," she said dryly, "but I do not believe you."

Latouche rose and bowed. He was smiling quite benignly now.

"Come with me," he said softly.

Wondering what he was about, Aurore followed him to an inner room. A fire was burning in the grate. Four tables were scattered about, three of them occupied by young men writing diligently. After startled glances at Aurore, they resumed their separate tasks.

"My sub-editors," Latouche informed her, gesturing grandly. "They are preparing tomorrow's issue of the *Figaro*."

The *Figaro* was a journal Latouche had recently bought. Since coming to Paris Aurore had read it with interest and amusement. Editorially it ridiculed the existing government of Louis-Philippe, the Citizen King whose rule no longer pleased Aurore and her friends.

Latouche pointed to the vacant table. "Sit there, madame. Write me a little satire on the present political situation. If you have completed it within one hour, bring it to me. If you have failed, go home and seek me out no more."

With that he marched from the room. The three young men

looked at Aurore across the room. One laughed sneeringly, another scowled and muttered, "Women!" The third winked wickedly. The wink, along with the friendly smile on the youth's lips, was all the encouragement Aurore needed. She seated herself and seized a pen.

The present political situation? Suddenly she recalled that the Citizen King, alarmed at the possibility of another revolution, was taking unnecessary military precautions, while the police were constantly exposing "conspiracies" which soon proved to be harmless. Aurore's pen flew over the paper. Now enjoying herself thoroughly, in less than an hour she had written four hundred words.

"Too long," Latouche pronounced, without even reading her masterpiece. "Write it again."

Aurore returned to him an hour later in despair. "I shall never make a journalist. In trying to reduce the length, I have succeeded only in adding a hundred words."

"I am sometimes at fault in that direction myself," Latouche admitted surprisingly.

Then he began to read. At the same time he lined out words and phrases with a blue crayon. It should have been a red one, Aurore thought miserably, for as far as she was concerned Latouche was lacerating her heart rather than her work. Finally he sat back in his chair and chuckled deeply.

"So the Prefect of Police is soon to issue a new decree is he? Splendid! One thing is certain. The *Figaro* will sell a few extra copies. This is the best sentence of the lot!" And still chuckling, he read: " 'The Government undertakes to discover not more than twelve conspiracies each month.' "

"I thought the last sentence was the best, monsieur."

"Perhaps, perhaps." And again Latouche read aloud: " 'Each Monday, Wednesday and Friday the police will give their valuable time to forestalling treasonable assemblies, while each Tuesday, Thursday and Saturday, they will employ themselves wholeheartedly with breaking up the same.'" He looked at Aurore benevolently. "You are now a member of my editorial staff."

Aurore could scarcely believe her ears. "My foot is on the first rung of the ladder!"

"Possibly—possibly."

"I am very grateful, monsieur, but I must warn you that I still intend to write fiction."

"From what I have seen of your fiction writing, you are doomed to failure. There is no common sense in that little novel of yours."

"Who wants common sense in fiction, monsieur? People read novels in order to escape from reality."

"Obviously few people will ever get the better of you in an argument," Latouche muttered, not without admiration in his eyes. "Very well. Write another novel and let me see it."

Aurore was thrilled to see her satire in print even though it was published anonymously. There was delighted laughter in the cafes but a storm of anger at the Tuileries and the Prefecture. The Prefect of Police swooped down on the *Figaro* and suppressed it and court proceedings were initiated.

"Will I be sent to prison?" Aurore asked Latouche.

"More than likely, madame."

"Then I shall become famous overnight."

It soon became common knowledge that Aurore was the author of the anonymously published satire. Latouche, taking full advantage of this, appeared with her in many cafes where she was cheered and congratulated by boisterous students. Far from being angry with her for causing the suppression of his journal, Latouche chuckled with delight.

"As editor, I, too, must have a share of this notoriety."

"You're just as likely to go to prison as I am, monsieur."

"Ah well, we'll see."

Aurore returned from one such excursion with Latouche to

find her mother waiting grimly for her at the apartment. Jules, who had just met Sophie for the first time, was scowling and submitting to a fit of childish temperament.

"She actually threatened to thrash me," he shouted.

"Spank was the word I used," Sophie jeered. "One thrashes a man but only spanks an infant. A man," she pondered, staring in disgust at her daughter's male attire. "If I had the strength, I would certainly thrash this would-be gentleman."

"But why, Mother?" Aurore asked patiently.

"Are you not living openly in sin with this boy?"

"Like mother, like daughter," Aurore murmured.

"How unkind of you!" Sophie exclaimed. "It is years now since I lived in sin with a man." She looked at Jules again. "Are you keeping him, Aurore?"

"Not entirely. He earns a little money himself."

"But not enough?"

"No," Aurore admitted.

"Who does the cooking—you or the child?"

"I will not be called a child!" Jules raged.

"Jules does the cooking," Aurore said, "and a very good cook he is."

"You must put him in a pinafore."

Jules uttered a wild curse and flew from the room.

"You must teach him better manners," Sophie said severely.

"I shall do my best," Aurore promised, trying not to smile.

Sophie fell to thinking of the past. A slow smile crossed her face. "When I lived with the old general and had not quite made up my mind to desert him for your father, I often gave him—your dear father—a little spending money. Your grandmother was very difficult about an adequate allowance for your father."

"What are you trying to say, Mother?"

Sophie smiled brightly. "That I am not being entirely fair to you, Aurore."

"How very generous of you."

"You, on the other hand, are not being in the least fair in another direction. That shocking article of yours in the *Figaro!* Everybody is talking about it. People stop me in the street and say, 'Your daughter really did write it?' I deny it spiritedly but give myself away by blushing with shame."

"You will blush with greater shame when you read the book Jules and I are going to write."

"A book?"

"About a nun and an actress."

Sophie gasped in horror. "I forbid it. I absolutely forbid it!"

"I came of age several years ago, Mother."

"Are you going to use your joint names, Jules Sandeau and Aurore Dudevant?" Sophie asked anxiously.

Aurore smiled. "No, we are going to use a pseudonym. We are thinking of Jules Dupin."

"Dupin! That is even worse! Use Dupin and I'll sue you! By heaven I will!"

Aurore soon discovered the reason why Latouche was not angry with her. He had received private and confidential information. The Public Prosecutor himself, amused by the satire, had convinced the King that there was nothing treasonable in it. The ban on the *Figaro* was lifted. No prison, then, for Aurore, no pleasing martyrdom.

Thereafter she continued to write quite merrily at the government's expense, but her mind was still on fiction. She wrote some short stories and had the pleasure of seeing them appear in *La Revue de Paris* and *La Mode*. Then she and Jules made a determined onslaught on the first volume of their novel which they had decided to call *Rose et Blanche*. They showed it to Latouche. He frowned and sneered and refused for a time to commit himself.

"Are you still appalled at the absence of common sense, monsieur?" Aurore asked him.

"I am appalled at the extreme virtue of the saint and the extreme sinfulness of the sinner."

"I shall submit it to another publisher."

"Do so, by all means."

Aurore approached Ernest Dupuy of the publishing house of J. P. Roret et Dupuy. Expressing immediate delight, Dupuy demanded to know when the book would be completed.

"If you are prepared to offer a firm contract," Aurore said boldly, "I and Monsieur Sandeau will give all our time to *Rose et Blanche*."

"I see I am dealing with a business woman."

When the contract was drawn up and signed, Aurore realized that her foot was on the second rung of the ladder. She wept for joy and so did Jules. She had now spent six months in Paris so, keeping her promise, she returned to Nohant. Jules followed a few days later. Paris or Nohant, they were as inseparable as ever; their novel must be completed speedily.

IV

At Nohant they worked in a summerhouse. It was a trysting place as well as a study. The small building was conveniently isolated from the manor. The servants, warned never to disturb Aurore when she was working, were rarely permitted entry. The single room was furnished with two desks, two chairs, and a bed. Aurore swept and cleaned the place herself. Here she did all her writing and here Jules could slip in and out unobserved.

"I don't feel much like work today," he remarked one afternoon.

"Nor do I. I was at it from seven last night till six this morning."

Jules rose and stretched. "I feel like something else though."

They locked the door and undressed. Jules lay with his blond head on Aurore's breast. He talked rather petulantly about the novel which he was finding a difficult task. Absently she ran her fingers through his curls. She herself had done the greater part of the writing and was growing a little bored with Jules' temperamental outbursts about the strain of sustained writing. Bored? She was both shocked and dismayed that such a thought should have crossed her mind.

"My parents are somewhat disturbed about our novel," he murmured.

"Disturbed?"

"Dupuy has been advertising it already. The subject sent my mother to confession at once."

"And your father?"

"He forbade me to publish the book under my own name."

Aurore and Jules had already written a few stories together and had published them under the signature: "J. Sandeau." Now Aurore generously agreed that *Rose et Blanche* should carry that same pseudonym.

"Let us use only the initial and divide the surname in half," she suggested.

"J. Sand," he pondered a trifle sulkily. "Would I be recognized at all under such a pseudonym?"

"Jules Sand—if you wish," she compromised.

"Yes, that would be better!"

He began to make love, but carelessly and hurriedly like a man hastily devouring a meal the deliciousness of which meant little to him. When he had finished he moved away from her instantly, leaving her grasping as if at an elusive bird in flight.

"Did I hurt you?" he asked just as he had asked that first time.

"No, Jules," Aurore said, feeling hurt both physically and spiritually.

"Did I ever hurt you?"

"No."

He stretched and laughed boastfully. "Almost from the first I learned to practice a firm gentleness. Why, I'm entirely self-taught—like that odd fellow, Chopin."

"Chopin?" Aurore was searching her memory. "He, too, is a great lover?"

"No, he's a composer and a pianist. I heard him play in Paris. You were too busy writing to go with me, remember? Everybody says he's a self-taught pianist, but they admit, most of them, that he's an absolute genius. I suppose making love the way I do is like playing a musical instrument brilliantly."

Brilliantly! Aurore sprang up and began to dress. In her exasperation and disappointment she realized that she was growing bored with Jules in more ways than one. Quickly she turned from him in order to hide the tears in her eyes.

Seated at her own desk, she came to one of her quick decisions. "Jules, when we go back to Paris, we shall have separate apartments."

"You're tiring of me," he accused.

"Nonsense, Jules. We'll visit each other, love as never before, and preserve our individual freedom. Besides, I want to take my daughter to Paris."

"You don't want Solange to grow up under the influence of a 'bad' example?"

"When she grows up, I want her to be strong enough to choose for herself as I have been able to do. If a happy marriage is possible for her, I will be immeasurably pleased."

"Madame," Jules said, his manner ridiculously dignified, "I shall write the rest of my part of the book in Paris alone."

Aurore lingered on at Nohant long after Jules had departed. She found Casimir surprisingly meek. True, when they spent an evening together they had nothing much to talk about, but clearly he was living up to his part of their bargain. When at last she broached the subject of taking Solange with her to Paris he made no objection. Maurice, who was truly his, had a good tutor. But Solange, who had passed her third birthday, needed a mother's constant care.

"Why, we are almost friends now!" Aurore exclaimed.

"Weren't we friends before we made the mistake of marrying?"

In spite of his meekness, his seeming friendliness, and understanding, Aurore saw a cunning look in his eyes. What was he planning? What, in the name of heaven, would come of this marriage which, in every respect, was a mockery?

V

"I have never been so gratified in my life," Ernest Dupuy said warmly. "We are not making a fortune out of *Rose et Blanche* but we are doing very well with it. You have captured not only the housemaids and the cooks, but a portion of the intelligentsia as well."

"I?" Aurore asked.

"Oh come! You have contributed far more to the book than Jules Sandeau. Admittedly there are many faults in the writing, but such faults don't matter when a book is causing a mild sensation."

Aurore smiled. "I write because I must. Still, it is not entirely a question of living to write. Writing to live plays a part in it, too. Naturally I want to earn money by writing successful books."

Dupuy nodded approvingly. "I can see that we are going to have an excellent author-publisher relationship. The main fault of *Rose et Blanche* is the striking difference of styles. In a collaboration that is often inevitable. Your own style is patently superior. That is to say . . ."

"The more salable style, monsieur."

"Precisely! I must have another book, madame. One written by you alone."

"You shall have it sooner than you think," Aurore promised. "I wrote several chapters of *Indiana* before I left Nohant. Now I shall press on with the rest of the novel."

"*Indiana?* An intriguing title. May I hear something about the subject?"

Aurore smiled at him calmly. Publishers, to her, were no longer great men in whose presence one was forced to tremble with awe and fear. They were, first and foremost, businessmen once a previously unknown author had achieved success. "The plot is a deadly secret," she chuckled.

Dupuy all but tore his hair. "Authors, how I loathe them!"

Jubilantly, Aurore returned to her new apartment on the Quai Malaquais. This she had recently taken over from Henri Latouche. Here, since Jules was ill when she reached Paris, she had furnished a special little room for him, nursed him back to health and allowed him to stay in spite of her earlier decision. They had achieved a full reconciliation. Jules was touchingly grateful and, influenced by the success of *Rose et Blanche,* had become again a gay and sparkling companion.

Entering the apartment now, Aurore found her mother ensconced in a comfortable old armchair. She was bouncing Solange on her knee while the nursemaid whom Aurore had engaged stood anxiously by.

"I want to talk to you," Sophie said, her voice mysteriously low. Then giving the child to the maid, she instructed her to take the little girl out for an airing.

"Are you in debt again?" Aurore asked resignedly.

Sophie ignored the question haughtily. "I'm so glad Solange isn't Casimir's child."

"Is that all you want to discuss?"

Sophie frowned. "I am deeply shocked by *Rose et Blanche.* I prefer purity in novels I read."

Aurore nodded and smiled. "Of course! That is your own particular form of escape from reality."

Sophie sighed sadly. "I'm too old for the reality you mean. A very great tragedy, but one must contrive to make the best of the ravages of old age."

Aurore looked at her mother in considerable astonishment. This was something new, talking about old age. Her hair was a more vivid red than ever before and she was so heavily painted that a stranger could not possibly make an accurate estimation of her true age. Her eyes, however, looked tired and just a little frightened. She had complained lately of a pain in her stomach and Aurore had urged her to consult a doctor.

"Mother, did you visit the doctor I recommended?"

Sophie ignored the question. "Aurore, can you hear anything? Listen carefully." She was glancing indignantly at the door of Jules' room. "Strain your ears, Aurore."

"I can't hear anything, Mother."

"Ah, but I can. I'm an old hand at that sort of thing. The slightest rustle, the faintest of sighs, and I know instantly what is happening. I consider it shameful, absolutely shameful. You must throw him out at once."

Aurore opened the door. Jules lay in bed with the sheet tucked under his chin. He sat up in some surprise at the sight of her.

"I thought you were dining with Dupuy."

"Tomorrow, not today."

In sitting up, he had inadvertently dragged the bedclothes aside, exposing a girl's head and shoulders. Her nose was tip-tilted, her hair long, black and tousled. Jules shrugged and laughed jauntily.

"Don't wake her. I'll do it myself in my own good time."

Aurore was nonplussed and for the moment speechless. Icy fingers plucked at her heart, then anger overwhelmed her. "Come out when you're dressed," she said tensely. "I'll talk to you then if I'm calmer."

Aurore sent her mother away and stood by the window,

waiting and trying not to think. Jules emerged eventually, a sheepish smile on his face.

"You needn't take it so seriously, Aurore. She's only a laundress."

"Are you trying to humiliate me by choosing such a girl?"

"What a penetrating intellect you have! It's almost masculine. That's one of the things I dislike about you."

"One of them? There are others then?"

Jules nodded. "Your diabolical dedication to writing."

Aurore turned away. Why talk, why argue? Hurt and shocked as she was, she tried to regard Jules Sandeau as only a brief incident in her life. All she wanted now was to make an end of it, quickly and cleanly.

"Aren't you going to forgive me?" he demanded.

Aurore stared somberly out of the window. "I can forgive, Jules, but I can't forget. Take the girl away. If you come back yourself, you'll find the door locked against you."

"But where can I go?" he asked pettishly.

"Your friend Regnault will give you a bed until you find a place to live."

"We were going to Italy together," he reminded her. "In Italy you will forgive and forget. I know you will."

"Go to Italy alone."

"I can't afford it."

Aurore remembered then that but for Jules Sandeau she would not have come to Paris, would not have met Balzac and Dumas, would not have written the greater part of *Rose et Blanche* and so established herself as a writer. Anger still throbbed in her breast but gratitude was there, too.

"I'll pay your expenses, Jules."

"Now you are trying to humiliate me!"

"Am I succeeding?"

"Judge for yourself! Of course, I'll go to Italy at your expense. It will be a pleasure to travel alone. The greatest joy in the

178

world—not having a woman to order me about."

The laundress emerged, fully dressed and dowdy. Her cheeks were rosy, her eyes bold and challenging. Her voice was shrill and common.

"You said she was your sister," she sneered, taking full stock of Aurore's male attire. "Surely you meant your brother!"

Jules hustled the girl from the apartment, only to return a few moments later with a pleading if sulky look in his eyes.

"We have so many things in common, Aurore: art, music, literature. Frédéric Chopin is going to play in Marie d'Agoult's *salon* tomorrow night. Please come with me."

Frédéric Chopin— Memory stirred and dear old Deschartres sprang to life again. A polonaise, wasn't it, sent to him by a friend who was traveling in Poland? Aurore remembered it vividly. Casimir in one of his rages had thrown the music along with some of her books into the fire.

"Chopin's music will thrill you and soften your heart," Jules urged.

"I shall be too busy writing for music. Good-by, Jules. I'll send your things to Regnault's apartment."

Aurore ran to her desk the moment the door had closed behind Jules Sandeau. For the reader there was escape from reality in reading, but for the writer there was even greater escape in writing. Casimir, Aurélien, Stéphane and Jules. Among them, they had destroyed her faith in all men. But writing! *Indiana,* for the moment, was all that mattered. She decided then to keep the pseudonym "Sand," but to replace the "Jules" with "George." Henceforth her professional name would be George Sand.

14

Franz Liszt paused before opening the door of the small apartment in the Boulevard Poissonnière. He smiled sympathetically. Frédéric Chopin was giving yet another piano lesson and, as usual when confronted with a stupid pupil, had flown into a rage. Liszt listened for a moment to the rapid flow of abuse. There was despair in the poor fellow's voice as well as anger. The door was flung open before Liszt could touch the handle and a girl flew out. She was weeping copiously. A roll of music came hurtling after her. Liszt caught it, tucked it under her arm and entered the apartment.

"Ah, you, my dear Liszt," Frédéric said. "How glad I am to see you."

"You sound quite hoarse, Chopin."

Frédéric laughed grimly. "One of these days I shall lose my voice altogether."

Liszt smiled affectionately. He had grown fond of the Polish pianist since first meeting him a year or more ago in the rooms of Camille Pleyel, the celebrated music publisher and manufacturer of pianos. Already they had given a concert together in the Salle Pleyel and another at the Conservatoire, but mostly they played in the fashionable drawing rooms of Paris where each in his own way was becoming famous.

"That girl will never come back again," Frédéric said darkly.

"Can you afford to lose a pupil?" Liszt asked.

"No, but I would rather starve than be tortured by an idiot."

Franz Liszt, rich himself, was often sorry for his friend. Concerts were anything but lucrative and the music that Chopin had published up to now had brought in very little money. It was a terrible thing, Liszt thought, for an artist to have to give music lessons just to keep body and soul together.

"Is your health improving?" he asked anxiously.

"My health?" A frown wrinkled Frédéric's brow. "I never think about it."

Chopin was twenty-three now. He had been in Paris almost two years, having traveled from Warsaw by way of Vienna, Stuttgart and Strasbourg, and having spent some little time giving drawing-room recitals in each of those cities. While in Vienna, he learned of the Russian invasion of Poland; in Stuttgart, he was shattered to hear that Warsaw had fallen. The only consolation was that his parents and sisters had come to no harm. Nevertheless, he was tormented constantly by the thought of his country held in bondage. Unable to bear arms, blaming himself just as if he alone was responsible for the fall of Warsaw, he had poured all his agony and self-reproach into an étude in C minor.

"I am nothing but a lost soul," he exclaimed, thinking of this now, "capable only of playing the piano."

Liszt was startled, as indeed he often had cause to be, by Frédéric's rapid change of mood. Gay one moment, the young man was depressed and melancholy the next. Small wonder Chopin, with his frail body and violent extremes of emotion, was often in poor health.

"I came into a self-imposed exile," Frédéric went on dramatically. "Now, whether I like it or not, I must remain in exile."

"Oh come," Liszt protested, "your father is French. This country is just as much yours as Poland is. And Paris will soon be your city because of your music."

"I hate Paris!"

"Truly?"

Frédéric grinned. "At least, I find it a most peculiar place. Every Frenchman dances and shouts even if his bones are bare. Wherever I turn, I find the utmost luxury, the utmost poverty, the utmost swinishness, and the utmost virtue all huddled together. And the women of Paris . . . !"

"Ah, you have become an authority on that subject?"

"Delectable creatures, every one of them."

"Yet you remain aloof."

"How can they and music dwell together in peace and harmony?"

"I have never found any trouble in that direction," Liszt chuckled. "You need a mistress to look after you."

"A mistress?" Frédéric's eyes reflected his horror at the suggestion. "That would be scandalous. And besides, what would people think?"

"Some men are able to practice a cunning discretion."

"I refuse to listen to you, Liszt."

The older man tried not to smile. "But, seriously, you live too much alone."

"On the contrary, I go about constantly in society."

"I mean alone within yourself."

"Still there are times when I enjoy society, especially when I am not called upon to play the piano."

"Ah yes. Those famous imitations of yours."

"Perhaps I shall give up music and go on the stage."

Liszt smiled slyly. "Even comedians are expected to make love—on the stage."

Frédéric considered this seriously. "Pretending is, of course, another matter."

"Have you never been in love?"

"No, never. W-e-ll, yes. Once. No—two or three times. Perhaps a dozen. I can't remember."

But Frédéric was thinking of Maria Wodzinska. How old was she now? "With all our love," she had said when offering him that bouquet of flowers. He knew she had meant to say "With all my love," but she had been too shy and modest to reveal the truth. One rose from the bouquet was still preserved in a faded condition between the pages of a book. He had never written to Maria but had sent her messages when writing to her brothers. Impulsively he ran now to his little writing-table and dragged open the drawer. In it was the silver urn filled with Polish soil and the book that held the rose. He seized the book and held it reverently.

"I see you have been reading *Indiana,*" Liszt observed, coming up behind Frédéric.

"I never read novels," Chopin said scathingly. "As you see, most of the pages are still uncut." He glanced at the title and the author's name, GEORGE SAND. "It was given to me by a grateful pupil. Just why he was grateful I can't imagine since he caused me to break a chair. Who is George Sand?"

"A clever writer. Strange you haven't met her in one or other of the fashionable *salons.*"

"Her?"

"George Sand is a pseudonym. In private life she is Madame Dudevant, the mother of two children."

"Ridiculous!"

"I beg your pardon?"

"Dishonest, too."

"Dishonest?"

"Is she ashamed of her book?"

"Indeed no. She is very proud of it."

"Then why use a man's name? I might as well call myself Frédérica something or other."

The rose fell from the book. Liszt picked it up and shook his head in mock gloom. "So sad to think that love, like this flower, can fade and die."

"How wrong you are!" Frédéric said angrily. "My love for Maria will never fade and die."

"Maria?"

Frédéric blushed. Never before had he mentioned the name to anyone. Now Liszt had trapped him into betraying his secret. Then he remembered a bold and important decision he had reached earlier in the day while playing a waltz dedicated to Maria. He snatched up a letter he had received the day before from his mother. It contained news of Maria. She and her mother, along with her brothers, were planning a visit to Carlsbad. It would be of great benefit to Frédéric's health, Justina Chopin had suggested, if he too went to Carlsbad to take the waters. Indeed, it was imperative that he should visit the spa since his father in need of a cure was going there also.

"I shall go to Carlsbad," he announced.

Liszt nodded. "That is where the dear Maria lives?"

Frédéric began instantly to dissimulate. "No, she lives in Geneva. Her father, the count, was a very important man in Warsaw. The Russian invasion drove him away. He and his family now live in exile at Geneva but have hopes of returning to Poland some day."

"Geneva is quite a distance from Carlsbad," Liszt said solemnly.

Frédéric laughed. "Why, so it is, my dear Liszt."

II

Justina Chopin obeyed her husband's gentle command and hid behind the curtains in the inexpensive apartment they had rented in Carlsbad. She waited expectantly, trembling with excitement. A few moments later, Frédéric hurried into the room and flew into his father's arms. They embraced again and again, weeping for joy.

"You haven't changed in the least, my boy," Nicolas Chopin asserted.

Peeping through the curtains, Justina shook her head sadly. Frédéric had grown thinner and was much paler now. If only he had a loving wife to look after him! Maria Wodzinska, she thought. Who would be better for him than Maria?

"I have a surprise," Nicolas now said solemnly. "Prepare yourself for a shock."

Justina revealed herself at once. "Frédéric, darling Frédéric!"

"Mother!" There was more wild embracing, more joyous weeping.

"I would have brought your sisters, too," Nicolas said, "but that was impossible."

Two years or more had elapsed since Frédéric's decision to come to Carlsbad, for the Countess Wodzinska had put off her visit many times. So had Nicolas Chopin; he had wanted to save enough money to bring his wife with him. Meanwhile, Frédéric had steeled himself to write daring little letters to Maria and had received in reply some sweet notes, all of which he had carefully preserved with the dead rose and the urn of Polish soil. And thinking of what his friend Liszt had said about love fading and dying but refusing to believe it, he had composed another étude, this time in F minor, especially for Maria. This he had brought with him to Carlsbad even though he knew he must still work on it, searching as ever for perfection.

"The Countess Wodzinska is anxious to see you again," Nicolas remarked casually.

A guarded look crossed Frédéric's face. "Naturally I am just as anxious to see her."

Justina smiled brightly. "Only the countess, darling?"

Frédéric blushed. "Oh, I have a great affection for her sons also."

Observing his son's embarrassment, Nicolas nodded wisely. "And they for you, Frédéric."

"You will find the little Maria changed," Justina murmured. "You will scarcely recognize her now that she is grown up."

"She's as pretty as a picture." Nicolas spoke admiringly.

"Intelligent, too, and very fond of music," Justina added.

"Your music in particular," Nicolas smiled.

That evening the Countess Wodzinska received the Chopins in a private drawing room at her hotel. She greeted Frédéric warmly and remarked, after one glance at his pale, drawn face, that he must take the waters regularly before returning to Paris.

Frédéric bowed. "Father forced me to drink a whole pint this afternoon. I found the bitterness nauseating."

"One grows accustomed to it, Frédéric."

Frédéric bowed again but his eyes were on the young woman who, smiling and blushing, stood at the countess's side. Maria! And not merely as "pretty as a picture," but beautiful—ravishingly beautiful! She wore a light summer dress. Her dark hair glowed, her blue eyes sparkled bewitchingly. Frédéric kissed her hand gallantly. They both spoke at the same time, uttering the same words.

"Do you remember . . . ?"

Everybody laughed and the countess remarked that the two young people would have many childhood memories to recall now that they had met again after almost five years. Then she drew Frédéric's attention to the piano in the room.

"I had it brought in so that you might play for us."

Frédéric smiled politely. Why must he be regarded as a sort of machine, available at any moment of the day or night to sit at a piano and produce music? All he wanted to do right now was to carry Maria away and tell her that he loved her.

"If you will be so kind ... ?" the countess said, smiling fondly. "Maria often plays your music but only you, dear Frédéric, can do full justice to it."

Completely won over by her flattery, the young pianist seated himself on the piano stool and began to play.

"The waltz you dedicated to me!" Maria exclaimed.

"So it is," Frédéric agreed, not quite having realized what he was playing.

The countess sighed deeply when he finished. "I can hear so many things in it: the murmur of lovers' voices to begin with, followed by the striking of a clock and the sound of carriage wheels on cobblestones." She sighed again. "The clatter of the wheels seems to me to drown the sound of distracted sobbing."

Frédéric had heard only her first phrase. The murmur of lovers' voices! Did that mean that she suspected already how much he loved her daughter? That she and her husband, rich and aristocratic as they were, would accept him as a son-in-law? He began to play again, frantically. He would never find the courage to speak of his love. Never!

The Chopins spent five weeks at Carlsbad. Frédéric saw Maria daily and often they were alone together. No restraints were placed on their friendship, yet Frédéric failed to utter the words burning in his heart. During the last evening, he played—for Maria alone—his new étude.

"This," he said, his voice muffled, "is a portrait of your soul."

Maria brushed his cheek lightly with her lips. "You know a great deal more about my soul than I do."

He turned to her eagerly. "But your heart? What of your heart, Maria?"

She laughed chidingly. "How slow you are, Frédéric. My heart is yours. It always has been."

"You love me, Maria?"

"Deeply."

187

"And—and you'll marry me?"

"I could never marry anyone else."

Frédéric took her in his arms. They kissed gently, like children.

"You forced me to speak, but you haven't spoken yet yourself," Maria murmured, her head on Frédéric's breast. "I know you love me but you haven't said so. A girl likes to be told, Frédéric."

"I have told you, Maria. In my music. Over and over again!"

"The words would make even better music."

Frédéric made the greatest effort of his life. "I love you, Maria."

She drew away from him, her eyes brilliant. "Thank you, Frédéric."

"You will be a poor man's wife," he warned.

"As if I care about that!"

Frédéric turned to the door. "We must tell your mother!"

They found the countess on the terrace of the hotel. She smiled knowingly and declared that it was clear enough what they wanted to say, but she insisted that for the time being the engagement must remain a secret.

"I love you as if you were my own son," she told the young man. "You have my consent, but it would be premature to make an announcement before my husband has been consulted. The count is very much the master of the house."

"Or so he imagines," Maria chuckled.

The countess smiled. "I anticipate no difficulty in that direction."

Frédéric was delirious. He left for Paris the next day in a gay and confident mood. Henceforth, inspired by Maria's love he would write the most brilliant music of his whole life.

15

"You actually appear to be enjoying your cigar, my dear George," Sainte-Beuve remarked skeptically.

The author of *Indiana* smiled as nonchalantly as she could. Her face had not yet turned green in spite of the queasiness of her stomach. It was, after all, only her second cigar; the first, given to her at an earlier literary party, she had only pretended to smoke.

She glanced about the little gathering at Sainte-Beuve's dinner table and felt very much in her element. No longer did she sit at the feet of such literary giants as Sainte-Beuve, Dumas, Balzac, and Mérimée in the guise of a timid outsider. She was one of them. The success of *Indiana* and her more recent semipolitical articles had made her so. They accepted her on her own terms and without exception called her "George," just as if Aurore Dudevant had never existed. But then, she told herself, she was George Sand; only rarely did she think of herself as Aurore Dudevant. Her glance fell on Alfred de Musset, the young poet whose work she was beginning to admire. He was studying her intently from his place at the bottom of the table, yet at the same time pretending indifference. She gazed back at him in an attempt to stare him out of countenance. He blushed

189

and averted his eyes. Delightful!

"What are you writing now, George?" asked Mérimée who was seated next to her.

"Another novel."

"May I know the title?"

"Lélia."

"Tell me about it."

"What is there to tell?"

Dumas leaned across the table, his dark eyes flashing. "George Sand, my dear Mérimée, is the only man of letters who never talks about her work."

"I leave the talking to my readers—and, of course, the critics."

Mérimée laughed. He took the cigar from her and began to smoke it himself.

"You must thank me, George, for saving you from a bilious attack," he murmured, his eyes challenging.

A perceptive man, this Prosper Mérimée, George thought, but apart from that, cold and conceited. It was ludicrous that Sainte-Beuve should be trying once again to throw them together, claiming that they, much of the same age, had a lot in common. She had told Sainte-Beuve often that she was no longer interested in men, that Jules Sandeau had driven all thoughts of romance from her mind, but he was a persistent little fellow, always saying that one of these days he would find the right man for her.

"When you were Aurore Dudevant, you went about in male attire," Mérimée said reflectively. "Now that you are George Sand, you wear petticoats again."

"Not always."

"But generally at these literary gatherings. Is it your wish, when alone with a group of men, to remind us that you are still a woman?"

"Perhaps."

Mérimée's eyes were challenging again. "You look most striking in black. Striking . . ." He dwelled on the word. "No, I mean—forbidding." He shrugged eloquently. "You are, let us say, still in mourning for Jules Sandeau."

"Sandeau is certainly dead as far as I am concerned."

"There were others before him. All your affairs, like your marriage, have been disastrous."

George looked at him steadily. "You appear to think you know a great deal about me."

"We writers are great gossips."

Her lips curled scornfully. Nobody in Paris could possibly know anything about her past except for the Sandeau incident. Jules himself, as she well knew, had talked freely, embroidering the truth with fantastic fiction. His present mistress—Marie Dorval, the actress who was supposed to be her friend—had talked freely, too. "According to the gossips, every man I meet eventually becomes my lover. What of your own affairs, monsieur? Disastrous like mine?"

"My dear George, I have succeeded always in extricating myself before disaster fell upon me."

He was boasting, George thought. According to Sainte-Beuve, Mérimée liked to be known as something of a Don Juan— though only in certain circles. His life, so she had learned, was divided into two strictly separated parts. In high society, where he had many aristocratic connections, he was the respectable archaeologist, the eminent man of letters who was likely during the next few years to become an outstanding master of French style; in Bohemia, however, he was a rake making a sort of butterfly progress from one complaisant woman to another.

Sainte-Beuve rose now and led the way to the *salon* where presently one or other of his guests—less inhibited than George Sand—would give a reading from his latest collection of stories or poems.

"Wait," Mérimée said, detaining George at the table, "I want to talk to you."

"I cannot prevent you from talking."

"By which you mean I cannot force you to listen?"

"Oh, I'm prepared to listen."

"Attentively?"

George nodded. "I may have use for a character such as you in one of my books."

"It would have to be a very daring book," Mérimée laughed. "However, it is your character we are discussing at the moment. Now those failures of yours— You failed, I suspect, because you expected too much of the men concerned. You sought an ideal. You wanted the spiritual as well as the physical. That was stupid. All you needed—that is—all you need now is the physical."

"I need neither," she said, nettled.

"You can manage very well without the former, but deny yourself the latter and your writing will suffer."

"In short, if I go to bed with Prosper Mérimée, a brilliant novel will be the outcome. Is that what you think, monsieur?"

"It is not a question of thinking, Madame Sand; I know it to be the undeniable truth. Having made a precise and painstaking study of the mechanics of physical love, I am now, as you will live to discover, a most skillful lover."

Mérimée began to make little sketches on the tablecloth with his forefinger. The indentations were as graphic as if he were using a pen. George was revolted, yet at the same time attracted. She saw from the guarded look Mérimée gave her that he expected her to be shocked, so she smiled serenely in an effort both to disappoint him and prevent him from realizing that he had succeeded.

He rose from the table. "The streets of Paris are dangerous for a woman alone at night. Pray permit me to escort you to your apartment."

Well, George thought, why not? She knew herself to be a passionate woman, with the passion, unrelieved, growing sour within her.

But when the fiacre drew up in the Quai Malaquais, she remembered her young daughter. Not here, she thought, sick at the full realization of what she had been about to do. Solange would be asleep but the nursemaid had sharp ears. She offered Mérimée her hand.

"Good-night, monsieur. I am not so easily conquered."

His eyes darkened for a moment, then he shrugged. "At all events, madame, you leave a door open."

"The door is closed and locked."

"I shall knock on it gently at first, then heavily. Finally I shall break it down."

"You make me quake with fear."

"No, madame, anticipation."

Thereafter Prosper Mérimée pursued George Sand relentlessly and without any trace of gallantry. He was a young stallion, or so he claimed, with pounding hoofs and flaring nostrils, and he spoke of himself as the thoroughbred of thoroughbreds. The whole of Bohemia was watching and waiting he boasted. None of their friends doubted that he would succeed. It was merely a question of when and where.

Casimir came to Paris while the stallion was still pounding his hoofs and breathing flames of passion.

"Now I have my husband to protect me," George mocked, meeting Mérimée briefly at Tortini's.

Casimir was in a thoroughly disgruntled mood. He brought with him a list of complaints, most of which concerned his wife's way of life in Paris.

"You have forgotten your promise of long ago," he said. "Six months in Paris, six months at Nohant. How often do you visit Nohant these days? I've half a mind to take Solange from you."

"You can't do that, Casimir."

"Indeed I can if I take legal action."

"Nohant is mine. The income from the estate is mine. Do you wish to be deprived of the large portion I allow you for yourself?"

"Bitch," Casimir said, "arrogant, selfish bitch!"

Growing calmer, he suggested that, if it came to a legal battle, he might well establish his right to secure the entire income for himself as well as the guardianship of the two children. In the end, after an exhausting argument, George agreed that Casimir should take Solange on a visit to the Baronne Dudevant at Guillery. Although actually thinking of Prosper Mérimée, she tried to deceive herself that she had allowed her husband to take the child solely because the country air would strengthen her.

"And so," Mérimée said when they met again at one of Sainte-Beuve's parties, "you have sent your husband away."

"He went of his own accord."

"But not without some little encouragement from you?"

"True."

"For one reason only?"

"For one reason only," she said honestly.

Once again Prosper Mérimée accompanied George Sand to the Quai Malaquais. It was no longer necessary for the thoroughbred to batter down the door, the "stable" door as he called it. Frantically eager only a few moments ago, George felt a strange reluctance as she led him into her small, cluttered-up *salon*. She placed an easy chair at Mérimée's disposal and brought him a bottle of wine.

Later, as he sipped at the wine and superciliously pronounced it no better than *vin ordinaire,* George loosened her hair and, with Mérimée watching, changed into a negligee of Spanish design. Then hurriedly she found a second bottle of wine. Perhaps if she could make the stallion drunk he would fall asleep in his chair.

"I'd be no more use to you than a plaster saint," he laughed, "if I drank any more of this vile stuff."

George saw then that he had scarcely touched the glass she had poured for him from the first bottle.

"Mérimée a plaster saint?" she forced herself to scoff.

Unceremoniously he pushed her into her bedroom.

"Light! We must have light!" he commanded.

George lit a lamp. Mérimée undressed hurriedly and tore off her negligee.

"You're smaller than I thought. A small Venus who has grown a trifle plump. Not that it matters. I loathe scrawny women."

Masterfully he flung her on the bed, but that, as he fell upon her, was the end of his masterfulness. He moaned and threshed about until, finally defeated, he dropped back at her side. George repressed a desire to giggle insanely. She even felt a little sorry for this impotent boaster until she heard him cursing her.

"It was your immodesty, your damnable immodesty!" he raged.

"My immodesty?"

"To change in front of me like that!"

"It was you who wanted light—you who wanted to see."

"You behaved like a whore. You postured, you tantalized. Never yet have I had a whore."

Mérimée rose and dressed slowly, deliberately. There was anger in his eyes. George dragged on her negligee. When he was fully dressed, she followed him out to the *salon*. He delved deep into a pocket, found a five-franc piece and tossed it onto the mantelpiece.

"Even that is more than you are worth," he said scathingly, "but I was never ungenerous."

A few days later George went to have an ice with Sainte-

Beuve at Tortini's. The gossip had already started. Mérimée had apparently confided in Dumas, and Dumas, the greatest gossip of them all, was busily spreading the story. Prosper Mérimée had spent a wild night with George Sand but the wildness had been his alone. George, neither a man nor a woman, had proved an unsatisfactory companion in the pursuit of love. Not ungenerous, however, not ungallant, he had tossed a five-franc piece onto her carpet and she, always eager to earn a few francs either by the use of her pen or her body, had snatched it up.

Sainte-Beuve, however, was humble and contrite. "Please forgive me, George. I made a sad mistake when I tried to force Mérimée upon you."

Hurriedly she excused herself and went back to her apartment. There was only one means of escape—work. She re-read all that she had so far written of her new novel, but concentration was difficult. With her mind in confusion, the thread of the story eluded her. All she managed to write that day was nonsense. She grew desperate and tore up the pages. Her talent, which had seemed so promising, had disappeared. Mérimée was the cause. Never again, because of him, would she write another intelligible word.

II

"I don't believe the story," Alfred de Musset said warmly. "I know Mérimée too well to place any faith in the accounts he gives of his amatory adventures."

"Thank you," George said lightly, both pleased and embarrassed by his words.

The editor of the *Revue des Deux Mondes,* to which journal George Sand had contributed many articles, was giving a dinner party for his staff and free-lance contributors. George, who had remained something of a recluse since the Mérimée fiasco, had steeled herself to attend, knowing that she must sooner or later face the delighted smiles of her "friends," and had found herself seated next to Alfred de Musset. A glance at Sainte-Beuve, who was smiling and nodding further down the table, told her that accident had played no part in giving her de Musset as a table companion. Sainte-Beuve, in his determination to find the "right" man for her, was absolutely incorrigible!

She looked covertly at de Musset now and just as shyly as if she were Aurore Dupin newly released from the convent. He was her junior by at least six years and something of a dandy. His fair hair and beardless chin reminded her of Jules Sandeau, but there, fortunately, the resemblance ended, for he had rather plump cheeks and full, red lips. He wore a dark blue frock-coat with a velvet collar, and light blue trousers so tight and narrow that his thighs bulged within them. She had already seen him carrying a gold-handled cane and wearing a tall hat set at a jaunty angle. It was one thing to admire de Musset's verse, quite another to admire his appearance. She, George Sand, had no use for dandies.

"Is *Indiana* as shocking as people say?" he asked, affecting a blasé air.

"You haven't read it?"

"No. Is that an unforgivable sin?"

"It is at least a timely reminder that I am not as widely read as I like to think."

"You are that very rare phenomenon—a modest writer."

George felt her heart warming to him. "I'll send you a copy of *Indiana.*"

"Do so, and I'll send you a sincere and honest report."

They went on to talk about art, music, and literature. Soon George was beginning to find the young man highly intelligent. How could it be otherwise, she asked herself wryly, when he listened attentively to all she had to say and pronounced most of her comments both wise and penetrating?

"What do you think of our infant prodigy?" Sainte-Beuve asked her later that night.

"I'm inclined to like him more than I expected to at first. I think his dandyism is mostly affectation. Nevertheless, my poor Sainte-Beuve, you will never throw us into a love affair."

Sainte-Beuve looked at her seriously. "De Musset is too disillusioned to want anything like that."

George went home in a happier mood. Her mind was so clear that instead of going to bed, she sat at her desk and wrote as she had never written before. She worked until dawn, corrected the pages and smiled in wonder. Thank you, Alfred de Musset!

Remembering her promise, she sent a copy of *Indiana* to the young poet and found herself waiting as anxiously as if she were still a callow young writer for his report. Two days later the book was returned to her. A short note was enclosed.

> I do not ask your forgiveness for what I have done. Please meet me at Tortini's at noon tomorrow.
>
> Alfred de Musset

For what he had done? George turned the pages of *Indiana* and found that de Musset, using a blue crayon, had presumed to correct her priceless novel just as if it were still in manuscript form. Countless adjectives were lined out and here and there whole phrases. Impudent young puppy! Infant prodigy indeed! Nevertheless, she was intrigued by his presumption and presently admitted to herself that *Indiana*, successful as it was, had been over-written. Alfred de Musset, with his poet's ear for the music of words, had taught her a much-needed lesson. *Lélia*, when completed, would most certainly benefit from a ruthless revision. She told this to Alfred when they were seated at a table on the terrace at Tortini's the next day.

De Musset raised his eyebrows. "How humble you sound."

"Humble—me?"

They laughed together as if at a great childish joke, but Alfred soon grew serious and referred to one of the characters in *Indiana*.

"This hero of yours and all the misery he suffered—was it fiction or fact, George?"

"Fact?" she questioned uneasily.

"I read of a love striving to grasp and hold a fond illusion. Fiction or fact? I read of an endless, fruitless seeking, of agony and despair, of a desperate recourse to the pleasures of hell and hopelessness. Were you remembering it all, writing vividly from your own experience?"

"Partly," George admitted, shattered by his perception.

"Writing but still not escaping the past?"

"You're an awful child," she said shakily. "Not an *enfant prodige* so much as an *enfant terrible*."

Alfred smiled sadly. "One can escape the past as well as the present when writing, but when the writing is finished, they both are all about you again, tormenting you. I know that from bitter experience."

"You do? Young as you are?"

"In many ways I'm older than you, George."

Impulsively she leant across the table and rumpled his hair. "Now you look like an angel."

Alfred sighed dramatically. "A fallen one, George."

Then he began to talk about himself. He was a great trial to his mother and brother and only when he could no longer afford to live alone did he reside with them. His little circle of admirers—Romantics, all of them—called him a genius, but those who scoffed at him—and their name was legion—called him a trickster. He was, he thought, a little of each, and sounded neither boastful nor sorry for himself as he spoke. He was much influenced by Byron—Byron the man, not Byron the poet. Hence his fanciful way of dressing, his pursuit of women and his debauchery. No woman had yet been faithful to him. They only played a game, so he had turned his back on them forever. Opium gave him far more satisfaction. Ah, the dreams, the soaring delights of opium!

George laughed lightly. "You are only pretending!"

"Pretense, if practiced long enough, becomes reality."

"But opium! Really, Alfred, you must give it up."

"Now you are trying to mother me. Well, that's a new experience."

"Promise not to resort to opium again. Come! Promise!"

"I thought perhaps we might smoke a pipe together."

"Never!"

"The escape is beyond belief."

"Never!" George repeated.

Alfred looked at her somberly. "You prefer to go on suffering the romantic restlessness that tortures both of us?"

"Romantic restlessness?" she echoed. "Yes, that's an apt description. I try again and again to forget my past mistakes, but they pursue me into the present and they will torment me in the future. But still, Alfred, I prefer—as you put it—to go on suffering."

"How strong you are! Please give me a little of your strength and help me to go on suffering too."

"On one condition."

"And that is?"

"No more opium."

Alfred was all eagerness. "I accept your condition gladly!"

They shook hands across the table: Alfred and George, two men reaching a serious agreement with one another: Alfred ready to be mothered, George more than willing to do the mothering. No talk of love, no romance between them. A marriage of two minds, if you like, but that and no more. Thereafter they met frequently and, when unable to meet, they exchanged long letters: George and Alfred, the greatest friends in the world—if not exactly mother and son.

16

MADAME SOPHIE DUPIN had come to her daughter's apartment in a towering rage. She said she was ready to die of shame and humiliation.

"*Lélia* is a dreadful book," she cried. "I only wish I could have prevented its publication."

"It is certainly enjoying a *succès de scandale*," George said calmly.

"I can well believe it. The moment I finished reading it I suffered a terrifying heart attack."

"At all events, you read it from cover to cover and you appear to have survived the heart attack."

"God was merciful, but even so my life has been shortened by several years."

"The book will earn a lot of money."

Sophie's eyes narrowed. "That, at least, is something." She departed in a happier frame of mind, having been assured of an increase in her allowance.

George, meanwhile, half-regretted having published a book into which she had put so much of herself. She was indeed her own heroine, Lélia, while many of the characters represented the conflicts of her own nature, her search for God, her striving for spiritual perfection, and her belief that the Church was in part degenerate.

In their reviews the critics either praised the book unduly or attacked it viciously. Gustave Planché, whom George had met through Sainte-Beuve and grown to like as a friend, wrote that the whole of *Lélia* was the cry of society in its death throes and therefore assured the author a place among the immortals. On the other hand, Capo de Feuillide, whom she had never met, wrote that *Lélia* was a rank obscenity, a burning coal dropped from the fires of Hell. Condemning it out of hand, he warned any adult unwise enough to read it to destroy it before his children came upon it.

George's friends roared indignantly and Gustave Planché, bolder than the rest, challenged Capo de Feuillide to a duel. The challenge was accepted. The weapons were pistols. Capo de Feuillide's shot hit a tree, Gustave Planché's disappeared high in the air; but de Feuillide, clapping both hands to his breast, screamed that he had been mortally wounded. He was carried away groaning. Bohemian Paris rocked with laughter and *Lélia* continued to sell to the publisher's delight and satisfaction.

Belatedly, Alfred de Musset danced with rage.

"The right to dispose of your enemy was mine," he cried, when he came one day to George's apartment. "By what right was my right usurped?"

George knew from his eyes with their pin-point pupils that he had been smoking opium again. Instead of reproaching him, she spoke soothing words and put him to bed in the room once occupied by Jules Sandeau. There was no need to worry about Solange, for the child was still in the country. The next morning Alfred woke refreshed and calm.

"Fight if you must," George said, "but use a pen, not a pistol."

He smiled sheepishly. "I confess that firearms terrify me."

He looked at his clothes which George had folded neatly and placed on a chair. "You actually undressed me?"

She nodded. "Just as if you were a baby."

"Am I to stay here?"

Sainte-Beuve had long since told George that Alfred was in debt. "Can you afford to keep a separate apartment?"

"No."

"Do you wish to return to your mother?"

"Heaven forbid!"

"Then stay here you shall."

"You want to keep a strict watch on me."

"My aim is merely to look after you."

"My heart is dead, George."

"So is mine."

But was it? She could feel it beating painfully in her breast. Happiness and a sensation of foreboding battled for supremacy. Was it coming to her now—the one great love of her life?

"There'll be gossip," Alfred warned.

"Gossip is always with us. Vile as the world is, our friendship will stand the test."

"Perhaps," Alfred said uncertainly.

"We have our liberty. Nothing else matters."

"There are times when liberty stifles one."

During the next few days they worked at separate desks in George's *salon*. Then Alfred, who had written nothing of any worth, said woefully that he had never been able to write except in complete isolation. Accordingly, George rearranged his room until, like her room at Nohant, it became part-study, part-bedroom. Even so, he suffered small fits of temperament. The light was not strong enough at night. So George bought more lamps, lit more candles, until the light in Alfred's room was dazzling. Then he said that he could only write freely and well when partly intoxicated. George set aside the wine that Mérimée had despised and ordered a special vintage direct from Bordeaux.

"Wine, George? No, no! Wine dulls the senses. What I need is *eau de vie*."

Indulgently she provided him with a goodly supply of *eau de vie* but insisted on dosing him with salts each morning to tone up his liver. Making a face and protesting shrilly, Alfred submitted like an obedient child. When he grew pale and strained from overwork, she sent for a doctor and cooked nourishing broths and special chicken dishes. His well-being at every moment of the day was her sole concern. She had never been so happy in her life.

Occasionally they went about together in Bohemian society, ignoring the knowing smiles of their friends. But more and more they felt the need of no company but their own. How could their hearts be dead, George asked herself, when the greatest friendship the world had ever known bound them together?

One evening, after Sainte-Beuve had chided her about their "exclusiveness," George gave a party. Alfred was so excited at the prospect that she wondered if she had been monopolizing him too much. Then, too, it occurred to her that as a novelist she had perhaps withdrawn unwisely from the world. There were twelve guests—writers, artists, actors, and one lone philosopher. It was a gay affair.

Alfred insisted on dressing as a page of a bygone era and pranced and postured in a multi-colored doublet, a revealing cod-piece, smooth silk hose, and pointed leather slippers. George herself wore an outlandish costume of yellow silk. An ornamental belt holding a jeweled dagger emphasized the slimness of her waist. A weblike mantilla covered her head and the Turkish slippers on her feet matched the belt.

Alfred, the page, served at table and presently, his high spirits bubbling over, he poured a jug of water down the neck of the solemn philosopher. Later, when that drenched gentleman had departed, he found his sketching pad and with rapid strokes drew caricatures of everybody. All in all, it was a joyous and carefree evening. There was no serious talk, no heated discussions, only lighthearted and at times drunken laughter.

When the last guest had gone, George lay contentedly on the divan smoking Turkish cigarettes, while Alfred roamed restlessly about the room, picking up books and flinging them down again. Of a sudden he seemed nervous and ill at ease.

"What's the trouble, Alfred?" George asked anxiously.

He came and knelt at her side. "If I kiss you, will you protect yourself with that dagger?"

"It's only a toy dagger, not very sharp."

Her voice was so low that the words were scarcely audible. Alfred darted to her desk, sat down and began to write.

"A sudden inspiration, Alfred?"

"No." He went on writing. "I have been brooding over the subject for weeks."

When he had finished he offered George the sheet of paper. She took it from his trembling fingers and began to read. It was not a new poem, but a letter:

What I have to say may seem stupid to George Sand. She may think I am trying to make pretty, lying phrases. She may laugh either indulgently or angrily. She may open the door and throw me out. The truth of the matter—and it is the truth—is that I am in love with George Sand. I have been in love with her from the moment I first saw her. I tried to cure myself by permitting only a steady friendship—I who could never be a platonic hero. I know, tragically, just how George Sand regards me. To her, I am a child, to be cared for and protected. If she loves me at all, it is only mother love, but I no longer have the strength to keep this declaration to myself. I love George Sand, I love her!

"I had to write it," he said nervously. "I can't *say* what I feel."

With that he rushed to his room and slammed the door.

George read the letter again. How blind she had been! This should have been as clear as day to her from the first. Mother love indeed! She adored him! She knew that now without question. In him she recognized the best of all the others. His faults mattered not at all; they were the faults—the heartrending faults—of youth. Yet she shrank from committing herself. She had been hurt too often in the past. Should she dare take the risk of being hurt again? But presently, following her heart and ignoring her reasoning mind, she went to the desk and slowly began to write.

What I have to say may seem stupid to Alfred de Musset. I have fallen in love with him. I have been in love before but never as seriously as this. The feeling goes so deep that I tremble in wonder. My heart which I had thought hardened is soft within me. And why? Alfred de Musset's tenderness and loyalty are the cause. He has been a true friend, an understanding companion. Now he must be more. No longer can Alfred de Musset and George Sand live together as brother and sister. I love Alfred de Musset with all my heart, all my mind, and all my soul. I can hide it no longer from him nor from the world.

Without hesitation she opened Alfred's door. All the lamps and candles were burning brightly. At the sound of her step, Alfred sprang up from his desk. She offered him her letter. He took it with a fearful expression in his eyes.

"George, have I lost a dear friend?"

"Read my letter, Alfred."

"It was wrong of me to declare myself. Suffering I understand but not love."

"Read my letter," she repeated.

Alfred read it slowly and avidly, then again, seizing on a phrase here and there in almost childlike glee and reading it aloud.

"Before we come together," George warned, "we must be sure, both of us, that our love is real and lasting."

"But it is! It is!"

George gave him the dagger. "Protect yourself if you must."

Appalled, she realized that her voice was harsh, that she sounded like the dominant, aggressive partner. But Alfred, now putting out the lamps and candles, seemed not to have noticed. He turned and faced her before dousing the last candle. George drew in a sharp, anguished breath. The passion in his eyes was startling. Reason plucked faintly at her mind. Was this pain she felt and gloried in more physical than spiritual? No longer caring, she took the child in her arms.

II

It was one of the gayest parties that the novelist and the poet had ever given in the apartment on the Quai Malaquais, yet George, ever sensitive to atmosphere, was troubled by an undercurrent of hostility. Who, she wondered, was the culprit?

Alfred himself was in the best of moods. Once again serving at table, he was wearing a short skirt and a maid's cap. Sainte-Beuve, inclined to be rather solemn these days, was nonetheless enjoying himself. Balzac and Dumas were gossiping merrily together at a corner of the table, while François Buloz, editor of the *Revue*, was pretending to be a learned professor lecturing all and sundry on the works of Victor Hugo. Her glance strayed now to Paul de Musset, Alfred's brother, whom she had never liked but entertained for Alfred's sake. She saw him lean across the table, a scowl on his face, and shake his fist at Gustave Planché.

"What did you call my brother, monsieur?"

Planché laughed pleasantly. "I called him 'M'm'selle Byron.'"

Paul de Musset's eyes flashed angrily. "A remark in the worst of bad taste."

"A joke, Paul, merely a joke. Alfred has called himself 'M'm'selle Byron' on more than one occasion."

"Better that, I admit, than 'M'm'selle Sand.' "

George pretended not to have heard. So Paul de Musset, disliking her as much as she disliked him, was the troublemaker. A momentary strained silence fell upon the company. Dumas's eyes darted wickedly. He, George thought, would have a new story to tell at Tortini's tomorrow. Of a sudden she grew weary of all her friends, even of Sainte-Beuve, the gentlest and most generous of them all. There had been too many parties since Alfred had become her lover. All she wanted was privacy, seclusion. Not that the gossip of friends or the hostility of Paul de Musset mattered very much, but other inroads were being made into her life.

New and unrecognized writers came daily to the Quai Malaquais with bulky manuscripts under their arms, all of them confident that she, the celebrated George Sand, would help them in their search for a publisher. Gentlemen of leisure, leering horribly, approached her in the streets and cafes, confident in their turn that she, the notorious George Sand, would admit them to her bed. Starving actors, artists, and journalists came up the stairs in droves, holding out their hands for a few francs. Not the least of her worries was her mother who loved and cursed her alternately according to the amount of extra money doled out. Where, then, was the much vaunted liberty? She was now more trapped by life than ever before. Looking quickly at Alfred, she wondered if he felt trapped also. A fond smile crossed her face. He was giving an imitation of Lord Byron, a somewhat cruel one, but that strained silence had fully broken. Everybody was laughing merrily—everybody except Paul de Musset.

Gustave Planché was the last guest to depart. He kissed George's hand in his usual gallant fashion and bowed before Alfred.

"*Au revoir*, M'm'selle Byron."

Alfred frowned slightly. "One of these days my brother will challenge you to a duel."

Later, his manner guarded, he went round the table gathering up the wine glasses and sipping a little wine as he went about his self-appointed task. That his mood had changed was obvious to George as she watched him anxiously. Unable to let well enough alone, she asked him if he was happy.

"Happier than I have ever been." His voice was distant. "And you, George?"

"It would choke me to tell you how happy I am."

Alfred leaped onto the table, scattering plates and dishes, snatched up another wine glass and squatted there, his skirt caught up above his hips. Smiling brightly, he arranged the skirt so that it looked like a loincloth.

"George, was Gustave Planché your lover before you met me?"

"Why must it be assumed," she asked steadily, "that every man I know has at some time or other been my lover?"

Alfred tossed off the wine. "That, my dear George, is the price you must pay for your particular sort of notoriety."

He was not drunk, George decided, not in the sense of unsteadiness and slurred speech, but clearly his brain had become inflamed. Gustave Planché, she felt constrained to point out, was a dear, good, loyal friend—that and no more. Alfred seemed not to be listening.

"Paul says you are ruining my life if you haven't already done so."

"What do you think, Alfred?"

"It was ruined before I met you." And softly he added, "Regarding Gustave, I don't believe you."

Then he laughed like a child and said again that he didn't believe her. Yet there was no hint of rancor in his voice. Still George wanted him to believe her. It was agony that Alfred, who had become so great a part of her life, should doubt the truth of the slightest words she uttered.

"Alfred . . ." she began.

"Yes?"

Quickly she changed her mind. "Alfred, you once said that there are times when liberty stifles a person, but what true liberty do we have now? We are stifled by the lack of it; or more correctly, by the lack of privacy."

"And—so?"

George considered her words carefully. "My daughter is being brought back from the country this week. The nurse-maid is a reliable, motherly person. In addition, I shall bring in a tutor. Boucoiran, I think. He was my son's tutor before my husband sent Maurice to the military academy. I shall be able to leave Solange here for a time without any worry about her well-being."

"And—so?" Alfred repeated.

"A little holiday at Fontainebleau. I'll rent a cottage there."

At Fontainebleau they threw themselves wholeheartedly, even insistently, into domesticity. The insistence, though she failed to realize it at first, was mostly hers, a sort of fever which Alfred caught only slightly. He soon grew restless and torn by a devouring jealousy that George, immersed in domestic bliss, failed to recognize. When the days were fine, they went riding in the forest, George wearing a blouse and trousers reminiscent of the old days at Nohant with Deschartres. The evenings they spent in solitude in the cosy little drawing room of the cottage, George writing, Alfred writing a little but mostly sketching.

"And here," he said one night, "we have Gustave Planché."

He showed George the sketch. It was a clever caricature of Planché, the supposed lover, wearing horns.

"Of course, he was your lover," Alfred said, his eyes shining. "You passed from him to me."

"Please believe me, Alfred, he was not my lover."

"Paul says he can prove it."

"Paul is intent on shattering our life together. Don't you think he may be quite insane with jealousy?"

"Paul was always jealous, but he never lies to me."

"Alfred," George said desperately, "I'll tell you about my life before we met. Everything. Every little detail."

Alfred laughed exultantly. "A confession, dear George?" He sprang up and strutted about the room. "How splendid!"

Every little detail? No, she decided against that. So briefly, not caring to dwell too lengthily on the past, she touched on Aurélien de Sèze, Stéphane de Grandsaigne, Jules Sandeau, and Prosper Mérimée. She pointed out that Alfred himself had said that he did not believe the gossip about Mérimée. He nodded and chortled.

"You absolve me, Alfred?"

"Gladly."

"And—the penance?"

He had already made up his mind about that. "You shall take me to Italy."

George embraced him warmly. "You call that a penance? It will be heaven, sheer heaven!"

Alfred held her away from him and laughed lightly. "I still don't believe you about Gustave Planché."

It was some time before George and Alfred were able to leave Paris. George was writing a novelette that had to be finished first; she had given Buloz who had agreed to publish all her work, a definite date for its publication in the *Revue*. Soon after its appearance, she signed a contract for a novel to be written during the Italian holiday and accepted Buloz's offer of a retainer of four thousand francs a year. A regular income, Buloz promised, would be sent to her during her absence, and since Casimir was keeping a tight rein on the income from Nohant, it would be most pleasing to have no immediate financial worries.

Casimir, informed of her plans, grumbled in a letter that instead of asking her husband's permission she was merely telling him what she proposed to do. However, he would only take steps to stop her from leaving France if she attempted to take the children with her. He came to Paris to discuss the matter, thus forcing Alfred to leave the apartment and take up temporary residence with his mother in the Rue de Grenelle. Casimir agreed that the tutor was trustworthy and efficient. Moreover, he had decided in any case to spend a little time in Paris himself if only to be near Maurice at the Henry IV Academy.

Paul de Musset, when told of the impending journey, raised immediate and violent objections. Alfred grew stubborn until Paul brought their mother into the argument. Madame de Musset, a widow in straitened circumstances, a thin, pale creature had both preached and always practiced a strict morality. She wept and refused to give Alfred her permission.

"You are over age," George reminded Alfred. "Is your mother's permission necessary?"

Alfred threw up his hands in despair. "I cannot go without it."

Supremely sure of herself, George went to call on Madame de Musset. She wore a plain gray gown, her attitude was demure, and she announced herself as Madame Dudevant, for she was well aware that she was known to Madame de Musset only as George Sand, a mannish creature given to male attire. She also knew that Madame de Musset was a snob with a taste for high living that she had never been able to afford. George therefore took with her a bottle of champagne and some expensive out-of-season strawberries.

Madame de Musset was considerably flustered. "This is extremely kind of you, Madame Dudevant. Do please forgive my failing memory, but when did we last meet?"

"We have never met before, Madame de Musset. But surely

you were well acquainted with my late father-in-law, the Baron Dudevant?"

"The Baron Dudevant! Such a dear kind gentleman!"

George, knowing that Madame de Musset had never met the baron, began to talk about Nohant, painting an exaggerated picture of a vast estate and impeccable, aristocratic connections. A passing reference to her great ancestors, the Elector of Saxony and Marshal de Saxe, had Madame de Musset on the point of genuflecting. Then softly George spoke of Alfred who was, she knew, his mother's favorite son and shamefully spoiled, even though his behavior had often caused her much pain.

"My husband and I are very interested in Alfred. We consider him the greatest poet of the century."

"How can you be sure of that, madame?"

"I am well qualified, for my professional name is George Sand."

"I cannot believe it!" Madame de Musset gasped.

"Many vile things have been said of me, but one must learn to live with vileness and get the better of it. However, that is another matter, a very personal sorrow. I have looked after Alfred during the last few months as carefully as any mother, but I cannot guarantee to preserve his health if he remains in Paris this winter."

Madame de Musset sprang up in alarm. "Alfred is ill?"

"Had you not noticed? He has a most distressing cough."

Madame de Musset wrung her hands. "I would send him to Italy myself, but I cannot afford the expense."

George inclined her head. "Fortunately, madame, I can. My husband and I, as I have already indicated, enjoy a comfortable income."

A sly look crossed Madame de Musset's face. "Since you and your husband will be traveling together to Italy . . ."

What a hypocrite! George thought, smiling sweetly. "Alfred would make a very gay traveling companion."

Madame de Musset tried for a moment to look stern. "Alfred is no more to you than a son?"

George very nearly lost her temper. Did Madame de Musset regard her as old enough to be Alfred's mother?

"He is, at all events, as dear to me as if he were my own boy."

Madame de Musset sighed and gave her permission.

Paul de Musset, as Alfred reported later, flew into a rage and declared that the siren by some devilish stratagem had got the better of their foolish mother.

"That is a wicked thing to say," Madame de Musset retorted angrily. "Madame Dudevant won me over by her sweetness and her concern for poor Alfred's health. She has been deeply wronged by gossip."

III

George and Alfred left Paris one bleak December morning. The stagecoach which was to take them to Lyons bore the number 13, a fact that caused Alfred to pout boyishly. He was not a superstitious fellow, but all the same ... A few moments later the coach lurched into a post, the horses reared and a water-carrier was knocked to the ground. Alfred recovered his good humor. Number 13 was unlucky for the water-carrier but not for them. George agreed and gave the injured water-carrier a few francs.

She had dressed sensibly for the journey. Her new pearl-gray trousers fitted perfectly, her Russian-style boots were comfortable, and her black spencer snug and heavy enough to keep out the cold. Alfred wore sky-blue trousers, a long traveling cloak, and a tall black hat. The two of them, he chortled, made a most dashing, adventurous sight in comparison with the other drably garbed travellers. Their picnic hamper contained meat pastries and champagne. Alfred, saying that his mouth was watering, opened the hamper within an hour. The champagne cork popped; they sang merrily as they ate and drank. How good life was! How free, how absolutely free they were!

From Lyons they sailed down the river to Avignon, continued their journey by stagecoach to Marseilles and there embarked on the packet for Genoa. Alfred was horribly seasick and lay below groaning. George tried to minister to him but he flew into a temper and screamed at her.

"I'm a humiliating sight. Leave me to die in peace."

George repressed a chuckle—after all, mere seasickness was anything but serious—and went up to the deck where she sat smoking cigarettes and taking notes for her new novel. Before they reached Genoa, Alfred begged her pardon for his bad temper. He was still slightly green in the face but he showed her a few lines which he had jotted down.

> George is on the deck
> Smoking her cigarette;
> Alfred, quite a beast,
> is sick in the stomach.

"A lovable beast, dear Alfred."

Seeing him scowl, she realized that her voice must have sounded detached and aloof. Hurriedly and contritely she tried to explain that she was deeply preoccupied with her novel. Alfred shrugged and, turning away, smiled invitingly at a pretty girl on the deck. What a child he was, George thought. Did he expect her to be jealous?

After disembarking, George decided to remain in Genoa for a while where she proposed to spend eight hours each day writing. Alfred remarked crossly that as far as writing was concerned she was a ruthless creature. "You never think of me when you're working!"

"Work is essential, Alfred. I must keep faith with my publisher."

It came as something of a shock to her to realize that indeed she never did think of Alfred when she was working. More and more, she admitted to herself, she was becoming two people: George Sand, the writer, and George Sand, the woman. However, to propitiate the young poet, she reserved her writing for the night and accompanied him during the day on sight-seeing tours. She continued this regimen when they left Genoa for Florence.

"But what am I to do at night?" Alfred asked. "Sit in a corner twiddling my fingers while you scratch away at your writing pad?"

"Why not write yourself?" She tried to keep the impatience out of her voice since it hurt her intolerably to see Alfred so discontented. Then she saw the look of anger and frustration on his face.

"I write only when inspired," he said acidly. "It's a different matter with you, isn't it! You turn a wheel, tug at a lever and the machine runs on for hours."

George's heart leaped painfully, but she tried to tell herself that Alfred's resentment was not serious.

"I won't do any writing tonight," she promised.

"That's up to you, George. I have a rendezvous with a dark-haired girl. Oh, she has no brains but she certainly has a lovely body!"

With that, he flung himself from the room and George saw no more of him for forty-eight hours. He returned wild-eyed, almost incoherent. His cheeks were flushed, his eyes bloodshot and his breath reeked of alcohol. Appalled, reproaching herself beyond all reason, George put him to bed in the hotel room adjoining hers. There he raved and screamed. Pointing to the pictures on the walls, his voice quivering with terror, he declared that ugly spirits lurked behind them.

"One of them is Planché—Gustave Planché wearing horns."

George sent for a doctor. Alfred was given a sedative. She

sat up with him all night, sometimes weeping, sometimes staring at him as if in a trance. Why would he not accept her as she was? Why would he not believe that she loved him more than anyone else in the world had ever been loved?

When he woke at dawn, he looked at her wanly. "I was unfaithful to you. There were two girls, not one. Can you forgive me?"

George kissed him lightly on the brow. She had parted with Jules Sandeau because of his unfaithfulness, but this was different. Alfred was a child, defiant yet dependent.

"I can forgive you anything, Alfred."

"You're unfaithful to me, too—all those hours you spend with your novel."

"You did it because of that? How silly!"

"No, I did it because of Gustave Planché. Only to think of him and you casts me into an endless nightmare."

"Be sensible, Alfred," George said. "How can you possibly be jealous of something that never happened?"

"It happened, it did happen!"

"Well, what if it did? I knew Gustave before I knew you. You knew other women before you knew me."

"You admit it, you admit it!"

"I do not admit it. I only said 'if.'" George sighed, but not too heavily. Alfred's jealous tantrums were flattery of a sort. "When you are well enough to travel, we'll leave for Venice."

They reached Venice late at night after a tiring journey from Florence. Alfred sat in the gondola which was taking them to the Hotel Danieli, his cloak wrapped tightly about him. But late as the hour was, she dragged him from the hotel and made him walk in St. Mark's Square. It was a clear, cold night. Stars danced in the deep azure of the sky and the moon, high in the heavens, cast a shimmering orange glow over the dome and towers of the ancient cathedral. She gripped his arm tightly.

"Alfred, here is all the inspiration you need!"

He freed himself roughly. "I'm aware of nothing but the stench of the canals."

George laughed with forced gaiety. "I can't smell a thing myself. In summer, perhaps, but this is winter."

"And winter brings disillusionment," Alfred said somberly.

"Disillusionment?" she echoed brokenly. "Why have you changed so suddenly?"

"Suddenly? The change took place in Genoa. I became fully aware of it in Florence. You and your spiritual love! Whom are you trying to deceive—me or yourself? I'm a man, my poor George, not an angel. And as a man, I no longer love you."

"I would rather you had said 'I'm an angel, not a man, and as an angel I love you.' Why didn't you, Alfred, why didn't you?"

He laughed bitterly. "There you go, in your mind planning another chapter of your novel."

George wondered if there was some little truth in this accusation. Well, what if there was? It was wiser, she thought, to regard life as fiction. Living became more bearable that way. The next morning she woke with a headache, a sore throat, and a running nose.

Alfred adopted an "I told you so" attitude. "It was madness to rush out in the cold air last night."

George grew feverish, and, in the delirium that followed, she constantly heard the echo of Alfred's voice: "As a man I no longer love you." She saw very little of him. He kept to his own room during the day, appearing only when the doctor called. At night he went out to drink with the casual friends he had made in Venice. He remarked once that the Venetian girls were the prettiest he had ever seen. He was, he said, enjoying his new-found freedom immensely. George recovered within two weeks and began to work again. She and Alfred were no longer lovers, yet she loved him as much as ever. The pain in her heart was more intense than anything she had ever experienced. On one occasion, longing for a reconciliation, she tried to flatter him by asking him to correct a chapter which she had just completed. Setting to work at once, with a gleam in his eyes, he wielded a ruthless pen.

"You are as careless as ever," he burst out. "Take this, for example. You have written 'very unique.' Nothing can be very unique."

"You are," George said softly.

"No, merely 'unique.' The word means without like or equal. It means single or alone in any quality. You cannot qualify it."

"You're talking like a dictionary, Alfred."

"It would do you no harm to study one."

"I'm studying you instead," she snapped.

Alfred rushed from the room in a temper. It was a week before George saw him again and then she scarcely recognized him. Two porters carried him into the hotel on a broad plank. He was unshaven, wild-eyed and flushed, and babbling incoherently. Pietro Pagello, the Venetian doctor who had attended George during her illness, followed the porters and their burden into the suite. In his halting French he explained that he had been called to a disreputable cafe where he had found Alfred on the floor.

"Drunk," George said in disgust.

"Alcohol has aggravated his condition, madame, yes."

"His condition?"

"Brain fever."

George and Pagello undressed Alfred, sponged his clammy body and put him to bed. Distracted as George was, she noticed that Pagello revealed considerable embarrassment as they bent together over the naked Alfred. Pagello was quite young for a doctor—not more than twenty-six. He had large, passionate, brown eyes and his hair was as fair as Alfred's.

"Can you save my poor friend?" she asked.

"Who knows? All I can do is try."

To be on the safe side, Pagello called in an elderly colleague, his senior at one of the hospitals. His name was Juannini. Fastidiously he made a thorough examination. Brain fever? It was a politeness, no doubt, to refer to delirium tremens as brain fever. His voice was dry, his eyes contemptuous. He would leave the patient, he said, to the good offices of Pietro Pagello. He himself had more important things to do.

"You knew all the time," George said to Pagello. "You were trying to save me embarrassment."

"Possibly," Pagello said shyly.

During the three weeks that followed, Pietro Pagello spent many hours with George at Alfred's bedside. It was necessary at times to restrain the patient. He raved and screamed and on one occasion sprang out of bed and tried to strangle George. Slowly after that he recovered his senses, leaving her utterly worn out by her almost unbroken vigil. As soon as he was convalescent, George resumed her writing. Pagello still called and often lingered for hours at a time. Asking herself why he should do so, she found the answer in the languorous but shy glances he cast upon her.

This was not lost on Alfred. He rushed out to the terrace one morning and pointed wildly at the single cup standing on the table between George and Pagello.

"You have been drinking out of the same cup!"

"Nonsense," George said lightly. "This is the cup you yourself drank from earlier."

"What a fool you must think me!" Alfred sneered. "The maid took my cup away an hour ago. I saw her. You passed from Gustave Planché to me. Now you have passed from me to Pietro Pagello." He turned to Pagello and bowed mockingly. "Permit me to place my bed at your disposal."

Once again it might well have been Casimir speaking, Casimir who had addressed Aurélien de Sèze in much the same way. Pagello rose, started to kiss George's hand, decided against it and departed in confusion.

"You break my heart, Alfred," George wept.

"A heart of iron is unbreakable."

"You are still very ill. I can see that, Alfred."

"On the contrary, I am in full possession of my senses. This, Madame Sand, is the end. Or do I mean Monsieur Sand? I shall leave for France at the earliest possible moment."

"Have you money for the journey?" George asked stonily.

"God will provide."

"No, Alfred, Monsieur Sand will provide."

"That," he laughed, "is precisely what I meant."

George was longing for Paris herself. In Venice she was beginning to feel as isolated as if she were at the other end of the earth. Letters took up to three weeks to reach her. She missed her friends and especially her children. Yet she felt a pressing need to remain longer in Venice and write a novel with a Venetian setting. Pietro Pagello himself had suggested such a book. He was, she thought, an excellent model for a Venetian lover. Guiltily she shied away from this thought. Must she take Pagello in order to write more "authentic" fiction? Or must she take him just to satisfy an entirely physical yearning?

"Alfred," she said, coming down to material essentials, "Buloz is slow with his payments. I owe money to Dr. Pagello and to the hotel. What little I have in hand until more arrives is just enough for one person to travel from Venice to Paris."

"In other words—myself."

"The decision is yours, Alfred."

But now that George had provided him with sufficient money for the journey to Paris, Alfred became an attentive, deferential escort in Venice. He bowed and kissed her hand in public. He suggested that a reconciliation had already been achieved, a reconciliation that would come to full fruition when she joined him in Paris. But his parting words were a stinging blow in the face.

"You thought you were my lover. But no! You were only my mother. I've known that from the first. My mother—only my mother!"

17

"YOU MIGHT AT least pretend enjoyment, Chopin," Liszt said.

Frédéric settled more deeply in his seat. "I prefer honesty to pretense."

"But what of politeness?"

The applause rose again. Frédéric shrugged and clapped his hands politely. He had come to this concert at the Conservatoire reluctantly, agreeing only after Liszt insisted that he needed a change from the deadly routine of piano lessons. He glanced guiltily at his friend. What a prig he must have sounded! It was a matter neither of honesty nor pretense; as he had sat dreaming of Maria, he had heard scarcely a note and he had already forgotten the name of the new and, according to Liszt, quite promising young violinist.

Time was slipping away all too rapidly. Would Count Wodzinski never reach a decision? Maria, in her letters, wrote that she was just as impatient as Frédéric, but she urged him to wait with fortitude. She was now in Warsaw with her mother and brothers; the count himself was still in Geneva. The countess had written to him, but up to now he had refused to commit himself one way or the other. Meanwhile, he was expected to reach Warsaw any day and Maria was confident that once she talked to him she would have no real difficulty in winning him over; her father had always been fond of dear Frédéric.

With somber pleasure Chopin thought of Maria's last letter. She was anxious about his health. He must consult a doctor if his cough grew any worse and he must drink at least a pint of gamboge water every day. He loathed the resiny taste but he drank it dutifully, and as he sat in his cold apartment teaching, he wore the fur-lined slippers Maria had sent him. Dear, dear Maria!

At this moment Liszt dug Frédéric in the ribs. "Look, there's George Sand!"

"Who?" Chopin asked, resentful of being brought back so sharply to reality.

"George Sand, the novelist. Or perhaps I should call her Madame Dudevant tonight. She's actually wearing a dress."

Frédéric, his curiosity aroused, looked critically at George. She was seated three rows in front of them, talking animatedly to her male companion. He had heard a great deal of gossip about her since Liszt had first mentioned her. One of his pupils, more concerned with scandal than with piano lessons, had called her an ogress, a tigress, a veritable man-eater. Frédéric bobbed his head this way and that now in order to get a better view of her. She turned, caught Liszt's eyes and smiled. Liszt waved gaily.

"Who is the gentleman with her?" the younger man asked.

"An Italian doctor called Pagello. He's her latest protégé. Some say her latest lover. She brought him back from Venice."

"I've heard it said," Frédéric remarked tartly, "that you were once her lover."

"Sheer gossip," Liszt laughed. "She and I are the best of friends. That and no more. Would you like to meet her?"

Frédéric sat up primly. "A creature like that? Certainly not!"

"You misjudge her," Liszt said gently.

"She has a husband and two children."

225

"The husband is a brute. It was a marriage of convenience. What if she has had a number of lovers? George is a brilliant and sensitive woman. She told me once that she is looking for the absolute so far as love is concerned. Love, mark you, in all its aspects."

Chopin laughed smugly. "I myself have found it."

When the concert came to an end and before the final applause had died away, he rushed out to the street and hurried on foot to his apartment. What if a letter had arrived from Maria during his absence? The fact that no postal deliveries were made at night did not seem to matter. He had an instinct about such things, a sure instinct. That was why he had not wanted to go to the concert with Liszt. It was even possible that Maria, arriving after a long and tiring journey, would be waiting at his door!

He found the letter the moment he flung open the door. The concierge, often too drunk to know what he was doing, had forgotten to deliver it earlier. Frédéric tore open the envelope and read the contents avidly. Maria's father had at last rejoined his family in Warsaw. Her mother had organized a party to welcome him in a fitting manner. Oh, such a gay party! Maria herself had played some of Frédéric Chopin's music, pride and love in her heart. Inevitably there had been a lot of speechmaking. Count Skarbek, fuming at the dullness of the speeches, had himself made a really witty one. There would be other, more significant speeches, Maria added, once her father gave his consent.

"And who," Frédéric asked himself, "is Count Skarbek?"

II

George, happy as always to see Franz Liszt, paused for a few words with him before she and Pagello left the concert chamber.

"Who was your friend who hurried away just now?"

"Frédéric Chopin."

"Ah, the celebrated pianist. You must bring us together sometime, Franz. I should like very much to hear him play."

Liszt laughed wryly. "He's a difficult fellow to corner but I'll do my best."

Pietro Pagello hired a fiacre and drove with George to his apartment, a tiny one quite close to hers on the Quai Malaquais. Punctiliously he had refused to share her apartment. He was thinking, she suspected, of his own reputation rather than hers, of himself as a very young doctor with a promising medical career ahead of him in his native Venice.

In actual fact she had shared his apartment in Venice during the five months she had remained there after Alfred's departure. But now Pietro Pagello was concerned solely with his reputation in Paris, afraid that the doctors from whom he was learning so much at the French hospitals would withdraw their patronage if it became known that the notorious George Sand was his mistress. She smiled. Actually it had been herself who, without bringing her name into it, had contrived the introductions to the important doctors and surgeons of the city. She was grateful to Pagello for the help and solace he had given her in Venice. She also had a deep affection for him but she did not love him in the sense that she loved Alfred de Musset. How could she when the doctor was such an independent fellow?

George had met Alfred again soon after returning to Paris. His mother had called to say that her favorite son was ill, and George, wearing a maid's cap and apron, had nursed him there in his mother's apartment as devotedly as she had nursed him in Venice. Now, on the one hand, she had Alfred chaste and reformed, for the things of the spirit; on the other, Pietro, healthy and strong, for the earthly demands of the flesh. The choice, when she thought about it, was not a pleasing one. In abandoning her search for perfection in one man, she had, she felt, betrayed herself.

"This," said Pagello as he helped her from the fiacre, "is our last night together."

George nodded. "Since you are so set on leaving for Italy tomorrow."

"What choice have I?" Pagello asked soberly. "I have learned all I possibly can in Paris and am eager to take up that important hospital appointment in Venice."

"A man, especially when he is a doctor, must think only of his career."

"You are a very understanding woman, George."

"I could, perhaps, return with you."

A hint of alarm showed in his voice. "My dear George, I am engaged to be married. The negotiations were concluded soon after we left Venice."

George smiled faintly. "Have a happy marriage. Live a long and useful life."

Pagello bowed and led her up the two flights of narrow stairs to his quarters. After lighting the candles, he looked eagerly about the room.

"Now you must see my beautiful tools!"

He flung open a polished wooden box. The tools within were surgical instruments of the finest workmanship, some of them unobtainable in Italy. Piled up near the box were a dozen or more brand-new medical books. Opening one, he turned the illustrated pages lovingly.

"How fortunate that my pictures sold for such a good price! Fifteen hundred francs! Except for that I could not have bought these books and tools nor paid for my journey back to Venice."

"How fortunate indeed," George murmured.

Pagello's independence was at times irritating; he had refused to borrow money from her or accept it as a gift. Accordingly, looking ahead, she had persuaded him to bring four pictures from his Venice apartment. Although they were all but worthless, she, employing a secret agent, had bought them herself and hidden them away in her apartment.

"Will you take a glass of wine?" he asked, his hospitality a trifle forced.

George shook her head. "Work is waiting for me at home." She held out her hand. "Let us say good-by without preamble. Partings can be painful if protracted."

They shook hands. Pagello averted his eyes; George averted hers.

"Thank you for everything!" he called after her as she clattered down the stairs.

Much to her surprise she found Alfred de Musset sitting at her desk when she reached her apartment. His hair was tousled, his shirt open at the neck. Her heart missed a beat. She had never seen him look so young and vulnerable. Steadily and purposefully he was leafing through the sheets of a loosely bound manuscript. He glanced up briefly.

"You were at the concert with Pagello. I met Liszt. He told me."

"What of it?"

"Pagello is no more interested in music than he is in literature."

"So I discovered long ago."

Alfred went on reading, then looked up briefly again.

"I've brought a lot of my things and taken possession of my old room again. I thought it a necessary precaution, a sure means of preventing you from giving it to Pagello."

"Pietro is leaving Paris tomorrow. I've seen him for the last time."

"Splendid!" Alfred turned another page. "What new masterpiece have we here?"

"My journal to Alfred de Musset."

He laughed shortly. "I thought as much. There's anguish and suffering in every line." He sprang to his feet. "Please, George,

I'm not really laughing. My heart is torn asunder. Why did we do those dreadful things to each other? Why, George?"

Her voice faltered. "It's the way of the world, my boy."

"No, George. Not the world at large—the world we created for ourselves. My God! when I think of it all, tears choke me and my knees tremble so that I can hardly stand!"

He was standing as firm as a rock and his voice, though quivering with emotion, had no hint of tears in it. Melodrama, poetic melodrama, George thought lovingly.

"Listen!" he cried, and began to read aloud: " 'If you were to feel real love for me, I would willingly cut off the hand that offends you. If you would show me a little affection, I would willingly live like a nun. I realize that there is nothing so dead as a love that has died, but I must have your friendship. I need it in order to endure the love in my own heart and prevent it from killing me . . . ' "

George listened in silence. And she had accused him of melodrama! She had begun the journal in a desperate mood and had continued it day by day. How much of it was fiction? How much truth? But did it matter? She had felt it all when she was writing the words and she felt it all again now, much more agonizingly, as she listened to Alfred's voice ringing through the *salon*.

He came to take her in his arms. "Did you go to bed with Pagello just now?"

George drew back from him. "Would you believe me if I said no?"

"I'd believe anything you said, George. I've finally come to my senses. Planché, for instance. Of course, you never slept with him! This spiritual reconciliation! Oh, it's very noble, very inspiring, but I want more. I need more. I thirst for you as no woman has ever been thirsted for before. Let me live with you again, George, please!"

He took her in his arms, and resting there, she wept for joy.

At last, after much travail, much indescribable misery, here was the ideal love she had sought from the first. It was heaven on earth. Her questing heart had found fulfillment. Only peace, a heavenly peace, had come to her.

III

"I can only repeat what I said in my letter," Casimir asserted coldly. "I have changed my mind about the agreement we signed last February."

Though reluctant to leave Paris and Alfred, George had hurried to Nohant, following her receipt of the letter, to discuss her husband's change of attitude. The agreement had been a simple one. While continuing to live separate lives, they would make a division of George's property. She herself would take control of the Nohant estate—Casimir had been neglecting it badly of late—while he was to receive the income from the Hôtel de Narbonne, the Paris property left to George by her grandmother. The Nohant estate yielded nearly ten thousand francs a year, the Hôtel de Narbonne almost seven thousand. Casimir was to maintain Maurice; Solange was to remain entirely her mother's concern. It had all seemed very satisfactory until Casimir, unpredictable as ever, had changed his mind.

"You told me you were longing for Paris and a carefree bachelor existence," George reminded him.

"I find that I am fonder of Nohant than I thought."

"We signed an agreement, Casimir."

"What of it? As your husband I have the privilege of disregarding it. I also can continue to control Nohant—in fact, everything that is yours."

"You want more money from me? Is that it?"

Casimir smiled. "Possibly."

"Furthermore, since you still control my whole estate, you want to deprive me of an income sufficient for my needs."

"You earn plenty of money from your writing."

"Otherwise I should be reduced to penury. I've half a mind to resort to the law. A husband's privileges are one thing, but what of a wife's rights?"

"I doubt if a wife possesses any. You should have thought of that before marrying."

"Indeed I should," George said bitterly. "Today women are forced to live a life of imbecility. They are despised if they remain ignorant and are mocked if they try to improve themselves. In love they are reduced to the level of courtesans. As wives they are treated in the main as servants, not as companions. They are used shamefully and exploited ruthlessly."

"Well, well, you can always use your pen in the interest of women's rights. Meanwhile, resort to the law by all means if you think you can achieve anything."

Thus challenged, George conferred with the family lawyer in La Châtre and he, feeling incapable of dealing with the tricky situation, sent her to Louis-Chrysostom Michel who practiced law in Bourges. George suggested that, since divorce was not permitted in France, legal separation was her only recourse. Instead of listening, however, Michel harangued her about the political situation. He also said, smiling charmingly, that of all her books his favorite was *Lélia*.

"That is merely changing the subject," George said dryly. "I came to you for advice and help, not to be lectured on the iniquities of the King."

"Do you consider our Citizen-King a saintly creature?"

"No, monsieur. I think him something of a fraud. What's more—I have struck many a blow at his government since the publication of my first article in *Figaro*."

Michel looked at her dreamily. "We shall never have true liberty in France until the Seine runs red with blood."

George was horrified. "I myself aim at liberty through love."

"Love?" he mocked. "You believe in love?"

"I do, monsieur, but not love as most men know it."

"You also believe in the equality of the sexes, or so I have been left to assume after studying your more serious writing."

"Equality in civil rights certainly."

"You are battering your head against a stone wall."

It was the same whenever they met. Michel discussed either politics or George's writing but never the intolerable situation which existed between her and Casimir. Nevertheless, she found him fascinating, a man of granite who was at the same time something of a saint. And what a magnificent talker he was! Ready to thunder one moment, to smile beatifically and persuasively the next.

"Much as I admire *Lélia*," he told her during one of her frustrating visits to his chambers in Bourges, "I know—and you know—that you are wasting your time writing novels."

George guessed instantly what he was about. "So you want me to write political pamphlets."

"If you have the ability," he challenged.

"Do you hold it a sin that I should own a considerable amount of property?" she countered.

"Do you, madame?"

"No," George said soberly. "I have never been a hard taskmaster to my servants. I have even allowed them to take advantage of me many times. All I want is to keep a little of what is my own, whereas my husband . . ."

But it was useless. Michel changed the subject instantly and spoke of the insurrection that had taken place at Lyons where thousands of workmen of all descriptions had gone on strike, setting up barricades in the streets. The troops had been called out and much slaughter had followed. Finally the ringleaders had been arrested; they would soon be brought to trial in Paris. Michel himself, a republican leader of no mean stature, was

233

going there to take part in the defense.

"You," he told George, "shall write articles for the republican press."

George shook her head stubbornly. "No, I shall not. What would I prove, either to your satisfaction or mine, if I did? I shall continue to write novels, prove nothing and thereby do neither good nor harm."

"Cynic!"

"Fanatic!" she retorted.

Michel looked at her steadily. "We feel strangely drawn to each other."

"Strangely," George admitted.

She followed him to Paris, there to watch though not to take an active part in the trial; and there she nursed Michel when he fell ill during the rigors of the legal battle. She was confident that she would win him over in the end. The agreement with Casimir was not due to come into force for several months. Her personal affairs could wait, and meanwhile there was Alfred whom she had neglected far too long.

IV

Franz Liszt paused and listened at Frédéric Chopin's door before knocking and entering. All seemed deathly quiet within: no sobbing pupil, no distracted teacher's voice, no sound of a chair being crashed against the wall. He turned the handle slowly and entered on tiptoe.

"My dear Chopin!" he exclaimed in alarm.

Frédéric was lying face down on a little strip of carpet. His shoulders were heaving convulsively. A torn letter lay near him on the floor. More concerned than ever, Liszt helped him to his feet.

"Chopin, what in the world has happened?"

"It's only my cough," Frédéric said evasively, his eyes brilliant with tears. "A more violent spasm than ever before. Leave me alone. I'll recover soon." Quickly he remembered the need to offer hospitality. "Help yourself to a glass of wine." Then he laughed wildly. "I'm sorry, Liszt. There isn't any wine." And violently he added, "Try some gamboge water. There's a gallon or more of that."

Snatching up the pieces of the letter, he took them to his writing-table and fitted them together. Before reading the shattering words again, he glanced cautiously over his shoulder. Liszt had gone obediently to the little kitchen in search of that abominable gamboge water.

The letter was from one of Maria's brothers. Reading it Chopin had learned that Count Wodzinski had finally reached a decision, a flat refusal to allow his daughter to marry him.

Let us be reasonable, Frédéric. We all love you dearly and will never cease to honor your name, but Father takes the view that the little Maria must be well provided for when eventually she marries. He also takes the view—and do forgive me for mentioning this—that her future husband must be healthy as well as a man of substance.

Reading again, he came to the brief postscript which Maria had added to her brother's letter:

You were always kind to me, Frédéric, and very patient, too. I shall never cease to be grateful to you for that. Good-by, dear friend, good-by.

Liszt came back from the kitchen. Holding it at a distance as if it were poison, he carried an untouched glass of gamboge water.

"This is really good for your cough?"

Frédéric looked at him wildly. *"Moja bieda!"*

"What does that mean, Chopin? You make it sound like a curse."

"It means 'my sorrow.' "

By no means deceived, Liszt, nevertheless, tried to make light of the situation. "It would be mine, too, if I took one sip of this revolting stuff. The smell alone is nauseating."

The distraught Chopin dashed the glass from his friend's hand. "I'll never touch a drop of it again!"

Liszt looked at him sympathetically. "Lying on the floor is no greater cure than gamboge water. On the other hand, a little musical evening might make you forget your—er—cough."

"I'm not well enough to go out."

"We could hold a musical evening here."

"Here?"

"Leave everything to me, my dear Chopin. I'll invite a few suitable guests."

Frédéric, glancing about the restricted space, tried to be practical. "How many guests?"

"A dozen or so."

The young pianist laughed scathingly. "I have a piano stool and three or four chairs."

"What of it? Our friends, especially those with artistic pretensions, don't mind sitting on the floor. Maybe I'll have a few more chairs sent in."

Chopin felt trapped. "I won't play a single note myself. You, my masterful Liszt, must do the entertaining."

Liszt hesitated for a moment. "Would you mind if I invited George Sand?"

"That impossible woman?"

"Whether you like her or not, it would be a kindness to invite her. She's very unhappy at present, having finally parted with Alfred de Musset."

"My dear Liszt, no. I do not want to meet her."

Liszt smiled faintly. Relentless once her mind was made up, George would go on badgering him unmercifully until she had what she wanted. There was only one thing for it—a surprise party here in Chopin's apartment.

V

George Sand sat in an armchair close to the piano, as withdrawn from the world as Frédéric Chopin who sat at the other side of the room. Taken completely by surprise, he had greeted her politely enough on arrival, but he had sat down immediately afterward swamped in gloom. What, she wondered, was he brooding about? Were his thoughts as depressing as hers? Did the greatest love of his life lie in ashes at his feet?

Franz Liszt had already played, somewhat thunderously, George thought, and now Nourrit was going to sing. George pushed back her chair, lit a cigarette from a nearby candle and allowed herself the luxury of sober introspection. Alfred de Musset had gone forever from her life. So much then for ideal love and heavenly peace! She ought to have known from the beginning that no reconciliation with Alfred, however heady, could last. Deliberately she closed her ears to Nourrit's soaring voice. On her return from the country, there had been another ecstatic reunion, but when the first flush had burned itself out, little had remained except the old smoldering flame of Alfred's jealousy and, more heartbreaking still, a demanding curiosity. He became of a sudden the "master" of the house, posturing ridiculously; his "wife" must be subservient to him in all things, she must confess everything. Had George slept with Pagello before he, Alfred, left Venice or was it immediately afterwards? What sort of a lover was he? Oh, Alfred had suffered, possibly even more than he had intended her to suffer but solely because he loved to suffer. "A new refinement of pleasure," she remembered him saying. Often enough he was contrite and begged forgiveness, but once forgiven, he broke out again even more wildly and accused her of conducting a liaison with Michel.

Nourrit had finished. A little stir of excitement was passing through the room, for the blonde Marie d'Agoult, Liszt's most expensive mistress, was leading Chopin to the piano. George lit another cigarette. She was no more interested in Chopin's music tonight than she was in Nourrit's singing. Alfred, she reflected now, had become a greater drunkard than ever before. A child still, but a child who had grown beyond all control. Once, after the wildest of drinking orgies, he had suggested a suicide pact. The world, he said, was an ugly place. The people in it were ugly, nasty, and spiteful. So why remain in it? Why not blow out one's brains and solve the riddle? Did Heaven await them, or Hell, or nothingness? Nothingness would be preferable.

Startled suddenly, not by the memory of how she had almost agreed with Alfred and made an end of things, but by the sound of Chopin's music, George stubbed out her cigarette and listened intently. Every fiber of her body thrilled in immediate response. What a sinful waste it would have been to have died in Alfred's arms before hearing this demanding, maddening, heavenly music!

"A new polonaise," Marie d'Agoult whispered.

Spellbound, George sat forward in her chair. Frédéric Chopin! As clearly as if it had happened yesterday, she remembered the polonaise that Deschartres' friend had sent from Poland. She could still feel the frustration she had suffered at not being able to play it properly and the sorrow that had tormented her years later when Casimir in that rage of his had burned the music along with her books. All too soon the pianist rose from the piano. The applause was deafening, although there were less than a dozen people in the small, neatly furnished room.

George looked at Chopin with devouring interest. Liszt had

238

told her that he was twenty-six, younger than herself by six or seven years, and Marie d'Agoult had remarked that he was unquestionably a virgin. There was a dreamy, nay, a spiritual look in his luminous blue eyes. The brooding sorrow, clearly defined earlier, had either disappeared or been skillfully masked. His fair hair was as silky as a girl's and the transparency of his complexion was suggestive of a creature not of this world. His every movement, graceful in the extreme, set him apart from the common herd. He looked like a prince, a fairy prince. If one touched him, would he vanish? Impulsively George rose and embraced him, first on the left cheek, then on the right. He drew back as if affronted.

"Master," George sighed, "you are greater even than Liszt."

"Franz will never speak to you again," Marie d'Agoult said dryly.

"Each is great in his own way," somebody remarked. "That is why they remain friends."

George had eyes only for Chopin. "You wrote that divine music for me."

Chopin looked startled. "This is our first meeting, madame."

"I knew you when you were twelve."

"You were in Warsaw fourteen years ago? I have no recollection of it, madame."

"No, I was at Nohant, in the province of Berry."

"No doubt our clever George flew from Nohant to Warsaw on a broomstick," Liszt chuckled.

George was still looking at Chopin, her heart leaping painfully in her breast. "Not a broomstick, a magic carpet. I was transported by music. I'll tell you about it sometime, Chopin. Nohant is my country estate. I shall be going there with my children soon. I hope to persuade Liszt to join us. Come with him."

Frédéric's eyes dilated. "My commitments force me to remain in Paris."

"Surely a little holiday in the country will be good for your health."

"My commitments . . ." he began, his hands fluttering.

George had heard all about those exacting but wasteful commitments. "Perhaps then I shall remain in Paris and take piano lessons from you."

A guileless smile illuminated the sensitive face. "Would you have me rage at your incompetence and break still another chair?"

Entranced by his smile, she said unsteadily, "Please come to Nohant. The country is lovely."

"Possibly—at some future date," he said airily.

"When you have had time to recover from a broken heart?"

"A broken heart?"

"In my own way, Chopin, I, too, am an artist and possess at least a little perception."

Chopin stirred uneasily. "I am about to go to London. A—a concert there. Pleyel is arranging it."

Liszt glanced quickly from George to his young friend. Had he made a mistake in bringing them together? Time alone would tell. A concert in London indeed! Pleyel had wanted it certainly, had already hopefully obtained a passport for Chopin. But Chopin himself, nursing his private sorrow, his *moja bieda*, had sworn that he would never leave Paris.

VI

Casimir Dudevant was in a black and ugly mood. He sat at the head of the table glowering and casting dark glances upon George, upon the children, even upon the neighbors who had been invited to dinner. The cause of it all, George suspected, was their recent argument about his administration of the estate. The children, sensitive to the lowering atmosphere, were eating in silence: Solange, now a pretty child of eight, almost furtively, while Maurice, thirteen now, was digging stoically into his baked apple.

"Maurice," George said, "you need a little more cream on that rather dry apple."

"Oh yes, Maman! Please!"

"Cream," Casimir pronounced heavily, "is an expensive luxury."

"But Papa," Maurice protested, "it comes from our own cows."

Casimir sprang to his feet. "How much, my son, do you think it costs to keep a cow?"

"Maman said . . ."

Casimir cut him short. "Your sainted mother is more acquainted these days with *la vie bohème* than country life. Leave the table. Go to your room and stand in a corner."

The boy looked appealingly at George. "Must I, Maman?"

Before George could speak, Casimir flew into a rage, slapped his son's face and advanced threateningly on George herself.

"Leave the table yourself, madame. I won't be defied like this in my own house!"

"Am I defying you, too?" George asked quietly. "The house, in any case, is mine."

Casimir seized a gun from the wall and pointed it at his wife's heart. "I have the means here to make it mine, by God!"

"And at the same time sign your own death warrant."

Casimir darted forward and prodded George in the chest with the barrel of the gun. His finger curled round the trigger and he shouted a string of obscenities. One of the guests, an old family friend, leaping upon him, struggled with him and finally gained possession of the gun. It all happened so quickly that George was able to persuade Solange that it was just a game the adults were playing, but she could see that Maurice, pale and trembling, was not deceived.

"Your father is ill," she told him when Casimir had stamped

241

from the room.

Later, after the children had been sent to bed, George's friends held a council of war. All were concerned for her safety and all agreed that she must waste no time in taking legal action against this crazy husband who, in the presence of reliable witnesses, had come close to murdering her.

Casimir, as it turned out, was more frightened by what he had done than either George or her friends. The next morning he mumbled a contrite apology, saying that he was horrified at the violence he had attempted. He was morose but apparently quite tractable, leaving George to feel that she had the upper hand.

"Are you still determined to break our agreement, Casimir?"

"I—I don't know," he stammered.

"Whether you are or not, a legal separation is the only solution."

"Whatever you wish, Aurore."

This was almost too good to be true. "You understand that I shall bring the action myself?"

"I cannot prevent it." A momentary sly smile crossed Casimir's face. "Wives have some legal rights after all."

Puzzled by the smile, George said quickly, "We shall be able to arrange a fair distribution of my income."

"Are you trying to bargain with me?"

"I said a fair distribution. I realize that you will always be in need of money while your mother is still alive."

"True." The sly smile came again. "You are more than generous."

Once more George consulted the family lawyer at La Châtre, he agreeing that he could now handle the case since Casimir had resorted to violence. It would have been useless to take the case to Michel again; he had been committed to prison because of the part he had played in republican activities. Meanwhile the children were sent to Paris, Maurice to his military academy,

Solange to a girl's boarding school. As for Casimir, he went docilely to Paris, for it was necessary under the circumstances that he and George should not continue to live under the same roof. George's petition was heard before the court at La Châtre. Would Casimir make a sudden dramatic appearance? She waited anxiously, knowing that he could seriously damage her case by entering a defense and charging her—even though he might be unable to prove it—with adultery. However, he remained aloof in Paris chiefly, she could only conclude, because of the money she had promised him. The hearing was surprisingly and gratifyingly brief. Their original agreement was maintained, with the addition that George was granted the custody of Maurice as well as of Solange.

It had all been much too easy, she thought, remembering Casimir's sly smile. She was to remember that smile again when, striking maliciously, he demanded far more than a fair share of her income. As a result, the case was reopened in La Châtre. Casimir, who had lodged himself at the village inn, made a number of wild accusations, some of them true enough, many of them patently ridiculous. Yet, instead of asking for a legal separation on his own account, he insisted that the marriage should continue; in short, that the wife whom he described in court as a prostitute should return obediently to his bed. His wildness and his failure to substantiate his accusations destroyed his own chance of legal victory. The court showed George every sympathy, granted her a legal separation, and once again gave her the custody of the children.

"I shall appeal to the higher court at Bourges!" Casimir raged and did precisely that.

While waiting for the appeal to be heard, he took possession of Nohant, claiming that, to all intent and purpose, it was his and would assuredly remain so after he had defeated George in court. She herself found lodgings with a friend in Bourges and went to see Michel newly released from prison. His appearance shocked her. The strain of the part he had taken in the long trial in Paris and his subsequent imprisonment in Bourges had taken their toll. George tried at once to mother him but he would only allow her to nurse him back to health.

Their relationship was a lively battle of wills, each thriving on it as they shouted and argued, Michel trying to bully George and George refusing to be bullied. The question as to whether Michel would appear for George in court remained unspoken between them for some time. Then, almost without willing it, they became lovers, each striving for mastery but neither succeeding. It was not a coldly physical affair, such as Mérimée had tried to initiate; there was emotion in it, the emotion of anger.

"You have met your match at last, Madame Sand."

"So have you, Monsieur Michel." Then an alarming thought struck George. "Did you become my lover in order to prevent yourself from appearing for me in court if the need arose?"

"An interesting point," Michel chuckled. "Fortunately we have been secretive. Your husband is unaware that I am your lover and can make no charge against you on that count—nor against me—in court."

George's heart leaped. "You will appear on my behalf?"

In reply Michel said, "No trousers for the hearing. I want you to look helpless if not demure. I suggest a flowing white dress with a touch of black at the neck and sleeves. And yes—a veil edged with black."

Michel was magnificent at the hearing of Casimir's appeal, just as George had expected him to be. Pointing a quivering finger at Casimir, he decried his vices in ringing tones and, turning to George, he praised her virtues to the skies. Fists were shaken at Casimir and tears were shed for the poor, ill-treated wife. Even so, the bench failed to reach a decision and the evidence was set aside for further deliberation. Had Michel failed her after all?

"How long is the adjournment likely to last?" she asked him.

"Indefinitely."

"I can't believe it! What if Casimir secures evidence about you and me and brings it before the court?"

"I admit to some slight fear of that," Michel said, but he was smiling broadly. "Your husband, however, is afraid that further deliberation of the present evidence will swing the final decision against him. I have had a consultation with his lawyer. Monsieur Dudevant is prepared to withdraw his appeal and reach a private settlement."

"You think I should agree?"

"Judge for yourself. Agreement would make secure your legal separation."

"Very well," she said.

And so, with Casimir's withdrawal, the original agreement came into force: Maurice and the income from the Hôtel de Narbonne for Casimir; Solange and Nohant for George. At least her freedom, insofar as freedom was possible for her under French law, had been achieved. Certain property divisions were still to be made, but that she gladly left to the lawyers as she prepared to return to Paris. Before she left, however, she met Casimir at Nohant at his own request. She found him briskly businesslike.

"I am fair and just," he said. "I trust that you are also."

"What do you mean by that, Casimir?"

"The household effects must be divided equally."

Accordingly they went together through the manor, counted the blankets, the sheets, the pillowcases and the counterpanes, and divided them equally. They reached the kitchens, there to count and divide the crockery and the cutlery. Finally they came upon seventeen pots of jam. Casimir arranged them neatly in two rows of eight. The seventeenth he balanced in his hand for a moment, nodded gravely and smashed it against the stone wall.

"I am fair and just," he repeated.

George parted from Michel in much the same manner as she had parted from Pagello. They shook hands in a manly fashion. If they met again in the future, they would meet on friendly terms but they would never be lovers again. Had she really loved him with the whole of her being? She was inclined to doubt it now. It had been passion and desire, not love. Loneliness and unhappiness, along with considerable admiration for the persuasive, explosive, egotistical Michel, had driven her to it. Never again could she love, not in the way she had loved Alfred de Musset.

At the last moment, as she turned to glance back at Michel, she recalled that the ringing tones of his voice in court had reminded her of Frédéric Chopin's music, had moved her emotionally in almost the same way. Chopin! Such an unsatisfactory young man! She had written to him, inviting him again to visit Nohant, but he had failed to reply. Unsatisfactory, yes, but what a pianist! what a composer! She remembered his broken heart and his cough. He needed friendship and comfort such as she alone could give. She would seek him out again, break down his timid yet stubborn opposition. It would be, when she came to think of it, the most important mission of her life.

18

Frédéric chopin and Franz Liszt were about to enter Marie d'Agoult's apartment. A frown crossed Chopin's face. He paused on the threshold and drew back.

"I should not be here tonight," he said fretfully. "I should be at home working. Except for my dislike for breaking a promise, I'd return to my piano at once."

"You worked all day," Liszt protested.

"Teaching, merely teaching. Pleyel is growing impatient. I must snatch every moment from teaching for real work."

Liszt refused to listen. "You need a little relaxation. Marie's parties are always gay, and Marie is very fond of you."

"Oh, I'm very fond of her, too."

"But at times just a little disapproving, eh?"

Laughing uncertainly, Chopin denied this stoutly, but it was true enough. Marie d'Agoult was a dear creature, gay and charming, but she had deserted her husband and child in order to become Liszt's mistress.

Gently but insistently the older man led his friend into the apartment. Marie herself came forward, tottering a little on her high heels, to greet Frédéric warmly. A moment later he was surrounded in the spacious *salon* by admiring guests. One of them begged Frédéric to entertain them with his amusing "portraits."

Obediently he sat down at the piano, but instead of playing a "portrait," he began to improvise a ballade which, when perfected, he would dedicate to Maria Wodzinska. There was a lingering sadness in the opening bars, then boldly, soaring above the sadness, a story of reunion and indescribable happiness emerged. Dear, dear Maria! The letters he had received during the last few months from her brother had included postscripts from Maria herself. She was missing him, thinking of him and as anxious as ever about his health. Even her father had expressed a similar anxiety and was following his musical progress proudly. Maria loved him still; Frédéric knew that without the slightest doubt; he had already convinced himself that the engagement, never official, still existed secretly. It might be some years before they were able to marry, but marry they would and with her father's blessing. That was why he was working so hard teaching incompetent pupils and writing music for Pleyel. Money—how essential it was! But money would in time overcome at least one of Count Wodzinski's objections.

"The portraits! the portraits!" Marie d'Agoult cried insistently.

What an imperceptive fool she was at times, Chopin thought. Why could she not recognize the happiness in his heart and let him play in peace? It was then that he saw George Sand. She was seated a little apart from the other guests, a contemplative look in her dark, glowing eyes. She wore light gray trousers and a loose-fitting black coat. But worse than that, she was smoking—of all things—a long cigar. Very well then, a portrait, a portrait of George Sand!

The portraits differed from the imitations he had played with such boyish enthusiasm at home in Warsaw only in that people were not asked to guess. Far from it, the subject sat before him and, studying him or her, Frédéric gave musical impressions of character. They were always amusing even if ruthlessly penetrating.

"Madame Sand first," he said commandingly.

"Am I to pose?" George asked.

"No, remain exactly as you are," Frédéric instructed, thinking that she was posing in any case.

He began to play. Pretending indifference, George listened intently, bringing to mind all the musical knowledge she had absorbed, however imperfectly, since she had first heard her grandmother play the harpsichord so many years ago at Nohant. Her eyes hardened and her lips curled. What an uncanny gift he had! She recognized her long nose and her large eyes, except that he was making her nose over-long and her eyes too bulbous. She listened to herself as, in her male attire, she strove to walk like a man, a man far too self-assertive in his lengthening stride. A flush, scarcely discernible beneath her olive complexion, tinged her cheeks. The cigar was in evidence now, as long as a flagpole, and the smoke from it, too, choking everybody in the room, herself included. Frédéric finished with a flourish, rose smilingly and bowed. Everybody applauded wildly.

"Thank you, monsieur," George said as harshly as she could. "Extremely clever, but a caricature, not a portrait."

Slightly conscience-stricken, the pianist said, "I played what I saw, madame."

"And I, as a writer, write what I see. Someday I may give you a word painting of your portrait."

"An artist is often swayed by personal prejudice," Liszt interposed gently.

"True," George agreed, striving to remove the harshness from her voice.

Frédéric was growing flustered. "Forgive me if I offended you, Madame Sand."

"I am not in the least offended, except in another direction."

"And that, madame?"

"Your refusal to visit me at Nohant."

"I was in London."

George inclined her head. "They received you well there?"

"Tolerably well, thank you."

George was studying the drawn and pallid cheeks. "Are you in better health these days?"

"I was never in better health, madame."

Defeated by his grim politeness, George turned away. Seeing Pierre Leroux, she engaged him at once in a lively political discussion. She was becoming much influenced by Leroux, a republican leader whom she had met through Michel. His theories, much less violent than Michel's, appealed to her greatly, for they pointed the way to a socialism based on Christian principles.

Meanwhile Chopin had seized Liszt by the arm and hurried him to an isolated corner of the room.

"You were somewhat cruel to George," Liszt commented.

"Never mind that! Was I brought here tonight because of her?"

"No, but it was inevitable that you should meet her someday in this *salon*. George has given up her old apartment on the Quai Malaquais and now has a much larger one here in the Hôtel de France. As a matter of fact, this *salon* lies between the two apartments. Marie and George share it. That is why there are several literary personalities here tonight—Balzac, Dumas, and the rest. Come, let me introduce you to Balzac. You'll find him amusing."

As it happened, Honoré de Balzac was just leaving, so Chopin, feeling a pressing need to escape if only from his own rudeness, took the opportunity of leaving with him.

"Are you walking or taking a fiacre?" Balzac asked when they were out in the cool night air.

"Walking, monsieur."

They walked together in silence for some moments, then Balzac remarked with a chuckle that he had no need to ask what Frédéric Chopin thought of George Sand. "A caricature, but a skillful one," he murmured.

"I was inexcusably rude," Frédéric said hastily, "but I do find her repellent."

"So do many men. Be warned, Monsieur Chopin, she is not a lovable woman."

"Why should I be warned?" his companion asked faintly.

"Clearly she is pursuing you. I repeat—she is not a lovable woman. Therefore it is hard to love her. How can she possibly be lovable with her marriage a failure and her many love affairs failures also?"

Alarmed though he was, Chopin tried to be fair. "Is it not unjust to blame it all on her? You appear to hate her, Monsieur de Balzac."

"On the contrary, I like and admire her in many respects. There is, I admit, another side to her nature. She is generous and kind, if much too managing. She has a beautiful soul, but it is a woman's soul, not a man's as she tries to believe. I predict nothing for her but disenchantment and disillusionment, and the same for any man who becomes too deeply involved with her."

"You are beginning to make me feel sorry for Madame Sand."

"That is not my intention," Balzac said weightily. "I only hope that, because of George Sand, I shall not be called upon to feel sorry for you."

II

It was five in the afternoon. George had worked all the previous night. Now, helped by her maid, she had just finished dressing. Her mother often accused her of ruining her health by turning night into day and refused to believe that George had never felt better in her life. The maid placed her "breakfast" tray in front of her. On the tray near the coffee-pot lay a letter. The handwriting was unfamiliar. George opened the letter curiously.

Forgive me. My rudeness was inexcusable.
—Frédéric Chopin

George's heart leaped with pleasure. During the last three days she had felt deeply hurt by his musical caricature; now that he had begged her forgiveness, the memory of it delighted her. Coming to one of her quick decisions, she ordered a fiacre and gave the driver Frédéric's address.

She heard the music as she climbed the stairs. It was the ballade Chopin had played before embarking upon her portrait. The door was slightly ajar. She pushed it open and stole softly into the room. Chopin at the piano had his back to her. The music flowed through her. She stood entranced until finally, throwing up his hands in exasperation, he swung round on the stool.

"Bravo!" she said.

Frédéric stared at her blankly. "I can't get it right. I keep altering, correcting, but I can't get it right."

George affected a mocking tone. "Such scrupulousness! Such artistic integrity! Is it always like this? You compose a faultless piece of music, then alter and correct?"

The young composer sprang up. "Madame Sand! I didn't recognize you at first."

"Because, for once, I am not wearing trousers?"

He sank back on the stool, facing her. His eyes were haggard, his brow moist with sweat, but even so, with his finely laundered shirt open at the neck and his fair hair tousled, he looked

252

so like a tired little boy that George's heart went out to him.

"Play it again," she begged. "Please, Chopin."

Frédéric, turning, struck the opening notes, then suffered a severe spasm of coughing.

"You're ill," George cried in alarm. "I knew you were exaggerating when you said you had never been in better health."

He swung round with a gesture of angry denial the moment he could speak again.

"Not ill, just a little weary. I worked all last night, gave lessons today until five o'clock."

"You'll kill yourself, Chopin."

"How else can I earn money?"

"Is money so necessary?"

Chopin smiled naively. "I'm saving up to get married."

His voice was so boyishly eager that her heart went out to him again. It was almost as if he had become her son, her elder son.

"Do I know the girl?" she asked.

He shook his head. "She lives in Warsaw. A—well—a childhood friend. Her name is Maria Wodzinska." And he added proudly, "Her father is a count."

"And—rich?"

"Very rich."

"Then why this frantic need to earn money? Maria will bring you a substantial dowry and you will be free to write still greater music."

"I want to be independent," he said lamely.

"That, my dear Chopin, is nonsense. Nevertheless, money is not the chief consideration. Is this Maria right for you? Does she understand you?"

"She means everything in the world to me. That is all I know."

"Your music comes first. Does she understand that?"

"How cross you sound, madame!"

253

George looked at him shrewdly. "Does her rich father have some misgivings because you are poor? Is that why you are working so hard?"

Frédéric shook his head. He was seized by another spasm of coughing. More alarmed than ever, George feared that he was on the verge of collapse. As gently as she could, she urged him to go to bed and asked for the name of his doctor. Surprised at his own submissiveness, Frédéric obeyed.

The doctor came and diagnosed a touch of fever undoubtedly caused by overwork and nervous strain. He prescribed rest and a special mixture to reduce the fever. George remained in the apartment during the night, working and each hour tiptoeing into Chopin's bedroom to see if he was sleeping peacefully. He sat up in feverish agitation when she entered at eight the next morning.

"Have you been here all night?"

"Of course. You were far from well enough to be left alone."

"But—but what will people say?"

George, touched by this shrinking, old-maidish attitude, laughed and told a ready lie. "My maid was here. I sent for her. She slept on the couch."

"But where did you sleep?"

"I didn't sleep. I never sleep at night. I worked at your little writing-table."

Chopin sank back on the pillow with a groan. Suppose she had opened the drawer and read his private letters, especially the treasured letters and postscripts from Maria! Then he took heart. Of all the horrible things people had said about George Sand, no one had ever accused her of dishonorable peeping and prying.

"Did you bring writing paper with you?" he asked cunningly.

"No, but fortunately I found a writing block on the piano."

He sighed in relief. "You were very welcome to it."

From then on, breaking her normal routine, George went

to Frédéric every morning and remained with him until night-fall. She nursed him expertly and, when he was well enough to eat properly, cooked him nourishing food just as his mother would have done. There was even broth tasting very like his mother's special broth. He submitted with childlike patience and luxuriated happily in the careful attention she gave him. Balzac was right; that other side of her nature was a beautiful soul. But what pleased him most was the thought that, if his health continued to improve so rapidly, the second obstacle to marriage with Maria—if not the first—would soon be removed.

When Chopin was well enough to get up, George asked him to play for her. He did so without the slightest hesitation, for he was longing to get back to work and was wracked by the fear that his fingers were growing stiff and inept. Listening in rapt silence, George recognized a gay little country tune. She could feel the spring sunshine on her cheeks and see the tender spring flowers. It seemed to her that she was dancing on the lawn at Nohant with Chopin.

"You bring my beloved Nohant right into this dark Paris apartment," she said ecstatically when he had finished.

"What is your real name?" Chopin asked without turning.

"Dudevant."

"I mean your given name."

"Aurore."

He turned and smiled at her shyly. "What a lovely name! Goddess of the Dawn! I was playing for you then without knowing that George was really Aurore."

George smiled fondly. "Poetic license. Your music spoke of a spring morning, not the dawn. How could you possibly play like that without seeing Nohant? I beg you to come there with me. The country air will do you good. Your doctor said so."

But he shrank instantly from the suggestion. "I have done no work during the past two weeks, given not a single lesson."

"You could work freely at Nohant."

"But not give lessons."

"I could find you more pupils in the district than you could cope with."

"Possibly, but I would lose my regular pupils here in Paris."

George guessed his real reason for refusing. "The manor house is a large one. I have many servants and a few friends will be staying with me when I go there for the summer. You would be adequately chaperoned."

Taking fright, Chopin said querulously, "I—I am a creature of habit. The thought of leaving Paris, my doctor, my own special piano, terrifies me."

Was it that, George wondered, or was it herself? Had she, for all the tenderness she had felt and tried to convey, presented herself as a veritable virago?

"Think about it," she pleaded. "I know you will love Nohant. After a week there, you will come to believe that you have never lived anywhere else." Then she saw by his startled expression that she had said the wrong thing. "Think about it," she repeated.

Publishing business kept her from visiting Chopin again for several days. When at last she was able to call at his apartment, she found the door locked. Seeking out the concierge, she learned that "Monsieur Chopin" had left suddenly for London with Camille Pleyel. So that was it, she thought; more concerts abroad, more luster added to his growing fame. Pleyel would fleece him again, just as he had fleeced him in the meager payments he had made for those priceless compositions. But over and above that, did Chopin really believe that he, genius that he was, could earn enough even in a whole lifetime to provide for a rich man's daughter?

19

"I wonder what sort of a portrait Chopin would play if faced with our handsome Creole?" Marie d'Agoult asked.

"A most unpleasant one, I should imagine," George answered shortly.

Félicien Mallefille, the Creole, was fencing with Liszt in the middle of the *salon*. George, who had met him only two or three times before, considered the man both repulsive and arrogant. She studied him now as he moved back and forth, thrusting and parrying, his steps as dainty as a dancing master's. Born in the Île de France twenty-four years earlier, he had come to Paris when he was nine to complete his education. He wore a long, pointed beard, a shade lighter than his long, dark hair, and a thick bush of a mustache. His complexion, what little could be seen of it, was swarthy. The dark hair of his chest extended above his cravat to intermingle with his beard. His eyes were large, dark, and piercing.

Did all that hair indicate an intensely manly man? George could not decide but she thought that the long, grotesque beard made his thin figure look even shorter than it was. Mallefille styled himself a dramatist, for two of his plays had already been presented, although neither had been a financial success.

"When are you going to Nohant?" Marie asked George now.

"Later in the month. I shall be taking the children first to Fontainebleau."

"Both of them? Your husband has no objection to Maurice going, too?"

"Apparently not," George said dryly, "but he reserves the right to summon the boy to Guillery at a moment's notice."

"Guillery?"

"The Dudevant estate near Nérac in Gascony. Casimir is spending most of his time there these days attending to his family estate."

The old baroness had died at last. Casimir had come into his inheritance and with it the title: Casimir, Baron Dudevant! She herself, now the Baroness Dudevant, still preferred being known as George Sand. Nothing could be less important than an empty title.

"I expect you will engage a tutor for the children," Marie suggested.

"I'm looking for one now."

Marie smiled innocently. "Why not Félicien? He is a very learned young man and needs suitable employment."

"I loathe Mallefille!"

"So much the better," Marie said sweetly. "Even your most tolerant friends would turn up their noses if you conducted an affair with your children's tutor."

"Dear Marie, how wise you are," George said just as sweetly. At that moment, Mallefille, disarming Liszt, came to sit at George's feet.

"Do you fence, Monsieur Sand?" he asked, pronouncing the "Monsieur" teasingly rather than contemptuously.

"No. At least, not since I was quite young."

"What did you think of my play, *Glenarvon?*" Mallefille asked.

George shrugged indifferently. "I have neither seen it nor read it."

The young man's eyes flashed angrily. "I, on the other hand, have read all your books."

"And—your opinion of them?" Marie d'Agoult prompted.

His eyes softened. "I adored every word."

George, rarely influenced by flattery, merely shrugged again.

"Félicien has just finished writing a novel himself," Marie ventured.

Mallefille looked up at George, his eyes liquid and quite pleading now. "I wonder if you would be kind enough to read it and express an opinion?"

George tried not to sound ungracious. "I am really much too busy. I have a large manuscript to copy for the press."

Mallefille smiled. "Is your handwriting legible?"

"Extremely so."

"Then why not let me do the copying?"

"In order that I may have time to read your own manuscript?"

"Precisely!"

Reluctantly George agreed and reluctantly she began to read Mallefille's novel, *Le Dernier Sauvage*. She found it expertly written, if rather trite, and quite publishable. Impulsively she offered to present *Le Dernier Sauvage* to her own publisher, and, quite carried away, decided to engage Mallefille as her children's tutor as well as her own secretary.

That done, she left Paris for Fontainebleau, accompanied by the children, her maid, and the tutor-secretary. There she rented the cottage she and Alfred de Musset had once occupied. This she did as a special test and was gratified to discover that her memories of the things she and Alfred had done and said in that quiet environment stirred her neither one way nor another.

While the little party was at Fontainebleau, George's publisher returned *Le Dernier Sauvage* with a little note of regret. No doubt it could—competently written as it was—enjoy a small success, but he himself was not prepared to publish it.

"I thought your recommendation would do the trick," Mallefille said gloomily.

"So did I."

"He won't publish it even for you. I can't understand it."

"There are other publishers, my boy," George told him encouragingly. "We must send it off again."

"You're so kind," he sighed. "Such a great, good friend."

That special liquid expression was in his eyes again. George's heart warmed to him. She was no longer finding Félicien Mallefille repulsive.

A little later word reached her at Fontainebleau that her mother was desperately ill. George hired a post chaise immediately, leaving the children in the care of her maid, a reliable, loyal creature, and the tutor.

George found her mother in a dreadful condition. According to the doctor, she was suffering from cancer and close to death. But Sophie, in spite of the pain she suffered, was as concerned as ever about her appearance.

"My hair is in a shocking state, Aurore. Do something about it."

"I'll send for a hairdresser."

"Not just any hairdresser—René Rollinat. Expensive, but he thoroughly understands my requirements."

George sent for Rollinat who looked more like a farmer than anything else. Sophie's faded, brittle hair was soon dyed the brightest possible shade of red. The incorrigible woman, studying her reflection in a hand mirror, nodded approvingly.

"Now I look young again. Your dear father will have no trouble in recognizing me when we meet again in Heaven."

Visitors called frequently. They were gay, over-dressed, vulgar, and, without exception, brainless. All of them were strangers to George. To each, Sophie said proudly, "You must meet my daughter, the Baroness Dudevant." But toward the end, she wept a little and told George that one great sin lay heavy on her heart.

"It is true, Aurore, that I have rarely approved of you since you grew up, but I admit that I have been responsible for much of your unhappiness. I should never have allowed you to marry Casimir. I gave my consent for one reason only. Do you know what it was?"

"No, Mother."

"The knowledge that if you married him you would become a baroness some day."

"Why think of that now?"

"Oh, I'm not asking you to forgive me," Sophie said haughtily. "I have confessed and made my peace with God. That is sufficient."

Incredible woman! George thought emotionally. "You loved me when I was a child," she said brokenly. "I have many happy memories."

Sophie wept again. "There is another sin, too. During Casimir's appeal at Bourges, I could have given evidence of his cruelty, neglect, and unfaithfulness. Do you know why I didn't?"

"No, Mother."

"He offered me an additional allowance to remain silent."

"Did you ever receive it?"

"No, not a single franc."

One evening toward the end of August, Madame Sophie Dupin fell into a coma. She lingered on, however. It was one of the times when George was watching over her that a wild-eyed Mallefille arrived suddenly and dramatically in Paris.

"George, the children have disappeared!"

"Disappeared?"

"Kidnapped, both of them."

"By whom?"

"I suspect your husband."

Worn out by lack of sleep, George felt herself numb and incapable of dealing with this serious situation.

"What makes you suspect my husband?" she asked vaguely.

"Maurice said he had seen his father near the cottage. Solange saw him, too. She talked to him about a holiday at La Châtre."

George emerged momentarily from the engulfing haze. "Go to La Châtre. Call on the Mayor for help if need be. I cannot insist on recovering Maurice, but Solange—that is another matter."

Sophie died without regaining consciousness. George, stirring herself into spasmodic activity, made the necessary arrangements for the funeral. Many of her friends joined the cortege to the cemetery at Montmartre. The funeral caused a considerable stir in Paris if only because Madame Sophie Dupin had been the mother of George Sand.

It was a beautiful summer's day. George felt the hot sun on her face and saw butterflies making streaks of brilliant-colored lights above the grave. One had wings as red as her mother's hair. George wept bitterly. But for what, she asked herself —the dead past or the uncertain future?

She hated the thought of returning to her apartment at the Hôtel de France since both Franz Liszt and Marie d'Agoult were in Italy. But when she arrived there, Mallefille and Maurice were waiting for her. Why, she asked, why Maurice and not Solange? Maurice, it seemed, had been left by his father with the Duvernets. They, in turn, had been on the point of sending him back to Paris with a servant when Mallefille reached La Châtre . . .

"But Solange—where is Solange?"

"Papa has taken her to Guillery," Maurice said.

George, cold with rage, consulted a lawyer. A court order

for her daughter's return was obtained. Armed with this, she set out by post chaise for Nérac. Leaving Maurice with friends, she took Mallefille with her. The Creole screamed at times for Casimir's blood. George smiled tolerantly. Félicien Mallefille, her would-be champion! At one village inn where they were to spend the night, this violent little gentleman, looking very fierce with his beard thrust out, informed George that only one room was available.

"I told the innkeeper we were man and wife."

"In that case, my boy, man and wife shall ride on through the night."

And ride on they did, Mallefille either dozing or sulkily refusing to make conversation. Reaching Nérac, he sprang to life, taking instant control of the situation. Waiting on the *sous-préfet,* he presented the court order and demanded that the nearby Château de Guillery be surrounded by a band of gendarmes. Surprisingly enough, since the name of Dudevant was a powerful one in the district, this was done immediately.

"My forceful little Creole," George said mockingly but not without a certain amount of admiration.

Together they drove out to the château, passed through the police cordon and rapped the heavy knocker of the massive door. A manservant refused them entry. Mallefille, brushing past him, demanded an immediate interview with Casimir. George stood aside, watching with interest.

Mallefille slapped the court order into Casimir's hand. "M'm'selle Solange? Produce her at once!"

Casimir tore the order to shreds and grinned at George. "You appear to have a knight in shining armor. Where did you find him?"

They were grouped together in the hall. Coats of armor stood in the corners, and firearms and swords of all description hung on the walls. Mallefille, seizing on two rapiers, tossed one at Casimir who caught it clumsily.

"En garde, monsieur!"

George began to enjoy herself. What delightful theatre, what magnificent melodrama! Casimir, never a very proficient swordsman, put up a good fight, but he was no match for the nimble-footed Creole. George watched breathlessly. Then Casimir tripped and the rapier flew from his grasp. Snatching at it, he tripped again and fell. Mallefille stood over him, roaring like a bull, the point of his rapier pricking the humiliated man's throat.

"M'm'selle Solange—at once!" Mallefille rasped.

Casimir, rising shakily, retired without a word and came back presently with Solange.

"Take her out to the carriage," George instructed Mallefille. "I want to talk with the baron."

George waited until Mallefille and Solange had gone. "Why did you bring Solange to Guillery but not Maurice?"

"She's my daughter, isn't she?"

"Privately you have never admitted paternity."

Casimir smiled slyly. "It amused me to hurt you."

"That I can well believe. Has it occurred to you that I could sue you for abduction?"

"Do that, madame, and I shall obtain a court order myself to recover Maurice."

"You abandoned him at La Châtre. That, I must say, was a very fatherly gesture. Maurice is better off with me."

"So I imagine," Casimir sighed.

"What do you mean by that?" George asked.

"It so happens," Casimir grumbled, "that I am in temporary financial difficulties. The wretched old baroness left many debts and a number of ridiculous legacies that I am obliged to pay. Certain portions of the estate will have to be sold, but I want to take my time and obtain a good price. I have dismissed all the servants except the cook, the head gardener, and the man-

264

servant who admitted you."

George laughed dryly. "Are you asking me to lend you money?"

"No, I am not."

"Clearly you have some scheme in mind."

Casimir shrugged elaborately. "An arrangement possibly that would enable you to keep Maurice."

They argued for some time. In the end, driven by necessity, Casimir agreed to surrender his interest in the Hôtel de Narbonne for the sum of forty thousand francs.

"You will recover it from rents in a few years," Casimir complained. He fingered his neck tenderly. "If you are living with that bouncing little monstrosity, he will lead you a merry dance when you tire of him."

George held out her hand. "Good-by, Casimir."

He turned from her with a snarl. "I never want to see you again."

"How splendid that we should part for the last time so amicably!"

During the more leisurely journey back to Paris, the little party of three came one evening upon the village inn at which George had earlier refused to stay. Three rooms were vacant now. George said that two would be sufficient; one for Mallefille, the other for herself and Solange.

Mallefille violently disagreed. "No, one for Solange who is old enough to sleep alone, the other for you and me. The innkeeper still believes us to be man and wife."

"Are we to fight a duel over it?" George asked, amusement showing in her eyes.

After a pleasant country meal and a little more wine than she was in the habit of drinking, George put Solange to bed and changed into a feathery, very feminine negligee. Then, stirred by a rising excitement, she went to Mallefille's room.

"You were magnificent, getting the better of Casimir like that," she said. "It was quite an adventure."

Mallefille took her in his arms. "The real adventure is just beginning."

20

"CHOPIN IS ILL again," Marie d'Agoult remarked. "I begged him to see his doctor but he refused to listen. Perhaps you can succeed, George, where I have failed."

George and Mallefille had just returned to Paris from Nohant where they had spent the winter, both of them working and, apart from their tempestuous love-making, living a more or less placid domestic country existence. George, however, had never ceased to think of Frédéric Chopin and his music. She had written to him soon after his return from London, inviting him again to Nohant, but his reply had been vague and evasive.

"I'll go and see him at once."

"Why should either you or Marie worry about a sickly musician?" Mallefille asked sulkily.

George tried to be tolerant and patient. Félicien had been depressed and grumpy ever since the rejection of his novel by yet another publisher. He had complained bitterly that George's name, great as it was, meant less than nothing where his own work was concerned. Then pleadingly he had asked her to help him in a very special way. She seized upon this request now, hoping to propitiate him.

"Félicien, I'll do what you asked. I'll allow my name to

appear on the title page with yours."

Mallefille's face brightened instantly. "Now it will be published and have an immense success!"

Chopin failed to hear her when she entered his apartment. That in itself was not unusual, but she could see at a glance that apart from his being ill something had upset him deeply. He was sitting at the writing-table, his head in his hands, his shoulders quivering. She stole up behind him and touched him lightly on the shoulder.

"Chopin, what has happened?"

Frédéric dashed her hand away without turning. "Leave me alone."

"Tell me," she repeated, "what has happened to upset you so much."

A letter lay before him on the writing-table. He had received it not an hour ago from Maria Wodzinska's brother. He read it again, slowly, the words running into each other. Maria had recently become engaged to Count Skarbek, the man who had made such an amusing speech on her father's return from Geneva. The wedding would take place very soon. Maria, on the whole, was well content with this marriage of convenience. She had added a postscript to the letter:

You must be patient with me once again—and understanding, Frédéric. Childhood attachments, as Papa says, rarely develop into mature love. Even at Carlsbad we were still children, playing the childish game of being in love. It was pretty, and I find it touching to remember it, but it was only a game. I played your waltz before penning these lines and I remembered what Mama said in Carlsbad. The murmur of lovers' voices followed by the striking of a clock and the sound of carriage wheels on the cobblestones, then the clatter of wheels drowning the sound of distracted sobbing. Were you thinking of me, a mere child at that time, when you created such poignant music? No, Frédéric, no! You were expressing the agony you felt at being compelled by your ambition to leave Poland, your native land. . . .

268

Chopin, turning at last, faced George and thrust the letter into her hand, not realizing that he was opening his heart to her even more than he would ever have opened it to his mother. As soon as she had read the letter, he snatched it back from her. Opening the drawer violently, he took the dead rose from between the pages of *Indiana*. Angry now, he gathered together all Maria's letters and with the rose made a little parcel of them.

Seeing that he was shivering violently, George found the remains of the medicine the doctor had ordered before and gave Chopin a dose. He took it docilely enough.

"Now I'll send for your doctor."

Chopin rose and almost fell. "No, I want to work. Among other things, work is an escape."

"So I have always found, but you'll do no work tonight. Do go to bed, you great idiot!"

Chopin allowed her to help him to his bedroom. She lit a candle, then withdrew until he was undressed and in bed. But when she prepared a little broth for him, he was unable to swallow it; he was still shivering and very nearly delirious. George snuffed out the candle, removed all but her underclothes and slipped into bed with him, her movements slow and cautious. He made no gesture of rejection when she took him tenderly in her arms, and presently, relaxing like a baby, he fell asleep with his head on her breast. It was for her a strangely beautiful experience. There was heavenly music in it and a wordless poem. She doubted if she would ever want or ask anything more of him.

At dawn, scarcely having slept herself, George got up, dressed and sent the concierge for Chopin's doctor. It was the middle of the morning before he arrived. Alone with him after he had examined the sick man, George asked the doctor to tell her frankly about his patient's condition.

"Merely another bout of fever, madame."

"Nothing more serious than that? Come, man, tell me the truth!"

"Well—perhaps a lung infection."

"I was afraid of that myself. Country air is more essential than ever."

"It is, madame. Indeed, I absolutely insist upon it."

"Then I beg you to tell him. It is most unlikely that he will listen to me alone."

When the doctor had gone, George broached the subject of the long-delayed visit to Nohant. Much to her delight he showed a pathetic eagerness to accede to her wishes. However, thinking of the proprieties, he declared that he would travel separately to her country estate.

"You would not be unchaperoned during the journey," she pointed out. "My children will be traveling with me, their tutor also."

"Even so . . ."

"Very well," she said quickly, fearing that he would change his mind if she pressed him further. "Come with Franz and Marie."

Frédéric agreed as if grasping at a straw; then blushing and avoiding her eyes, he said faintly, "Were you with me last night?"

"Only in spirit, Chopin."

"Ah! So it was merely a dream!"

"But a comforting one, I hope?"

"A very comforting one," he said, sounding grateful.

II

The Countess Marie d'Agoult sat in a corner of the *salon* at Nohant only half listening to Chopin as he worked at the piano. She was a jealous woman and now she was in a mood to make mischief. More and more she was growing to resent George's friendship with Liszt even though she did not believe the gossip that George and Liszt were lovers. She was irked, too, by the way George had monopolized Mallefille who was, after all, her protégé. It was obvious enough that George and Félicien were sleeping together, even if they were practicing the utmost discretion. The isolated summerhouse was undoubtedly their rendezvous. They worked together there at separate desks—or so the story went. Worked together indeed!

Chopin rose from the piano. "Marie! I hadn't noticed you."

Marie tossed her blonde curls. "What a blow to my pride. I love to be noticed!"

He grew instantly contrite. "I merely meant . . ."

"Dear Chopin, I know what you meant. Not having been noticed, I was obviously not a disturbing element."

He smiled charmingly. "An audience of one is not so terrifying as a concert hall crammed with critics."

"You are actually terrified when playing in public?"

"Only during the first moments. As soon as I become immersed, I forget everything but the music."

Marie smiled innocently. "Tell me, do you find dear George a disturbing element?"

"George? On the contrary, I find her most restful."

Marie clapped her hands in apparent delight. "George restful? You must have nerves of iron!"

Vaguely troubled but unable to decide just why, Frédéric walked to the window and gazed out across the lawn. It was early evening, with long shadows cutting dark paths through the sunlight. Summer was drawing to a close; soon he must return to Paris. He hated the thought of it. Here at Nohant he had been happier than ever before in his life, quietly happy and almost contented. For the first time since leaving Warsaw, he had grown to feel that he belonged to somebody—not just to one "somebody," but to a little, entirely domestic family group. How foolish of him to have resisted Nohant so long! It was just as George had predicted. It seemed now as if he had never lived anywhere else; now he no longer even missed his own family quite so much. George's children, perhaps a little suspicious of him at first, seemed now to like him, while George herself had done everything possible for his comfort.

Marie joined him at the window. "What of Félicien? Do you find him restful, too?"

"One could hardly say that of Monsieur Mallefille," Chopin admitted.

"The poor boy has been more fretful of late than usual. I suspect him of being jealous of you."

"Of me?"

"He is very possessive where George is concerned."

"He—the children's tutor?"

Marie gave the thin cheek a playful little slap. "What an innocent you are, Chopin! Aren't you jealous of him?"

"I have no reason to be jealous."

"So very angelic of you, dear Chopin! You live in the clouds! But how fortunate for you that you do."

Marie appeared to be speaking seriously now, all thought of gossip set aside. Frédéric grew more troubled than ever. What, precisely, was she trying to tell him?

"George is my friend," she went on earnestly. "I try constantly to help her but I always fail. She is her own worst enemy. She uses her lovers as if they were pieces of chalk. George scratches away on the blackboard of their lives and when she is finished—that is to say, when she is tired of them—she grinds the chalk to dust beneath her feet."

"Do you write novels too?" Frédéric asked icily.

"Now I have offended you. But all I want to do is help you."

"Surely you mean—warn me?"

"Possibly."

"George is the kindest creature on earth. I won't listen to your nonsense any more. I—I'm only sorry I dedicated those études to the Countess Marie d'Agoult!"

Marie smiled sadly, but on the whole she was well content.

Chopin, after his fashion, would brood over what she had said and his regard for George Sand, his trust and admiration, would never be the same again. She glanced at the door. George and Félicien were just entering the *salon*. It was clear from George's grim expression and Félicien's flushed cheeks that they had been arguing fiercely.

"The idiot wanted to challenge Charles Duvernet to fight a duel," George exploded.

"He looked at George impertinently and intimately," Mallefille shouted, "and that I will not permit from any man!"

"Worse still," George said acidly, "Charles made the unfortunate remark that he had not enjoyed *Le Dernier Sauvage*. His great sin, however, was that he thought that I—not Félicien —had written the book!"

Le Dernier Sauvage, published recently, had not been well received by the critics but was nevertheless enjoying a mild success.

Mallefille turned on Chopin. "And what is your opinion of my novel?"

"I have not yet read it," Frédéric replied, "but like Monsieur Duvernet, I was unaware that you were the sole author."

Marie heaved a deep sigh. "So are many people. George is taking most of the credit when all of it should be Félicien's."

"Credit?" Chopin questioned. "Perhaps George, out of her generosity, has done harm to her own reputation."

Mallefille, tugging a glove from his pocket, flew at Chopin and slapped his cheek with it.

"Name your seconds, monsieur! Let them wait on mine!"

George stepped angrily between the two men. "Go to the summerhouse, Félicien! Do some useful work for once."

Mallefille bowed ironically. "I am yours to command, master." He turned at the door. "No, by heaven! I meant— mistress!"

Utterly confused, Chopin looked at George. "Am I obliged

to fight him?"

"If you feel so inclined," Marie purred.

"Félicien will recover presently," George said, darting a furious look at Marie. "I'll not permit brawling at Nohant. Nor will I permit the sacrifice of genius to vaunting incompetence."

Chopin turned away unhappily. The peaceful life at Nohant had been shattered. He could no longer exist in an atmosphere that had become suddenly quarrelsome and gossipy. He was sorry for George, immeasurably grateful to her, too, but he knew that he must leave for Paris even earlier than necessary. After dinner that night he told her of his plans, saying lamely that he had neglected his pupils far too long.

"As if they matter!" she said indignantly.

"I have taken too great an advantage of your generous hospitality," he added, even more lamely.

"But I want you to stay here forever, Chopin. Your health has improved so much during the summer."

"Yes, hasn't it? I'm so grateful to you for all you have done for me. I shall be able to face the coming winter in Paris with a lighter heart."

"Chopin . . ." George begged woefully.

"I must go. I must!"

There was more stubbornness in the young artist than George realized. Reluctantly she allowed him to go, then angrily she attacked Félicien and Marie, accusing them both of driving him away. She directed her anger against Marie with even greater force than against Félicien.

"You were the chief cause," she said. "Why must you set yourself to hurt me like this?"

"Hurt you?" Marie echoed, hiding her delight. "I'm your best friend, George. You know I am. You are wasting your time on Chopin. Believe me, he is an unstable creature. There is nothing permanent in him but his cough."

"And nothing permanent in Félicien but his jealousy."

"What could be more flattering in a man than jealousy?"

"Trust," George replied, "and the love it breeds."

III

Maurice had suffered a mild attack of fever, so George, not too greatly worried by his condition, decided to take him to Paris for a consultation with Chopin's doctor. It was as good an excuse as any, she thought, for following Chopin back to the capital. Accordingly she set off from Nohant with her two children. Mallefille, quarrelsome and ready to challenge any man who glanced at her, accompanied them. In her heart George knew that the Félicien "episode" was coming to an end, but her chief concern was Chopin.

She went to his apartment one night and found him in a sadly dejected mood. It was miserable weather in Paris. The chilly atmosphere with its mist and drizzle had brought back the cough. It had almost entirely disappeared during the summer at Nohant. Commenting on this, George affected a gently reproachful tone.

"You see what happens, Chopin, when there is nobody to look after you."

"I can look after myself, George."

"You haven't missed Nohant then?"

"Nohant?" Frédéric sprang up and kissed her impulsively on the cheek. "I've missed you, only you! Being alone in Paris has been torment, the greatest torment I've ever suffered."

"You have forgotten about Maria, then?"

"Maria?" He burst out. "Who in the name of heaven is Maria?"

"The girl you were in love with," George said quietly. "The girl you wanted to marry."

"That was self-deception. A game, a childish game. I've

275

grown up now. I'm in love for the first time in my life. No, the only time. There'll never be anyone else."

He took her in his arms but quickly she held him back.

"Am I making a fool of myself?"

"I want to be sure," she said. "Not of you so much as of myself."

"You, of course, have been in love many times!"

"I cannot deny it. All I want to be sure of is that this time it will endure."

"You love me! You love me!" Chopin cried triumphantly.

"In more ways than one."

He nodded. "Chopin, the helpless child, Chopin, the invalid . . ."

"Chopin, the genius, too."

"But what of the man—Chopin, the man?"

"You must give me time to think."

"Think? Why should one pause to think when one knows?"

He took her fully in his arms and kissed her on the lips. Chopin, the man! Masterful, demanding! Chopin casting to the wind all thought of what was right or wrong; Chopin, in his excited, feverish condition, obeying only the urgent demands of the flesh. George abandoned herself to him with a like urgency.

Presently, as she lay in his arms, she whispered, "I didn't want this to happen. I never even dreamed of it."

"But now, Aurore?"

"Are you ashamed, Chopin?"

"We have joined our lives together fully, completely. Must I be ashamed of that? Must you?"

"I couldn't bear it if you felt the slightest shame, Chopin. This is holy and sacred to me."

"To me also," Chopin said, trying to come to terms with his religious scruples. "This is marriage, Aurore. We are bound together for life. Unfaithfulness is as impossible as divorce."

"Thank you," George said humbly, "for bringing back from the dead that romantic child of so long ago. Chopin," she went on, thinking this a good time to broach a subject close to her heart, "the doctor is worried about Maurice's health. He has recommended a warmer climate for my son during the coming winter."

"Then take him to a warmer climate by all means."

"But how could I leave you behind when you are in greater need of such a change than Maurice?"

"For the boy's sake, I am willing to make the sacrifice," he said stoutly.

"You may be, Chopin, but I am not." George hesitated a moment, weighing her words. "God forgive me for being more concerned about your health than Maurice's." She could tell by the way he moved at her side that he was both pleased and flattered. "Why not come with us to Majorca?"

"Majorca?"

"That is where I propose to take Maurice for the winter."

"Will Liszt and the Countess d'Agoult be joining you there?" Frédéric asked.

George sighed. "Liszt himself would be welcome . . ."

"Liszt himself—yes."

"But not Marie. She is no longer my friend."

"No one can blame you for that," Frédéric said heatedly. "She is no longer my friend either."

"Still—it would make me very happy if you would come with Maurice and me to Majorca."

Chopin was tempted. He could not bear the thought of being separated again from George now that this tremendous thing had happened. He was held back only by the fear of what people would think and say, and, above all, by what his mother would write to him if the story reached her ears.

"Is the tutor going with you?" he asked.

"No. I've finished with him."

Frédéric laughed. "I was about to insist on that."

Chopin thought himself master of the house now, George thought, smiling in the darkness. "You'll come with us?"

Frédéric hesitated, seeking an excuse he no longer really wanted. "My piano . . ."

"It will be a simple matter to transport a piano to Majorca. Pleyel will help you in that." She held her growing impatience in check. "Well, Chopin?"

"I have a number of things to attend to in Paris. I—I'll join you in Majorca."

George smiled again in the darkness. "Just as you wish, Chopin. But why not somewhere en route? Perpignan, for instance?"

Thinking that he was saving face, Chopin agreed instantly. "Yes, why not Perpignan! I should like to visit the old fortifications with you."

George left him during the night and the next day began to make swift preparations for the journey. She had first thought of leaving Solange at school in Paris, but she decided she must have all her children with her—her three children—for Chopin was almost as much her child as her lover. She tried in vain to keep her plans secret.

George had sent Félicien Mallefille to Nohant on some quite unnecessary business, hoping to slip away during his absence, but he returned before she was ready to leave for Majorca and made a wild, dramatic scene.

"Marie d'Agoult has told me everything, everything!"

"Marie was always a trouble maker. Be sensible, Félicien. Let us part good friends."

A shrewd look crossed his face. "Let us have one last night together before you go."

"No, Félicien. You ask the impossible."

He laughed triumphantly. "I am well aware of George Sand's peculiar sense of honor. Never two lovers at the same time."

Mallefille left her apartment. He had no option; she had packed his belongings and locked the door against him. But whenever she went out, there he was, waiting to follow her wherever she might be going. Finally, when she thought she had succeeded in eluding him one evening, he bounded after her into Chopin's apartment.

"Ludicrous but true!" he screamed.

"Chopin is leaving soon for Warsaw," she said angrily. "I merely came to bid him au revoir."

Mallefille, more fierce and aggressive than George had ever known him, carried two rapiers under his arm. He flung one at the startled and bewildered pianist.

"We shall dispense with seconds! Fight, man, fight!"

George snatched the rapier from Chopin. "You fool, Félicien! This is not one of your ridiculous plays."

He turned to her with a suddenly woebegone expression on his face.

"*En garde*, Monsieur Sand!" he said half-heartedly.

He began then to leap about clumsily, lunging out with his rapier as if uncertain of what he was doing. This was not the gallant fellow George knew, thrusting surely and terrifyingly. His breath struck her face and she realized he had been drinking. Not since her youth at Nohant when Hippolyte had taught her a little sword play, had she engaged in fencing. Even so, she thought it would be child's play to get the better of Félicien in his present condition. Chopin, to whom physical violence was abhorrent, watched in horrified silence for a few moments. Then unable to bear the thought of George sustaining even the slightest injury, he seized a cushion and flung it at the flashing rapiers. Mallefille turned with a curse, lost his balance and fell heavily. George pounced on him at once and held the tip of her rapier against his neck.

"Apologize!" she commanded.

"By God! No!" Mallefille gasped, partly winded by his fall.

"Come, apologize!"

As he struggled to sit up, the rapier pierced his bearded chin and drew a little blood. George stood back, afraid of causing him further injury. The Creole touched his chin and stared at the blood on his finger. A frightened look came to his eyes.

"Blood!" he exclaimed.

George looked at him in amazement. "One would think you were in danger of bleeding to death," she remarked pityingly.

"For all you know or care, I may be!"

"You are a skillful fencer—with foils. But how many duels have you actually fought?"

"None," he admitted sulkily, "but at least I made short work of your husband."

George placed the two rapiers on the piano. "You'd better go, Félicien."

21

NOVEMBER THOUGH IT was, the weather in Majorca was as warm as Paris in early summer. Palma, Frédéric thought, was a heavenly place. He was lounging lazily in the sun, waiting for George to come back from a shopping expedition with the children. He glanced about the sun-drenched garden. It was something of a wilderness, ill formed and uncared for; but beyond it were palm trees, cedars and aloes, oranges, lemons, and pomegranates, while above the cloudless sky was a turquoise blue. The whole scene was so unreal to him he could scarcely believe in its existence. No painter, however skillful, could truly capture it on canvas.

Although he wanted to write to his mother about this entrancing paradise, he had already decided that his family must believe him still to be in Paris. When he wrote he would mention only his work, and his letters, enclosed in letters to a Paris friend, would be forwarded from Paris to Warsaw. He was protecting George's reputation, he told himself, as much as his own. He sighed almost contentedly. Only one thing was missing, his precious piano without which it was impossible to do satisfactory work.

"Chopin!"

It was George followed by the children. They were laughing together and carrying baskets of meat, bread, and vegetables.

"Now I can cook for my family," George said gaily. "No need for us to exist any longer on fish and garlic."

Chopin had never complained, but George knew that he had quickly grown tired of the staple diet of the Majorcans and was often nauseated by the smell of the oil in which the fish was cooked. Nevertheless, his health had improved during the three weeks they had been in Palma. His cheeks were faintly rosy, his cough had almost disappeared, and he had even put on a little weight.

"Did you inquire about my piano?" he asked.

"I did, but it hasn't come yet. The customs officers will notify us the moment it does."

George led the way into the house where they had rented two sparsely furnished rooms. Frédéric and Maurice slept in one, she and Solange in the other. It was actually a boarding-house and would have been thoroughly uncomfortable except for the beautiful weather. The trestle beds were hard and the straw-covered chairs rickety. Maurice had complained of this, but not Frédéric. The fact that George and he were together was all that mattered; life, beneath the beneficent Mediterranean sun, was idyllic.

"Why did you buy all this food, maman?" Maurice asked querulously. "You know very well they won't let you invade the kitchen."

George's eyes danced merrily. "It so happens, my boy, that I have at last managed to find a villa." As she spoke, she was looking at Frédéric rather than at her son. "You'll like that, won't you?"

"A villa!" Frédéric exclaimed, thinking of the simple delights of a purely domestic existence. "That will be heavenly."

They moved that very afternoon, George hiring a donkey-cart to transport their baggage. The villa lay at the foot of a hill with the emerald-colored mountains rising above it. It was an old building, a mixture of Spanish and Arab design, partly covered in creepers. The owner, a Señor Gomez, on hand to receive them, explained that the name of the villa, *Son Vent*, was Catalan for "House of the Wind."

"Does that mean we are likely to be blown off our feet?" Chopin asked gaily.

Señor Gomez, a man with many rings on his fingers, shrugged evasively. "One must be prepared for a little wind at certain times of the year."

Once George had bought some additional furniture from the suspicious, hard-bargaining Majorcan dealers, they were able to settle down in reasonable comfort. The surprising fact that the windows were innocent of glass scarcely worried them. Many houses in Palma had been constructed in the same manner. It was an indication, they thought, that the mild weather would continue and that no serious winds would blow. George started work immediately and prayed, since Chopin was showing signs of growing fretful, that the piano would come soon.

They were sitting on the little terrace one night watching the bobbing lanterns of fishing boats out at sea when heavy drops of rain began to fall. They went indoors hurriedly, unaware that they had reached Palma just before the wet season normally set in. During the night the rain became torrential and a strong, cold wind arose, moaning in the trees and lashing the villa. There were no fireplaces, only braziers. After several days, the smoke made Chopin choke painfully. At first he tried to hide his discomfort, but soon it was evident that his cough had returned worse than ever.

"Merely a touch of catarrh," he told George. "It will disappear when the rain clears and the sun shines again."

Trying to deceive himself, he had fallen into the habit even while in Paris of referring to his cough as "catarrh." George, however, was not deceived and sent at once for a doctor. He was noncommittal. Going away solemn-faced, he returned with two other doctors. They were, George discovered, the only three doctors in Palma and, such being the superstition of the Majorcans, their power was limitless. The doctors spoke only a little French, she spoke even less Spanish, but somehow they made their wishes known to her so that she could pass on their commands to Frédéric who spoke no Spanish at all.

"They want you to spit into a handkerchief, Chopin."

He obeyed ungraciously, then scowled as the doctors one by one examined his sputum.

"They want to examine your chest, too. You must cough while they do so."

Chopin bared his chest and coughed repeatedly while, turn by turn, the doctors tapped and listened.

"Consumption," the first doctor declared.

"Catarrh," George insisted.

"Consumption," he repeated. "And consumption is a contagious disease."

He took George aside. He was aware, he said, that Señor Chopin was not her husband, but he had been given to understand that he was certainly that in all but name. Sternly he warned her against sleeping with Frédéric for both their sakes. She thanked him icily. They had not slept together in any case since leaving Paris. Though he had wanted to frantically at times, Chopin had ruled against it because of Maurice and Solange.

"He must be bled and blistered," the same doctor concluded.

"Barbaric and useless," George said, escorting the three men of medicine from the premises.

Frédéric, joining her at the door, spoke sadly. "I knew it all along, George. It is a family failing. My sister Emilia died of it."

"I have no intention of letting you die of it, Chopin."

Then she glanced back at the room in despair. The plaster

was peeling off the thin walls; dampness oozed from floor and ceiling; the smoke of the braziers swirled in the chilly air blowing in through the open windows. A warmer climate indeed! If only somebody had warned her what to expect. She had only succeeded in making poor Frédéric worse.

"Shall I take you back to Paris, Chopin?"

"It's a long journey to make in my present condition," he said doubtfully.

George, putting him to bed, nursed her patient for a week. The weather improved and so did the invalid's health. He was able at last to get up and take short walks in the fitful sunshine. Soon, however, people backed away from them in the streets. Fists were shaken angrily; curses were hurled after them.

"Am I a leper?" Chopin asked pitifully.

"They are ignorant and superstitious. Take no notice of them."

Then one day Señor Gomez came to the villa and, refusing to enter, addressed George loudly and indignantly from the garden. So excited did he grow that his tolerably good French all but deserted him and it was some time before she fully grasped the demands he was making of her. She must vacate the villa at the earliest possible moment and take the "consumptive gentleman" with her. Moreover, she must burn Chopin's bed, have the inside walls replastered and replace the bed linen—all at her own expense.

"What is he raging about?" Chopin asked.

"I haven't the faintest idea." George turned the question aside. "But obviously we are no longer welcome here."

"Because of me," he said sadly.

"Nonsense! The Majorcans are angry with us because we have never been seen going to church."

"I should like to go to church myself," Frédéric ventured.

"To worship the God of hate and fear?"

"To me, George, God is love."

"To me, also."

She wondered if he were reproaching her because, in the sense of going to church, she was no longer a practicing Christian. It was a subject, she thought, that must not be discussed unless he initiated a discussion himself. Chopin, with his simple, unquestioning faith in orthodox religion, would have difficulty in understanding her attitude.

Later in the day she went for a long and solitary walk in order to think things out. Dare she risk endangering Chopin's health by taking him back to Paris? He was almost well enough to travel, but the long journey by sea and road would tire him. Worse than that, it was now mid-winter in Paris. She decided that they must remain for the time being in Majorca and make the best of things. But where could they live? Who in Palma would rent them even one room?

Coming upon the Customs House, she made yet another inquiry about Chopin's piano. It had arrived at last. When she examined the large packing case, she became hopelessly involved in an argument with a customs officer. One thing seemed abundantly clear: the authorities, swayed by Chopin's illness and as eager as Gomez to drive him away, were unwilling to release the piano. She suspected that a little money, distributed discreetly here and there, might help; yet where could she have the piano sent?

In desperation she called on the French consul. He received her charmingly, expressing a genuine concern for her predicament. He had read some of her novels and once, while in Paris, had heard Frédéric Chopin play at a concert.

"Madame, I am anxious to help." Then he smiled. "Would it amuse you to live in a monastery?"

"A monastery, monsieur?"

The consul gave George a brief account of the Charterhouse of Valdemosa. The village of Valdemosa, three leagues from Palma, was situated high in the mountains where the air was

286

healthier and a little cooler. The Charterhouse was no longer used as a monastery and, since nobody had wanted to buy it as a private residence, the cells were rented to tourists during the summer months. If she wished, Madame Sand could rent for a very nominal sum a group of cells recently vacated by a political refugee. She would, however, be expected to buy the furniture. The actual rent? The lease of the cells would cost her less for a whole year than the villa had for a month.

"You may not want to make up your mind immediately," the consul said. "Meanwhile, I suggest that you and your party seek temporary refuge here at the consulate."

George, thanking him warmly, hired a carriage and took Frédéric and the children to inspect the monastery. They traveled over narrow, deeply rutted roads winding through acre upon acre of asphodel lilies. Chopin recognized the lilies immediately and, admitting their beauty, said gloomily, "They are known as the flowers of the dead." Nevertheless, he grew more cheerful as the road extended up into the mountains. It was a warm sunny day, the air exhilarating, and the scenery magnificent. Looking back they caught a glimpse of the sea; the view became breathtaking when at last they rattled through the village of Valdemosa and reached the monastery.

The Charterhouse of Valdemosa was an ancient building covered in creepers. There were three cloisters enclosed by a gallery along which the meditating monks had once walked in slow procession. Now only a sacristan remained. He and an apothecary and an eccentric-looking woman who introduced herself as Maria-Antonina shared the solitude. It was Maria-Antonina who showed the visitors the cells vacated by the political refugee. They were large vaulted rooms with stout and apparently draft-free oaken doors. In the days of the monks, they had served as bedroom, chapel, and refectory. Now they were furnished adequately enough for George and her family. Most important of all, the windows were glazed. George went to one of them. The garden below was filled with pomegranate and orange trees. The distant sea was a deep blue, the sky more mauve than pink. Was Chopin going to like it?

"Heavenly!" he said, joining her. "Here I shall live and dream and compose my music."

George sighed in relief. "And here I shall write as I have never written before."

"Is the monastery haunted?" Maurice wanted to know. "Does a ghost walk when the moon is full?"

"We have only a witch," Maria-Antonina said, her eyes gleaming wickedly. "She is Catalina, one of the two village girls who work for me. Are you afraid of witches?"

"No," said George, answering for her son. "We are not even afraid of ghosts."

Maria-Antonina looked disappointed. "It has been my habit to drive away unwelcome people by mentioning the witch."

"You disapprove of us?" George challenged.

Maria-Antonina pursed her lips. She studied George, Frédéric, and the children at length. George's male attire was scandalous and indicated wild immorality, but then it must have cost a lot of money. Frédéric's formal clothes impressed her deeply, especially his immaculate white waistcoat. Obviously these queer foreigners who had traveled all the way from Paris were immensely wealthy. She smiled, her eyes flashing greedily.

"You are more than welcome," she purred. "I shall do all in my power to look after you." Piously she crossed herself and added, "For the love of God."

George turned to Chopin. "Do you think you can be truly happy here?"

"Truly happy? Without my piano?"

George, having delayed the news for such a moment, told him that the piano had arrived. "I shall have it brought to Valdemosa as soon as the authorities release it."

They returned to Palma. Then, after spending a few days at the French consulate, they started off again for the monastery. The sun was shining; the view from the windows seemed more magnificent than ever. The wind and the rain were little more than a nightmare now only vaguely remembered. Majorca was even better than they had first expected it to be.

II

Maurice, a promising young artist at sixteen, was putting the finishing touches to his sketch of Frédéric. It was late evening. There had been heavy falls of snow during the last few days. The silence, both indoors and out, was deathly. George and Solange, taking a little storm lantern with them, had gone for a walk, leaving Frédéric and Maurice alone together in Frédéric's room. The pianist was seated at the piano but he had long since ceased to play. As far as the sharp-eyed Maurice could see, he was in something of a trance. Was he going to have another of his morbid fits? It would be amusing, Maurice thought, if that happened.

After two months at Valdemosa Chopin was ill again, but to Maurice, his condition seemed more mental than physical. Had Catalina, the alleged witch, cast a secret spell upon him? Whatever the cause, Frédéric had become a prey to violent flights of fancy. From time to time he saw visions, just as if the monastery really were haunted; at such times he would draw back from these specters in terror. Maman blamed this on his failing health, but Maurice did not agree.

Chopin turned away from the piano. "Your mother and Solange have been away far too long. Could they be lost in the snow?"

"More than likely," Maurice said cheerfully, hoping to pre-cipitate the anticipated fit. "Would you like to see my sketch?" He placed his sketching pad on the music rack. "A striking resemblance, don't you think?"

Chopin stared at it blankly. "Who is it?"

"You, my dear Fritz."

"Fritz" was the name Maurice and Solange used when addressing Chopin. There would often be an ill-disguised sneer in Maurice's voice, while Solange, a flirtatious eleven, displayed every sign of coquetry, as if she were competing with her mother.

"I can't recognize myself," Frédéric said vaguely.

The sketch was a caricature rather than a genuine likeness. Every stroke revealed Maurice's growing jealousy and resentment. He had come to regard Frédéric as an intruder, a fact that he was careful to hide from his mother. There were times, too, when he even resented Solange. Nobody, he vowed, must be allowed to come between him and Maman. The way she pampered Fritz was sickening. There had been other men, but Maurice had seen little of them, and in any case they had soon disappeared. This was different. This association seemed horribly permanent. Yet one thing seemed odd. In spite of all the watching and listening he did, he had discovered nothing to indicate that Fritz and Maman were sleeping together.

"Did you see the eagles today?" Chopin asked.

"I saw the big one, Fritz."

"Ah yes, yes! The Angel of Death!"

"That's what I call him, too," Maurice said quickly.

"Swooping, always swooping, Maurice."

With that, Chopin began to play again. Maurice was right, he thought. George and Solange were lost in the snow. Worse, they were already dead. A shiver ran down his back, a wave of depression rose in his chest. Frantically now he poured all he felt and suffered into the music. He was dead himself. Fleeing from the big eagle, the Angel of Death, he had drowned in an icy lake. Now his ghost was seeking to join the ghosts of George and Solange out there in the snow. Soon, with tears streaming down their cheeks, the three of them would come to gaze in silence at poor Maurice.

"Maman!" Maurice cried suddenly.

Frédéric merely glanced at the door. George and Solange had come back much sooner than he had expected, leaving his ghostly self behind in the snow with only the eagles for company. He was lost and would never find his way to them. Wildly he went on playing until finally, out of sheer exhaustion, he turned on the stool, his face hidden in his hands.

Taking off her cloak, George shook it. She and Solange had been caught in the heavy rain that had come after the snow.

"Play the last few bars again, Chopin," she said, smiling to hide her anxiety over her dejected "child."

The young composer looked up. "I knew you were dead. I am dead myself. My body is floating in the lake. Great drops of water are falling on my breast. Listen!" He attacked the keys more wildly than ever. "The raindrops!"

"They really are falling on the roof," George laughed. "You heard them and the sound crept into your music. It's the most wonderful prelude you have ever composed. Such a splendid example of imitative harmony."

Chopin sprang up instantly. "Imitative harmony! I never imitate! Everything I play comes to me from within. Everything!"

George sighed in relief. Unwittingly, by making him angry, she had restored his balance. He was, thank heaven, himself again though still wild-eyed and trembling. He had of late become something of a recluse. That, she thought, was the greater part of his present trouble. The villagers of Valdemosa, like the people of Palma, had ostracized him because of his illness. Once they had even come in a body to the monastery, chanting that the "consumptive" was bound for Hell. As a result, Frédéric rarely ventured out-of-doors. He spent his time either working frantically or lying listless on his bed.

"The silence is shattering," he said when the children had gone to bed. "Silence indeed! It beats on my ears constantly like the insistent beating of a drum."

"It affects me like that, too," George said, taking note of the fact that he could no longer hear the heavy raindrops on the roof. "Is this visit to Majorca a failure, Chopin?"

"If you say so, George."

An impasse, George thought, with neither of them willing to admit the truth. But failure, utter and complete? No, it was wrong to think that. She had done some quite promising work in spite of all the other calls made upon her time. Maria-Antonina's two village girls, like Maria-Antonina herself, were sly thieves and useless domestically. So, while nursing the invalid, George did all the cooking and cleaning herself and also spent six hours a day giving the children lessons.

As for Chopin himself, he had written preludes and ballades, impromptus, polonaises and mazurkas, and more important still a sonata in B flat minor with which he was not yet satisfied. George was proud to think that she was in part responsible. But how much longer could he go on working, harassed as he was by increasing ill-health and the persecution of the Majorcans?

Glowing with love and understanding, she went to him and embraced him. "Chopin? Your need is great, Chopin."

Frédéric returned her kiss with passion. "So great I cannot give expression to it in mere words."

"As if words were necessary!"

George stayed with him long after the storm had spent itself, but waking suddenly, he drew away from her as if in horror.

"Chopin, what is it?"

"A dream, Aurore." His voice was low and stricken. "A dream so real it must have happened. I saw myself going to confession. I heard myself being told what I already knew— that I had committed an unpardonable sin. It must never happen again, not with the children living under the same roof."

"Chopin . . ."

"You are stronger than I. Be stern with me if I find myself weakening. Come, Aurore, promise!"

"Very well, I promise."

A few days later George learned that the road to Palma had been blocked by the bad weather. Mountain streams, turned into roaring torrents, had made it impassable. Stores could no longer be brought to the village and soon there was little to eat but pork and tough old hens slaughtered because they had stopped laying. The pork made Chopin sick and the roasted fowl choked him. Thereafter he existed on stale bread and the fruit George bought from the villagers at outrageous cost. Anxious and desperate, she prayed for an improvement in the weather. But at last she decided that they could no longer remain in Majorca.

She came upon the composer one afternoon at the piano. The music he was creating was magnificent, even awe-inspiring, but she shuddered at the melancholy chords.

"What is it, Chopin?"

"A march. The sonata has troubled me sorely. This march should improve it."

"It sounds funereal."

"Precisely—a funeral march."

George shuddered again. It was apt enough. Their life at Valdemosa was slowly becoming a funeral march.

"You shall finish it in France," she said. "The weather is clearing. In a day or so the road to Palma will be passable."

"Whatever you wish," Frédéric said, like a submissive child.

At the end of the week, with their personal belongings packed and the piano stowed away in its massive case, George tried unsuccessfully to arrange transportation to the coast. The villagers of Valdemosa, eager earlier to drive them away, now regarded their departure as an insult. Not even the burly men, paid an exorbitant fee to pack the piano, would give further help. Maria-Antonina, pretending visionary powers, declared that the foreigners would die at the monastery and be buried in unconsecrated ground. Still, after holding out her hand greedily for a few francs, she arranged for George to go to Palma as an "extra" in a farm cart crammed with squealing, acrid-smelling pigs.

There, through the good offices of the French consul, the author obtained the use of a broken-down two-wheel cart. Plainly the piano would have to be left at the monastery.

The final journey from Valdemosa to Palma was torment to Frédéric. He sat without complaint in the cart as it bounced and lurched perilously over roads more deeply rutted than ever. On arrival, however, he suffered an alarming hemorrhage, and in the course of the day he used and destroyed a dozen handkerchiefs.

Once again the friendly French consul came to their aid. He gave them shelter at the consulate while they waited for the master of the *El Mallorquin* to announce a sailing date. He also introduced George to a local banker to whom she sold the abandoned piano for a small sum. Then when the sailing date was announced, Frédéric was given a battered, uncomfortable birth for the crossing to Barcelona and told that it must be destroyed the moment he had finished with it. Fuming with anger and planning to write a scathing account of their stay in Majorca, George promised to pay for the replacement.

"In advance," the master of the vessel demanded.

There were no other passengers. The cargo consisted of a hundred or more pigs. The stench was nauseating and the continual squealing nerve-racking, for the seamen, thinking to prevent the swine from being seasick, whipped them unmercifully. The children endured the rough voyage remarkably well, but Frédéric was so weak from the loss of blood that he could not stand or walk.

Half-crazy with worry, George caught sight of a French warship lying in Barcelona harbor. She wrote hurriedly to the captain for help. Instantly Chopin was taken aboard and the naval surgeon, by sitting up with him all night, finally stopped the hemorrhage. Later, when he was well enough to be moved, the sick man was carried ashore to a hotel, and still later was put aboard a passenger vessel bound for Marseilles. The captain placed his own cabin at Chopin's disposal, but the ship's surgeon, who had managed to stave off another hemorrhage, warned George that her invalid was close to death.

At Marseilles George found accommodation at the Hôtel de Beauvau. There Frédéric brightened considerably. Delighted to be on French soil again, he showed marked improvement. Dr. Cauvières, whom George had known during his student days in Paris, took over the case here and pooh-poohed the suggestion that he was close to death. But he warned George against trying to go north to Paris until the spring.

After a piano was hired, Chopin began to work seriously. George did too, now that his health was improving daily. Finally, near the end of May, the little party traveled first to Arles and from there, in George's own coach that she had sent for, to Nohant. Paris, for the time being, could wait.

22

Followed by george and her daughter, Frédéric walked slowly up the thickly carpeted stairway to the Salle Pleyel. It was February 21, 1842, the day before the composer's thirty-second birthday, and he was about to give another concert, only his second in Paris itself in several years. The Salle Pleyel was already crammed with the most fashionable audience imaginable. Such wild applause greeted Chopin the moment he was recognized that he and George and Solange had difficulty in making their way to the platform where chairs had been placed for the favored few.

"I do hope Fritz is well enough to give this concert," Solange whispered as she seated herself on her mother's left.

George looked anxiously at Frédéric now standing at the open grand piano and bowing gracefully. The strain of the last concert he had given a year ago had exhausted him so terribly that she had urged him, fruitlessly, not to give another. What did concerts matter when his fame was unshakably established? Chopin, the composer, was more important to the world than Chopin, the pianist, even when playing his own works. The state of his always precarious health was George's constant concern. Fortunately he had suffered no breakdown as serious as the one marking their departure from Majorca three years ago.

"He really does look like a prince, doesn't he!" Solange murmured, her manner as possessive as ever where Fritz was concerned.

George agreed and patted her daughter's hand indulgently. Chopin was dressed in gray, the frock coat a darker shade than the trousers. The waistcoat, scarcely visible, was of black velvet. The spotless white cravat added a touch of femininity not unpleasing to George. She smiled as she recalled his instructions to the tailor. The trousers were to be plain and simple, certainly not striped, and the waistcoat devoid of any pattern. Stripes and patterns were much too showy. He had aimed at neatness and elegance and had indeed achieved both. The smallness of the tailor's account had delighted him. George, unknown to him, had made a separate payment.

Silence fell over the crowded hall now as Chopin seated himself at the piano. First he played a new ballade, then three new mazurkas. George's anxiety grew apace as she watched and listened. A touch of feverish color tinged his hollow cheeks and a fine coating of sweat was spreading across his brow. Much to her relief he was given a brief respite while Madame Pauline Viardot sang. Then after playing three études and a prelude, he was allowed to rest again while Franchomme, the cellist, performed. But the audience wanted only Chopin and he was forced to play an impromptu and four nocturnes.

When at last it was seen that he literally could play no more that night, members of the audience flocked about him on the platform, congratulating him and begging him to give another concert soon. Franz Liszt was among them; he slowly edged his way to Chopin's side. A coolness caused by Marie d'Agoult's mischief-making had sprung up between the two pianists, but Liszt, thinking only of music now, was as unstinting as ever in his praise.

Frédéric was glancing vaguely from George to Liszt. He had heard scarcely a word. His head was spinning and there was an insistent stabbing pain in his chest.

George drew Liszt aside. "You see how exhausted he is? Help him to the carriage. I doubt if he could walk down the stairs unaided."

Chopin was still breathing painfully when he reached the Rue Pigalle with George and Solange. Since returning from Majorca, he and George had formed the habit of spending their summers at Nohant and their winters in Paris. At the beginning of the first winter, George had rented two small houses here in the Rue Pigalle for herself and the children, while Chopin had rented an apartment nearby. Later, in order to be closer to George, he had moved into one of the two houses; he occupied the ground floor and Maurice, the upper story. Thus, though on the surface only, the proprieties were scrupulously maintained. Nobody was deceived. Their friends, especially George's, were apt to laugh at "Mademoiselle Chopin" behind his back.

"Shall I make some coffee?" Solange asked now, when Chopin had been helped to a chair.

"No, I'll make it myself," George decided. "Off you go to bed. It's school again tomorrow, remember."

"School! How I hate it!" Solange exclaimed dramatically, and left the room with dragging steps.

Chopin drank only a little coffee and touched no food.

"No lessons tomorrow," George warned.

"I must keep faith with my pupils," Frédéric protested weakly.

It annoyed George that he should be so determined to give piano lessons while he was in Paris. He wanted, he had said, to be self-supporting, so lessons were as necessary as ever. When she tried to argue with him now, he affected not to hear. Then, as presently he succumbed to a violent fit of coughing, George stole a quick look at his handkerchief. Not a single speck of blood, thank heaven! Nevertheless, he had grown so exhausted that she had to help him undress. Later, when he was calmer, she rearranged the pillows, kissed him on the brow and bade him goodnight.

"I'm worried about Solange," he said, detaining her.

"Worried?"

"Is she receiving proper religious instruction at Madame Bascans' boarding school? From something she said this morning I gathered that Solange neither goes to confession nor takes any part in the services."

"True," admitted George, wondering how best to avoid a religious argument.

"By her own choice or yours?"

"Mine," George conceded. "Madame Bascans, a liberal-minded woman, agrees with me that religious ceremonies excite Solange unduly."

"But George, you must not bring her up as a pagan!"

"I am not bringing her up as a pagan and you know it," she said quietly. "As a matter of fact, I think I have succeeded in arousing her enthusiasm for the mission and teachings of Jesus. I want it to grow and expand into a full understanding of Christ's philosophy of equality. Above all else, I want to make her feel, as I feel, the poetical beauty of the Divine Man's life and death. The ceremonial tends to overshadow true Christianity, especially in a girl of Solange's dramatic imagination."

Chopin looked puzzled and confused. "But what of religious discipline? My mother taught me that it was the basis of all discipline."

"It seems odd for you to talk about disciplining Solange when you spoil her so!"

Chopin smiled sheepishly. "I love her dearly. I want her to find happiness."

"Happiness," George pondered. "Can you define it, Chopin?"

He became instantly fretful. "Can you?"

George shook her head. "I try again and again, but I always fail." She kissed him on the brow again. "Sleep well, chéri."

"You're not going to stay with me?" Chopin said, struggling to sit up.

"You know what would happen if I did."

He looked up at her pleadingly. "It's an excellent opportunity, Aurore."

"So it's 'Aurore' now—not 'George.' "

Chopin laughed. "George? I've never heard of such a person."

"What do you mean by an 'excellent opportunity'?"

Carefully he avoided her eyes. "Maurice is away visiting his father at Guillery. Solange has gone to bed next door. We have this little house entirely to ourselves."

She resisted the temptation to call him a hypocrite.

"I'm much better now," he insisted, a dark look in his eyes. "I'm beginning to feel stronger."

"That's what you said the last time, Chopinski," George laughed, using her special pet name for him. "Then you fainted in my arms—remember?"

"I do not remember," he said obstinately.

"You alarmed me terribly," she said, and added lightly, "Do you want to kill yourself? I, dear Chopinski, will not be a party to your untimely death."

"As you wish, George."

"Ah, now it's 'George' again!"

Chopin pouted. "You make me feel like a child in the nursery!"

George smiled tolerantly and decided on a new line of attack, half-convincing herself that she was the first woman in the world to tell such a lie. "Has it not occurred to you that I am just as modest as you are in spite of what many people say of me?"

Frédéric looked vastly puzzled. "You mean . . . ?"

"Must I labor the point? It isn't possible, strong as you may feel, willing as I may feel, at this time of the month."

Understanding dawned upon him and he blushed richly.

"I'm so sorry," he mumbled, and sounding as if he believed that the greatest tragedy in the world had overtaken both of them.

"But apart from that," George went on earnestly, "you have raised me to such unbelievable heights with your music that I have come to feel that emotion without passion is a heavenly ecstasy seldom granted to a poor mortal like me."

"Emotion without passion," Frédéric repeated. "How deeply ashamed you make me feel of myself, dear Aurore."

"All the same, there must still be passion in your music. You gave the most magnificent performance of your life tonight, but what about your future work? All I hear these days is the depressing tinkling of your pupils."

"Some of them do a little better than that," he said huffily.

"Even so, Chopin . . ."

"Yes, yes," he admitted gloomily, "I am no longer capable of teaching and composing at the same time."

A little wheedling, George thought, was necessary now. "Paris for teaching, Nohant for real work. Which is the more important?"

Frédéric stirred uneasily in his bed. Thinking about it, he was surprised to discover that only at Nohant had he been able to set down on paper the music that racked his soul and demanded expression. He laughed almost gaily.

"At Nohant, I have only one pupil and never yet—inept as she is—have I been compelled to reduce dear Solange to tears."

George was well satisfied. "I think we should return to Nohant a little earlier than usual this year. What do you say to that, Chopinski?"

This suggestion excited him immensely. "Tomorrow if you

wish. I am always calm and serene when we are together at Nohant."

And so, toward the end of the week, with Solange at her boarding school and Maurice still at Guillery, George and Frédéric started off on yet another journey to Nohant.

23

"MAURICE AND HIS drum!" Solange exclaimed. "How can I possibly concentrate on a lesson with that infernal noise to disturb us? One would think he was a schoolboy, not a grown man of twenty-three!"

Chopin smiled sympathetically; he himself had not yet found the noise disturbing. Maurice, who had recently completed his military service at the Pépinière Barracks in Paris, had come home to Nohant with a drum. He was practicing on it now in the garden. Chopin listened intently. The rhythm had a strange, insistent appeal. Maurice was producing music not normally associated with a drum.

"I'm growing bored with Nohant," Solange said. "What about you, Fritz?"

"The tranquillity is much to my taste, chérie."

"But not to mine, Fritz! What does a girl of eighteen want with tranquillity? It's such a dreary round, this family life of ours: Paris in the winter, Nohant in the summer. Years of it in the past, and years and years more of it stretching into the future. Nothing exciting ever happens."

"You will soon have a family life of your own," Chopin reminded her.

A scowl crossed the girl's pretty, rather boyish face. "I sometimes find Fernand just a little dreary, too."

Chopin was mildly shocked. Fernand de Préaulx was Solange's fiancé, a quietly spoken, well-mannered young man of whom he very much approved. George herself had not favored the match in the first place, but Chopin, siding with Solange as he almost always did, had won her over and gained her consent. Fernand came from a well-to-do middle-class family. In time he would inherit a considerable fortune and he was also a devout Catholic. Suitable, Chopin thought, eminently suitable!

"I think you deceive yourself about the tranquillity," Solange remarked, her fine, dark eyes almost as penetrating as her mother's. "Often when you are in Paris you yearn for Nohant, and often enough here at Nohant you yearn for Paris."

"Have I ever said so, chérie?"

"No," Solange admitted, "but I know you better than you know yourself."

Chopin smiled uneasily. What she said was true enough, but he never yearned either for Paris or for Nohant when he was working really well. All else was forgotten then—even George's friends, many of whom he found uncongenial. Her Paris friends were much too clever, much too politically unstable, and much too irreligious, while her country friends, excessively hearty, were just a little coarse. Nevertheless, he had tried to be tolerant and had never complained. To complain, he told himself, would be ungrateful since the seven years he had spent with George had been the most musically productive of his life.

"How many times have you been in love, Fritz?" Solange asked, growing tired of the piano lesson and springing up from the stool.

"Only once."

"Maman?"

304

"My love for your mother is the same as yours, Solange."

Solange doubted this, but so far as she was aware, her mother and Fritz had never slept together.

"Fritz, who was the girl?"

Chopin laughed gaily. "Bless my soul, I can't remember."

"Then you're as fickle as I am! You do think I'm fickle, don't you?"

Solemnly Chopin began to count on his fingers. "Now let me see—how many broken love affairs? For that matter—how many broken engagements?"

Solange heaved a tragic sigh. "Not love affairs, Fritz, only affairs of the heart. There is a difference, you know."

"True," her companion agreed and, to Solange's delight, he blushed slightly.

"And the two engagements—they weren't even affairs of the heart. Louis Blanc, for instance. Why, he's nearly forty. One of Maman's special pets, of course, and a socialist, mark you, a socialist! What a tremendous quarrel that caused! Remember? But I did get my way in the end."

Chopin did remember. Solange, taking a shrewdly calculated risk, had said that she would only marry Louis Blanc if her mother gave all her money to the poor. That had been too much for George, sincere as she was in her concern for the working classes and ready always to write in support of their cause. Of what use would she be to them, she had retorted, if she beggared herself?

"And what of Victor de Laparde?" Chopin asked.

"Poets may be romantic but in my experience they are very self-centered."

"Such a vast experience!"

"Wretch!" Solange shrieked. "In any case, Victor's parents were horrified at the thought of their dear, pretty son marrying the daughter of the infamous George Sand."

"I don't think you should speak of your mother like that,"

Chopin protested mildly.

"But she is infamous, Fritz."

"Merely outspoken.

"Politics bore me," Solange went on, "except that I loathe socialism. Is Maman really a socialist, Fritz?"

Chopin considered this gloomily but brightened when he recalled how George had once complained that socialism overlooked the importance of the individual, striving as it did to impose the happiness of all mankind on each human being. "Your mother is a republican rather than a socialist," he said finally.

"Well, that's bad enough. I'm sure you don't approve since you are such an ardent royalist."

Chopin grew gloomy again. "It is not my place to approve or disapprove."

"Well, never mind. We were talking about me, not Maman. Fickle as I am, I have always been constant to one man."

"And who is he?" Chopin asked innocently.

"You, dear Fritz!"

Chopin chuckled and pinched Solange's cheek. She sighed, though not very despairingly. Fritz as a lover had no appeal to her, but Fritz, her mother's "dear child," was another matter. Solange had always thought that she had a greater right to him. It would be amusing to take him from her mother some day— platonically, of course. But up to now there had been no real reason for wanting to do so.

"That drum!" she burst out. "Maurice is becoming quite fanatical."

Listening intently again, Chopin seated himself on the stool vacated by Solange. The rhythm, getting the better of him, was driving all else from his mind. He played a few tentative bars, began again and tried urgently as he battled against the drumbeat to hear nothing but the music he was creating. It was necessary to drive out the sound of Maurice's drum, otherwise he would fall foul of the inclination to accuse himself of imitative harmony. He was still playing, oblivious of all else, when George came into the *salon* with her young cousin, Augustine Brault. Maurice, joining them presently and holding Augustine by the hand, stood listening with the others until Chopin, partially satisfied with his new work, turned from the piano with a look of quiet triumph in his eyes.

"A mazurka in A minor!"

"Inspired by my skill on the drum," Maurice declared, his eyes bright with resentment.

"We-ell—yes," Chopin admitted.

" 'Imitative harmony,' " Maurice taunted softly.

The older man smiled in spite of himself. "If you wish, Maurice. Certainly I would not have composed this new mazurka except for your drum-playing just now."

Somewhat mollified, Maurice bowed deeply, leaving George, who had long ago sensed her son's hostility, to breathe more freely. It was fortunate, she thought, that Chopin, lost so often in his dream world of music, had never noticed Maurice's attitude.

"Can you actually remember all you have just played, Monsieur Chopin, and later set it down on paper?" Augustine asked with a simper.

"Not exactly, but I shall keep on working at it until it is right."

"Incredible!" Augustine was making eyes shamelessly. "Are you in better health today, monsieur?"

Chopin shrugged. "I am always in better health when I'm working."

Momentarily displeased with Augustine's coquetry, Maurice glanced at his sister. "Augustine and I are planning a picnic for tomorrow. Would you care to join us?"

"And spoil your fun?" Solange flashed back.

She resented Augustine even more than her brother resented

Chopin. It had always seemed to her ridiculous for her mother to adopt this cousin who, until recently, had been little more than a stranger. It was all very well to be stirred by family feeling and responsibility, but to bring this common creature to Nohant and treat her as a second daughter was inexcusable and cruel. Augustine belonged to the past, the shameful past of Grandmother Dupin. She should have been left in her Paris slum, not "rescued" from her supposedly neglectful parents. Solange had argued with Maurice about it, but he, fascinated by Augustine's common prettiness and bold flirtatiousness, had told her to mind her own business.

"Why not invite Fernand to the picnic?" Chopin suggested.

"If I do that, we shall suffer a very dull outing," Solange complained.

"Really, Solange, I don't know what to make of you," George exclaimed.

"It is not unusual," Chopin said, "for a girl to grow a little apprehensive before settling down to married life."

Solange tossed her head. "What a frightening prospect—settling down to married life with the unexciting Fernand! I want to move about in Paris society; I want to travel abroad. But Fernand! He was born and bred in the district. His only ambition is to vegetate for the rest of his life."

"You were very eager to become engaged to him," George pointed out. "And remember that I was against it."

"But not Fritz," Maurice said pointedly. "He brought about the engagement."

"True," Chopin admitted rather smugly. "I have always wanted for Solange what Solange has wanted for herself."

"As things seem to be turning out," Maurice snapped, "it would have been better if you had not interfered in a purely family matter."

Chopin looked hurt. "I am not a member of the family?"

"At all events, you are not the master of the house!"

Chopin, more hurt than ever, turned without a word and walked quickly from the room, his shoulders quivering slightly.

"That was cruel of you, Maurice," George said quietly.

"I find his interference insufferable, Maman."

"I think you should apologize."

"Never!"

In that moment George saw her quiet, contented little world falling in ruins about her. She had not realized that her son's hostility went so deep. Something must be done about it—and at once.

"I want to talk to you, Maurice. Come to the summerhouse. Nobody will disturb us there."

Maurice accompanied her sulkily, a little boy anticipating a spanking and not in the least relishing the prospect. George repressed a chuckle and glanced at him covertly as they walked through the garden. At twenty-three, he was slim and graceful, straight of back and soldierly in appearance, just as her dimly remembered father had been. When in a good mood he was full of fun, high-spirited, and very enthusiastic about whatever project he happened to have in mind. She realized then that he was almost always in a good mood, except when face to face with Frédéric Chopin. Was she biased, she wondered, simply because he was her son and mistaken in believing him to be the nicest person she was ever likely to meet?

"Your resentment of Chopinski distresses me," she said almost apologetically when they reached the summerhouse.

"I'm sorry about that, Maman, but I can't help myself."

"When did you first feel this way, Maurice?"

Maurice flung himself into a chair. "I first felt it really seriously at Majorca."

"Chopin was ill while we were there, Maurice, humbly grateful and never, as you put it, 'interfering.'"

"Ill, yes. And you nursed him and pampered him, while I was left to my own devices."

"I gave more time to you and Solange than to him."

Maurice laughed. "Lessons!"

"We discovered many things in common through those lessons, things that brought us close together."

"But not close enough, Maman. I can't bear it for anyone to be closer to you than I am."

George was appalled. Agitatedly she walked to the window and from the window to a mirror on the wall. Was it possible that, in her concern for Chopin, she had neglected her son? She stared intently at her reflection in the mirror. Obviously Maurice thought so, but was it true? Why, when she searched her heart as she was searching it now, her son meant more to her than anyone else in the world.

"Heavens," she exclaimed, "a gray hair!"

Maurice came up behind her. "Old age is creeping upon you, Maman."

"I'm only forty-two!"

Maurice's eyes in the mirror were impish. "Not a great deal older than me. Only nineteen short years. It's nice to have a young mother. Pluck out the gray hair and look even younger."

"I'm much too plump. Plumpness makes me look middle-aged."

"Take more exercise."

Maurice grasped his mother's shoulders and turned her from the mirror. Diligently he searched for the gray hair, found it and plucked it out.

"Now two more will spring up in its place, Maurice!"

"That's a fallacy, Maman."

They laughed about it, but presently George grew serious again. It seemed to her that a heartening strength was coming to her from her son, her grown-up son. Never before had she felt the need to gather strength from anyone. Yet now, at forty-two, with the first gray hair having made its appearance . . . Or perhaps it was her own strength, given to Maurice and returned by him to her. It was different with Chopin; none of the strength she gave him ever came back to her. Often enough daily association with him left her mentally exhausted.

"We are very close now, Maurice. Can't you feel it?"

"I can feel it," her son replied emotionally.

Her heart grew light at the thought that a deeper understanding had been reached. She must grasp at it, hold it firmly. The tie of blood was the greatest tie of all. She wanted both Maurice and Chopin; each needed her in his own way. But how much longer would the frail Chopin live? Chopin, the baby in swaddling clothes, the baby who would never grow up. . . . Come what may, even though her heart was more her son's now than her "baby's," she must remain with Chopin till the end.

"Are you feeling happier now, Maurice? Have we cleared the air with this little talk?"

Maurice nodded, but he was frowning slightly. "I want to make one thing clear. I never resented Fritz being your lover."

"If he ever was my lover, Maurice."

"Am I embarrassing you, Maman?"

"A little."

"How silly! This is a man-to-man talk. George Sand on the one hand, Maurice Dudevant on the other." He frowned again. "If he was never your lover, that makes the tie all the stronger. Love affairs come to an end and then—voilà!"

"It is quite some time since we—that is, since we were lovers."

Maurice looked at her quizzically. "Who imposed the abstinence—you or Fritz?"

"You must make up your own mind about that, my boy."

They walked back to the house hand in hand. Chopin was at the piano again. They paused for a moment listening as the music flowed out through an open window. He was working on the mazurka, altering, adding, and improving.

"I still think you should apologize, Maurice."

"I can't do that, Maman."

"Not even to please me?"

"Naturally I want to please you, but still . . ."

"Then praise the new mazurka."

Maurice nodded and smiled. "A fitting compromise. Flattery is always more pleasing to Fritz than apology."

And that, as George had long ago learned, was the truth.

Flattery, however, made no impression on Chopin now. He sat in brooding silence on the piano stool, glancing from mother to son while Maurice, tongue in cheek, spoke of the new mazurka in glowing terms. They were still hand-in-hand, like lovers who had just discovered each other, he thought, and would remain inseparable forever. There they stood, isolated from the world, isolated from him. The depression which had plagued him so sorely at Majorca got the better of him again and much more frighteningly. He saw himself alone and friendless on a barren mountain peak. Eagles were swooping about him, each a separate, menacing angel of Death.

Struggling for control, he caught Maurice's smiling eyes and held them for a moment. Maurice himself—was he the eagle that would strike first and carry him away? He sprang up wildly and ran to his room. No time must be lost if he was to preserve himself from the beaks and claws of the circling eagles!

George, following him, found him gathering together his few possessions.

"Chopin, what are you doing?"

"Packing. Nohant is destroying me. Only in Paris can I save myself."

"Chopinski . . ."

"You can't hold me here!"

"It isn't my intention to hold you anywhere."

"Thank you."

312

"Except in my heart."

"Your heart! Clearly you no longer love me!"

"I love you as I have always done—in a very special way."

"And now you love Maurice in a very special way."

"You're out of your mind," George said, her voice rising sharply. "Maurice is my son."

"Nevertheless, you must choose between him and me."

"You would actually force such a terrible decision upon me?"

"Yes, George, I would!"

"I refuse to make it."

With a sinking heart George helped Chopin pack, trying meanwhile to tell herself that once in Paris, and calmer, he would regret this outburst and cling to her more than ever.

The moment he was actually gone, George wrote a letter to their mutual friend, Madame Marliani, begging her to look after her "Chopinski." His bed must be properly aired before he slept in it; he must be provided with all the hot water he needed; and if his health had suffered during the journey from Nohant to Paris, a doctor must be summoned at once. After that, George tried unsuccessfully to work. Again and again she scribbled the biting words on the paper: "You must choose between him and me." If he failed to relent, how then would she choose? Heartbreaking as it was, she could find only one answer to that. Her son came first.

24

MADAME MARLIANI, wife of the Spanish consul in Paris and a fashionable hostess, was giving a dinner party at her house in the Rue Saint-Lazare. Some years ago Frédéric and George had moved from the Rue Pigalle to the Rue Saint-Lazare. When in Paris, they had occupied separate apartments on either side of Madame Marliani's house. Thus the old Spanish lady, who was fond of them both, had become, much to many people's amusement, an unofficial chaperon. Quite often she made a point of entertaining their friends, but on this occasion she was entertaining entirely on her own account, with Chopin the guest of honor.

George, having reached Paris that very afternoon with her family, had accepted a last-minute invitation. It was as good a way as any, she thought, of taking Chopin by surprise. A month had passed since his headlong flight from Nohant. He had failed to answer any of her letters, but he was, according to Madame Marliani, contrite and a little ashamed of himself. Only pride had prevented him from apologizing and seeking a reconciliation.

The *salon* was already crowded when George entered, followed by Maurice, Solange, and Augustine Brault. She caught sight of Chopin at once. Immaculately dressed as ever, he was standing a little apart from the rest, deep in discussion with Delacroix, the painter. He looked up as George approached and blushed faintly. She smiled and, inclining her head, she addressed herself solely to Delacroix.

"My son is eager to make a real study of art. Will you accept him as a pupil?"

"Gladly, my dear George."

"Then pray tell him so."

"Imperious as ever," Delacroix chuckled and went off to join Maurice who was arguing heatedly with a bearded young man.

"You followed me to Paris," Chopin said accusingly.

"On the contrary, I came for one purpose only—to buy Solange's trousseau."

Chopin bowed politely. "The engagement has not been broken?"

"No. I refused to permit it. You—approve of my attitude?"

He smiled faintly. "Am I the master of the house?"

George inclined her head again and turned from him. He seized her hand quickly, furtively.

"Aurore . . ."

"Yes?"

"I've missed you so much."

"I've missed you, too."

He laughed shakily. "Now we're friends again."

George's heart melted. "Have we ever been anything else?"

Chopin pressed her hand before releasing it. "I could leap for joy!"

"Save your energy until after dinner. Madame Marliani, as usual, will expect you to play for her guests."

"In other words—to sing for my supper."

"That's a novel way of putting it, Chopinski."

"Yes, isn't it! It amuses me. I rocked with laughter when Jane asked me if I must always sing for my supper."

"Jane?"

"My Scottish pupil. French, spoken with a Scottish accent, is delightful."

"And Jane herself?" George asked carefully.

"A most promising pupil. Rich, too. She insists on paying me outrageously."

Before more could be said, Solange approached with the bearded young man. Maurice hovered in the background, his eyes flashing angrily.

"Maman," Solange said excitedly, "you must meet Jean Clésinger. He's a sculptor. He's longing to do a bust of the notorious George Sand." Solange's eyes slanted coquettishly. "Of her daughter, also."

George eyed the sculptor warily. His beard reminded her most unhappily of Félicien Mallefille. It also reminded her even more unhappily of Alfred de Musset, for Alfred, whom she had met by chance a year ago—only to be snubbed, had grown a beard too. She took an instant dislike to Jean Clésinger, thinking his eyes too bold, too domineering, and grew angry beyond all reason with her daughter's coquetry.

"You'll sit for me, madame?" Clésinger said, his voice booming and commanding.

"Only if she is suitably chaperoned," Solange murmured, angering George afresh.

"Since I prefer my sitters to sit *au naturel*," Clésinger roared, "a chaperon is permissible."

Solange laughed in delight. "For the mother or for the daughter?"

"Could I concentrate on my work if the daughter were unchaperoned in that condition?" Clésinger demanded coarsely.

"This is scandalous!" Chopin muttered.

"Scandalous!" Maurice echoed, edging closer.

Despite her own anger, George felt a little upsurge of joy. Maurice and Chopin were seeing eye to eye for once and in a family matter!

Further conversation was prevented by Madame Marliani who at that moment summoned her guests to the long table in the elegant dining room. Conversation was general during the meal, but later, when coffee and liqueurs had been served, it turned inevitably to a discussion of George's new novel then appearing in serial form in the *Courrier français*.

"Surely you, my dear George, are your own heroine, Lucrezia?" Madame Marliani remarked.

"Scarcely," said George, hating as usual to talk about her work.

"It seems to me that Lucrezia's character is in part your own," Madame Marliani demurred. "Also certain of her experiences."

"It is being said," Delacroix laughed, "that George's life, installment by installment, is becoming an open book."

"My friends appear to know more about me than I do myself," George retorted dryly.

"And the hero, Prince Karol," Madame Marliani went on, "seems patterned on Frédéric. What do you think yourself, Chopin?"

Chopin laughed apologetically. "I haven't read any of the installments. I get so little time for reading, and I was never in any case much interested in novels."

George was beginning to feel alarmed. What, precisely, had she written about herself and Chopin? Naturally she drew on living people and personal experiences for her novels but only in the sense of inspiration. The stories, when written, bore little resemblance to actual fact—or so she told herself naively. Besides, at times she was given to working in a trance and rarely re-read what she had written before publication. Straining her memory, she failed to recall much about *Lucrezia Floriani*. She was already immersed in writing another book.

"There is no doubt in my mind," Maurice said lightly, "that Prince Karol and Frédéric Chopin are one and the same person.

Maman unwittingly has drawn a most skillful picture of Fritz."

"She has?" Chopin's eyes danced with pleasure. "I'm flattered, deeply flattered." He turned eagerly to George. "Why not let me have the original manuscript? It would be agony to wait for the installments to come out."

"Very well," George agreed reluctantly. "Maurice has the manuscript. He copied it for the press."

II

George was sitting for Jean Clésinger, but not *au naturel*. It was the final sitting and presently she would be allowed to view his work. Disliking him still, she had not wanted to sit for him, but she had been won over by Solange and by the sculptor himself. Clésinger had paid her extravagant compliments and sent her flowers every day for a week. She studied him carefully now as he worked, uneasily aware that while she found him repulsive, her daughter thought him vastly exciting. He was thirty-four, noisy, exuberant, always ready for a heated argument. But he was undoubtedly a talented sculptor. Formerly a cavalry officer, he had taken to sculpturing like his father before him, and recently, having exhibited a nude, had achieved considerable notoriety. It was a daring piece of work—a serpent was coiled around the legs—so daring that, for the sake of decency, Clésinger had been obliged much against his will to add a conventional fig-leaf.

Solange came into the room now carrying a bottle of wine and three glasses on a silver tray. All the sittings had taken place in George's *salon* where the light was better, or so Clésinger claimed, than in his own shabby studio. Nevertheless, he had made George promise not to inspect the unfinished bust, so it had stood here day after day, covered by a shawl.

"Maman is not going to be very pleased," Solange commented as she placed the tray on a table.

"Reality is unpleasing to most people," Clésinger chuckled.

"You were not supposed to look either, Solange," George complained. "Clésinger dislikes people peering over his shoulder."

"True," Clésinger agreed. "I shall insist on the door being locked against everybody when I work on your daughter's bust."

Solange clapped her hands. "What a delightful innuendo!"

George rose angrily. Solange, under Clésinger's influence, was growing as vulgar as Casimir, this even though Casimir was not her real father. Was the girl falling in love with the sculptor, or was it merely an adolescent infatuation? The sooner she was married to Fernand de Préaulx the better. The respective family lawyers were even now drawing up the contract, and the moment it was signed, George would hurry her daughter home to the comparative shelter of Nohant.

Clésinger stood back from the bust. "Perfection at last, madame!"

"So very modest of you, monsieur," George said dryly.

"Are you afraid to look, Maman?" Solange taunted.

"I am not afraid of man or beast," George asserted.

Solange clapped her hands again. "Such a lovely beast, isn't he!"

George ignored this sally and studied Clésinger's creation in silence. Perfection? No one could doubt it. There she was, an aging, tired woman, every line, every wrinkle accurately portrayed. She glanced at Delacroix's portrait on the wall. It had been painted many years ago. Had she ever looked as young as that?

"Well, Maman?" Solange demanded.

"I'm not yet a grandmother," George said acidly.

Clésinger bowed. "If Madame Sand is dissatisfied, payment will not be demanded."

"A bargain is a bargain, monsieur."

Clésinger bowed again. "A pity. I should dearly love to retain this bust and exhibit it."

"Exhibit it?" George was horrified.

"Perhaps in any case, madame . . . ?"

"Never!"

"Be reasonable, Maman," Solange expostulated. "People see you every day looking exactly as Jean has portrayed you."

"I quite agree."

George swung round. The speaker was Chopin. He had entered the room silently, carrying, George saw, the original manuscript of *Lucrezia Floriani*. He placed it now much too carefully on the stand holding Clésinger's study. Then he stood back, pale-cheeked and wild-eyed, and examined the bust with exaggerated concentration.

"Is Jean any more ruthless in his work," Solange challenged her mother, "than you are in yours?"

"In my opinion," Chopin said hotly, "he is much less so."

George took fire at once. "You know how to be ruthless yourself, Chopin. Your musical portraits, heaven help us, are often most unpleasant caricatures."

Chopin was silent. It was, George thought, a senseless argument. She saw the whole ludicrous situation as a scene in a melodrama. Her *salon* had become a stage. Who next would steal out of the wings to make yet another contribution to this tragic farce? As if in answer to this question, Maurice strolled into the room, stared at the bust in silence for a moment, then turned angrily on Clésinger.

"You have been needlessly cruel, monsieur!"

"Your mother has no reason to complain," Chopin said, carefully avoiding George's eyes. "She herself was needlessly cruel in *Lucrezia Floriani*."

"That, as the English say, is a matter of the cap fitting," Maurice retorted. "In this case, the cap does not fit. I gave Clésinger credit for being an artist. What art is there in this monstrosity? What sign is there of my mother's beautiful and generous soul?"

George smiled gratefully. Maurice was the only one who really understood her. She glanced in turn at Chopin, at Solange, and at Clésinger, recognizing resentment, defiance, and self-satisfaction in their eyes. But for Maurice, the world would be a lonely place. How many true friends did she possess? Not a single one except her son!

"No one doubts that Maman has a beautiful and generous soul," Solange murmured. "She is also fair and just. She believes in liberty and preaches the doctrine of individual freedom of choice, doesn't she?"

"What are you trying to say, Solange?" George asked, sensing a mocking tone in her daughter's voice.

Solange stepped quickly to Clésinger's side. "Shall I tell her, or will you, Jean?"

Clésinger grinned widely. "The prerogative is mine." He turned to George and bowed deeply. "Solange and I have fallen in love. We seek your permission, madame, to marry."

George laughed sardonically. "You choose a most appropriate moment to break this startling news."

"Tact was never one of my virtues, madame."

"Solange is already engaged," George said coldly.

"I could never marry Fernand," Solange said warmly. "I knew that even before I met Jean."

"I still have no intention of permitting you to marry Monsieur Clésinger."

"What about your belief in liberty and individual freedom of choice?" Chopin asked heavily.

George looked at him angrily. More than once he had expressed a dislike for Jean Clésinger. Now, by springing to Solange's support, he was perversely opposing a mother's authority.

"This is a family matter," Maurice said, carefully keeping

anger from his voice. "We have no thought of consulting Fritz. Nor has he the right to expect to be consulted." He smiled at Chopin. "Oh come, be reasonable, Fritz!"

Flushing, the older man turned on his heels and hurried from the room. George hesitated for a moment, then followed him. Nothing further was said until they were in his own apartment. Even then, faced with his sulky expression, George experienced some difficulty in speaking.

"Our friendship is too precious to be shattered by a family quarrel," she said at last. "Do you seriously believe that Solange would be happy married to Clésinger?"

"Who can say?"

George tried again. "Are you opposing me because of *Lucrezia Floriani?*"

Chopin fell into another of his brooding silences. He had been hurt and shocked by the novel because in his mind George had deliberately modeled Lucrezia upon herself, Prince Karol upon him, and the plot certainly followed the true story of their personal relations: Lucrezia, at the time of her meeting with Karol, was disillusioned and no longer seeking love; Karol, pale, slender, and melancholy, had no physical attraction for her. She grew fond of him in a tolerant, protective manner, but her attitude throughout the novel was more that of a mother than a mistress. At times his fits of bad temper irritated her, yet she bore them stoically, believing that God had appointed her both to save Prince Karol from his past follies and to nurse him when he was ill however ungrateful he might be. What pained her most was his failure to understand her and his contempt for her Bohemian way of life. He was jealous of her good health and accused her, when pettishly angry with her, of insensibility. In trying to make a god of him, she had sacrificed herself needlessly and stupidly. In the end, broken-hearted because of his harsh treatment, she died.

This hurt Chopin more deeply than anything else in the

book. In reality George was killing him, not he her. Worse still, the whole world was laughing at him behind his back. Once again he was almost as afraid to go out in public as he had been at Valdemosa.

"Chopinski . . ." George pleaded.

"What is done is done. There's no point in discussing it."

"*Lucrezia Floriani* is only a novel."

"Would you have written it if you hadn't met me?"

"No," George admitted.

"Then let us say no more."

George, recognizing defeat, changed the subject. "I'm taking Solange back to Nohant tomorrow. You'll join us as usual during the summer?"

"Of course." Chopin faced her briefly and held out his hand. "Meanwhile—*au revoir*."

III

George was trying to work at her desk in the summerhouse at Nohant, but never in her life had she found concentration so difficult. It had been like this every day during the last week, with the middle of the afternoon the most trying time of all. She was inclined to blame the doctor for changing her working hours. No longer was she capable, he claimed, of working all night. If she continued to do so, she would undermine her health and suffer a serious breakdown.

Setting aside now all thought of further work, she leafed through a pile of unanswered letters, one of which called more urgently for a reply than the rest. It was from Sainte-Beuve. The dear old fellow had written to congratulate her because the fame of her more serious work was spreading throughout the world. Sainte-Beuve quoted a number of reviews and comments as far afield as Russia and America. Dostoevski, after reading one of her social novels, had stayed awake all night, excited and inspired, while Turgenev had called her a saint in whom all egotism had been consumed in the inextinguishable fire of her faith in the Christian ideal. There was praise, too, from Walt Whitman, the American poet.

George took up her pen. "My dear Sainte-Beuve, I am less a saint now than I ever was, my egotism has not been destroyed, and there are times when I regard myself with repugnance . . ."

Her thoughts strayed to *Lucrezia Floriani* which she had reread after leaving Paris. The portrait of Prince Karol, she admitted now, resembled Chopin much more closely than she had believed or intended at the time of producing the novel. Should she write to Chopin and apologize? She decided against it. "What is done is done." Even a passing reference to the book would make him more touchy than ever and more than likely keep him away from Nohant this summer. Would he come in any case? She glanced at the calendar. In his last brief letter he had promised to leave Paris on the first of the month. It was now the seventh.

She rose from the desk and wandered aimlessly about the summerhouse. She missed Chopin, but she missed her son even more. Maurice had gone to stay with his father at Guillery. Her thoughts grew gloomy. She was ill and tired. Was she, like Lucrezia, really going to die? "It's only nerves, Maman," she could hear Maurice saying. "Physically you're as strong as a horse." She smiled grimly. Nerves! That, no doubt, was the truth of the matter. Or was it a case of ingrowing vanity as Marie d'Agoult would have claimed?

Knowing that she would do no more work that day, not even finish her letter to Sainte-Beuve, George wandered out to the garden. It was early afternoon. A light breeze made music in the branches of the old elm trees; the May sunshine was warm on her bare head. Nohant was as lovely as ever. If only she had the strength to forget the past, make no plans for the future, and just live for the present, accepting God's gift of this indestructible beauty!

Laughter floated out from Solange's open window as George approached the house. Solange and Clésinger! They were the present. It was better, she decided, to live in the past or grope searchingly in the unknown future than even to think of the present. Jean Clésinger had come to Nohant, storming and shouting and once again demanding Solange's hand in marriage. And George, without Maurice to support her, had weakly allowed him to stay for a few days. Now Solange was sitting for him, but always with George's maid in the room to keep an eye on them. "Even to you, madame, I am quite irresistible," Clésinger had boasted. George smiled wryly as she reflected that in her younger days she might well have found him as attractive as Solange did. But marriage for her daughter and Clésinger? No, that was out of the question.

The laughter, loud and arresting, floated out again, irritating George unreasonably. Why should they be happy when she herself was miserable? Clésinger must go. He had been here far too long. She would tell him so at once. She entered the house quickly and went up the stairs to the large, airy room converted into a private *salon* for her daughter. Quietly opening the door, she saw at once that her maid was no longer present. Then she saw Solange. The girl was seated near the window in an abandoned pose, naked to the waist!

"Dear Maman," she laughed the moment she caught sight of George, "we expected you to remain in the summerhouse for hours."

"You sent my maid away?"

"Can you blame us? She has a distressing habit of breathing loudly through her mouth. Jean found the noise distracting. Besides, she would have shrieked in horror at the sight of my nakedness."

"The most beautiful breasts I have ever seen," Clésinger said and went on calmly with his work. "Eventually, madame, you

325

will have the joy of seeing your daughter's neat little derrière in marble, too."

"You appear quite speechless, Maman," Solange chuckled.

Wordlessly, George seized a shawl and flung it about the girl's shoulders.

"Thank you," Solange said pertly. "My breasts are covered in goose pimples. I don't want to catch a cold before my honeymoon."

"We shall marry within two weeks," Clésinger went on, still chipping away at the marble, "whether or not you consider your daughter sufficiently compromised."

The uncertain tone of his voice made George laugh. The whole thing was a trick, a childish trick.

"You saw me in the garden," she said. "You laughed loudly in order to attract my attention. And then you prepared this shocking little scene especially for me."

Solange's face fell. "Why can't you confine your cleverness to writing novels, Maman?"

"My hand," said George, "has not been forced."

Solange's eyes hardened. "I want to talk to you alone, Maman. Please leave us, Jean."

"Well?" George asked, when Clésinger had lounged from the room.

"I shall ask my father's consent. He'll give it. I feel sure he will."

"Indeed he will not! Your father, in any case, has no say in the matter."

"I mean my real father."

Taken so suddenly by surprise, George felt unable to deal with this new attack. "What in the name of heaven are you talking about, Solange?"

"Stéphane de Grandsaigne is my father, not Casimir Dudevant. It's common knowledge in the district."

"Gossip—mere gossip!"

"No, the truth, Maman. Are you ashamed of it?"

"No, by heaven! Are you?"

"So it is the truth!"

"I expected to take the secret with me to the grave," George said sadly. "Why did you force it from me?"

Solange burst into tears. "I didn't force it from you. It was a slip of the tongue on your part. I wanted to know, yes, and at the same time I didn't want to know." She was sobbing violently now. "I—I want you to take the secret to the grave. I know I shall myself."

George flung her arms round the girl. "You really are ashamed?"

"Yes, Maman."

"You've been brooding over the gossip for a long time?"

"Yes."

"What a strange child you are. It never occurred to me that you were so conventional."

Solange freed herself. "Naturally it wouldn't."

"Conventional, yet your behavior just now . . ."

"I wouldn't have let Jean touch me!" Solange cried hotly. "I had to steel myself to take off my blouse. I'm sorry I did now. I have only succeeded in cheapening myself in Jean's eyes."

"I doubt that very much," George said dryly.

"You don't understand him, Maman. He respects me. I suggested that we elope, but he wouldn't hear of it."

"A most conventional suggestion, Solange."

"Oh, I wouldn't really have eloped with him!"

George shook her head in despair. "What am I to do with you, Solange?"

The girl smiled hopefully through her tears. "Give your consent. Allow me to follow my heart as you have always followed yours."

"My heart has often been my worst enemy."

"Mine never could be." A cunning look that George failed

327

to see flashed momentarily in Solange's eyes. "If you had your life to live all over again, Maman, would you refuse to follow your heart?"

"No."

Solange put on her blouse and straightened her hair. Then she embraced her mother and kissed her on the cheek. She had won—she knew she had.

"Shall we go to Jean and tell him that you have given your consent?"

George felt herself weakening. What peace would she have at Nohant if she continued to refuse? Clésinger would only linger on. There would be one violent scene after another. Then Maurice would return from Guillery and there would be even more violent scenes. "What of your belief in liberty and individual freedom of choice?" she could hear Chopin asking. That dictum, as he and others well knew, was precious to her.

"Come, then," she said and went with Solange.

Clésinger bowed and kissed George's hand. "Now we shall discuss Solange's dowry."

George laughed scornfully at the undisguised greed in his eyes. "My daughter shall have the Hôtel de Narbonne. It will provide a sufficient income for both of you."

Clésinger bowed again. "You are as generous as ever, madame."

George agreed to an early marriage. It would take place here at Nohant on the 20th of the month. She wrote to Maurice, but she hoped fervently that he would not return from Guillery in time for the ceremony. She also wrote to Chopin, urging him to be present, since he loved Solange and had always wanted for her what she wanted for herself. In his reply, a brief and courteous one, he mentioned certain inescapable commitments in Paris. Then, writing separately to Solange, he expressed the hope that she would be happy with Jean Clésinger for the rest of her life and added that he would be very pleased to see her when she came to Paris with her husband. George was hurt when Solange gave her this letter to read. The inference was clear enough. It would give him pleasure to see the daughter but not the mother. He was being more childish than ever, she thought. She decided to write and tell him so.

George, however, found she now had other things to occupy her mind and time. Maurice arrived before the 20th and actually brought his father with him. Much to her relief, the quarrels she had anticipated did not arise, but the hostile silence when the family dined together was almost more than she could bear. Casimir, whom she had never expected to see again, was surprisingly affable when alone with her. It was not unpleasing to hear him speak of Clésinger contemptuously and call him "that abominable stonecutter." Maurice still disapproved of the sculptor but said that he was no longer very greatly concerned.

"After all, I shall soon have you entirely to myself, Maman."

That was true enough, for Augustine Brault with whom Maurice had been mildly in love had recently married with George's full approval.

Solange insisted upon a religious as well as a civil ceremony. She was, she said, a good Catholic in spite of her mother's unorthodox beliefs. Casimir had smiled owlishly and departed immediately after the ceremony. The past was the past, he said, and he would always think of young Aurore with love in his heart.

Solange and her husband left the next morning for their honeymoon, but they returned within two weeks to gather together Solange's personal possessions. Entirely under Clésinger's influence now, the girl proved herself equally greedy and laid claim to many family heirlooms that in the course of time would belong to Maurice. A violent quarrel broke out over a pair of silver candlesticks. Maurice seized them from Clésinger; Clésinger tried to snatch them back. They wrestled together for several moments, with George striving to remain coldly detached. Finally Clésinger broke away, swept up a hammer from a packing case and struck out at Maurice with it. George flung herself between them and received a blow on the shoulder. Maurice flew from the room cursing and returned with a pistol. Once again George intervened and succeeded in taking the pistol from her son. Steadying herself, she addressed Clésinger as sternly as she could.

"You must leave Nohant at once, monsieur."

"My place is at my husband's side," Solange cried dramatically. "If Jean goes, so must I."

"The choice is yours."

"I never want to see you again, Maman!"

Solange and Clésinger departed during the night, taking with them the silver candlesticks and, in addition, a quantity of sheets, blankets, and counterpanes. Maurice was all for giving chase, but George succeeded in restraining him.

"We have peace at last, Maurice. Let us be content with that."

She was still anxious, however, about Chopin. She had lost Solange. Was it really possible that she had lost him too?

IV

Chopin was writing a letter to George when Solange, stealing softly into his apartment, took him completely by surprise. He smiled in delight, sprang up and embraced her warmly.

"When did you reach Paris?"

"Not an hour ago. I came to see you at once. Jean sends his kindest regards. We both hope you will visit us often."

Chopin laughed uncertainly. "I thought I might have offended you by not being at your wedding."

"I was disappointed, Fritz, but not offended. I do understand how painful it would have been for you, visiting Nohant again."

"It is more painful remaining away from Nohant," he said truthfully.

330

"It isn't for me, Fritz." Solange burst into convincing tears. "We were treated shamefully there, Jean and I."

"By Maurice, you mean?"

"By Maman as well. And all because of some silver candlesticks that have always belonged to me." She looked obliquely at Chopin. "That must sound silly to you, Fritz."

"Tell me about it," Chopin said comfortingly.

"I was packing them with some of my other belongings when Maurice objected. He was more angry with Jean than with me and actually threatened him with a pistol. If I hadn't torn it from his hands, he would have shot poor Jean."

Chopin found himself trembling with indignation. "How dreadful! You might have been injured yourself."

"Maman joined forces with Maurice. She always does, of course. There was an awful scene. It ended with Maman ordering Jean and me from the house. She said she never wanted to see us again."

"I can't believe it!"

"Nor could I at the time. God forgive me for saying this, but Maman is a very hard, unfeeling woman."

"Hard? Unfeeling?"

"You think me unjust, Fritz? Have you forgotten *Lucrezia Floriani*?"

"No," Chopin said soberly, "I haven't forgotten it."

"There's worse to come," Solange went on, well satisfied with the progress she was making. "Maman intends eventually to write the story of her life. I heard her discussing it with Maurice. Just imagine what will happen when she does! How often do people tell the truth when they write autobiographies? I shudder to think how many lies Maman will tell about me and Jean. Or, for that matter, about you, dear Fritz. Everybody who has displeased her will be made to suffer. Naturally she herself will emerge as a character entirely angelic."

Chopin turned, walked slowly to his writing-table and took

331

up the unfinished letter. A phrase here and there held his shocked attention: "I have behaved like a spoiled child . . . I have reproached you for many things; now I reproach only myself . . . Pray write, dear Aurore, and tell me I am forgiven . . ." Wild laughter surged up in his throat. He tore the sheet to shreds and scattered the pieces at his feet.

"I shall never see your mother again, Solange. I can thank her for only one thing—the gift of a very dear friend, her daughter."

25

GEORGE, ALIGHTING from her carriage in the Rue Saint-Lazare, suffered a moment of indecision, even of timidity. Should she seek out Chopin at once, should she wait until she was re-established in her own apartment, or should she call on Madame Marliani who had written her that he was "terribly ill"? Maurice decided the issue. Catching sight of her from the window, he rushed out to greet her. He led her eagerly into her apartment.

"I knew you wouldn't be able to stay away from Paris any longer, Maman! You should have been here during the riots. The excitement was awe-inspiring."

"Would I have helped the cause by getting myself knocked on the head? Would you yourself, for that matter?"

"Oh, I was very cautious. I watched but took care not to participate."

It was February, 1848. Revolution had swept through Paris. The King had abdicated and it seemed as if a new republic would soon be an accomplished fact. George, having worked constantly for the republican cause, was pleased enough with the political turn of events, but it was Madame Marliani's letter that had brought her hurriedly to Paris, not the fall of Louis-

Philippe.

Earlier, and contrary to her usual habit, she had decided to spend the winter at Nohant even if it meant temporary separation from Maurice. Chopin's coldness and his refusal to answer her letters were the deciding factors, not her claim that she worked better these days at Nohant than in Paris. Now all that was changed. Chopin was a dying man Madame Marliani had written. It would break her heart, George thought, if he died while still unreconciled.

Later in the day, still tormented by indecision, she called on Madame Marliani and learned that Chopin had given a concert on the 16th. But he had not been well enough to face the ordeal; immediately afterwards he had all but collapsed.

"I advised him against playing," the old lady sighed, "but since the King and Queen were to attend, he considered it his duty to perform."

"Their Majesties actually did attend?"

Madame Marliani shook her head. "With all those riots going on?" She sighed again. "How rapidly events have moved! A few days ago, a monarchy; today, political confusion. Poor Chopin is most distressed. Such an ardent royalist, as you well know. And besides, what will happen to him now, with so many of his aristocratic pupils in flight? He will have more difficulty than ever in making ends meet."

George rose. "I must go to him at once."

"That would be unwise, George. I fear he would refuse to receive you."

"That is a risk I must take."

"Be guided by me," Madame Marliani urged. "Let us practice a little subtlety."

"Subtlety?"

"When Chopin is well enough, he calls to see me—usually in the late afternoon. Be patient, my dear. The next time he calls, I shall send my maid to tell you. Then you may come upon him here as if by chance."

And so, a few days later, the "chance" meeting was brought about. Chopin, however, was about to leave when George hurried up the stairs. They met in an anteroom and stared at each other in silence for several moments. George fought back her tears as she studied him. It was impossible to believe that Chopin was only thirty-eight. His eyes were deeply sunken, the skin of his hollow cheeks more transparent than ever, and his shoulders pathetically rounded. Finally, as if only just recognizing her, he bowed courteously and asked her, with the impersonal politeness of a stranger, if she was in good health and spirits.

"Never better," George said chokingly. "And—you?"

"Need you ask? I survived the last concert. No doubt I shall survive many more. Each morning I am born again. Each night I die another little death. One day is sufficient in itself."

"You actually plan further concerts?"

"Naturally, but not in Paris. I am going to England again."

George seized his hand; it was icy. "You're not well enough, Chopin!"

He freed his hand, the fingers quivering like the wings of a trapped bird. "Let me be the best judge of that."

George smiled sadly. "What if I were to forbid you to go?"

He seemed not to have heard. "Have you had news of Solange?"

"She wrote to me some time ago. She thought it her duty to let me know that she was pregnant."

"You haven't heard from her since?"

"No."

"You are now a grandmother. Solange has given birth to a daughter. I am delighted to give you this news."

Again Chopin bowed with the impersonal politeness of a stranger and made his way down the stairs, moving deliberately lest he give the impression that he was running away.

"Chopin!"

He turned at the bottom of the stairs. George followed him out to the street. He felt himself trembling but succeeded in keeping his voice steady. "Naturally you are anxious about Solange's health. Pray forgive me for not having mentioned it. She is, under the circumstances, very well indeed."

George seized his hand again. "I—I thought that our separation would heal the wound, make a tranquil friendship possible."

Chopin's hand lay lifeless now in hers. Involuntarily she let it fall. Bowing for the last time, he turned and walked along the Rue Saint-Lazare and crossed the Place d'Orleans, still moving with deliberate slowness. He was indeed running away but she must never suspect it. Nor must she suspect that, from the first moment till the last, he had wanted with all his heart to embrace her.

George lingered on in Paris. She forced herself to take a hectic interest in the new regime, talked "man-to-man" with the republican leaders and even acted as secretary to one of them. In the end, however, fearful of running entirely by chance into Chopin, she returned despondently to Nohant.

Old friends gathered about her but she found little consolation in their company. Where, she asked herself, had she failed not only with Chopin but with all the others? Was it possible that the fault had been hers, always hers? Was that the fate of one who, in an unfeeling, material world, tried always to follow her heart?

This questioning mood persisted until, rising early one morning, she snatched up a small wicker cage in which fluttered a sparrow. She had found the bird in the garden, injured during a stormy night. He was chirping merrily now and fit again for freedom. Young Aurore rather than aging George Sand walked with growing eagerness across the garden and entered the little glade where Corambé's altar had once stood. A few smooth stones were still scattered about. She gathered them roughly together and, kneeling, opened the cage. The sparrow flew out but hovered for a moment on her outstretched hand.

"More reluctant than Chopin," she whispered, "but you shall have your freedom just as he has had his. I could hold you by force, I could have held him by force, but freedom—freedom is the gift of God."

The sparrow flew up, circled and disappeared.

What, she wondered, had she learned of life and love and true religion since those far-off days when she had worshipped at Corambé's altar? Where had she failed—where? She resolved then to begin the long-planned story of her life, writing carefully and impartially, with charity toward others, dignity toward herself, and honesty before God.

II

Supported by Solange and his favorite pupil, Adolf Gutmann, Chopin stood at the window of the apartment that he had rented on returning from abroad. It was on the second floor of a house in the Rue de Chaillot. The view over Paris was magnificent. He could see the Tuileries, Notre Dame, the Pantheon, the Invalides, and many other famous landmarks. The music of the vast panorama sang in his heart.

"Must I really leave all this?" he asked pitifully.

Gutmann reminded him that the apartment was only a summer residence. Winter would soon be upon them. He would be much more comfortable and warmer in the new apartment his friends had found for him in the Place Vendôme.

"Since I can scarcely stand without your help and all I really need is a bed, does it after all matter where I die?"

Seeing the quick tears glisten in Solange's eyes, Chopin was instantly sorry for having spoken of death. It was, in any case, the first time that he had admitted, even to himself, that death was close at hand. Previously he had agreed with his doctor that he was merely suffering from a lingering exhaustion caused by concerts given in London, Manchester, Edinburgh, Glasgow, and finally London again. That exhausting tour had been the greatest triumph of his life. He had even played before Queen Victoria and her husband, Prince Albert. Searching his memory, he wondered why he had hurried back to Paris. To evade his Scottish pupil, Jane Stirling, of course. Such a dear creature, Jane—helpful, hospitable, and generous, but there was that look in her eye that suggested marriage.

"Come, Fritz," Solange said.

Docile and unprotesting, Chopin allowed Solange and Gutmann to help him down the stairs and out to the waiting fiacre. On reaching the new apartment, he was surprised at first to find that he was being put to bed by his sister Louise. Then he remembered that Louise, who had married Kalasanty Jedrzejewicz some years ago, had come to Paris recently to nurse him.

"Madame Jedrzejewicz," he laughed, trying to make a joke of the name. "I must be more French than Polish these days. I can scarcely get my tongue round it."

It was the end of September, 1849. From then on, his sister and Gutmann were constantly at his side. Solange came frequently to see him as he lay in bed fighting for breath and striving to retain a stream of coherent thought, and friends and acquaintances came by the score. So many faces, some of them unrecognizable. Where, he wondered, was Aurore?

"Have you made your peace with your mother?" he asked Solange one afternoon when she came with a bouquet of flowers. "Did I not beg you to, or am I dreaming?"

Solange hesitated for a moment. Her mother had come to see her soon after the death of her baby daughter. They had wept in each other's arms. They were friends again, and George,

338

using her influence with the republican leaders, had secured a government appointment for Clésinger. Clearly Fritz had forgotten about the death of her baby. Why pain him then by reminding him of it, or by a mention of republicanism which he hated?

"I have made my peace with Maman," she said.

"I'm so happy to hear it."

Chopin waited expectantly. Did not Solange realize that he was longing to see Aurore again? One word from her and he would abandon his stupid pride forever and say "Yes, yes!" After waiting in vain, he tried to say, "Tell your mother I'm dying; bring her to me," but to his horror, he found that further speech had for the moment become impossible.

That was October 14. The next day speech failed him again, yet by weak gestures he managed to make some of his wishes known. His uncompleted manuscripts must be destroyed. Gutmann and Louise carried out this order reluctantly. A priest must be brought to his bedside; the priest came and against the background of the suppressed sobbing of Chopin's friends he intoned the prayers for the dying. Alert for the moment, the dying man imagined that he had recovered his voice. He could hear it ringing bravely through the death chamber. Aurore had once sworn that he would die in nobody's arms but hers. How, then, since she had absented herself, could he possibly be dying?

III

George was at Nohant when the news reached her. Anger rose in her breast even as she wept. Why had nobody told her that the end was near? She had written to Louise Jedrzejewicz only to receive a stilted reply saying that Frédéric's health was much the same as usual. Mutual friends had told her a similar story. Why the conspiracy of silence?

Dumbly she read Solange's fateful letter again:

On the evening of the 15th, his voice returned, painful and weak. He forbade us again to tell anyone that he was dying. He asked one of his former pupils, the Countess Potocka, to sing for him. The piano was dragged to his bedroom door . . .

On the 16th he received the last sacrament and was heard to whisper "Amen" . . .

During the night he asked for a drink. Adolf Gutmann held a glass to his lips. He died shortly after three in the morning. Gutmann swears that his last word was "Nohant" . . .

His face in death was more beautiful, more tranquil than we ever knew it in life. My husband took a cast of it, and casts, too, of his fine hands . . .

The funeral will take place at the Madeleine. His own Funeral March, orchestrated by Reber, will be played, and the organist will play the Preludes in B and E minor . . .

He will be buried at Père Lachaise, the little urn of Polish soil with him, but his heart will be taken to Warsaw to rest in the nave of the Church of the Holy Cross . . .

No, George thought, his real heart was here at Nohant. His last whispered word had given it into her keeping forever. Growing a little calmer, she went to the piano and took from the trinket box lying on it a lock of Chopin's hair he had given her years ago. She placed it in an envelope and with trembling fingers inscribed the words: POOR CHOPIN! OCTOBER 17, 1849.

Presently, opening the piano, she tried in vain to play the Funeral March. Had she, by allowing the separation to continue, prevented Chopin from living a little longer? Or would she, if she had been permitted to see him, have hastened the end through the emotional stress of their meeting?

It was useless to speculate. Chopin had said, "What is done is done; there is no point in discussing it." He had also said,

"Each morning I am born again; each night I die another little death; one day is sufficient in itself." Her fingers were still clumsily attacking the keyboard. How right he had been! If she could believe that, the future would at least be bearable.

George swung round at the sound of a light footfall in the room. Maurice! She must not let him see her grief. One must keep one's grief to oneself, the more so when one was the mother of a family. Had he seen the tearstains on her cheeks? Apparently not, for he was smiling and shaking a finger at her teasingly.

"What a terrible row you were making on the piano, Maman!"

George forced a quick laugh. "There's a storm brewing. I was indulging in a little imitative harmony in advance of the event."

"Harmony? Fritz would call it cacophony."

Reaching up, her attitude as secretive as Chopin's had always been, George hid the inscribed envelope beneath an article she had written in support of Louis-Napoleon, the Bonaparte pretender now President of the Republic.

"Cacophony!" Maurice repeated, greatly amused with the remark.

George closed the piano and rose from the stool.

"Chopin is dead," she told her son harshly, "but the world goes on."

Footnote

FOLLOWING Frédéric Chopin's death, George Sand entered upon a more settled period of her life. Maurice married and provided her with grandchildren upon whom she doted, while Solange, separating from Jean Clésinger, returned to Nohant. Her interest in politics continued, but she turned in disgust against Louis-Napoleon when he made himself Emperor, thus destroying the Republic. At times, defiantly, she called herself a communist, declared that true communism was Christianity, and predicted that within a hundred years France would become a communist state. But searching as ever for perfection, she knew in her heart that the error of communism was the same as the error of socialism: it overlooked the importance of the individual. George Sand, one of the greatest individualists of the day, could have come to no other conclusion.

Much of the money she continued to earn by her pen she gave to impoverished republicans living in exile. She made new friends, among them Heinrich Heine. Before his death, he wrote that her works "set the world on fire, lighting many a prison where no cheer had ever entered." At the age of sixty-five, she made a special note in her scrapbook: "And now I am growing old, but by some freak of nature I am stronger,

343

physically and mentally, than ten years ago. It seems to me, as I look back, that one changes from day to day, and every few years becomes a new being. Now, in my final phase, I can no longer find any trace of that anxious, agitated woman who was dissatisfied with herself and impatient of others. Old age, or a glimmering of wisdom? Goodness and sincerity are all I seek. I am becoming impersonal; I can bear the evil of my life and appreciate the good. I believe in God and the life eternal, and more than anything else, I believe that some day evil will be vanquished. Death, when it touches me, will be kind and gentle."

But death for George Sand was neither kind nor gentle. She died, as her mother had died, of cancer. A devil, she said, was clawing at her insides. She was within a month of her seventy-second birthday, and she left behind her an unfinished novel. They buried her at Nohant in a grave close to her grand-mother's. The service, at her daughter's insistence, was a Catholic one. Important men of letters came from Paris for the funeral. They included Gustave Flaubert, Ernest Renan, and the younger Dumas, and one of them delivered an oration written by Victor Hugo:

I weep for the dead and salute the deathless. It cannot be said that we have lost her. One cannot lose a living idea, and that is what she was. Free now, George Sand has found release from the flesh. In death she lives on forever.

4546